✒ THE ✒
AFFINITY BRIDGE

Newbury AND Hobbes
Investigation

Also by George Mann and available from Titan Books

The Osiris Ritual: A Newbury & Hobbes Investigation (November 2015)
The Immorality Engine: A Newbury & Hobbes Investigation (March 2016)
The Executioner's Heart: A Newbury & Hobbes Investigation (available now)
The Revenant Express: A Newbury & Hobbes Investigation (August 2016)

The Casebook of Newbury & Hobbes

Sherlock Holmes: The Will of the Dead
Sherlock Holmes: The Spirit Box
Encounters of Sherlock Holmes
Further Encounters of Sherlock Holmes

Ghosts of Manhattan
Ghosts of War
Ghosts of Karnak (forthcoming)
Ghosts of Empire (forthcoming)

THE
AFFINITY BRIDGE

GEORGE MANN

TITAN BOOKS

THE AFFINITY BRIDGE: A NEWBURY & HOBBES INVESTIGATION

Print edition ISBN: 9781783298273

E-book edition ISBN: 9781783298280

Published by
Titan Books
A division of Titan Publishing Group Ltd
144 Southwark Street
London
SE1 0UP

First Titan edition: July 2015
10 9 8 7 6 5 4 3 2 1

George Mann asserts the moral right to be identified as the author of this work.

Visit our website:
www.titanbooks.com

What did you think of this book? We love to hear from our readers. Please email us at: readerfeedback@titanemail.com, or write to us at the above address.

To receive advance information, news, competitions, and exclusive offers online, please sign up for the Titan newsletter on our website: www.titanbooks.com

A CIP catalogue record for this title is available from the British Library.

Printed and bound in Great Britain by CPI Group (UK) Ltd, Croydon, CR0 4YY

FOR JAMES GEORGE ALEXANDER MANN

PROLOGUE

INDIA, JUNE 1901

The flies. Always the damn flies.

Coulthard slapped at the insects buzzing incessantly around his face and checked his rifle for the fifth time that hour. The heat was proving even more oppressive than usual, and the hair at the nape of his neck was damp with perspiration, his uniform tight and uncomfortable. The other two weren't faring much better, either: Hargreaves was perched on a nearby rock, taking a long swig from his water bottle, and Taylor was pacing backwards and forwards, kicking miserably at the dirt. Only two days remained before the start of their return journey to England, and the lieutenant was still riding them hard, forcing them to go out on patrol in the stifling midday sun. Coulthard cursed under his breath. The man was an egomaniac.

From the craggy outcropping on which he stood, Coulthard could just make out the village they had trudged their way here from: a small collection of farms and ramshackle buildings that leaned awkwardly against each other like rows of uneasy siblings. Behind him, a line of trees marked the edge of the village boundaries, and to his left, a series of distant specks denoted a smattering of local farmworkers tending their crops in fields of leafy green. The place had an air of expectancy about it, like somehow it was holding its breath in anticipation of something yet to come.

Yawning, he turned to his companions, resting his rifle against a nearby rock. "So, what's the first thing you're going to do when we get back to London?" They'd had this conversation a hundred times in the last few weeks, and he already knew what Har-greaves was going to say. Still, it was a conversation that reminded them all of home, and as far as Coulthard was concerned, that was no bad thing.

Hargreaves looked up from his water bottle. He mirrored the other man's smile. "The minute I step off that airship, I'm heading for a pint in the Fox and Hound. I've missed the sorry beggars that prop up the bar in there, and I've missed a good pint of English ale." He chuckled at the memories. "After that, who knows? Maybe I'll take the train out to Berkshire and spend some time on my parents' farm." He glanced over at Taylor, who was still kicking up clouds of dust with his feet, a preoccupied expression on his face. Hargreaves dabbed at the perspiration beading his forehead with the back of his sleeve and then leaned in conspiratorially. "Not sure about him, though." He indicated the other man with his water bottle. "He's not in a good way. Too wet behind the ears for the things he's seen out here." He lowered his voice even further. "May be the asylum for him, when we finally get him home. Poor sod."

Coulthard let the comment pass without a response. They'd *all* been too wet behind the ears for the things they'd seen out here. India was a world apart from England, even with its thin veneer of Empire. He couldn't wait to get home, to get away from the heat and the noise and the ever-present flies. He watched Taylor for a moment, pacing backwards and forwards like an animal trapped in a cage. Hargreaves was right, of course: India had clearly broken the man. He wasn't sure if there was anything to be done for him now. But the asylum? Even the thought of it made him shudder. He'd visited an asylum once, back in Wandsworth, and the screaming of the inmates still rang out in his dreams sometimes, during the long nights when he lay there, trying not to think of all the terrible things he'd seen. If Taylor were headed for the asylum, what hope was there for the rest of them?

Repressing another shudder, Coulthard turned his attention back to Hargreaves. "Well, if luck be with me, my Ruth will be waiting at the airship port when we arrive." He smiled at the thought of her. In another week, he'd be holding her in his arms, spinning her around in the pale winter sun. His heart felt as if it would burst in his chest. That was the thing that would keep him sane, the thing that he was out here fighting for: his life back in England, and the lives of everyone he loved.

Hargreaves smiled. He'd heard all of this before. He reached for his water bottle again, and Coulthard turned to survey the horizon once more.

There was a shuffling sound from behind him. At first, Coulthard assumed it was Taylor, still kicking awkwardly at the sun-baked soil with his boots. Then he became aware of a quiet whimpering sound, like that of a frightened animal, and he felt his hackles rise. He turned around slowly on the spot. His heart was hammering in his chest. What he saw was enough to send him running for the asylum himself.

The creature that was menacing Taylor was like something raised from the very depths of Hades itself. It was dressed in the torn rags of an Indian peasant, and may once have been human, but now looked more like a half-rotted corpse than like anything resembling a man. The creature's skin was desiccated and peeling, its eyes bloodshot, its hair hanging in loose stringy strands around its face. Its teeth were bared in a rabid snarl, and it was bearing down on a terrified Taylor. Coulthard presumed that it had crept out from the cover of the nearby trees when they hadn't been paying attention. Taylor was on his knees before it, using his arms to cover his face from the beast as if simply trying to will it out of existence.

Coulthard scrambled hurriedly for his rifle, fumbling as he tried to bring the barrel to bear on the horrifying creature. Hargreaves was already on his feet and rushing forwards, his sword drawn, ready to take a swing at the monster. Shaking, Coulthard tried to remind himself to breathe, to hold himself steady as he planted his feet and took aim. He let off a shot, jarring his shoulder with the sudden recoil. The creature staggered back for a moment, then surged forwards again in a frenzy, lashing out at Taylor, who had given himself over completely to his terror and seemed unable even to attempt to defend himself from the diabolical thing. Coulthard watched in shock as the creature raked its nails across Taylor's face, digging its bony thumbs into his eye sockets and sending him spinning to the ground, his once-handsome face reduced to nothing but a bloody ruin. He gave a final wail before crumpling to the dirt, silent.

The creature turned its attention to Hargreaves. Blinded by rage after witnessing the fate of his fellow soldier, Hargreaves swung his blade at the lurching monster with all his might. It struck home, cleaving deep into the creature's chest, biting through skin, muscle and bone, but it hardly seemed to slow the beast at all. To Coulthard's amazement, it showed no signs of pain, or even distraction, as Hargreaves struggled to pull his weapon free from where it had wedged inside the creature's shattered rib cage. Coulthard let off another shot, to no avail, and finally accepted the uselessness of the firearm and abandoned it to the ground instead drawing his sabre and rushing quickly to his fellow's side.

Using his momentum to carry his blade forward, he speared the monster directly through the gut, driving his sword home until the hilt itself was buried deep inside the creature's abdomen. He twisted it, trying desperately to slow the assault of the vile thing, to draw some sort of reaction from it. All the while, it continued to rage at Hargreaves, who had given up trying to pull his weapon free and was now pummelling the monster's face with his fists as he endeavoured to wrestle free from its talonlike grip. A moment later, his movements turned to spasms when, unable to gain useful purchase on the creature, it pulled him close and tore his throat out with single wretched bite.

Coulthard, aghast, pulled his sabre free of the creature's guts and aimed a blow at the arm that still held the limp body of his friend. The blade sliced clean through the arm, lopping off the limb at the elbow and dropping the dead Hargreaves to the dirt. Dark blood sprayed from the wound, but the monster itself seemed entirely unperturbed by its injury. Baring its teeth, it pounced on Coulthard, clamping its mouth on his forearm as the man struggled to bring his weapon up before him in defence. Howling in pain, Coulthard kicked at the creature, desperate to break free. He could smell the carrion-stench of the thing, see the feral hunger behind its darting inhuman eyes.

Acutely aware of the horrifying manner in which his friends had died, Coulthard's instincts screamed at him to run. With a concerted effort, he grabbed a handful of the creature's hair and wrenched his arm from its mouth, tearing skin away from bone as an enormous hunk of his flesh was rent away in the creature's jaws. Almost swooning with the pain, Coulthard drove the blade of his sword through the monster's chest and then turned and fled, his feet pounding the dry earth as his legs pumped as fast as they could, sending him careening down the side of the outcropping and onwards towards the village, his left arm dangling uselessly by his side.

Behind him, the unusual beast, still with the hilt of the sabre protruding rudely from its chest and the stump of its missing arm spouting ribbons of dark blood, turned and grabbed the hair of Taylor's fresh cadaver and began to drag it slowly towards the cover of the trees.

CHAPTER 1

🔔

The room was full of ghosts.

Or so Felicity Johnson would have had him believe. Sir Maurice Newbury, weary from a day spent scouring the dusty stacks of the British Library, drummed his fingers on the table with a quiet impatience. The dinner party was not working out at all as he'd anticipated.

Around him, the other guests sat in a wide circle, spaced evenly around a large round table, their faces glowing in the dim light of the gas-lamps. Overturned tumblers, tarot cards, holly leaves and other assorted paraphernalia littered the table-top, and their host, her shrill voice piercing in the otherwise silent room, was attempting to raise the dead.

Newbury, decidedly unimpressed by the charade, glanced at the other guests around the table. Their faces were difficult to read in the half-light, but many of them appeared captivated by the performance of the woman as she waved her arms about her, wailing, her eyes shut tight, her body tensed; possessed, apparently, by some kind of unearthly spirit. She was currently engaged in babbling something about Meredith York's dead brother, and the poor woman was entirely taken in, sobbing on her husband's arm as if she truly believed she were receiving messages from beyond the grave.

Newbury shot a look at the man seated beside him and shrugged. Sir Charles Bainbridge was a Chief Inspector at Scotland Yard, a favoured agent of Queen Victoria herself and one of the most rational men in Newbury's acquaintance. He didn't think for a minute that his old friend would be taken in by any of this nonsense. He was older than Newbury, about ten years his senior, and was greying slightly around the temples. His moustache was bushy and full, and his eyes were bright, shining with mischief and the glassy patina of alcohol. Acknowledging the pained expression on his friend's face, Bainbridge offered an amused smile, the flickering light casting his face in stark relief. Clearly, he was considerably more forgiving of the indulgences of their host. Newbury shook his head in exasperation.

A few moments later, Miss Johnson fell back into her chair with a gasp, her eyes suddenly flicking open, her hands raised to her mouth in affected shock. She turned to survey her guests. "Did I–?"

Meredith York nodded emphatically, and a moment later, when the gas-lamps were turned up and the room was once again cast in a warm orange glow, the small audience paid tribute to their host with a hearty round of applause. Newbury sat back in his chair, relieved that the spectacle was over. He rubbed a hand over his face, feeling a sense of lethargy creeping over him. The other guests were already deep in conversation as he surveyed the scene with the air of someone ready to take their leave. He didn't want to be drawn out on his opinions of the evening's pursuit, lest he inadvertently cause offence. He patted his friend on the arm.

"Charles?" The other man turned to meet his gaze. Newbury stifled a yawn. "My lodgings beckon me. I'm intent on taking a stroll. Would you care to join me?"

Bainbridge allowed himself a brief chuckle at the other

man's expense. "That keen to get away, Newbury?" He shook his head in feigned disapproval, but his smile was barely concealed. "I had a feeling that you'd find this all rather objectionable. Come on, let's bid our friends good night and take our leave."

The two men stood together, and Felicity Johnson almost leapt out of her seat when she spotted them out of the corner of her eye. She briefly patted Meredith York on the back of the hand before turning to regard them. "Oh, gentlemen, must you go so soon?"

Newbury edged around the table and took her hand. "I am afraid that duty calls, my dear Miss Johnson. Both Charles and I have early appointments to keep in the morning. Thank you for a pleasant evening." He paused, unsure how to go on. "It has been an . . . entertaining diversion." He inclined his head politely and turned to reclaim his coat from the butler standing by the door. The woman's face fell, and she stammered briefly before replying. "Always a pleasure, Sir Maurice." She turned to Bainbridge, who was just collecting his cane from the hat stand in the hallway. "And you, Sir Charles. I do hope we will see you both again soon." And with that, she returned her attention to the adoration of Meredith York and her other guests.

Outside, the pavement was covered in a layer of hoary frost. Newbury turned his collar up against the biting winter chill. The moon was full in the sky, the night was clear and people bustled along the street, their breaths making foggy clouds in the cold air. Newbury drew the crisp air deep into his lungs, obviously relieved to have escaped further embarrassment at the hands of Miss Johnson.

Bainbridge, his cane clicking rhythmically against the ground as he walked, turned to Newbury as they made their way back towards Piccadilly. "Really, Newbury, did you have to cut her so?"

"Oh, Charles, the woman's a buffoon! She's trifling with things she has no real concept of, making light of Mrs. York's bereavement. Games like that are dangerous and hurtful." He shook his head, sighing. "I did not aim to cause offence. I simply wanted to let her know that we were not taken in by her little merriment. You know as well as I do, there were no spirits present in that room."

They stopped as a ground train trundled by, the huge steam engine roaring as the fireman stoked the flames, the carriages behind it bouncing along the cobbled road, their wooden wheels creaking under the strain. Newbury caught stuttering glimpses of the people inside the small carriages as they rushed by, snug inside their little booths, speeding on towards their destinations. The driver, on the other hand, was wrapped up warm against the elements, sitting atop the engine itself on a large dickey box, a huge steering wheel clasped between his gloved hands. They watched as it rattled away into the night, causing hansom cabs and more traditional horse-drawn carriages to divert from their paths. Newbury smiled. It was time for the past to make way for the future.

The two men crossed the road and continued on their way. Newbury decided it was time to change the subject. "So, tell me, Charles, any new developments in the case at hand?"

The other man sighed. "Not as such. Can't seem to get past this ridiculous story about the glowing policeman. It's making life very difficult for my constables. They keep being accosted out on their rounds. No one will answer their questions, and the men themselves don't want to go out at night, lest they find themselves running into this damnable fellow. Superstitious prigs!"

Newbury looked suddenly serious. "Charles"—he patted the other man on the shoulder—"look who has his ire up now!

Don't be so swift to discount these stories, at least before we have any real evidence to the contrary."

Bainbridge looked incredulous. "Heavens, Newbury, surely you're not putting any stock in these ridiculous tales? They are clearly as much poppycock as Miss Johnson's spirits!"

Newbury hesitated. "Look, Charles, I know I was dismissive of Miss Johnson, but I've spent the entire day scouring shelves in the British Library, looking for references to a glowing policeman, and I assure you, there is more to it than meets the eye."

Bainbridge stopped in his tracks. He leaned on his cane. "How so?"

"There's a case from about twelve years ago. A bobby who was murdered by a gang of petty thieves—found himself in the wrong place at the wrong time. You know the sort of thing." Bainbridge nodded. "Well, for a month *after* the body was interred, a 'glowing bobby' was seen looming out of the fog around the Whitechapel area, his pale skin shining an iridescent blue. One by one, the bodies of the thieves turned up, all strangled, all dumped in the same area of the city. Witnesses reported sightings of the dead constable, come back from the grave to seek revenge on his aggressors. After the last of the thieves turned up dead, the 'glowing bobby' was never seen again." He paused. "Until now, that is. I pieced the story together from various newspaper reports."

Bainbridge shrugged. "It was probably the other boys from the station, using the story as a cover to take revenge for the murder. They don't take kindly to one of their own being put in the soil."

Newbury nodded. "That may well be the case, but until we know more, I think we need to follow this line of inquiry. It may turn out to be nothing but poppycock, but we shouldn't dismiss it until we've had the opportunity to investigate a little further first."

"Very well." Bainbridge covered his mouth with the back of his hand as he coughed. "Come on, let's get out of this cold."

Newbury sauntered along beside him. "Would you care to join me for a nightcap at the White Friar's? They have a shockingly good brandy."

Bainbridge was about to reply when a sudden powerful gust of wind knocked them both back a step, and the older man found himself clinging to his hat to ensure it wasn't lost in the draught. He looked up. "Damn airships! I wish they wouldn't fly them so low over the city."

Newbury laughed, following his gaze. The underbelly of an immense vessel was scudding overhead, scintillating in the reflected light of the city and temporarily blotting out the moon, casting the two men in a dark shadow. The airship companies had been enjoying a period of rapid growth in recent months, with demand for air travel almost exceeding their capacity to build new vessels and clear space for berthing fields. The appearance of a sizeable ship such as this was becoming a frequent occurrence in the skies over London, as the Empire grew larger and an increasing number of people found profitable business abroad. With the haulage companies taking to the skies, too, there was no longer any need to relocate to foreign climes on a permanent basis, and many businessmen had taken the opportunity to set up subsidiary companies in India, America and the West Indies. Newbury himself had never travelled on one of the vessels, but he was certainly enamored with them, and watched in wonder as this one drifted lazily overhead, en route, he supposed, to a berthing field south of the city. He glanced back at Bainbridge, who had finally finished repositioning his hat. "Well? To the White Friar's?"

Bainbridge shook his head. "Not tonight, old friend. You've given me much to think about, and I must say that that pudding of Miss Johnson's is sitting rather heavily on me now. Don't have quite the constitution I used to."

Newbury smiled. "You'll hear no argument from me." He held out his hand, and the other man grasped it firmly. "Let me know if there are any further developments in the case. In the meantime, I bid you well and good night." He turned and made off in the direction of the White Friar's Club, gazing up at the sky in wonder at the vapour trails left in the wake of the passing airship.

CHAPTER 2

◆

Newbury leaned back in his chair and, with a sigh, spread his morning copy of *The Times* out before him on the desk. After retiring from the White Friar's Club the previous evening, he'd found he was unable to sleep. Nonetheless, with the coming of the dawn, he had risen, dressed and caught a cab across the city from his Chelsea lodgings to his office at the British Museum. He had little doubt that his housekeeper, Mrs. Bradshaw, would curse him colourfully in her delightful Scottish tones for failing—yet again—to inform her of his plans, but he also knew that she was growing used to his unpredictable comings-and-goings, even if she feigned exasperation to his face.

Outside, the sun was settling over the city, and the streets were gradually coming to life as people set about their daily business. Soon the museum would be bustling with his fellow academics and, not long after, with members of the public, come to gaze in awe and wonder at the treasures on display in the gaudy exhibits. Newbury had been an agent of the Queen for nearly four years, and whilst he was typically engaged in some case or other—whether helping Scotland Yard or left to his own devices—he continued to maintain a position at the museum all the same. He was an experienced anthropologist, with a particular speciality in the religion and supernatural practices of prehistoric human cultures, and he often found his academic work had resonance with his work in the field. At present, he was engaged in writing a paper on the ritualistic practices of the druidic tribes of Bronze Age Europe. He'd hardly found time to touch it for a week, however, what with the string of bizarre strangulations occurring around Whitechapel and his desire to aid his old friend, Bainbridge, in the hunt for the killer. Discovering that the culprit may have supernatural origins had only solidified his resolve to see the case through to the end, and what's more, the revelation put the case firmly and directly into his specific area of expertise. Since briefing the Queen with a missive the previous day, any time he spent aiding Bainbridge with his investigations was now considered official business.

Newbury yawned. It was still early, and his secretary had yet to arrive at the office. He was anxious for a cup of tea. He regarded the newspaper before him, paying no real attention to the article he'd been trying to follow, which concerned a politician involved in some lurid financial scandal. He was dressed in a neat black suit, a white shirt and crimson cravat. His hair was dark—the very colour of night itself—and swept back from his face, and he was clean-shaven. His eyes were a startling emerald green. A casual observer would have placed him in his early thirties, but in truth, he was approaching his fortieth year. He looked up at the sound of someone bustling into the adjoining room and called out, "Good morning, Miss Coulthard. I'd like a pot of tea when you're settled, please." He returned, distractedly, to his reading.

A moment later, there was a brief rap at his door. He didn't look up from his newspaper when the door itself swung open and someone crossed into the room. "Thank you, Miss Coulthard. I trust you are well?"

The woman cleared her throat. Newbury's eyes flicked up from the print. "Oh, my dear Miss Hobbes. I do apologise." He fumbled for a moment, unsure how to remedy his error. "I'm afraid I'm still getting used to the notion that another person will be sharing my office. Do come in." He half stood behind his desk, embarrassment clearly written on his face, as his recently hired assistant, Miss Veronica Hobbes, crossed the room and took a seat before him. She was pretty: brunette, in her early twenties, with a dainty but full figure, and dressed in a white blouse, grey jacket and matching skirt.

She smiled. "Please don't apologise, Sir Maurice. It takes more than a little case of mistaken identity to offend me."

Newbury returned her smile. "Very good. Let's get you settled in, then, shall we? But first . . . I don't suppose you're at all handy with a kettle?"

An hour later, fortified by a constant supply of Earl Grey, the office had become a hive of activity. Newbury was working through his notes from the previous day, trying to make sense of the various newspaper reports and apparent sightings of the "glowing bobby" around Whitechapel. He was wearing a frown, lost in thought and deep concentration.

Veronica was hard at work, clearing the spare desk across the other side of the room, unpacking her small box of belongings and filing the many sheaves of abandoned notes she continued to find in drawers and random piles all around the office. She had placed her jacket over the back of her chair, rolled up the sleeves of her blouse and attacked the mess like it was some sort of villain in need of appeasing. Newbury was suitably impressed by her fastidiousness.

It was into this scene that a distraught Miss Coulthard came running, late, her hastily tied bun coming loose so that strands of her hair flapped around her face as she came to rest in the doorway, breathless. Both Newbury and Veronica looked up in concern.

Newbury was on his feet immediately, worry etched on his face. "My dear Miss Coulthard, whatever is the matter?"

The woman cowered, as if afraid of what she had to say. Veronica offered her a heartfelt smile.

"Oh, sir, it's my brother Jack. He disappeared yesterday, and we've every fear that he may have succumbed to that terrible plague."

Newbury shuffled uneasily. "I understand your concern completely, Miss Coulthard. Look–" He indicated his visitor's chair. "–come and take a seat for a while, and Miss Hobbes here will fetch you a hot cup of tea." He glanced at Veronica apologetically, and she waved dismissively before hurrying off into the other room to organise another pot of tea.

Newbury put a hand on Miss Coulthard's arm to reassure her. "Now, why don't you tell me exactly what you know?"

The diminutive woman looked up at him, a pained expression on her face. "In truth, sir, there ain't that much to tell. Jack went off to work yesterday morning as normal–to Fitchett and Browns, the lawyers–and never came back. We had a restless night, worrying what kind of a mess he'd got himself involved in, as he's never been one to loiter before coming home of a night. My sister-in-law and I took ourselves down to the law offices first thing this morning, to enquire as to his whereabouts, and it seems he never even made it that far." With this, she let out a racking sob, bringing her gloved hand up to her face to stifle her tears. "They had no idea where he was, or why he hadn't shown up for work the previous day."

Newbury sat back in his chair, looking thoughtful. "I'm sure we'll find a suitable explanation, Miss Coulthard, if we apply ourselves. Now, tell me, what makes you think it's the plague?" He looked up at the sound of the kettle whistling in the other room and caught sight of Veronica listening to their conversation from the doorway. He nodded approvingly and then returned his attention to the crying woman before him.

"There have been terrible things happening in our neighbourhood, sir, terrible things indeed. Revenants, they're calling them. Victims of the plague, found staggering around in the fog of a night, like wild animals, baying for people's blood. Bloodshot eyes, peeling skin—they're like walking corpses, wandering around in the darkness, waiting for passers-by. The plague transforms them into mindless monsters." She crossed herself to ward off the thought of the horrifying creatures.

Newbury nodded. "I'm well aware of the phenomenon, Miss Coulthard. It's thought the plague was brought here from India, borne over by returning soldiers. It inspires a terrible brain fever and a degenerative state in the flesh. Was Jack bitten by one of these walking cadavers?"

"Not that we know of. Jack knows better than to loiter in the dark these recent months. But I fear he must have encountered one on his way to work that morning. The fog was thick around Brixton, and it may have been upon him before he had an opportunity to flee."

Newbury shook his head. "Unlikely, Miss Coulthard. As I understand it, the victims of this plague find the light painful to their eyes and will avoid stepping out during the daylight hours unless desperate or provoked. Remember, they are driven by animal desires, and not those of a rational human being. Besides, anyone bitten by one of these creatures will incubate the illness for a number of days before showing any symptoms. If your brother was indeed harassed in the street, he would have likely retained his senses and sought medical assistance at a nearby hospital. I'm sure, therefore, that there must be another explanation as to his disappearance."

Miss Coulthard was still shaking. "You really think so?"

Newbury smiled. "Indeed. There are many things that can keep a man away from his home for a night, Miss Coulthard, and whilst some are less savoury than others, I'm sure in this case, there'll be a reasonable explanation." He paused whilst Veronica placed a steaming cup of tea on the desk before Miss Coulthard. "Now, see yourself right with that cup of tea, and then take the rest of the day off. If there's still no news tomorrow, come and see me again and we'll file a missing-persons report with Scotland Yard."

Miss Coulthard braved a smile. "Thank you, sir. It's just . . . we're all so on edge, what with the strange things that have been happening. Time was when we would have laughed it off. But with these revenants walking the streets . . ."

"I know, Miss Coulthard, I know. The plague has us all concerned for the well-being of our loved ones and friends. I promise I'll keep my ear to the ground for any clues that may help you to locate your brother." Newbury stood and edged around the desk. "You stay put for a moment, Miss Coulthard, whilst I have a few words with Miss Hobbes." He crossed into the adjoining room, straightening his jacket and pulling the door shut behind him.

Veronica looked up. "What is it?"

"I'll wager it has something to do with drinking or gambling, or both." He shook his head.

"Is there anything we can do to help?"

"No. I'm convinced the situation will resolve itself. Another day or two, and the man will show up at his own door, hungry and not a little sheepish. Either that or they'll find him in a cell across the other side of the city, too embarrassed at his own behaviour to tell his family where he's been."

There was a rap at the outer door to the office. Veronica glanced quizzically at Newbury before crossing the room and allowing the door to swing open, revealing a messenger standing in the hallway, a small card clasped in his right hand.

"Message for Sir Maurice Newbury, ma'am."

"Thank you. I'll see that he gets it." She took the card from the young boy and turned to Newbury, who had sidled up behind her, his interest piqued. He took the card from her and turned it over in his hand.

"It's from Bainbridge." His face had taken on a grim aspect. He looked up at Veronica. "Get your coat. There's been another murder."

CHAPTER 3

The cab clattered noisily over the cobbled street as its pistons churned furiously and the driver swore at the mechanism in a half-hearted attempt to make it run faster. In the back, Newbury and Veronica sat in silence, jolted by the speed at which the vehicle rumbled towards its destination and by the unevenness of the road. At the front, the driver sat upon his dickey box, pulling levers to direct the angle of the wheels as the steam-powered pistons fired with noisy abandon and the cab bounced along on steel wheels softened with rims of polished hardwood. Veronica couldn't help thinking that, whilst it might have taken them a few minutes longer, a traditional horse-drawn carriage may have offered them a more comfortable alternative to the loud, dirty transport within which they now sat. Newbury, on the other hand, was a keen supporter of progress, and whilst even the driver seemed to be having difficulty keeping the contraption under control, Newbury appeared to be relishing every moment of their tumultuous journey.

Outside, the fog was still thick and cloying, a yellow tubercular cloud that sat heavy over the city, a shroud over the populace and a haven for the creeping things of the dark. Veronica watched through the window, seeing only the impression of grandiose buildings looming out of the smog, or the occasional vehicle flitting by on the road, its passengers hidden behind darkened windows or wreaths of smokey fog. Gas-lamps flickered in the damp air, a network of disembodied halos that lined the edges of the streets. Underlit carriages rode on a carpet of rolling fog. It was mid-morning, but it seemed to Veronica as if the day had somehow stalled, the sunlight replaced by a remarkable twilight that appeared to have descended all across the city. She looked up, presuming that the regular slew of airships that filled the skies these days had been grounded temporarily by the impenetrable weather, or else they had risen up above the smog to where the skies were clear and free of city air. She glanced at Newbury, but his face seemed suddenly serious. She folded her hands on her lap and waited.

Presently, as they raced towards Whitechapel and the scene of the murder, the fog became gradually less dense and the buildings closed in, the streets becoming narrower, the towering mansions and sweeping terraces of Bloomsbury giving way to less monumental structures and more factories, breakers' yards and public houses. Whitechapel was not the sort of place that Veronica would visit by choice. It was one of the seedier locales of the city, a refuge of beggars, criminals and whores. She shivered when she considered what they might find there. Pulling her coat tighter around her shoulders, Veronica drew the curtain across the window inside the cab, and Newbury raised an eyebrow in her direction, evidently interested to know what had spooked her. She pretended not to notice.

A short while later, the cab juddered to a halt and the driver clambered down from his perch and opened the door for the two passengers. The engine was still running, and outside, the noise of it was even more intense. It sounded like some great industrial machine, churning out clouds of steam and soot into the already bleak morning.

Newbury made good on the fare and no sooner had he climbed down from the carriage than Bainbridge was at his side, leaning on his cane, his overcoat pulled tight around his wiry frame. He looked like he'd been here for a while already.

"Ah, good, Newbury. We can press on." He paused for a moment at the sight of Veronica, unsure how to go on. He inclined his head politely. "Good morning, Miss Hobbes."

He turned to Newbury. "Can I have a word?"

Newbury smiled. "Indeed." They moved to one side.

"My dear fellow, do you think it's a good idea to bring a lady to a scene such as this? She could find it terribly alarming."

Newbury chuckled. "Charles, I may have known the girl for only a few weeks myself, but already I know better than to exclude her." He smiled. "Trust me, Miss Hobbes can look after herself."

Charles shook his head, as if dismayed at what the modern world was coming to. "So be it." He sighed. "Come on, this way."

He led them on to where the body was lying, sprawled out on the cobbles like a broken doll, its neck contorted into an awkward posture, the face a picture of anguish and pain. Surrounding the scene were three constables, their hands clasped firmly behind their backs, each of them keeping a wary eye on the surrounding fog and what it may or may not be hiding from view.

"Any witnesses?"

"No."

Newbury knelt closer to examine the body. The man was dressed in pauper's clothes, dirty from the workhouse, with black filings underneath the fingernails. He was clean-shaven and appeared to be in his mid-twenties. Newbury turned him over gently, examining the soft flesh around the throat, probing with his gloved fingers. He looked up at Bainbridge, who was standing over them, watching intently. "The neck's been broken, but the cause of death is definitely strangulation.

Look at these marks here, here and here." He indicated with his hand. "This bruising suggests the victim was grabbed forcefully around the throat and struggled somewhat before finally being despatched. There's nothing of the perpetrator left at the scene, but it certainly matches the profile of the other killings."

Veronica cleared her throat. "Has he been robbed?"

Both of the men turned to look at her in surprise. "Good question, Miss Hobbes. Let me check." Newbury fished around in the dead man's pockets for a moment before withdrawing a small leather wallet from inside the man's waistcoat. He opened it up. Inside was a smattering of low-denomination coins.

"He had little enough about him, but whoever—or whatever—killed him clearly wasn't interested in making a profit."

Bainbridge tapped his cane thoughtfully against the cobbles. "So what did they have to gain?" The frustration was clearly evident in his voice. "Are they just killing people for the hell of it?"

Newbury stood, handing the wallet to Bainbridge. "No, I doubt that very much. There has to be a motive here somewhere. We just can't see what it is, as yet."

"Well, I hope one of us starts seeing it soon. This is the seventh victim this month. Things are getting out of hand. I'm going before Her Majesty this afternoon, and currently, all I have to tell her is that the body count keeps getting higher!"

Newbury looked pained for his friend. "Look, I'm making some progress with my research that could suggest a couple of avenues for your men to investigate. Why don't you call on me later at the office and I can talk you through it? Right now, I think it best that you get that cadaver moved to the local morgue and have the surgeon begin the post-mortem directly. A body lying around in the fog might be too much of a temptation for these 'revenant' creatures to bear." He glanced around at the nearest constable, who was shuffling uncomfortably on the spot.

Bainbridge shrugged. "Yes, yes, you're quite right." He turned to the constable on his left, waving his cane. "You, man. Go and organise some transport to get this body moved." The other man hesitated, as if he were about to protest. Bainbridge was having none of it. "Well, go on, then!" The constable scuttled off into the fog. Bainbridge turned back to Newbury and Veronica. "I'd better go with them, make sure the surgeon gets the correct instructions. Can you find your own way back?"

Veronica nodded. "Of course we can, Sir Charles. But first, would you object terribly if I put a few questions to your men?" She moved over to stand beside Newbury.

Bainbridge looked confused, but assented readily. "No, no, my dear. Anything at all, if you think it may prove useful in helping to solve the case."

Veronica nodded appreciatively and then stepped around the body and approached one of the remaining two constables.

"Good morning, ma'am." He looked vaguely uncomfortable at the thought of being questioned by a woman.

"Good morning, Constable . . . ?"

"Pratt, ma'am."

"Good morning, Constable Pratt. I'm in need of some assistance. You see, my colleagues over there are labouring under the impression that I'm fully up to date with all the minutiae of this murder enquiry, but, as I'm relatively new to the job, I seem to be missing some of the pertinent facts. I was hoping you could help me out of my predicament?"

"Certainly, ma'am. Where would you like me to begin?"

Veronica affected ignorance. "Well, we could start with the victims. How many are there now?"

Pratt hesitated before going on. "Well, ma'am, there are seven official victims, all of them strangled to death and

31

abandoned in the street, just like this one. All from the same area of the city."

"Official victims?"

"Yes, ma'am. Folk around here are saying there's actually around three times that number, if not more. Sometimes the families come and move the bodies before the police happen upon them, other times the corpses are stripped and robbed and end up floating down the river."

"And what of witnesses?"

"People aren't too forthcoming, ma'am. They're attributing these killings to a phantom, the glowing policeman. Talk like that makes them clam up good and proper when a man in uniform comes knocking on their door. Not only that, but people are scared to come out at night. On one hand, they're worried about the murderer; on the other, about the revenants that are walking the streets at night, hiding in the gutters like animals. Places like this, they ain't safe, ma'am. People keep themselves to themselves."

Veronica smiled. "So do *you* think this is the work of the glowing policeman, Constable Pratt?"

"I'm not qualified to say, ma'am. But I do know folk who claim they've seen him out here, wandering around in the fog, his face and hands glowing with ghostly blue light whilst he waits for his next victim."

"Thank you, Constable. Most useful." She made her way back to where Newbury and Bainbridge were standing, a wry smile on her face. "It sounds as if these bodies may be just the tip of the iceberg."

Bainbridge nodded, obviously impressed. "You continue to confound me, Miss Hobbes."

Veronica smiled. "Let's just hope it proves useful in bringing the killer to justice, Sir Charles."

"Indeed. Indeed."

Newbury doffed his hat to his old friend. "Charles, we'll

take our leave. Watch your back out here, won't you, and remember to call by the office this afternoon for a talk. I'm sure we can start moving forwards in this matter, hopefully before another sorry individual loses his life."

"Thank you, Newbury. Your assistance is most appreciated."

"Say no more." And with that, Newbury and Veronica turned on their heels and disappeared into the fog-laden morning in search of a cab.

"I liked your trick with the constable back there." Newbury was in a much more talkative mood, now that the two of them had managed to hail a hansom cab and were on their way back to the museum.

Veronica was relieved that, this time, they'd been able to settle on a more traditional vehicle, pulled by horses, instead of the more temperamental steam engine they had suffered before. She regarded Newbury from across the carriage. "I've always believed that it's worth keeping one's ear to the ground, finding out what people are saying. Invariably, in my experience, that's where one may find the truth, or at least the kernel of the truth that has given rise to the tall tales."

Newbury nodded in agreement. "An admirable tactic, and one that I'm convinced will bear fruit. But consider this–" He paused for dramatic effect. "–what if, in this instance, the tall tales were actually based on fact?"

Veronica's eyes betrayed her incredulity. "Come now, sir, you're not suggesting the glowing policeman is the real source of these murders?"

"Indeed not, although at this stage, I'm loath to rule *anything* out. What I'm getting at is the notion that the stories could have been inspired by *past* events, occurrences from many years ago that have left a residual, latent fear amongst the folk of this particular district."

"You've found something, haven't you, in your studies? Some reference that sheds light on what's going on at the moment?"

"A reference that *may* shed light on what's going on at the moment. In truth, it may also turn out to be entirely unrelated, although I find that difficult to believe, given the nature of the murders and the circumstances surrounding the deaths. I've already mentioned it to Bainbridge, but he puts no stock in the idea."

Veronica leaned forwards in the carriage. "Do tell."

Newbury smiled. He was beginning to believe he'd made the right choice in hiring Veronica as his new assistant. "About twelve years ago, there was a disturbing case in the Whitechapel area, in which a gang of petty thieves were discovered breaking into a house. Instead of fleeing the scene, they turned on the policeman who had found them, and viciously beat him to death. The thieves were never brought to justice, but for a month after the policeman's body was interred, a 'glowing bobby' was sighted around the streets, walking his beat and searching out his murderers, one after the other."

"What happened?"

"They all turned up dead. Strangled, just like the victims we've seen in the last couple of weeks. Such was his vengeance, it was said, that the murdered policeman had actually risen from the grave to seek revenge on his killers. Once they were all dead, the 'glowing bobby' disappeared, never to be seen again."

A ground train rattled by their cab, startling the horses and causing them to whinny noisily and pull up by the side of the road. The driver shouted down his apologies and waited for the other vehicle to pass before coercing the animals back out into the road.

Veronica sat back in her seat. "The parallels are uncanny."

"Indeed. But there are holes. Why would the spirit return

now, after all this time? Did it ever really exist, or was it just a cover used by the dead man's colleagues to track down and dispose of his killers? What, if any, are the connections between the victims? I can't see a good reason for the spirit of the dead policeman to be taking these innocent lives, both men and women. I'm not convinced the profile actually fits."

"But you are convinced that it is *possible*? Have any other policemen been murdered in the area lately? Could it be the same phenomenon, but a different set of people involved?"

Newbury straightened his back. He looked thoughtful for a moment. "My dear Miss Hobbes, what a splendid deduction! We'll get Bainbridge looking into it first thing this afternoon. I've been so wrapped up in trying to draw parallels between the two cases that I'd overlooked this most obvious of angles."

By this time, their cab was approaching Bloomsbury and the British Museum could be seen through the window, an epic, monolithic structure rising out of the grey afternoon. Newbury took his watch out of his pocket and examined its face. He glanced at Veronica. "I don't know about you, but I'm feeling rather peckish. Spot of lunch?"

Veronica grinned. "Sir Maurice, I'm famished."

With Miss Coulthard gone for the day, the office was silent when they returned from lunch, with just the ticking of the grandfather clock in the corner to break the monotony. The two rooms were connected by an interior door, the main office being a fairly large open space with Miss Coulthard's desk placed centrally to face the door. The walls were decorated with an array of spectacular artefacts, ranging from mediaeval weaponry to a glass display cabinet filled with smaller antiquities from Egypt, Greece and Rome. A small stove had been fitted in the far corner, and a series of bookcases were overflowing with ageing, dusty tomes.

Newbury had just finished arranging his hat on the hat stand when Veronica, who had already gone through to the side room where their desks were located, reappeared in the doorway, brandishing an envelope.

"It's got the Royal seal on it. Someone must have delivered it whilst we were out." She handed it to Newbury. He opened it immediately, dropping the envelope to the floor.

"It's from the Queen." He unfolded the letter and began to read.

To our faithful servant,

It is requested you abandon all current activity and proceed immediately to Finsbury Park. An airship has crashed this morning in suspicious circumstances, and one suspects foul play. Early reports suggest no survivors.

Full report expected in due course.

This is a matter of grave importance to the Crown.

Victoria R.

Newbury folded the note in half and slipped it into his jacket pocket. Veronica eyed him quizzically. He reached for his hat.

"We're off the murder investigation. At least temporarily." Veronica looked somewhat disappointed by the news. Newbury continued. "There's been an airship crash in Finsbury Park. I'm afraid we're going out again." He pushed his arm into the sleeve of his long black overcoat and headed for the door. "Come on, I'll explain on the way."

CHAPTER 4

From over two hundred yards away, it was clear that the airship crash was a disaster of phenomenal proportions. Black smoke spiralled through the sky in a dark liquid trail, a smudge across the landscape, clearly denoting the point of impact and consequent explosion. The heavy fog was starting to lift now, but the scene it uncovered had Newbury wishing it had stayed put.

The wreckage was scattered across a wide area of parkland, isolated flames still licking in little glowing puddles where firemen had yet to extinguish the smaller pieces of debris that had come to rest in the area surrounding the main carcass of the downed ship. Hose carts circled the wreckage, whilst onlookers milled about a police cordon that had been established around the entire perimeter of the park. A tree was on fire on the far side of the site, and firemen were currently engaged in trying to bring it under control before the flames spread to the neighbouring evergreens.

The airship itself was now nothing but a burnt husk, its shattered substructure an exposed skeleton, stark against the surrounding parkland. It reminded Veronica of a beached whale she had once seen when she was a child, half-rotted in the sea air, its huge rib cage exposed to the elements.

Newbury clambered down from the cab, choking on the thick smoke that lay heavy in the air all around them. The stench of the burnt vessel was almost unbearable. He turned to help Veronica down beside him, offering her a handkerchief to cover her face. She took it gratefully.

"What in God's name happened here?" Her voice was muffled from behind the small piece of linen that she held over her mouth and nose. Her eyes watered, stinging with the smoke.

"Airships such as this one get their lift from gasbags filled with hydrogen. The gas is highly inflammable, and in a major impact such as this . . ." He shook his head. "Well, you can see the results for yourself. I've read about a handful of similar incidents. The most recent was in Bulgaria, I believe, where a pilot missed his berthing tether and instead lowered the ship onto the ground spike, ripping the gasbags open and engulfing the entire vessel in flame."

Veronica looked grave. "But all those passengers . . ." She was staring out over the chaotic scene before them, unsure what to make of it all. She drew her coat around herself, an unconscious gesture that revealed her horror at the sight of the wreckage and the carnage it represented.

Newbury was lost for comforting words. He paused and then looked around, straining to see over the bustling crowds of people. "Come on; let's see if Bainbridge is here yet."

Together, the two of them circled the cordon, looking for signs of the Chief Inspector. Newbury kept a hand on Veronica's arm as they pushed their way through the press of locals, who had turned out in droves to catch a glimpse of the downed ship. Newbury supposed he couldn't blame them; for many it was a frightening near miss, with such a devastating explosion occurring so close to their homes. The vessel could easily have come down upon a row of terraced houses instead of the relative safety of the park. For others, it was surely a unique opportunity to witness something that they would usually only read about in newspapers, a sensational spectacle to tell their grandchildren of in years to come. From a purely detached perspective–ignoring, for a moment, the human cost of the tragedy–history was unfolding before their eyes.

They pressed on, fighting against the swarm of people in an attempt to find someone who looked in charge. Moments later, they found whom they were looking for.

The police had set up a temporary base underneath a bandstand, just inside the cordon at the far end of the crash site. Wreaths of dark smoke still curled through the air, and here, the stench of the wreckage was even more intolerable than when they'd first arrived. Newbury tried not to imagine what was causing the diabolical smell. He made his way over to the cordon line and called to get the attention of one of the men stationed there.

"Hello? May I have some assistance here, please?"

Two men in suits, deep in conversation, looked around to eye the newcomer. One of them flicked his wrist to a uniformed officer, and the man came plodding over to where Newbury and Veronica were standing.

"Yes?"

"I'm attempting to locate Sir Charles Bainbridge. Can you tell me, is he present at the site?"

"No, sir. I don't believe he is." The other man looked irritated, as if anxious to get back to his post.

"Ah. Well, in that case, is there anyone else I could talk to?" Newbury reached into his jacket pocket and produced his credentials, which he waved at the constable. The monogram of Queen Victoria was clearly visible on his papers. "My name is Sir Maurice Newbury, and I'm here on the business of the Crown."

The constable stared at him, wide-eyed. "Of course, sir. If

you'd like to come this way?" The officer lifted the cordon and both Newbury and Veronica dipped their heads to pass underneath the rope barrier. Veronica, straightening herself on the other side, made a point of repositioning her hat. Newbury supposed she was trying to keep herself busy and prevent her mind from wandering back to the horrors on the other side of the bandstand.

The two men in suits were still talking as the three of them approached. Veronica glanced around. She could see that the police were struggling to get the situation under control; they were few in number, and the constables were barely managing to keep the onlookers back from the cordon. Meanwhile, higher-ranking officers tried to coordinate the other emergency services and ensure that nothing was removed from the wreckage that would prove useful in uncovering the cause of the disaster. Veronica was sure that the investigation was already under way, but it seemed to her as if the police had their hands full just trying to stop the crash site from getting out of control.

The bobby who had led them over from the barrier made a point of clearing his throat, and the two men in suits ceased talking for a moment to take them in. The man on the left, dressed in pin-striped grey, with a full beard and dark green cravat, looked Newbury up and down discerningly. He seemed about to say something when the constable stepped in. "Sir, this gentleman is here on behalf of the Crown."

The man nodded, an unreadable expression on his face. "The Crown indeed. Well, we can certainly use all the help we can get. Abominable affair." His face cracked into a sad smile. He held out his hand. "Inspector Foulkes of Scotland Yard."

Newbury took his hand. "Maurice Newbury."

"Ah, Sir Maurice. Yes, Sir Charles has told me all about you. Glad you could make it." He put his hand on the shoulder of the man he'd been talking with when they arrived. "This is

Mr. Stokes, representing the company that built and operated the airship in question."

Veronica noted that Stokes was harbouring a dark frown.

Newbury took his hand, inclining his head politely. "Mr. Stokes." He stepped back, allowing the others to see Veronica, who had been standing behind him in the shadow of the bandstand throughout the course of the exchange. "This is my assistant, Miss Veronica Hobbes. She'll be aiding me in my enquiries. Please ensure you extend to her all the necessary courtesy and freedom she requires to properly execute her role."

Foulkes looked startled by this new development, but quickly spluttered his assent.

Newbury turned to the man named Stokes. "Mr. Stokes, I'd appreciate it if you could elaborate on some details for me. Have you any notion yet of what occurred to bring about this sorry situation?"

Stokes looked immediately uncomfortable. He was a short, lean man, shorter than both Newbury and Foulkes and only a few inches taller than Veronica. He wore a brown suit and white collar, with black shoes that, Veronica noted, were filthy with mud, grime and ash from the crash site. His moustache was trimmed to perfection and waxed at the ends, and his bushy eyebrows did much to accentuate his apparently permanent frown. He shuffled nervously on the spot. "Alas, we're only just beginning to piece together the sequence of events that preceded this tragedy. There is nothing in the wreckage to indicate what may have happened onboard, and we can see no obvious reason why it should have plummeted out of the sky as dramatically as it did. Unfortunately, there are no survivors left to question, either."

Newbury shook his head, his face serious. It was obvious he didn't care for Stokes's dismissive tone. "What of the ship itself? What was it, and where was it bound?"

"The ship was named *The Lady Armitage,* and according to my charter, it was bound for Dublin. It was a passenger-class vessel, the smallest size in the fleet, and appears to have been carrying around fifty individuals when it crashed."

"Fifty . . ." Veronica was appalled.

Newbury continued. "And what of your employers, Mr. Stokes?"

Stokes offered Newbury a black look. "I'm a representative of Chapman and Villiers Air Transportation Services, of Battersea. Mr. Chapman himself has engaged me to assess the situation here today and to act as his mouthpiece during the ongoing investigation. Any questions pertaining to the company can be directed at me. I am also the firm's legal representative."

Newbury glanced at Veronica, a sardonic expression on his face, and then turned his attention to Inspector Foulkes. "Do you know if Sir Charles will be attending the scene?"

"Not initially, sir. He has ceded responsibility for the case to me for the time being. He's still caught up in this damnable Whitechapel situation. They found another body this morning."

"Indeed. Miss Hobbes and I were present at the scene." He glanced back at Stokes, who was attempting to clean the dirt from his shoes by rubbing them on the grass. "Do we know how long it's been since the vessel came down?"

The other man didn't look up from his ministrations. "Witnesses are reporting seeing the vessel come down between ten and ten thirty this morning." He emitted a *tut*ting sound as he continued to rub the side of his shoe on the wet grass, to no avail.

Newbury flushed red. "Damn it, man! Fifty people are dead! Show some decency, and pay attention to the issue at hand."

Stokes ceased wiping his shoes and looked immediately flustered. He stammered something incoherent, which Newbury decided to take as an apology. Foulkes tried to cover his laughter at the man's expression with a loud cough.

Newbury met Foulkes's eyes. "I think the next logical step is for me to examine the wreckage."

"I'm sure that will be acceptable to Mr. Stokes." The Inspector shot the lawyer a sideways glance. "But I will warn you, Sir Maurice, it is a disturbing experience. I toured the remains of the vessel as soon as it was cool enough to go aboard, and I assure you, it's no place for a lady." He made a point of stressing these last few words.

Newbury was unperturbed. "I appreciate your candour, Inspector Foulkes. Of course, it's up to the lady to decide for herself. Allow me to consult with Miss Hobbes in private for a short while." With that, he turned his back on the two men and drew Veronica to one side, under the shadow of the bandstand.

"Miss Hobbes. Veronica. I would not presume to ask you to follow me into the horror of this wreck. I did, after all, hire you to assist me in my academic pursuits, and not to risk life and limb clambering after me into the still-smouldering carcass of a downed airship." He paused, giving his words time to sink in. "I'd be very happy if you preferred to wait for me here instead."

Veronica crossed her arms. "That's all very well, Sir Maurice, but what if you miss something fundamental? Surely a second pair of eyes would prove useful, especially when one considers the sheer size of the wreckage?"

Newbury smiled, trying to conceal his pleasure at her response. "Very good. Well, better pucker up that resolve, my dear. It's going to be dangerous, dirty and pretty horrific in there." He was about to move off when another thought occurred to him. "Oh, and hang on to that handkerchief, too. I suspect the smell will be unbearable as we get closer."

Newbury returned to stand beside Inspector Foulkes. "Miss Hobbes will attend the scene alongside me."

Foulkes looked ready to object, before Newbury caught his eye. "I assure you, I'll look after the lady's well-being. Now, what's the best way into the wreck from here?"

Stokes answered. "The ship came down nose-first, so the rear of the ship retains the bulk of its shape whilst the sub-frame at the front of the vessel has compacted, making it difficult to enter. I'd suggest you find your way around the left-hand side"–he indicated with a wave of his hand–"and enter through the main cabin door on the side of the gondola. I'm not sure what it is you're hoping to find in there, though, Sir Maurice. In truth, it's nothing but a burnt-out husk."

Newbury shrugged. "I'll know it when I see it, no doubt. Thank you for your assistance, gentlemen. We shall return presently, before the light begins to wane." He turned and offered Veronica his arm.

Foulkes watched as the two Crown investigators, entirely incongruous in their formal attire, began walking slowly towards the huge shattered structure on the park green, cautiously stepping around the still-smouldering piles of debris as they walked.

CHAPTER 5

The wreck of *The Lady Armitage* was like the carcass of some ancient, primordial beast; the skein of rubber-coated fabric that served as the outer skin of the vessel now burnt and torn like peeling flesh. The sub-structure of iron girders jutted into the sky like broken ribs, blackened by the soot and heat and buckled from the impact. The engine housing, at the rear of the wreckage, looked relatively intact, although in truth, it was hard to tell, as much of it was buried in the earth where the impact had driven it into the ground. The passenger gondola, usually situated underneath the belly of the ship, had been forced upwards and backwards, puncturing the underside of the vessel and contorting awkwardly where it came into contact with the iron struts of the interior frame. The whole thing was a terrible mess, and Newbury had to use every ounce of his experience to maintain a level head as he walked towards it.

Steam and smoke still rose from deep inside the wreckage. As Newbury and Veronica approached the misshapen outer door of the gondola, Newbury felt the need to warn his assistant once again of the dangers they may face inside. "Make sure you don't touch anything. It may still be hot from the fires. And watch out overhead, too; the wreck hasn't settled yet, and as the metal cools, fragments of the vessel may still collapse inwards, trapping us inside, or worse."

He covered his nose and mouth with the crook of his arm to stave off the terrible smell of death and burnt rubber. Veronica followed suit, once again holding Newbury's borrowed handkerchief to her face. The hem of her skirt was already thick with mud and soot where it trailed on the ground, her boots filthy with grime. She tried not to notice.

The door into the gondola had buckled badly. There was nothing but a blackened frame there now, where once there had obviously been an elaborate door and mechanism. Veronica peered inside, seeing nothing but darkness and iron girders. "Are you sure this is the best way in?"

"It looks like the *only* way in, as far as I can tell." He looked around, confirming his suspicions. "I wouldn't trust that man Stokes for a minute, but I can't fault his directions in this instance. Here, let me go first." Newbury tentatively put a hand on the outer rim of the door. "Still warm." He gripped it more firmly with both hands and swung himself through the twisted metal opening. Veronica watched him disappear inside.

"Oh, well. For Queen and Country, I suppose." She grabbed the doorframe and swung herself in behind him.

Inside, Veronica found it difficult to get a sense of the scale of the ship. She was standing in what she assumed had been the lobby, although now, with fire and structural damage, it was difficult to tell. *The Lady Armitage* may have been small by airship standards, but on the ground, it was still an immense vessel, and the passenger gondola was equally well-proportioned. Newbury was heading towards the compartments at the front of the gondola, if she had her bearings right. She watched him climbing over blackened furniture and the still-warm cinders of other unidentifiable objects. He turned back. "I'm off to try to find the pilot's control room. You take a look around. We'll meet up again shortly." She looked the other way, trying to see a path through the scene of destruction. "Oh, and Miss Hobbes?"

"Yes?"

"Be careful."

She smiled to herself, pleased with his evident concern.

The lobby—or what remained of it—was a long rectangular room with doors in each of the far walls. Since Newbury was heading fore, she decided to take the other option and see what she could find towards the rear of the vessel. She supposed, as she trod carefully over the ash-covered floor, that she was heading towards the part of the ship reserved for passengers, since the bulk of the gondola's interior space seemed to lie in this direction. Fighting her way past the crisp shell of a wooden sideboard, and ducking under a nest of trailing metal cables, she came to a stop in front of the door. It was still relatively intact, although flames had obviously licked black soot up and down its fascia. She hesitated. She knew she was likely to happen across a body or two on the other side. Taking a deep breath, she steeled herself. Her palate was growing used to the stench now, and her clothes were so thick with grime, dust and soot that she'd given up paying attention. She reached out and tried the handle, then immediately withdrew her hand. It was still hot from the fire, and even through her red-leather gloves, she knew it would scald her hand. Not only that, but the door appeared to have sealed shut with the heat. Stepping back, and looking around her to ensure no one was watching, she hitched her skirt up above her knees and sent her booted foot flying into the centre of the door. It gave a little in the frame, splintering where the wood had been stressed by the heat. She tried again, this time putting her full weight behind her as she drove herself forwards into the door.

It gave, bursting open and slamming back against an iron girder that blocked the way on the other side. She wondered, for a moment, if Newbury would come running at the noise, but after a short while had passed and she could hear no sound of him, she decided to press on. Pushing back against the door, she decided she'd try to squeeze through the gap she had created between the doorway and the girder. She tucked her hat underneath her arm, her dark hair spilling out of its carefully prepared coiffure.

She manoeuvred herself into the opening. Inside, she could still feel the residual warmth from the burnt-out interior. The floor was covered in a sticky mudlike residue, which she supposed had been created when the water from the hose carts had mixed with the soot and ash, forming a film of black grime upon the ground.

She looked around, and then dropped the handkerchief to the floor with a gasp. She stared in horror at the sight before her. Row upon row of passenger seats were filled with the remains of the dead. Horrific, skeletal cadavers sat fixed in their final death throes, gripping the seats in front of them, screaming at their neighbours, or else spilled out onto the floor, where they had tried to find somewhere to run. It was as if someone had set out a grisly diorama, a charnel house audience locked away in this horrible room, awaiting an appointment with God. She approached slowly, forcing back the rising bile in her throat. Her eyes filled with tears. It was the most appalling sight she had ever seen. She wondered why the people were nearly all still seated, why they hadn't tried to bail out of the ship as it crashed, or at least taken cover in the hope that they may survive the impending impact. The corpses were all blackened and burnt, cooked flesh still clinging to the bones, terrified screams still fixed on their faces. She had no way of telling which of them had even been male or female, save for the occasional piece of jewellery still hanging around a woman's throat.

Leaning close to one of the bodies, she noted the answer to her earlier question: The person had been tied into their seat, fixed by a hoop around their left foot to the base of the seat in front. She checked another, and another, and found that they were all the same. No wonder the people hadn't tried to run. They couldn't.

Veronica noticed a gentle patter of raindrops on her face. She looked up. High above, she could see the sky through the torn belly of the airship, the broken spokes of its internal structure poking up into the waning afternoon light. She realised almost immediately that the water droplets she had felt were not rain, but water from the hose carts, sprayed into the blazing inferno earlier that day and still dripping from the girders up above. She glanced around, looking for anything else that may be of use. She could see a hole in the left side of the room, where the firemen had obviously dug their way through from the outside in an attempt to find survivors. She wondered how those men had reacted to the scene that had faced them. Had they, too, been as appalled as she was? She finally gave in to her horror and vomited on the ground, her eyes stinging as she retched violently, over and over again, until there was nothing left for her body to expel. She stood, gasping, wondering if she'd ever be able to cleanse the smell of the burnt flesh from her hair and skin or, worse, from her nightmares. Perhaps she should have stayed outside after all.

She turned at the sound of the door banging against the girder. Newbury stepped into the room. He coughed, hacking on the smell of the still-warm bodies.

"My God." He rushed to Veronica's side. "Are you alright?"

Veronica coughed. "I'm not sure I shall ever be alright again. I just can't believe the devastation. So many people dead, burned alive in the fires. What a horrible way to die."

Newbury looked saddened. "It won't have been a lingering death. The collapse of the gasbags will have caused a series of massive fireballs to blow through the ship. That probably explains why they're all still in their seats."

Veronica crouched down beside a row of seats. "That, and the fact that they were all tied into position like common criminals." She showed him the loop of charred rope around the ankle of the nearest passenger.

"Stokes made no mention of the vessel being chartered as penal transport. Do you suspect he was trying to hide something?"

"I believe he was trying to cover his own back." She stood again, blinking. "What did you find in the control room?"

"Nothing."

"Oh." She moved to turn away, anxious to put space between herself and the grisly scene, and then paused when he continued talking.

"That's just it. Nothing. No pilot or co-pilot to be found. No bodies, no evidence to suggest they were ever there at all. It's as if the pilot simply abandoned the controls."

Veronica frowned. "Do you think that's why the ship went down? Because the pilot wasn't at the controls? Could he have bailed out before impact? Or could he be back here, unidentifiable now from the other passengers?"

"I suppose anything is possible." Newbury looked up, noticing that the light was starting to go. "Come on. I think we've seen enough, and this is far from my ideal of one's first time aboard an airship." He looked circumspect. "Besides, I do believe we have some more questions for Mr. Stokes."

Mr. Stokes was still standing around the police cordon when Newbury and Veronica edged up beside him. They were both filthy from climbing around in the wreckage, and Newbury was looking forward to retiring for the day, intent on a long soak in a hot bath. Stokes turned to regard them as they approached.

"Well, I do believe it's true what they've been saying. The Crown *is* prepared to get its hands dirty from time to time." He guffawed at his own joke.

Newbury was unmoved. "Foulkes?"

Stokes was obviously taken aback by Newbury's directness. "Um, no. He's had to go off somewhere. Something about a fireman getting injured in the wreckage."

"Well, Mr. Stokes, perhaps *you* could make yourself useful for a moment? I have another question, and it's very much in need of an answer."

The other man nodded, apprehensive now.

"What became of the ship's pilot? I've been down to the control room, and there's no evidence of a body. Indeed, there's precious little evidence that a pilot was even on board."

Stokes's complexion turned a ghostly shade of white. "The, um, the pilot is missing."

"Missing? How does a pilot go *missing*? Did he bail out before the crash?"

"Not exactly, Sir Maurice . . . If I can just—"

"Look, man, I'm in no mood for your ridiculous evasions now! Can you answer the question or not?"

Veronica put a hand on Newbury's arm in an effort to quell his rising temper. Stokes gave an audible sigh. "There is no way the pilot of that vessel could have bailed out before the crash."

"And why is that, Mr. Stokes?" This from Veronica, who had evidently decided to step in and calm the situation before things got out of hand.

"Because it wasn't a 'he.' It was an 'it.'" He rubbed his hands over his face in exasperation. "The pilot of *The Lady Armitage* was a clockwork automaton, designed by Mr. Villiers himself. They're remarkable units, capable of many basic and, indeed, higher functions. But they are *not* programmed to abandon their stations in an emergency. They're simply not capable of it."

Newbury looked incredulous. "An automaton piloting an airship! Why didn't you think to disclose this information before now? There's the probable cause for your disaster, Mr.

Stokes! The unit clearly malfunctioned."

Stokes shook his head defensively. "Oh no, Sir Maurice. That's simply not possible. The automata have been piloting airships for nearly six months now, and safety records have improved dramatically during that period. Up to eighty percent! The program is fully approved. We have all the necessary paperwork back at the office. I assure you, sir, that it's a simple impossibility that the unit malfunctioned. It's physically not possible."

"So where is the unit now, Mr. Stokes?" Veronica smiled in a placatory fashion.

Stokes cleared his throat. He was clearly unhappy with the course of the entire conversation. "I'm afraid I have no idea. My report will state that the device was destroyed in the explosion. Now look–" He waved a manifest in front of them. "–I really have to be getting on. I'm expected to provide a full passenger register for the police before the day is out."

"Of course. We're sorry to have kept you." Veronica took Newbury's proffered arm and began to walk away. Then, as if just remembering something, she stopped and looked back. "Oh, and Mr. Stokes? Just one more thing before you go?"

"Yes?"

"Could you tell me why all of the passengers were confined to their seats, with loops of rope around their ankles?"

Stokes looked as if he were about to choke. "A simple safety precaution, Miss Hobbes. In case of emergency, all passengers are required to insert their left foot into the safety brace underneath the seat in front. It stops people tumbling all over the craft if the pilot encounters dangerous turbulence whilst airborne."

Veronica nodded. "Thank you, Mr. Stokes. You've been most helpful."

She watched with Newbury as the little man scuttled away, keen to put distance between him and the ire of the moonlighting academics. The light was fading now, the sun low in the sky over the city. The crowds of people around the edges of the park had begun to thin and disperse.

"You understand, of course, that there's no feasible way in which the skeleton of a brass automaton could have been incinerated in that blaze? Especially when one considers that the majority of the human cadavers are still relatively intact." Newbury sounded contemplative now, rather than angry.

"Yes, my thoughts exactly."

"I'm beginning to think that Her Majesty's suspicions were correct. Something is definitely wrong here, and I'll wager it has its roots in the offices of Chapman and Villiers Air Transportation Services." He sighed, blinking to keep himself alert. "For now, though, I think it's time I retired to my lodgings. Can I drop you at home on my way, Miss Hobbes?"

She nodded, clearly exhausted. "Please do, Sir Maurice."

He held the cordon for her as they took their leave of the crash site and made their way to the nearest carriage.

The evening was still and cold as Newbury, attired only in a simple dressing gown, settled in his study before a roaring open fire. A book was open on his lap—*Trelawny's History of Esoteric Societies of the Seventeenth Century*—one of the many aged, leather-bound volumes that lined the walls around the room. Other shelves held more bizarre specimens: vials of chemical compounds, jars filled with preserved biological samples, a pentagram cast out of twenty-four carat gold, the bleached skull of a chimpanzee and much more besides. Paper files were stacked neatly in rows along one wall, containing reams of case notes, old academic papers, clippings and other assorted reference materials collected during many long hours of research. The study was his private haven, the room he filled with all the ephemera of his life. It was the one place where he could relax, where he felt free to become himself and where much of his actual deduction was carried out; over time, the study had become a place of revelation. He eased back in his armchair and turned the pages in his book.

Mrs. Bradshaw had retired for the evening after drawing him a bath and admonishing him enthusiastically for the state of his clothes. He smiled. She was forbidden from entering the study, but if she were to ever see its contents—not least the cluttered manner in which he liked to keep it—he wagered she'd flee his service at once. Not only that, but many of his files contained confidential information that needed to be kept away from prying eyes. He had no reason to doubt Mrs. Bradshaw's integrity, but he suspected the contents of his files would be enough to discredit the monarchy at least ten times over, and he feared what temptation could do to even the most loyal of people. For that reason, he kept the door to the room locked at all times, even when he was inside of it. He'd invited Bainbridge in once or twice, for he trusted him implicitly, and after the events of the previous summer—during which they'd hunted a madman intent on inflicting an Ancient Egyptian plague on London—he knew the man had a stomach for the bizarre.

Tonight, however, he was happy for the solitude. He sat watching the dance of the flames for a while. He couldn't help thinking of the ruined, tortured faces of the corpses in the wreck of the airship that he'd seen that afternoon. Veronica had taken it badly, but so, in truth, had he. He'd seen innumerable corpses in his lifetime, of course, but in this instance, it was a matter of scale; never before had he witnessed a scene quite so horrifying as this.

He reached for a small brown bottle from the shelf behind his head. The label was peeling, but he knew well what it contained. He unscrewed the lid and poured a measure of the liquid into the half-full glass of claret that rested on the side table by his armchair. The laudanum would help him sleep, or so he told himself as he raised the glass to his lips and took a long drink. In the morning, he would meet Veronica at the office, and they would head to Battersea, to Chapman and Villiers's manufactory. There he hoped to find out more about the mysterious automata and their creator, Mr. Pierre Villiers, an exiled Frenchman who—he had read—had been brought up on charges over a decade ago for experimenting on human wastrels in his Parisian laboratory. Still, that was for the morning. For tonight, he hoped, oblivion was near at hand. He drained his glass and sank back into the comfort of his Chesterfield, waiting for the laudanum to do its work.

CHAPTER 6

Given the heavy fog of the previous day, the morning seemed unusually bright as Veronica made her way up the steps outside the main entrance of the British Museum. Birds twittered in the trees overhead, and the sun poked through the clouds to sprinkle bright columns of light across the city.

After the horrors of yesterday, Veronica had retired to her lodgings in Kensington, where she'd bathed, eaten and gone directly to bed. Now, feeling somewhat refreshed, she hoped that the coming day would prove less fraught, and also less likely to inspire nightmares. The scenes from the crash site were still emblazoned on her mind, and she tried to push them to the back of her thoughts as she prepared herself for what the new day might bring.

Watkins, the doorman, was on hand to permit her entrance to the museum at this early hour, and he did so with a kindly smile. It was not yet eight, but she suspected Newbury would already be sitting at his desk, reading his newspaper as was typical of his morning routine. All the more surprising, then, was the scene that greeted her when she did finally open the door to the office on the basement floor. Newbury was nowhere to be seen, his desk undisturbed, his coat and hat distinctly absent from the stand inside the door. Instead,

Miss Coulthard sat at her desk, her face in her hands, tears streaming down her cheeks in desperation and dismay.

"Oh, Miss Hobbes. I'm sorry that you should happen upon me in this state." She looked up at Veronica as she came through the door.

Veronica quickly peeled off her coat and hat and pulled a chair up beside Miss Coulthard, taking her hand in her own. "I take it there's still no news?"

Miss Coulthard, sobbing, nodded briskly. "We've had no word. Neither have his employers. We all fear the worst, Miss Hobbes. I can think of no reason why he'd stay away this long, unless the revenants have got him."

"Now, Miss Coulthard, we don't know anything for sure. I do think it's unlikely that he's had a run-in with one of these 'revenant' creatures. I hear lots of talk about them, all over the city, but I'll admit I've yet to see one myself, and in truth, I'm starting to wonder if they even exist at all." She smiled warmly. "Have you seen one with your own eyes, Miss Coulthard?"

"No, Miss Hobbes, I can't say that I have."

"There you are, then. Neither of us can even verify their existence. So how likely do you find it that Jack may have encountered one on his way to work?"

"Well . . ." Miss Coulthard wiped her eyes, sniffling. "I suppose not likely at all. It's just . . ." She screwed her hands into fists, frustrated. "What *else* could have happened to him?"

Veronica rubbed the back of her neck. "Well, that's what we'll engage the police to find out today. I'm sure it'll turn out to be something quite innocent."

Miss Coulthard smiled. "Thank you, Miss Hobbes. I've been waiting here for Sir Maurice to accompany me, after what he said to me yesterday, but he hasn't arrived as yet. I fear he's made other arrangements or decided to go elsewhere this morning, on an errand or suchlike."

Veronica glanced at the clock, a slight frown crossing

her face. "No, no. We definitely arranged to meet here this morning. I'm sure he's just been held up. When he arrives, we'll put on a fresh pot of tea and then I'm sure Sir Maurice will send a note across town to his associates at Scotland Yard." Veronica noticed that Miss Coulthard had reached into her pocket and was now clutching a small sepia photograph to her chest. "Miss Coulthard, may I enquire as to the identity of the person in your photograph?"

The secretary looked down, staring at the photograph as if seeing it for the first time. She held it out to Veronica. "My brother, taken before he went off to war."

Veronica took the battered old picture and gave it an appraising look. A man, dressed in a field uniform, posed for the camera, a rifle cocked over one arm, his other arm resting against a large stone plinth. The backdrop was a large canvas showing paintings of trees and other unidentifiable flora. "He's very handsome, Miss Coulthard." She turned it over. There was an inscription on the back, written in a shaky hand. It read: *Jack Coulthard, January 1901*. "Where did he see action?"

"India. He was invalided out six months ago, after he was savaged by a wild animal whilst on patrol. The men he was with were all killed. We were blessed that he survived. They told us he was gripped by a terrible fever for days after the incident. When he returned home he was a shell of his former self. But he picked himself up and applied for an apprenticeship at Fitchett and Browns. They've done well by him, too. He's made quite a name for himself amongst the junior members of the establishment."

"I'm glad to hear it, Miss Coulthard. Now, I think this photograph will be useful for the police, if you can bear to part with it for a short while? They'll be able to use it to show Jack's likeness to their officers. It'll make it easier for them to spot him if they know exactly who they're looking for."

Miss Coulthard nodded. "I thought as much." She passed

Veronica the picture and watched as the other woman slipped it safely into her purse. "I don't know what we'd do without him. It'll ruin us if he can't be found."

"I'm sure it won't come to that. Now . . ." Veronica trailed off at the sound of footsteps on the other side of the door. "Ah, that sounds like Sir Maurice. Come on, let's get that pot warming." She rose to her feet just as the door swung open and Newbury stepped into the office. He looked haggard, as if he hadn't slept. Dark rings circled his eyes, and his face had taken on an unusual pallor. He lifted his bowler hat from his head and smiled. "Good morning, ladies."

Veronica looked immediately concerned. "Sir Maurice, are you unwell?"

He shook his head dismissively. "Only a malady of my own making, I fear, my dear Miss Hobbes. Nothing a strong cup of Earl Grey won't fix." He draped his coat on the stand beside him. "Miss Coulthard. Any news on your missing sibling?"

The secretary shook her head, fighting back further tears.

Newbury frowned. "Well, give me your address on a piece of paper, along with the particulars of the last time you saw your brother, his place of work and any distinguishing marks that may help the police to identify him. If you have it to me in the next half hour, I'll dash off a note to my friends at Scotland Yard."

"Thank you, Sir Maurice. I'm very much obliged to you."

"Say nothing of it, Miss Coulthard. It's the very least I can do." He rubbed his hand over his chin. "Now, Miss Hobbes, let us adjourn to my desk and see if we can't plan our next move."

"I'll be with you directly, Sir Maurice, just as soon as I've organised this pot of tea." She watched as he disappeared through the partition door, unsure what to make of his sudden change in demeanour.

* * *

"So what you're saying is that you're not convinced that the automaton was the cause of the disaster?"

Newbury nodded. His colour had returned, and he seemed imbued once again with his usual energy. Veronica had to admit she was relieved; when he'd walked through the door that morning, she'd been just about ready to hail a cab and ferry him to the nearest doctor. Now, after a recuperative cup of tea and a few minutes spent composing a note for Miss Coulthard, he was cheerfully engaged in outlining his current thoughts on the matter in hand. "What I'm saying is that I'm willing to hold off judgement until I've seen the evidence for myself. I've seen one or two of these automata demonstrated in my time, and they're certainly amazing creations. Technology moves quickly, these days. If you've any doubt, just look up at the sky." He gestured with both of his hands. "Chapman and Villiers is one of the pre-eminent air transportation organisations in London. If even a quarter of those airships above the city are under the control of an automaton, then in my book, that's a wondrous thing indeed!"

"I don't doubt you're right, Sir Maurice, but we must be sure not to let our enthusiasm for technological developments cloud our judgement in this matter."

He looked at her slyly. "I can see you've got a sharp sense about you, Miss Hobbes. You're absolutely right, of course. But equally I trust you will not damn the technology before we have carried out the due investigative process."

"Agreed. Even if Mr. Stokes is an odious wretch who did nothing but cloud my opinion of his organisation."

"Indeed. If we're lucky, we'll have no further dealings with the man today."

Veronica sipped her tea thoughtfully. "So, what of the Whitechapel murders? Have you thought any further on the mystery of the glowing policeman?"

Newbury shook his head, slowly. "Alas, I've had to forgo

that particular case, for the time being, anyway. If we get to the bottom of this airship issue quickly enough, I'll see what I can do to help. Otherwise, I'll just have to point Charles in the right direction and hope he can get to the bottom of it himself. He's got plenty of good men at his disposal, and if the case does turn out to have a supernatural origin, it won't be the first time he's come up against that sort of thing and won."

Veronica raised her eyebrows.

"A story for another time, perhaps." He stood, pulling on his gloves.

Veronica placed her cup back on the saucer. "One last question before we take our leave. May I ask why this crash is deemed so important to the Crown?"

Newbury paused for a moment, as if deciding how much he should disclose to this woman, whom—despite her having been in his employ for only a matter of weeks—he was already beginning to trust with his life.

Veronica took his lengthy pause as a sign of his disapproval. She flushed red. "Oh, please forgive me! Have I overstepped the mark?" She stood, nearly knocking her cup and saucer over as she banged awkwardly against the edge of his desk.

Newbury waved her to sit down again. "No, not at all, Miss Hobbes. The truth of the matter is simple: I don't know. I'll admit, I'm finding that question peculiarly frustrating. I can see no obvious connection between the affairs of the monarchy and the disaster that became of *The Lady Armitage*. Not only that, but the Whitechapel case is more definitely within my area of expertise." He sighed. "Nevertheless, one must do one's duty. And I must admit, I'm rather intrigued by this whole automaton business." He held the door open for Veronica and ushered her through.

Miss Coulthard was sitting at her desk, the nib of her pen scratching noisily as she attempted to transcribe one of Newbury's recent academic papers for the museum archives.

He shook his head as he collected his coat. "Miss Coulthard? Did you manage to have my letter sent to Scotland Yard as I instructed?"

"Yes, Sir Maurice. I sent it by cab as you requested."

"Very good. Then I must ask you what you're still doing here, scratching out one of my illegible essays when you should be at home, awaiting news of your brother?" He smiled warmly.

"Well, sir, this document was supposed to be completed for filing yesterday. I was concerned about getting behind in my work."

"Poppycock! Now, Miss Hobbes and I will be gone for the rest of the day, so I dare suggest you won't be missed. Go on, be off with you. I shan't take my own cab until I'm convinced you're well away from this place."

"Thank you, sir. I won't forget your kindness." She placed her pen carefully back in the drawer and fumbled with her papers.

A moment later, when Miss Coulthard had collected her belongings, the three of them left together, locking the door to the office behind them.

CHAPTER 7

From the Chelsea Bridge, the airship works were clearly visible in the morning light as a series of immense red brick hangars, squat beside the shimmering Thames, fumes rising like smoke signals from a row of tall, broad chimneys. Steam hissed from outlet pipes in great white plumes, whilst water gushed back into the river in a deluge of brown sludge. Huge airships were tethered to the roofs of the hangars, reminiscent of a row of children's balloons, bobbing languorously in the breeze.

Newbury looked out over the river. Ships and boats of all shapes and sizes drifted lazily along the shipping lanes, dipping gently with the ebb and flow of the water. It was busy, thick with the detritus of industry. It was noisy, too: horns blaring and gulls chattering over the constant clatter of horses' hooves as they rolled over the bridge towards their destination. He caught sight of one ship to which the others were giving a wide berth. He studied it for a moment through the window. Large red crosses had been painted on the sides of the hull, and the flag had been lowered to half-mast. He guessed it was a plague ship, carrying the corpses of the dead out to sea, where they would likely be dumped, unceremoniously, into the water. He knew from his discussions with Bainbridge that the corpses of plague victims had been turning up all over the city, particularly in the slums, where the people lived in squalor and the virus could easily spread from host to host. Stories of the "revenants" were spreading, too, with the daily newspapers parroting the rumours heard on the streets and sensationalising the epidemic for the gleeful consumption of cockatoos such as Felicity Johnson. They were right to fear, though; before the virus killed its host, it would completely unravel their humanity, transforming them into a monstrous killing machine. Their flesh would stop regenerating, their only thoughts becoming animalistic, feral; in short, they would be reduced to nothing but the basest of creatures, and with that loss of faculty, they'd become almost unstoppable, feeling no pain, showing no awareness of wounds that would kill an average man. It was as if the virus, somehow, kept them alive through all of this, waiting for an unidentified biological trigger. Then, after a handful of days had passed, the virus would complete its work and turn their brains to sponge, dropping their spent, lifeless bodies by the side of the road. It was a bad way to go. He hoped, for Miss Coulthard's sake, that she was wrong and that her brother had so far managed to evade infection. Everything he knew about the virus suggested if that if he *had* been infected, by now he'd either be dead in a gutter or else stalking the fog-shrouded streets by night, a mindless monster in search of food and blood.

Newbury closed his eyes for a moment, lulled by the motion of the cab. He imagined that Her Majesty would be growing impatient with the crisis by now, keen for the virus to burn itself out in the poorer districts of the city. She probably had a hundred scientists searching for a vaccination. If no solution were found soon, he had no doubt that she would place a cordon around the slums in an effort to slow the spread of the disease. Everyone was anxious, fearful of what might happen if the plague truly managed to get a grip on the city. Some projections suggested that up to 50 percent of the population could succumb to the illness: if not killed by the virus itself, then taken by one of the rampaging monsters it created. He suspected that it would be some time yet before the issue came to a head, and that the worst was probably still to come.

He looked up. Veronica sat in silence on the other side of the cab, lost in thought. Her hands were folded neatly on her lap, her face turned to the opposite window. She was wearing a powder blue jacket and white blouse, with matching culottes. He admired her modern sensibilities. Indeed, he admired much about her. Searching around for another distraction, he chose not to disturb her reverie. Instead, he unfolded his morning copy of *The Times* on his knee and inspected the day's headlines. Unsurprisingly, the editor had chosen to dedicate the front page to a huge article about the *Lady Armitage* disaster. The headline read AIRSHIP CRASHES IN FINSBURY PARK: SABOTAGE SUSPECTED, UPWARDS OF 50 DEAD. Newbury shook his head. Sabotage suspected? He wondered if Stokes had been feeding ideas to the press. He certainly wouldn't put it past the man. He hoped to find the company's directors a little less repellent but was expecting to be disappointed. In his experience, like invariably attracted like, and any associates of Mr. Stokes would either have to maintain a will of iron or an ego as enormous as that of Stokes himself.

He settled back in his seat, flicking through the pages of newsprint on his knee. He was still feeling delicate from the excesses of the laudanum, and silently chastised himself for giving in to his cravings. Miss Hobbes was astute, and his late arrival at the office and less-than-savoury appearance that morning had not gone unnoticed. He resolved to represent himself better in future.

The driver tapped loudly on the top of the cab, and both Newbury and Veronica looked up in surprise, dragged away from their thoughts.

"Yes?"

"Is this the place you're looking for, sir?"

He glanced out of the window. The cab had come to rest outside a small office building appended to a much larger complex of industrial hangars and factories. A sign above the door read CHAPMAN & VILLIERS AIR TRANSPORTATION SERVICES.

"Yes, thank you driver, this is the place." He sighed, and caught Veronica's eye, folding his newspaper under his arm as he did so. "Are you ready, my dear?"

"Absolutely."

"Well then, after you." He watched her clamber down from the cab to the street below. He had a feeling that today, one way or another, some of the missing pieces of the mystery would begin clicking into place.

The offices of Chapman & Villiers were an austere affair, housed within a separate structure that was divorced from the factory proper by a large courtyard and an elaborate set of cast-iron gates. Clearly the proprietors were intent on maintaining a strict distance between their visiting clientele and the factory workers, who, Newbury guessed, would likely have a separate entrance somewhere around the rear of the complex. It appeared, from the signs evident in the windows, that the office not only dealt with the company's commercial affairs but also served as a travel agency, of sorts, selling passage on its fleet of charter vessels to locations all over the globe, from Prussia to China, Jersey to Hong Kong. Newbury toyed with his gloves for a moment. "Well, Miss Hobbes, I do hope you have your detective's cap on?"

In reply, she stepped forward and pulled the office door open before her. It groaned loudly on its hinges. "Of course. After you, Sir Maurice."

He shook his head, taking the door from her and ushering

her inside. "Come now, Miss Hobbes, let's do things properly."

The main reception area was as sobering in appearance as one expected after taking in the view of the building from the outside: the walls were hung with a dark, burgundy covering that seemed to soak up all the light, and a scattering of chairs were situated beside low coffee tables and tall leafy plants. A set of short stairs led up to another, unseen level. A clerk sat in one corner with his back to them, talking to a customer in hushed tones about purchasing transport to the Far East.

But their attention was most immediately drawn to the man behind a mahogany desk in the centre of the room, his fingers forming a perfect pyramid before him on the polished surface, his pale face belying his apparent displeasure at receiving customers so close to lunch. When he spoke, his voice was thin and nasal. "Can I help you?"

Newbury strode up to the desk and placed his hat down beside a sheaf of paper files. The clerk looked at the item as if it were a horse's head, his disdain clearly evident.

"I'm here to see Mr. Chapman."

The clerk made a show of looking in his ledger. "Are you sure, sir? I have no meetings scheduled for Mr. Chapman today. He really is a very busy man." He shut his ledger as if that were simply the end of the matter. "Perhaps you'd care to make an appointment?"

"I'm afraid you don't seem to understand. It's imperative I speak with Mr. Chapman today." Newbury glowered at the man behind the desk.

"Imperative, you say, sir? Could I enquire as to what business you may have with my employer that could possibly be so urgent? If you're looking to make a complaint about a recent journey, then you can find the forms behind you on the table there."

Newbury sighed. "I'm here on the business of the Crown. It is a delicate matter that I wish to discuss with Mr. Chapman in private. Of course, if you'd prefer me to air his private business out here–?"

The man's entire demeanour changed. His face seemed to flush with colour, and his pursed lips split into a wide smile. He swallowed, and parted his hands in a conciliatory gesture. The timbre of his voice became immediately more welcoming. "Of course, sir. I quite understand. Allow me to go and enquire as to whether Mr. Chapman is available. May I offer him your name?"

"Sir Maurice Newbury."

"Please take a seat, Sir Maurice. I will only be a moment."

Newbury watched as the clerk scuttled out from behind his desk and crossed the office, glancing once behind him to see if Newbury was watching. He climbed the stairs and disappeared from view. Veronica lowered herself into one of the chairs, smiling to herself. Newbury paced the office, obviously impatient.

A moment or two later, the clerk appeared at the top of the stairs. He climbed down, his hands clasped behind his back, and approached Newbury tentatively, as one might approach a lion. "Mr. Chapman is in his office and would be only too delighted to make your acquaintance, Sir Maurice. I will show you up now." He beckoned for them to follow. Newbury remembered to reclaim his hat before helping Veronica to her feet.

At the top of the stairs, three doors led into what Newbury supposed were private offices. The clerk hesitated before the middle one, clearing his throat. He rapped politely, three times, and then opened the door with a flourish, stepping to one side to allow them to enter.

"Your visitors, sir."

Newbury followed Veronica into the room, his hat tucked carefully under his arm.

It was a large office, and ostentatiously furnished, cluttered with artwork and fine goods from all corners of the globe. Newbury glanced around, trying to get a measure of the place. A large marble fireplace dominated one wall, whilst above it, a portrait of the Queen looked mournfully down upon the visitors. A display case in one corner held relics from as far afield as Constantinople, Baghdad, Greece and Delhi; souvenirs, Newbury supposed, from journeys undertaken in pursuit of business in those far-flung nations.

Chapman himself lounged in a large Chesterfield, smoking a cigarette. His hair was blond and cut long around his shoulders, and he was dressed in his shirtsleeves and a black waistcoat. Newbury thought he had the look of a cat about him, languorously warming himself before the fire. He stood as Newbury entered the room, and moved quickly to shake his hand. "Sir Maurice Newbury, I presume?"

"Indeed." Newbury took his hand and shook it firmly. He stepped to one side. "Allow me to introduce my assistant, Miss Veronica Hobbes."

Chapman smiled and took her hand, holding it for just a moment longer than was necessary, before inclining his head politely. "Delighted, I'm sure." He gestured at the clerk, who was still standing in the doorway. "Now, can my man Soames fetch you any refreshments? A brandy, perhaps?" He glanced at the grandfather clock in the corner. "Not too early for that, are we?" He looked baffled, as if he'd only just realised the time.

Newbury shook his head. "A pot of tea would be fine. Earl Grey, if you have it?"

Chapman nodded briskly, and Soames disappeared again, clicking the door shut behind him. They heard his footsteps on the stairs as he descended to the office below.

Chapman beckoned for them to take a seat, folding himself back into his chair. He reclaimed his cigarette from the ashtray on the table and took a long, luxurious draw. It was clear to Newbury that the man didn't give much thought to convention: his entire manner was at odds with his station, and his appearance marked him as something of a fop. Nevertheless, he couldn't help feeling drawn to the man's bohemian charm. He could see immediately that there was a cool intelligence lurking behind the darting ice-blue eyes, and whilst he didn't put much stock in the man's taste in furnishings, he had to admit the fellow had an acute nose for business. Either that or he was spending his inheritance at a rate that would soon see him bankrupt or destitute. Chapman tapped his cigarette in the ashtray and regarded Newbury with a wistful smile. "So, Sir Maurice, I presume you are here regarding that terrible business with *The Lady Armitage*?" He looked suddenly serious. "A truly lamentable affair."

Newbury nodded. "Yes. Have you visited the site of the wreckage yourself, Mr. Chapman?"

"No." He paused to take another draw on his cigarette. "Unfortunately, I was previously engaged–a small matter to resolve with my banker–so I took the liberty of relying on my legal representative, Mr. Stokes."

Newbury stiffened. "Yes, I spoke with Mr. Stokes for a brief while yesterday."

Chapman smiled knowingly. "Terrible bore, isn't he? Seems to be the way with these legal chaps. Dependable, though. I trust he gave you everything you required?"

Newbury nodded. "In a manner of speaking. Nevertheless, I thought it wise to pay you a visit this afternoon, in an effort to get a better understanding of your operation, and to see for myself these automata that Stokes mentioned."

Chapman's eyes seemed to light up. "Ah, the automata. Villiers's prized creations. They are impressive machines, Sir Maurice, if you have not yet seen one?"

Newbury glanced at Veronica. "Indeed not. I would certainly welcome a demonstration."

"I'm sure that can be arranged." He reached over and crumpled his cigarette in the ashtray. "And you, Miss Hobbes. I'm sure you'd find the machines equally as impressive."

"I'm sure I would, Mr. Chapman."

Newbury looked up at the sound of rapping on the door, and then Soames entered, bearing their tea on a large platter. He crossed the room and placed it on the table before them. Chapman watched him turn and leave, waiting until the last moment to call after him. "Thank you, Soames."

Newbury scratched his chin absently. "So, Mr. Chapman, Mr. Stokes mentioned yesterday that one of these remarkable new automata was behind the controls of *The Lady Armitage* when she went down?" Veronica studied the other man's face, watching for a reaction.

He remained impassive. "Quite possible. I believe around half of the fleet is now piloted by the machines. We even have a Royal charter. Remarkable, really, when you come to think of it."

"Quite." Newbury paused. "Mr. Chapman, I'm not sure if you're aware of all the circumstances surrounding the disaster yesterday morning?"

Chapman looked puzzled. "Mr. Stokes provided me with a thorough report of his findings. I also spoke with Inspector Foulkes of Scotland Yard. I'd imagine myself to be in full possession of the facts."

"Did Mr. Stokes's report make reference to the fact that the pilot of the vessel appeared to be missing from the wreckage?"

Chapman fished around in his waistcoat pocket, searching out his silver cigarette case. He flicked it open and withdrew one of the small white sticks, then offered the case around to the others. When they didn't accept, he slipped it back into his pocket and struck a match with a loud rasp. Smoke billowed around his face as he regarded Newbury. "He made mention of the fact that the unit in question had been destroyed in the impact."

Newbury met his gaze. "I find that very difficult to believe, Mr. Chapman. I understand the skeletal frames of these automata are constructed out of brass?"

"Correct."

"Then why were there no remnants of the unit in evidence anywhere on board the ship? Both Miss Hobbes and I toured the wreckage, and I can assure you, there was nothing to be found."

Chapman poured the tea, his face thoughtful. "Well, if Mr. Stokes's assertions are correct, the unit may have burnt up in the fires that followed the crash."

Newbury sipped from his teacup. "Come now, Mr. Chapman. We both know that the heat in that wreckage would never have reached a temperature enough to incinerate brass. There has to be another explanation."

Chapman shrugged apologetically. "Perhaps it survived the incident and clambered out of the wreckage, wandering away into the park?"

"The police are certainly following that line of enquiry. Tell me, do you have any notion what may have gone wrong with the unit to cause it to lose control of the vessel, Mr. Chapman?"

Chapman shook his head. "As I understand it, Sir Maurice, the automaton was not responsible for the crash. We've had an impeccable safety record throughout the fleet since the implementation of these machines. I find it far more probable that, regrettably, there was a mechanical fault with the vessel itself."

"So you put no stock in the notion that the automaton unit may have malfunctioned?"

"I do not. Although in truth, you'd have to ask Villiers. He's the man who invented the things; he should be able to give you a better idea of their functions and limitations." He shrugged.

Veronica placed her empty teacup on the table. "So, Mr. Chapman, where would we find Mr. Villiers?"

Chapman smiled. "He'll be in his workshop behind the mechanical works. I can take you there, if you like, by way of the airship manufactory?" He stood, not waiting for a reply. "What do you say? A quick tour of the facility?"

Both Newbury and Veronica rose from their seats. Veronica met Newbury's eye. "Mr. Chapman, I think that would be an excellent idea."

CHAPTER 8

The hangar was cold, and Veronica hugged her jacket to herself, wishing she'd thought to bring a shawl or a more substantial overcoat along with her that morning. Her breath fogged in the air before her face. She tried to avoid shivering.

They were standing on a steel walkway above the main factory floor, where the huge shell of an airship gondola was currently under construction. It sat upon a large wooden pallet, squat in the centre of the massive room, scaffolds running over its surface like the strands of a vast spider's web, ensnaring the bowels of the partly erected ship. Men buzzed around the skeleton of the vessel like worker ants, swarming up the sides of the scaffolds to place glass panes into the wooden window-frames and pass doors, seats and other furnishings through to the workmen inside. Tools clattered loudly, and men shouted to each other above the noise.

Veronica stared down from the railing that ran along the side of the walkway. After her experience the previous day, she found the sight of the unfinished gondola incredibly eerie, reminiscent of the smashed wreck of *The Lady Armitage*. Many of the fittings were the same as those she had seen inside the shattered vessel, and from where she was standing, the internal layout looked practically identical. She could hardly bear to look at the passenger cabin, with its row upon row of empty seats, without visualising the scene inside of the burnt-out ship; the blank, ruined faces of the dead staring back at her, accusingly. She fancied for a moment that she could still smell the stench of the wreck, the aroma of cooked human flesh assaulting her nostrils and palate. Her stomach heaved.

She shook her head, realising that she was gripping the railing tightly with both hands. She had a sudden unnerving sense of vertigo, like she was tumbling over the railing towards the factory floor below. She closed her eyes. The moment passed. She caught her breath, drawing raggedly at the air. She knew it was no good giving in to melancholy. She'd seen the results of that before, long ago. What was done was done, and now the most important thing was to find out who was responsible for the disaster, and if necessary, aid Newbury in bringing them to justice. She breathed calmly, and hoped that the others hadn't taken note of her momentary lapse.

She watched a man below struggling to carry a large mirror across the factory floor, and wondered for a moment if the new ship was intended as a replacement for *The Lady Armitage*. She decided not; it was clearly too soon after the crash for the workman to be this advanced with the construction. She turned from the railing. "It's quite an operation you have here, Mr. Chapman."

Chapman, who had been deep in conversation with Newbury, turned and smiled. "Wait until you see the next hangar, Miss Hobbes. Now, that's really something to behold." He nodded at the workmen down below. "Come on, let's get a closer look." He led them along the steel walkway, their feet clanging loudly against the metal rungs as they walked. They made their way down a series of steps at the far end of the hangar.

Chapman crossed the floor to where the men were working and climbed up onto the wooden pallet, peering into the shell of the new gondola. He seemed pleased.

Down at this level, the air was filled with the smell of oil and wet paint, and the noise was tremendous: banging, sawing, shouting. There appeared to be an entire army of men at work. Newbury counted at least ten of them, dancing around each other, ferrying components back and forth, their faces damp with perspiration and grime. Not one of them looked up from their work to eye the newcomers as Newbury circled the construction, drinking it all in.

He looked up. High above them, the red brick walls turned to windows, allowing the natural light to seep in from outside. The roof was a skein of corrugated lead sheets, laid over a framework of wooden beams. The place was enormous, yet seemed bizarrely reduced by the sheer size of the gondola that was being erected inside of it.

Newbury finished circling the pallet and then moved to stand beside Chapman, clapping a hand on his shoulder to get his attention. The other man, who'd been standing with his hands on his hips, admiring the work of his craftsmen, stepped back, leaning in to hear Newbury's question.

"How long does it take you to build one of these? From start to finish, I mean?"

Chapman raised his voice so the other man could hear. "About three weeks. This is the smallest size in the fleet, a passenger-class vessel. The rest of the frame is being welded in the next hangar." He pointed to the other end of the vast room, where a huge archway led through to the next part of the site. Newbury could just make out some of what was going on inside, with iron girders being lifted into place around a wooden frame, the entire construction apparently suspended from the ceiling.

"Three weeks? That seems awfully quick."

Chapman nodded. "I know. We've spent the last ten years perfecting the process, ironing out all of the wrinkles." He coughed, and seemed to consider searching out another cigarette, before quickly changing his mind. "This one's bound for India." He nodded at the gondola in front of them. "It'll be out of here in a couple of days. We'll have an automaton fly it over the water. That way there's no need for the pilot to come back again, you see." He smiled. "It's a good package. The new owner is provided with a fully trained pilot, and we're not stuck ferrying people back and forth across the ocean."

Newbury nodded. He could see the economy in the system. "I admire your business acumen, Mr. Chapman. And your men certainly seem to know what they're doing." They both regarded the workmen still scurrying to and fro all around them.

Newbury glanced at Veronica out of the corner of his eye. He could see that she was feeling uncomfortable being around another airship so soon after her visit to the crash site the previous day. He decided to hurry things along. "Are we ready to move on, Miss Hobbes? I'm eager to see how the balloon itself is constructed."

Veronica smiled thankfully. "Yes, indeed. Mr. Chapman, please lead on."

They followed Chapman across the floor of the manufactory towards the archway and through to the next hangar. As they approached, Veronica gasped in wonder at the sight. The space itself must have been twice the size of the previous room, opening out into a cavernous hall filled with all manner of mechanical wonder and, at its heart, the massive skeletal frame of an airship balloon. Light shone down from the windows above in great shafts, penetrating the gloom and picking out the swirling dust motes in the air. Newbury stood beside Veronica as they looked up in awe. The immense structure of the airship was clearly taking shape, suspended from the ceiling on an array of large mechanical arms. Iron girders were being welded into place around a wooden frame, hot sparks showering the room below in a series of glittering waterfalls. Men, tied into harnesses and dangling from roof joists, clambered around the structure, gas tanks strapped to their backs, welding torches clamped firmly in their gloved fists. Other men operated large cranelike machines, lifting the iron girders into place for their colleagues to weld. Newbury had never seen anything like them; the operator sat inside a small cab on top of the machine, manipulating levers to control the arm, which terminated in a large claw used to grasp the iron girders and move them to precisely the required position. The machines themselves were fixed in place, bolted to the floor, and spluttered loudly as their steam engines turned over in the relatively enclosed space of the hangar. Chapman held his hands out, encompassing the scene before them. "Impressive, isn't it?"

Newbury couldn't help but agree. "Magnificent. A remarkable achievement."

Chapman smiled. "It is, rather." He rubbed his hands together in an unconscious gesture. "The difficulty, of course, is one of space. We have only enough room to assemble one vessel at a time. I've been thinking, recently, of constructing another facility on the other side of the river, but in truth, the advent of the automaton business has rendered that superfluous, at least for now."

Veronica was still regarding the skeleton of the vessel suspended overhead. She glanced at Chapman. "Are the automata also manufactured on the premises, Mr. Chapman?"

"Indeed they are, Miss Hobbes. Although I feel I must warn you that the scale of the operation is hardly as impressive." He indicated the airship. "The technology is still relatively new, and the units are expensive to develop. Mass production is unfortunately some years away. Nevertheless, orders have been growing steadily, and the production line has been constantly engaged since its inception." He cleared his throat.

"We'll pass through the area on the way to see Villiers in a few moments."

Newbury looked contemplative. "Tell me, Mr. Chapman, why it is that a highly successful airship business should make the move into artificial intelligence? It strikes me that the two disciplines make strange bedfellows. Why invest in something so new and speculative?"

Chapman paused before responding, as if weighing the question. "On one hand, in Villiers, I had the expertise and the vision to pull it off, and on the other, I saw the opportunity to make a return." He shook his head, not satisfied with his own answer. "No, it's more than that. After my father passed on, Sir Maurice, I found myself in the enviable position of inheriting an industrial empire, and with it, a significant fortune. I could have taken the opportunity to live a life of pleasure, wasting my time dallying with insignificant trifles, spending my days lounging around my estate. I admit, for a while I was tempted. But I also knew that if I devoted my life to such lackadaisical pursuits, I would soon shrivel up and die. I needed stimulation, and more, I had an overriding desire to aid progress. After meeting Villiers and being introduced to his revolutionary plans for a new breed of airship, I decided to invest a portion of my fortune in setting up this firm." He paused only momentarily, obviously in his stride. "I could see clearly, then, the impact that Villiers's incredible new designs would have on the air transportation industry, and with time and a lot of hard work, my faith was proved right. Chapman and Villiers Air Transportation Services became one of the most important airship operators in the world."

The others were listening intently. "So why risk that now? Why divert the resources of your successful company into something untested, unproved on the open market?"

Chapman shrugged. "Because I grew bored, and because Villiers kept pushing forward, irrespective of finances, time or effort. You'll understand that when you meet him. The man is fuelled by a passion for his work. He was like an unstoppable force, and it was only then, after watching him work himself into the ground, night after night, for months on end, that I finally realised how the automaton project could help us to fulfil our original ambition. I started to consider the almost limitless applications of these mechanical men. If they could learn to write, they could be employed as clerks. If they could learn to cook, they could replace servants. If we taught them the art of war, they could even march into battle against the Empire's foes. Think how many needless deaths could be averted? Surely these remarkable devices could aid in the technological revolution of the Empire? Surely that could only be of benefit to the wider populace, freeing them from the tedium of household chores, leaving more time for education and other, more profitable enterprises? I think you'll see, when we have Villiers give us a demonstration of the units, what a spectacular revolution awaits us, just around the corner, when the world becomes truly aware of what we're doing here in our little factory in Battersea."

Veronica met Newbury's eyes. "But Mr. Chapman, what of the people pushed out by these automata, and what of their families? If their jobs are taken away from them, to be replaced by these artificial men, many of them will be left destitute, with no hope of finding other work. Surely *that's* not in the best interests of the Empire?"

Chapman nodded. "Yes. I, too, have concerned myself with that, Miss Hobbes. Yet . . . we can't allow it to halt progress. Society will redress the balance, given time. Communities will change, and people will find worthwhile employ in any number of different industries. The automaton revolution will provide them with even more opportunities, and I'm convinced it will raise the standard of living across all classes throughout the entirety of the Empire."

Newbury looked unsure. "Grand claims indeed, Mr. Chapman."

"Time will tell, Sir Maurice, time will tell. But it is clear to me that you need to see one of these marvellous machines in action!" He was animated now, fired up on his own rhetoric. "Allow me to walk you through the automaton production site on our way to see Villiers. It's just this way."

Newbury arched an eyebrow at Veronica, and the two of them fell in behind Chapman as he continued his tour of the facility, picking a route through the array of spluttering machines that continued to swing iron girders into place high above their heads.

CHAPTER 9

◉

They passed along a corridor that stemmed off from the main airships works and eventually led them to a small warehouse space that appeared to have been hastily converted into a production line. Two large steam-powered presses thumped with reassuring regularity, pushing out components in a variety of shapes and sizes, from brass arm braces and finger joints to shiny torso plates and elaborate cogs. Men stood alongside the rolling conveyor belts that fed out from the machines, each one picking up components and checking them for flaws before sending them on to the assembly teams on the other side of the warehouse. There, small groups of men were busy welding the components together, testing the articulation of the joints and assembling the frames of the automatons. The room was hot; bustling with people and filled with the smell of oil and steam.

Chapman paused in the doorway. "As you can see, the automaton production facility is still a relatively minor concern when considered alongside the main airship works, but in time, I have hopes that it will grow."

Newbury paced alongside one of the presses, watching as the machine-head spun on its axis, pressing a new component from the mould on its fascia. He spoke to Chapman as they walked. "How many automata does the facility produce in any given day?"

"Fully functioning units?"

Newbury nodded.

"One or two. They can actually make upwards of ten frames on a good day, but Villiers himself installs the internal control systems, and it's delicate work. Any faster, and we'd jeopardise the integrity of the machines or risk damaging the complex mechanisms that make them run."

"I'm looking forward to meeting him. Villiers, that is."

"Let's see if he's here now. That's the door to his workshop." He waved to indicate the glass-panelled door up ahead. They approached, and Chapman rapped quickly on the glass before pushing the door open to reveal the workshop within.

The room was fairly small, after the grandeur of the airship hangars, and it was cluttered with components and other mechanical ephemera: cogs, tools, automaton torsos, pages covered in elaborately scrawled designs, a model airship hanging from the roof. In truth, the room had as much of the feel of a laboratory as that of a workshop, the sort of place where scientific breakthroughs were commonplace and genius was taken for granted.

Villiers himself stood at his workbench, fiddling with a brass skull. He was wearing a brown leather smock, not unlike a butcher's apron, and had a magnifier flipped over his right eye on a wire frame, the base of which wrapped around his head like the crude frame of a hat. His hair was coarse and black, and he was unshaven, with a vaguely dishevelled appearance. He was fairly short, although taller than Veronica, and his only acknowledgement upon hearing them enter the room was to grunt at the automaton head he was holding and choose not to look up from his work.

Chapman waited for a moment to see if his business partner would remember his manners. When it was clear the other man intended to carry on working on the brass head regardless of their presence, he stepped forward, trying to get Villiers's attention. He cleared his throat. "Villiers. I'd like to introduce you to Sir Maurice Newbury and his assistant, Miss Veronica Hobbes. They're here on the business of the Crown, investigating the airship crash I mentioned to you yesterday."

Villiers offered a half-shrug before continuing to dig around inside the brain cavity of the brass skull. There was an awkward silence. Then, a moment later, something popped free from inside the device and flew into the air, before falling to the floor by Veronica's feet. Newbury noted that it was a tiny gold lever of some sort. Villiers looked up, satisfied. "I'm sorry, what were you saying, my friend? Hmmm?"

He seemed to notice Newbury and Veronica for the first time. "Oh, please excuse me. I was lost in the middle of a delicate operation. . . ." His accent was thick, with a Parisian lilt. He placed the automaton head on his workbench, along with the tool he had been using.

Newbury stepped forwards, his hand extended. "No need for apologies, Monsieur Villiers. I am Sir Maurice Newbury, and this is my assistant, Miss Veronica Hobbes." Veronica inched forwards, and Villiers took her hand, gently. "As your associate here intimated, we're working on behalf of the Crown. We'd like to talk to you about your automaton devices and the airship crash that occurred yesterday in Finsbury Park." He stopped for a moment, glancing around. "I must say, though, Monsieur Villiers, this truly is a remarkable workshop. A credit to you, I'm sure."

Villiers smiled. "Thank you, Sir Maurice. I can spare a little while to talk, although I am sure my associate has already told you much the same as what you will hear from me."

Newbury nodded. "Nevertheless, I do feel your opinions on the matter will be of use. Are you aware of the circumstances surrounding the crash?"

The Frenchman shrugged. "In as much as Monsieur

Chapman told me yesterday."

"So you're aware that the automaton that was piloting the vessel appears to have gone missing from the wreckage?"

Villiers looked immediately uncomfortable. "Missing? No. Destroyed, perhaps? I know my creations, Sir Maurice. There is no way the unit could have gone 'missing,' unless someone spirited it away from the crash site for their own devices."

Newbury glanced at Veronica. That was an option they hadn't yet considered. Veronica was watching Chapman, trying to gauge his reaction to Villiers's words.

"So what do you believe happened, Monsieur Villiers? Did the automaton malfunction and cause the crash?"

"Impossible. There is no capacity for the units to malfunction. Physically, they can function only if their program is loaded correctly. They operate on a series of punch cards. If the card does not engage, the unit will immediately freeze. If that were the case with the pilot of *The Lady Armitage,* the vessel would never even have taken off in the first instance." He stopped, stroking his stubble-encrusted chin. "My assumption is that the vessel itself was at fault. Perhaps one of the steering pulleys had come loose, causing the mechanism to lose tension? If that were the case, the vessel would have been practically uncontrollable, and in high winds, it could have easily been knocked off course."

Veronica crossed her arms. "But as I understand it, Monsieur Villiers, the skies were calm yesterday morning. Otherwise the fog would not have settled on the city as it did."

Villiers shrugged. "Then it is a matter for the police to decide what occurred. I am in the dark. Whatever the case, I understand it was a terrible accident, and for that I am truly sorry." He hesitated. "I assure you, however, that the source of the problem is with the vessel, and not with the pilot." He regarded them sternly.

Newbury decided to change the subject. "So, Monsieur

Villiers. What of your exile from Paris and the claims that you experimented on wastrels? Is there any tru–"

"Come now, Sir Maurice, is this really necessary?" Chapman cut in, clearly trying to come to the aid of his friend.

"It's alright, Joseph." Villiers seemed unmoved by the question. He faced Newbury. "What of it? It was a long time ago, Sir Maurice, and very much a part of my past. I have spent the last decade in London, working to revolutionise the aeronautical industry with Monsieur Chapman. I no longer even think of Paris, and consider London my home."

Newbury nodded. "Very well, Monsieur Villiers." He noted that the Frenchman had chosen not to refute the claims. The man's arrogance was obvious, but not without foundation. He softened his tone. "So what inspired you to begin developing a new type of automaton, after years of designing airships? Mr. Chapman tells me you worked day and night to achieve your goal."

Villiers looked circumspect. "In truth, I have always dreamed of building the perfect automaton. For years, I have strived to reach this stage, and it was only when the airship business had established itself and the manufacturing process had been automated that I found myself with the time and resources to realise my dream." He glanced at Chapman. "Once my friend and I began discussing the application of these units—household servants, drivers, soldiers, clerks—we agreed it was time for our business to diversify. The added benefit, of course, was that the machines could be taught to fly the fleet of airships we had spent the last ten years establishing."

"It's an impressive achievement indeed, Monsieur Villiers. So tell me, are the units intelligent, self-aware?"

Villiers shook his head. "No, they are not sentient in their own right. They are simply machines that operate according to a complex set of algorithms and programs. Have you seen one operating, Sir Maurice?"

Newbury shook his head, and Chapman interrupted. "I was hoping that you would be able to give our guests a demonstration, Pierre?"

"Of course. Allow me to do so now." He moved over to the corner of the workshop where, Veronica realised for the first time since entering the room, an automaton was sitting in a chair, its head bowed. Villiers stood before it.

"Rise." His voice was a firm, emotionless command.

The unit's head jerked up at the sound of Villiers's voice, and it quickly rose to its feet. "Follow." He turned and walked back across the workshop towards them. The automaton followed suit, stepping forward into the light. The two visitors looked on, transfixed with wonder. The automaton was about the size of a man, skeletal, with a solid torso formed from interlocking breast and back plates. Its eyes were little mirrors that spun constantly on an axis, reflecting back the lamplight. Its mouth was nothing but a thin slot, and its remaining features were engraved into the otherwise blank mask of its face. In its chest, a glass plate revealed, like a tiny porthole, a flickering blue light, dancing like an electric current. Its brass frame shimmered in the light, and it moved like a human being, fully articulated, as it strode across the room towards them. Its joints creaked as it walked, and its brass feet clicked on the tiled floor of the workshop. It stopped about two paces behind Villiers and cocked its head to one side, regarding them silently.

Chapman clapped his hands. Newbury and Veronica looked on, feeling a little unnerved.

Villiers turned to the automaton. "Pick up that glass tumbler and pour me a brandy." He pointed across the room at a small table, which held the tumbler and a decanter, amongst other detritus. The automaton set to work immediately, crossing the room with a fluid gait, avoiding a pile of machine parts on the floor and approaching the table with the utmost precision.

Taking care, it reached down and picked up the glass between its brass fingers—which, Newbury noticed, were affixed with little leather pads to prevent them from shattering the tumbler—and poured a measure of brandy from the decanter. A moment later, it strode back across the workshop to offer Villiers his drink without ever spilling a drop.

Newbury was astounded. "Bravo. Bravo, indeed!" He glanced from Villiers to Chapman and back again. "This is indeed a revolutionary invention. What else can it do?" He was clearly enthused.

Villiers smiled. He took the drink from the automaton and pointed to a chair by his desk. "Take a seat." The automaton did as requested, positioning itself as if ready to receive further instructions. Villiers crossed to the desk himself, with Newbury close behind him, and searched out a letter. He placed this on a stand in front of the automaton, beside a typewriter on the desk. "Copy this." He indicated the sheet for the mechanical man. The automaton did not respond, its only movement the continual spinning of its mirrored eyes and the flickering of the iridescent light inside its chest.

"Ah. Please forgive me." Villiers handed his brandy to Newbury and leaned over his desk. He pulled open a drawer, pulling out a sheaf of punch cards. He rifled through, finally selecting one and brandishing it in front of him. "This particular unit has yet to learn how to carry out this task."

He pressed a panel on the back of the automaton, and it swung open easily, revealing some of the unit's internal workings. Newbury peered inside, fascinated. "Tell me, Monsieur Villiers, how does it learn? I was under the impression from your earlier comments that the device lacks its own intelligence, although it certainly appears to respond to complex voice commands."

Villiers took the punch card and fed it into a slot within the back of the machine. "As I mentioned earlier, Sir Maurice, the automaton operates on a series of predetermined programs. These programs are expressed as a series of punch cards that the internal mechanisms of the device can interpret and enact. The device has the capacity to file up to twenty-eight of these cards at any one time on a revolving spindle, and when asked to perform a task, it will check the programs stored on its spindle and see if the correct card is in its repertoire. If so, it will retrieve the card and carry out the task. If not, well, you've seen the reaction in that situation."

Newbury shook his head in disbelief. "A machine that learns. . . ."

Villiers clicked the panel shut. He repeated his earlier command. "Copy that."

There was a whirring sound from within the chest of the automaton. Then, suddenly, its hands blurred over the keys of the typewriter, and within a matter of seconds, the entire page had been typed. Newbury leaned forward, taking the page from the top of the typewriter and comparing it to the original letter. It was identical, in every respect, even to the extent of recreating an error, where a misspelled word had been omitted with a series of X's.

"Veronica, do you see this?" He held the pages up for her. "It's identical." He turned to Villiers. "What, it must be ten times faster than a human being?"

"Undoubtedly so."

Newbury shook his head. He was quite lost for words.

Veronica studied the two copies of the letter. "It's certainly very impressive." She seemed hesitant to be carried away by the spectacle.

Newbury was in his element. "Monsieur Villiers, tell me about the power source."

Villiers was obviously enjoying the attention. "The device is designed to power itself. When the automaton moves, a rotor inside its abdomen rocks back and forth, ratcheting the winding mechanism and causing the mainspring in the chest to become taut. Effectively, the unit is self-winding, and thus it will never power down, unless commanded to do so. If left inactive for long periods without instruction, the unit will eventually move itself to trigger the winding mechanism."

"So it goes for a little stroll? Quite wonderful."

Veronica looked at the automaton warily. "It certainly *seems* intelligent, Monsieur Villiers."

"Thank you, Miss Hobbes. A compliment indeed. The entire purpose of an automaton is to give the impression of intelligence, maintaining the illusion whilst the workings of the device are kept hidden from the audience."

"And what are those workings, Monsieur Villiers? We've seen the mechanism that enables the device to be programmed, but how does it come to understand your voice commands, or interpret the input from its mirrored eyes?"

"Ah, well, that is the secret, is it not?" Villiers put his hand on his hips. "The device is fitted with an incredibly complex mechanism that mimics the neurological structures of a human brain. It makes judgments by asking itself a series of logical questions and interpreting the results, enabling it to select a course of action. For example"–he leaned on the back of the automaton's chair–"if the device were commanded to walk across this workshop, it would automatically find a route around the workbench there, without having to walk into it or attempting to climb over it. This is achieved through a series of logical questions that the unit's brain is designed to follow. What will happen if the unit walks into the workbench? How will walking into the workbench prevent it from achieving its goal? What is the quickest alternative route to its destination? Switches trigger inside the brain to enable the automaton to settle on the most effective solution to each question, thus deciding its route around the workbench. In this instance, the unit would obviously decide to alter its course, rather than

face potential damage by walking into an immovable object."
Villiers smiled, obviously pleased with himself.

Veronica looked back at Chapman, who had taken a seat
by the door and was also smiling as he watched the others
receive their lecture from his friend. He had struck a match
and was in the process of lighting a cigarette. The glare of the
flame cast his face in stark relief.

Newbury placed his hand on the automaton's head. "Can
we see? I'd very much appreciate an opportunity to take a
look inside this remarkable contraption."

Villiers nodded, and went to fetch a tool to open up the
automaton's skull.

Veronica took the opportunity to catch Newbury's eye, and
he smiled knowingly. He was allowing himself a moment of
indulgence, but she knew from the look on his face that he
wouldn't allow himself to get carried away. He was ready and
alert, absorbing everything.

Villiers returned and set to work on the automaton's head.
It took him only moments to unclip the skull cap and unscrew
the safety catch that gave access to the unit's mechanical
brain. Both Newbury and Veronica couldn't help but gasp
at the sight revealed when the plate was lifted away. The
automaton's brain was like the workings of some incredible
watch, only orders of magnitude bigger and more complex.
They both leaned in, watching the cogs and levers as they
ticked over, minute switches flicking from one position to
another as the automaton regarded its surroundings. It was
like seeing human thought processes in action, like some sort
of bizarre window into the human soul. In some ways, it was
disturbing, to see a creation so complex and wondrous yet
without feeling, lacking the spark of life. On the other hand,
Newbury was amazed to consider that it could be argued
that the human brain was the same as this incredible device,
a series of clockwork switches and cogs rendered flesh and

blood. He watched for a moment longer, intrigued by the ticking of the tiny mechanical components as the automaton sat unmoving before them, unaware that they were looking deep into the very fabric of its being.

Villiers stepped in and replaced the skull cap. "We must not leave the internal components exposed to the air for too long. Moisture affects the workings, and the small mechanisms can easily become clogged with dust."

Newbury stood back, watching appreciatively as Villiers used his tool to replace the fittings. "I must thank you for your demonstration, Monsieur Villiers. It's been quite enlightening."

Veronica nodded her agreement. "Yes, thank you for your time. The experience has left me feeling quite breathless." She turned to Newbury. "Is there anything further you require of Mr. Chapman or Monsieur Villiers, Sir Maurice?"

Newbury looked thoughtful. He turned to Chapman. "I do not believe there is. If you would be kind enough to escort us back to your office, Mr. Chapman, Miss Hobbes and I will take our leave. I daresay you have pressing business to attend to."

Chapman stood, inclining his head. "Of course, Sir Maurice. It has been a pleasure to show such enthusiastic visitors around our humble business." He beckoned them towards the door.

Newbury turned to Villiers and shook his hand firmly. "Fascinating work, Monsieur Villiers. I expect we'll meet again."

He allowed Veronica to go ahead of him, and together they walked back towards the office complex, leaving Villiers alone with his clockwork automaton and his thoughts.

Outside, the afternoon was turning to twilight as Newbury and Veronica hailed a hansom cab. Newbury had offered Veronica his coat to stave off the chill, and as she mounted the steps into the cab, she turned to regard him, the horses whinnying as they stamped their feet impatiently by the side of the road. The sound of the foghorns on the river made it difficult to hear.

"So, what next? Do you think Chapman and Villiers have anything to hide?"

Newbury lowered himself onto the seat opposite her, and the driver whipped his reins, jerking the vehicle into motion. "I suspect they have a great deal to hide, my dear, but whether it pertains to the case at hand, I remain unsure." He ran his fingers over his chin. "I need time to consider our findings. I admit I find it difficult to see evidence of foul play. Unless you can offer any further insights that you think I may have missed?"

Veronica shook her head. "I don't believe so. I remain wary of Mr. Chapman. I find him both insincere and egotistical. I do believe he was holding something back."

Newbury agreed. "Indeed. There is clearly more to the man than meets the eye. He obviously believes himself to be a great philanthropist, or at least wishes to paint that picture of himself to others. He delivered his message with a little too much zeal for my taste."

Veronica pulled Newbury's coat around herself. "Do you think the automaton demonstrations have helped to shed a light on the disaster surrounding *The Lady Armitage*? I singularly failed to see the significance of anything they showed us, as spectacular as it all was."

Newbury thought on this. "I believe they succeeded in demonstrating how unlikely it is that the automaton itself malfunctioned. Although I'll admit, I'm still baffled as to what happened to it after the vessel had crashed. I wonder if there is any stock in what Villiers suggested, about someone spiriting it away before the authorities arrived."

"I wondered the same. Perhaps it's best we speak with Sir Charles again, to see if Inspector Foulkes has turned up any further evidence from the area around the scene?"

Newbury seemed distracted. He glanced out of the window. "Indeed. I'm sure we'll speak with both of the aforementioned gentlemen in due course." He seemed to relax a little. "Tomorrow I shall pay a visit to Buckingham Palace to talk with Her Majesty. It's been a difficult couple of days, Miss Hobbes, and I have no doubt that you would benefit greatly from a day of rest." He smiled, waving his hand to stifle her objections. "Besides, it'll give me a little more time to ponder our next move."

Veronica sighed. "Very well. Let us agree, then, that you will call for me if there are any new developments. We can't have you charging in alone."

Newbury laughed. "Indeed not, Miss Hobbes. That would never do."

He continued to chuckle as the cab rolled on towards Chelsea, and home.

CHAPTER 10

Newbury had visited Buckingham Palace on numerous occasions over the last few years, yet the grandeur of the place never failed to take his breath away. He was awed by the spectacle of it: looming out of the grey fog-shrouded morning, its towering façade was an imposing sight, a symbol of Her Majesty's might rendered in stone for the entire world to see.

He glanced up at the pillars that stood, sentrylike, over the main entrance. To either side of these were vast rows of windows, hiding all the secrets of the Empire behind their heavy curtains of red and gold. In the driveway, stable hands were exercising the horses, and a line of impressive carriages stood ready by the main gates. Newbury wondered if some sort of state function were being planned, or else if foreign dignitaries were expected to pay a visit later that day. He knew Her Majesty would not be impressed by either of those eventualities.

Nodding at the guard, who shivered as he opened the gate for Newbury to pass through, he made his way around the rear of the immense building, making haste for the private entrance that was situated near the servants' quarters, out of sight from prying eyes. He braced himself against the chill. The morning had brought with it a crisp frost, and the sun was yet to break through the dense cloud of fog that had settled on the city during the night. It was still early, but Newbury knew he was expected. It didn't do to keep Her Majesty waiting.

He approached the familiar oak door, glancing quickly from side to side to ensure that he wasn't being watched, and rapped gently with the brass knocker. After a moment, a small panel slid open and a pair of eyes appeared.

Newbury cleared his throat. "Morning, Sandford. It's Newbury here."

The panel slid shut again, and a few seconds later the door swung open, revealing a small foyer inside. The room was brightly lit with gas-lamps and, Newbury was pleased to see, the roaring flames of a fire. Sandford, the butler who oversaw this small secret area of the palace, ushered Newbury inside, clicking the door shut behind him. He held his arm out for Newbury's coat and hat. Newbury removed the garments and passed them to the butler, offering his thanks. The man was aged, now, in his seventies, with a shock of white hair and liver spots speckling his face and hands. He looked impeccable in his suit, however, and Newbury had the utmost respect for the man. He had stayed in service out of an unerring sense of duty to the Crown, and Newbury had often wondered if he had once been an agent of the Queen himself, back in the early days of the Empire. He certainly had a few tricks up his sleeve.

Sandford draped Newbury's coat on the stand in the corner and returned to his favourite position beside the fire. Newbury was rubbing his hands, attempting to soak up the warmth of the flames.

"Warm yourself there for a moment, sir. Her Majesty is expecting you in the throne room, but I daresay she'll wait a moment longer whilst you make yourself presentable." He winked at Newbury, and they both smiled. Newbury had received no official summons from the Palace, but he knew from experience that Her Majesty would be expecting a report on his findings at the crash site, as well as his consequent investigations. In fact, given the nature of the case, he was surprised that he hadn't received a summons before now.

Newbury straightened his suit. "Well, Sandford, I'm as ready as I'll ever be."

Sandford nodded, offering him an appraising look. "That you are, sir." He turned about on his heel, more deftly than his appearance would give him credit for. "I'll walk you there now, sir." They left the comfort of the fire behind them, exiting the foyer by a side door and out into a small passage that Newbury had walked along many times before. It snaked through the bowels of the palace, a secret route between the throne room and Sandford's little waiting area at the back of the great house. The corridor had been built for a different purpose, Newbury believed—an escape route from the throne room should the monarch ever find herself threatened and in need of escape. Now, though, it was primarily used to bring Her Majesty's agents into the palace for private audiences, concealing them from the rest of the household, who Newbury doubted were even aware that the passageway existed. Of course, it depended entirely on one's point of view. Newbury couldn't help but think that the secret corridor also prevented Her Majesty's agents from soaking up too much of what was going on elsewhere in the palace. Victoria was a monarch who liked to play her cards very close to her chest indeed.

Newbury couldn't keep his eyes from wandering as the two of them strolled along the passageway. The walls were lined with austere portraits of long-dead kings and queens, the figureheads who had helped to shape the nation in times past. Victoria herself was notably absent from the gallery, and Newbury wondered if that would be the first role of any new incumbent to the throne: to hang a portrait of this most powerful ruler in its rightful place, at the head of the gallery of her predecessors. Not that the queen showed any real signs of abdication or debilitating illness; the marvellous machines of Dr. Fabian took care of that. He was a scientific genius without precedent, and Newbury was only grateful that he was loyal to the Crown and not, as others with pettier minds might have been in his position, hungry for power in his own right. He'd met the man only once, fleetingly, but he knew at some point he was likely to meet him again. Most agents of the Crown found occasion to visit Dr. Fabian at least once or twice during the course of their career.

Presently, their feet scuffing the deep pile of the carpet, they came to rest before a door. The corridor ended abruptly here, and Newbury knew that the vast chamber of the throne room awaited him on the other side.

Sandford knocked boldly on the door, straightening his tie.

"Come." The command from within was direct, pointed.

The butler reached for the handle and clicked the lock, allowing the door to swing open into the room. All Newbury could see inside was darkness.

"Sir Maurice Newbury, Your Majesty." Sandford shuffled out of the way to allow Newbury to pass, and then pulled the door shut behind him. Newbury heard the sound of the butler's feet rustling on the carpet as he slipped away, heading for his rooms and the relative warmth of his fire. He stepped forward in the darkness, waiting for his eyes to adjust. Heavy curtains were drawn across all the windows, casting the place in dark shadow. The only light in the entire room was a gas lamp flickering in one corner, a lonely flame adrift on a sea of darkness. He had the sense of standing in a cavernous space, but being able to see only a few feet in front of him. He could hear the sound of Dr. Fabian's machines, wheezing and sighing as they rasped at the air, their bellows clicking as they rose and fell in the darkness.

Finally, Victoria spoke.

"Ah, my faithful servant. What news do you bring?" Her voice cut through the darkness like ice, sending a shiver up and down his spine. He turned towards the sound, and bowed.

"Majesty." He paused. "Precious little news, I fear." He sighed, deciding how to go on. "I attended the scene of the airship disaster, as requested, and discovered certain . . . irregularities."

"Go on."

"The body of the pilot was missing from the wreckage, and the passengers, or what remained of them, had all been tied into their seats. There were no survivors at the scene. I later discovered that the vessel had, in fact, been piloted by a clockwork automaton developed by the airship's operators, Chapman and Villiers Air Transportation Services." He hesitated, weighing his next words carefully. The wheezing sound continued steadily in the darkness. "Yesterday I visited the manufactory of the aforementioned business and saw one of these automaton units being demonstrated. I have no reason to believe the pilot of *The Lady Armitage* could have malfunctioned at the controls. The cause of the disaster remains unclear."

There was a creaking sound as Victoria wheeled forward in her chair, emerging from the shadows into the dim glow of the gas-lamp. Newbury fought the urge to gasp at her appearance. He had seen her before, of course, but the sheer extent of Dr. Fabian's work was a constant source of shock and amazement. The Queen was lashed into her wheelchair, her legs bound together, her arms free and resting on the wooden handles that enabled her to rotate the wheels of the contraption. Two enormous tubes protruded from her chest, just underneath her breasts, folding around beneath her arms to connect to the large tanks of air that were mounted on the back of the chair. Bellows were affixed to the sides of the contraption and groaned noisily as they laboured with the pressure, forcing air from the tanks in and out of her collapsed lungs. Her chest rose and fell in time with the machine. A drip fed a strange pinkish liquid into her bloodstream via a catheter in her arm and a bag suspended on a brass frame over her head.

She regarded Newbury with a steely expression. "Newbury." Her voice was full of gravitas. "We must impress on you the critical nature of this assignment. It is a matter of some importance to the Crown. We expect you to do your duty and identify the source of the disaster. Foul play remains a distinct possibility." Her mouth was a tight line, her face old and tired. Nevertheless, her eyes shone with a brilliant gleam that, even in the semi-darkness, gave evidence of the fact that her mind was still as sharp as her tongue.

Newbury was unsure how to respond. "Of course, Your Majesty. I will endeavour not to disappoint in this matter." He shuffled awkwardly. "If it's not impertinent to ask . . . may I know the origin of your suspicion of foul play? It may prove useful in identifying the next course of action."

Victoria moistened her lips with the tip of her tongue. "Very well. A member of the Dutch royal family—a cousin of this household, no less—has been missing in London for some days. Intelligence from other sources suggested he may have been on board *The Lady Armitage* when she went down. This morning, the mortuary confirmed his body had been identified in the wreckage." She hesitated before going on. "We need not impress on you the severity of this situation, Newbury. One suspects that sabotage of the vessel may have been an attempt to discredit this house. Worse, we fear the means of that sabotage may in some way be related to your . . . field of experience. We have given our word to the boy's mother that we shall provide a reasonable explanation for the disaster. You must find an answer, and quickly. What with all this business in Whitechapel and the plague spreading through the slums, your expertise is needed elsewhere. Scotland Yard are floundering without your aid. Hurry to it, Newbury. Bring us the answers we need."

Newbury bowed his head. "I will press on with all haste and due diligence, Your Majesty."

"Go, then, and report back to us soon."

He turned to leave.

"Oh, and Newbury, how is that new assistant of yours working out? A woman, isn't she?"

He smiled. "Miss Hobbes? Yes, delightful, Your Majesty. And full of spark. She'll be a great asset to us, in time."

Victoria let out a rasping chuckle. "We do hope so, Newbury. Women like that are difficult to find. Make sure you keep her close." With that, she turned the handles on the sides of her chair and retreated slowly into the darkness.

Newbury fumbled back to the door in the dim light, turned the handle, and left.

Sandford was waiting by the fire when Newbury emerged from the passageway. He turned to look at the younger man, and then picked up a tumbler from where he'd left it on the mantelpiece.

Newbury accepted it gratefully and took a long swig. The alcohol attacked his palate, causing him to splutter slightly. "Brandy?"

Sandford nodded, his lips curling in a wide smile. "For the cold, sir."

"Thank you. Very considerate of you, Sandford." He downed the rest of the drink, feeling the warmth spreading through his chest. He knew that Sandford was an old hand at this sort of thing, and that the reason for the brandy had, in truth, little to do with the cold. The man was simply used to seeing agents return from an audience with the monarch, and the brandy was a restorative offering to steady their nerves and put colour back into their cheeks. Newbury was thankful for the opportunity to do just that. He'd never found it difficult to talk with Her Majesty, but the sheer weight of expectation and nervousness always left his nerves jangling for the rest of the day. Today, of all days, he needed to head back to his lodgings and try to relax, to ponder all the disparate elements of the case and see what shape they were beginning to take. Not only that, but in answering one mystery, he had inadvertently opened up another. He now knew what had agitated the Queen so much about the airship disaster, but he was faced with an even more difficult question to answer: What was a Dutch royal doing on board a passenger-class vessel bound for Dublin? He needed a breakthrough, and at the moment, he wasn't sure where to look next.

Newbury placed the glass back on the mantelpiece and moved to fetch his coat and hat. Somehow, Sandford was there before him, and he thanked the butler as he helped Newbury on with his coat. "Sandford, my thanks. I'm sure it won't be too long before I'm giving myself over to your hospitality once again."

Sandford nodded. "Best of luck, sir." He opened the door for Newbury, momentarily allowing a gust of air into the room, stirring the newspapers that lay on the table. It was cold out, but the day was still young. His head buzzing with thoughts and the warm glow of alcohol, he stepped out into the grey fog and slipped away into the busy streets of London.

CHAPTER 11

The visiting room was cold and impersonal; clinical, even. Veronica was convinced that it wasn't supposed to feel so unwelcoming, even for a hospital. Her parents were paying a small fortune towards the upkeep of the place, after all. The least they could do would be to provide a few cushions and a bit of colour around the place to brighten things up. No wonder the majority of the patients were so miserable and lifeless.

Veronica firmly believed that people were inspired by their surroundings, and that a dull and dreary hospital would reflect badly on the mood of the patients, especially in an institute such as this, which catered for the clinically insane. She knew Amelia would agree. She resolved to make a point of talking to Dr. Mason about it at the next available opportunity.

Veronica sat with her hands on her lap, waiting for the nurses to fetch her sister. She felt uncomfortable and ever so slightly on edge, as she always did when she visited the asylum. She'd travelled to Wandsworth early that morning, taking care to ensure no one saw her leaving her apartments in Kensington and hailing a cab. She hadn't told Newbury where she was going, and consequently she hoped that he hadn't attempted to call on her with news of the case. If he had, she'd just have to tell him that she'd decided to go out for a stroll. She was meant to be taking the day to recuperate, after all.

She glanced around. One of the nurses sat on a stool by the door, looking out into the corridor. This would be her guard, she supposed, the woman posted there for the duration of her visit to make sure that her sister didn't stray towards violent tendencies, or that Veronica didn't try to sneak her any proscribed articles such as cosmetics, cutlery or photographs of the family. It was ridiculous, of course. Her sister had never hurt anyone in her life, and Veronica had no intention of causing difficulties for Amelia by bringing her any gifts that would cause her emotional unrest.

Dr. Mason believed that the less contact the patients had with their families, the easier they would find it to settle in to their new environment. In fact, the last time Veronica had spoken with him, he'd admonished her for the frequency of her visits, citing all manner of recent papers on the subject and claiming that the regularity of her calls was working against the treatment programme he had instigated for her sister. To Veronica, it seemed like an archaic way to try to make someone better, isolating them from the people who loved them. Besides, she knew it was a pointless exercise, anyway, although she didn't admit that to Dr. Mason. It wouldn't do to have him think that she disagreed with his diagnosis. Only, Veronica knew that her sister was far from the lunatic that the doctor had led her parents to believe. She wasn't mad. She just happened to be able to see into the future.

Veronica looked up at the sound of footsteps from the corridor outside. The nurse who was sitting on the stool turned to look at her in acknowledgement, and then a moment later another nurse in a white uniform led Amelia into the room. Veronica's heart leapt. She stood, moving to embrace her sister.

Amelia was painfully thin, and dressed in a loose-fitting

outfit comprising a grey woollen blouse and matching skirt that Veronica thought would be better suited to a prison than to a hospital. Her hair was raven-black and long, loose around her shoulders, and her pale skin and soft complexion gave the impression that she was even younger than her fragile nineteen years. She looked scared, although her face lit up as she entered the visitors' room and saw her sister coming towards her.

"Veronica! You came."

Veronica embraced her, feeling the press of her bony shoulder blades through the prickly fabric. "Of course I came!" She led Amelia to the sofa where she had been sitting and bade her to take a seat. "Are you eating enough? You're so terribly thin."

"I eat well enough, sister. The food here is passable." She forced a smile. "Anyway, what news do you bring from the outside world? Do our parents send word?"

Veronica looked uneasy. "No, Amelia, no word from home." She patted her gently on the back of her hand. "But I'm sure they will call soon." She lowered her voice to a whisper. "You know how Dr. Mason likes to hold them at bay."

Amelia glanced at the door. The nurse was still sitting on her stool, staring out into the corridor, as if there were something more interesting to engage her attention out there. Amelia sighed. "I don't understand it, Veronica. They must know by now that they've made a mistake. It's clear that I'm not a lunatic. I'm convinced the seizures are a medical condition. They must be able to control them with drugs or remedies of some sort. They *must*." She looked into Veronica's eyes. "I want so desperately to go home."

Veronica felt tears welling in her eyes, and she blinked them away, forcing herself to be strong for her sibling. "I know, Amelia. I know." She looked away, unable to see the pleading in her sister's eyes. "Your illness is unique. The doctors need time to study it, to find a way to help you. I'm sure they're doing everything they can."

Amelia nodded, biting her bottom lip. She brushed her fringe away from her eyes. "Well, that's enough about me! Tell me about yourself, Veronica. What have you been up to? This hospital is so drab and boring that I need to hear stories of the real world. I like to think of you going about your business out there, all pretty and professional in your smart clothes."

Veronica smiled. "I think your expectations of my life are rather fanciful, Amelia. I work in a museum. I've spent the last week transcribing Sir Maurice's essays and researching academic papers on the druids of Bronze Age Europe. It's good work, but it's quiet. Hardly the stuff of high adventure!"

Amelia nodded, a twinkle in her eye. "You forget, sister, that I'm able to see more than you think, even from in here. I fancy your recent exploits are far more engaging than you care to let on." She smiled, dismissing the issue. "So, tell me, have you scandalised the museum terribly with your forward-thinking ideas?"

Veronica laughed. "There have been a few raised eyebrows, certainly. Although I try to abstain from truly ruffling any feathers. I'd rather hold on to my position for the time being."

"And what of suitors?" The nurse by the door looked over, obviously interested in Veronica's response. "I hear that Sir Maurice cuts a dashing figure about town."

"Amelia, really." Veronica blushed. "Sir Maurice and I have a strictly professional acquaintance. He's a handsome man, I admit, but I–"

"–protest too much, clearly." Amelia cut in, chuckling. "Come now, sister, I'm only playing with you." She scratched at her arms, where the woollen shirt was evidently irritating her skin.

Veronica was suddenly serious. She put her hand to

Amelia's cool cheek. "Have you had any more episodes this week, Amelia?"

Amelia shrugged. "A few." She looked away, noncommittal.

"And . . ."

"And they were just as unpleasant and unwelcome as they usually are." She looked up at Veronica again, searching her face. "I do wish they could find a way to make them stop. The things I see . . ." She trailed off, clearly distraught.

Veronica hugged her close, her voice soothing. "I know Amelia. We're doing all we can, I promise."

She felt Amelia go limp in her arms.

"Amelia?" She held her by the shoulders. "Amelia?"

Suddenly, Amelia's thin body began twitching jerkily, her muscles going into spasms as Veronica tried to hold her still. Her eyes rolled back in their sockets, her mouth foaming as she shook wildly on the sofa.

"Amelia!" She glanced at the nurse, who had only just realised what was happening.

"Help in here!" The woman came away from the door, running to Veronica's side. She took hold of Amelia and eased her to the floor. She continued to twitch violently. "We need to restrain her so that she doesn't hurt herself."

Veronica dropped to her knees, clamping her hands over Amelia's legs. Her face was filled with concern. "What now?"

The nurse didn't look up from where she was struggling to hold Amelia's arms by her sides. "Now we wait for the doctor."

Amelia started to babble something incoherent in the midst of her tortured seizure. Veronica tried to make sense of the garbled words, tears now streaming freely down her cheeks. There was something about fire, screaming and trains. Other than that, it was impossible to tell what Amelia was saying, as her body, racked with nervous energy, fought against their grip in random, violent spasms.

Veronica heard footsteps. She didn't look up. A moment

later, two more nurses were by Amelia's side, one of them cradling her head whilst the other took over from Veronica, pinning her sister's legs to the floor. Veronica heard a familiar voice from behind her.

"Miss Hobbes. Please step away." She stood, looking round to see Dr. Mason hovering by the edge of the sofa. He looked serious. "I think it is time for you to leave now, Miss Hobbes. Your sister is in safe hands." Veronica glanced back at her sister's writhing body, held down by a small army of nurses. She looked torn.

"Really, it's for the best. We can see her through this unfortunate episode, and then afterwards she'll be in need of rest." For once, Veronica thought, the swarthy-looking man in the brown suit had a kindly expression on his face. She believed he really did want to help her sister. "You can call again in a week's time. I'm sure she'll be up and about again by then. If the weather is tolerable, you could even take her for a walk around the airing court." He smiled. "But now it is time to go. I'll walk you to the exit."

Veronica relented, glancing back at her sister one last time as Dr. Mason led her towards the door. Just as she was about to cross the threshold, however, she heard Amelia scream her name.

"Veronica!"

She looked back, startled. Amelia was trying to force herself up into a sitting position, facing her sister as the nurses tried ineffectually to hold her down. Her eyes were still rolled back in their sockets, showing nothing but a disturbing sheen of milky-white, but Amelia seemed to be looking straight at her, as if she could actually *see* where Veronica was standing in the doorway.

Shocked, she whispered her response. "Amelia?"

The reply was a tortured rasp, as if dragged from somewhere within the depths of the girl's nightmare. "It's all in their heads, don't you see, Veronica? You must see!" She collapsed back into her spasms, and shaking his head, Dr. Mason took Veronica by the arm, leading her away from the terrible scene of her sister's distress and on towards the secure exit of the hospital.

Outside, Veronica looked up at the asylum and used her handkerchief to wipe away the tears that were still stinging her eyes. The clock tower showed that it was fast approaching two in the afternoon, and she knew she'd be wise to head back to her rooms in case Newbury decided to call. She hated what was happening to her sister, back inside that terrible red brick building, locked inside a ward with no reasonable company, no decent clothes, no respect. She hated the fact that she couldn't do anything about it, either; that her parents had forbidden her from even discussing the issue with them, after she had railed so hard against their decision to place Amelia in the hands of these strangers in the first instance. Consequently, she hadn't had any contact with them for over two months, and neither had they been to visit her sister since her incarceration in September. She knew that, soon, she was going to have to write to them and insist that they pay a visit to the asylum to see their daughter. Amelia had enough to endure; it was unfair for her to have to suffer feelings of embarrassment, guilt and rejection, too.

Veronica regained her composure and proceeded along the gravel path towards the exit to the railed compound and the street beyond. She passed the airing court on her left, a large paved courtyard used to exercise the patients when the weather was clement enough for them to venture outside. She smiled. Next week, she would return to Wandsworth and take Amelia for a walk around this little yard, admiring the flowers and the birds as they had when Amelia was a young girl and Veronica would take her for morning walks along the country lanes by their parents' house. In the meantime, she would throw herself into the case with Newbury and spend some time deliberating on the meaning of Amelia's outburst. She could hear the words echoing around in her mind as she walked. "It's all in their heads, don't you see? . . ."

She had no idea what it meant, and whether it was simply the ramblings of a disturbed, frightened mind, or something far more pertinent to her immediate future.

Only time, she supposed, would tell.

CHAPTER 12

The next day, Veronica woke early and decided that, after breakfast, she would head straight to the office. She'd had no word from Newbury, and she was anxious to find out if there had been any further developments in the case. He may have been able to solicit further information from Her Majesty during his visit to the palace, and she wanted to press him to speak with Sir Charles, to find out if Inspector Foulkes had managed to uncover anything further at the scene of the crash.

Following her trip to the manufactory earlier that week, Veronica was still engaged with the notion that the vessel's automaton pilot may have crawled out of the wreckage, scrabbling away into the trees before anyone else arrived at the scene. It wasn't an outlandish idea; the automaton she had seen demonstrated had a hardy skeletal structure. She could see how the unit may have found itself confused, damaged but still functional, climbing out of the ruined cockpit before its more delicate components were consumed by the heat and the flames. Perhaps it had lain there inactive for some time before its pre-programmed systems engaged and it had been driven to move, not in an effort to escape the fire but simply because it was compelled to start the winding mechanism within its chest, as Villiers had described to them during the demonstration in his workshop. She would discuss these thoughts with Newbury at length when she arrived at the office.

Veronica pulled back the curtains in her living-room and looked out over the street. The sun was only just poking up over the clouds, but already the high street was bustling with people. Mechanical carriages trundled rudely along the road, puffing clouds of steam high into the air, their drivers shouting down at pedestrians to make way. She shook her head. She couldn't understand Newbury's obsession with progress. Of course, the automata were marvellous inventions, but she couldn't help wondering what would happen to all the people they would displace if they were ever properly applied to industrial work in the city. Besides, London was a city still finding its way out of the last century. In her eyes, before there could be any major scientific revolutions, there were other more pressing social inadequacies in need of resolving. For a country run by a woman, Britain was still a nation in awe of its men.

Stepping away from the window, Veronica walked to the small kitchen and put a flame to the grill. She'd take her toast and tea, and then, without further ado, she'd hail a cab to Bloomsbury and allow her head to be filled with the details of the case. That way, she thought, she might be able to forget the sight of her sister, her eyes shining white in the harsh light of the gas-lamps, screaming Veronica's name as she was pinned to the floor by a coterie of nurses and reassured by the doctors that the only reason she was suffering so much was because she was entirely insane.

The office door was locked when Veronica arrived at the museum. She fished around in her purse, searching out the key that she carried with her for the rare occasions when she was the first to arrive for the day. She turned the key hastily in the lock and stepped inside, closing the door behind her.

"Hello?"

The place was deserted. In fact, glancing around, she was convinced that it hadn't been disturbed since she was last there herself, with Newbury and Miss Coulthard, almost two days before. She knew that Newbury had given Miss Coulthard leave to take as much time as she needed in the search for her missing brother. The fact that she was not here did not bode well for her success in locating his whereabouts. Sighing, Veronica slipped her bag from her shoulder and placed it on the stand. She did the same with her coat and hat a moment later. Then, glancing at the grandfather clock in the corner, decided to press on for a while in the hope that Newbury would soon put in an appearance. If not, she would head over to his lodgings in Chelsea to see if she could find him there.

She set about making herself a pot of tea, and decided to take some notes, trying to put all of her haphazard thoughts about the case into some sense of order. That way, when she did finally manage to catch up with Newbury, she'd be able to present her ideas in something of a more coherent form.

An hour later, it was past nine o'clock and there was still no word of Newbury. Veronica had filled two sheets of paper with copious notes on the case of *The Lady Armitage*, recounting not only her own thoughts on the matter but also the chain of events that had led them to this point in the investigation. If she were asked to write a report on the case at a later date, the notes would prove an invaluable basis for the endeavour.

Glancing up at the clock again, she decided that it was time she tried to find out what had happened to her employer. She hoped that he hadn't been called away to another crime scene during the night, at least without attempting to get a message to her first. Even though she didn't relish the idea of encountering more cadavers, she also didn't want to find herself suddenly left out of proceedings. It wasn't like Newbury to leave her in the dark, though. She'd known him for only a matter of weeks, but already they had formed a mutual respect for each other, and no matter how secretive some of his pursuits may be, she knew that he wasn't in the business of shutting her out. She'd just have to track him down and find out what it was that had delayed him.

Veronica gathered her things and scrawled a brief note, which she left on Newbury's desk, just in case they accidentally missed each other as she made her way over to Chelsea. She locked the office door behind her, climbed the stairs to the ground floor—where the exhibitions were already beginning to fill with the noisy hubbub of the public—and left through the main entrance in search of transport.

Newbury's home was a delightful terraced house in a quiet suburban district of Chelsea. The entire street in which it sat appeared comfortably middle-class, residential and relatively unassuming. As she stepped down from the cab and paid the driver, Veronica tried to reconcile this fact with her knowledge of the man himself. Everything about the look of the house, at least from the outside, seemed to represent exactly the opposite of what she had taken to be Newbury's taste. The place looked decidedly *old-fashioned*: a traditional English home, with a small rose garden at the front of the property and a door painted in bright pillar-box red. An ornate black railing ran around the edges of the garden, and a short path led up to the door itself, terminating in a series of tall steps. A bay window looked out onto the street below, although the light was reflecting brightly on the glass panes, making it difficult for Veronica to see if there was anyone inside. She shook her head.

For a man so obsessed with the benefits of progress, Newbury kept a house that seemed a trifle understated and traditional. Still, she supposed it was good to challenge stereotypes.

Hesitating for a moment, the thought flashed through her mind that she might have given the cab driver the incorrect address. She searched out her notebook and double-checked the number on the door. It was certainly the address Newbury had given her, written in her book in her own neat copperplate: *10 Cleveland Avenue, Chelsea*. She shrugged to herself and approached the door, rapping the knocker briskly. Behind her, the cab rolled away down the road, its horse's hooves clattering noisily on the cobbles.

She waited for someone to answer the door. There was no response. She knocked again, louder this time. After a few more moments had passed and there was still no answer, she stepped away from the door and tried peering through the window instead, cupping her hands around her face to help her see. The room beyond the window had been dressed as a dining room, containing a long oval-shaped table, a small fireplace, a teak sideboard and a series of bookshelves lined with numerous leather-bound tomes. The door to the room was shut, and there was no evidence that the furniture had been disturbed that morning. She turned away, trying to decide what to do. It was clear that Newbury wasn't at home, and she had no idea where he may have gone, other than the office. She could head back there in the hope that he would eventually put in an appearance, or else she could return to Kensington and await his call. She chewed on her bottom lip thoughtfully.

Then, just as she was about to take her leave, the door clicked open behind her, and a rotund middle-aged woman dressed in the black uniform of a housekeeper appeared in the hallway, trying to catch her breath. "Oh, I'm sorry, miss. I was out in the back, dealing with the linens." Veronica noticed that the woman's sleeves were rolled up and her hands were still dripping with water.

She smiled. "I'm sorry to drag you away from your duties. You must be Mrs. Bradshaw? Sir Maurice has spoken very highly of you."

The woman looked perplexed. "Indeed I am, miss. And how can I be of service?" She spoke with a warm Scottish lilt. Her grey hair was scraped back severely from her face, worn in a black net, and whilst she certainly cast an imposing figure, it was clear she was a person of warmth and integrity. Veronica could see why Newbury liked her.

"My name is Miss Veronica Hobbes, Sir Maurice's new assistant. I was supposed to be meeting him at the museum this morning, but he hasn't arrived, so I thought it best to call instead, to ensure everything was in order." She craned her neck to see past the housekeeper and into the hallway beyond. It was gloomy inside, with deep burgundy wallpaper and dark wooden furnishings that added to the sense of the austere. There was no sign of Newbury, although she supposed he could have been elsewhere in the house, in the living-room or working out of sight in his study.

Mrs. Bradshaw glanced from side to side, looking along the street. She fixed her eyes on Veronica. "Miss Hobbes, the master told me to make you welcome if you ever had reason to call. I think you'd better come inside."

Veronica frowned. The woman seemed strangely on edge, as if Veronica's presence in the house would somehow make her uncomfortable. Nevertheless, she mounted the stairs to the door and stepped through into the dark hallway beyond.

Newbury's coat and hat were still hanging on the stand beside a small table and mirror. The post was lying unopened on the table. Veronica turned to Mrs. Bradshaw. "Is Sir Maurice at home?"

"Yes, miss, although I'm not sure he is receiving visitors."

She looked concerned, and it dawned on Veronica that something was not quite right.

She decided to press the woman further for an explanation. "Is Sir Maurice unwell? I assure you, Mrs. Bradshaw, that I have only his best interests at heart, and that you can rely on me to treat the matter with the utmost sensitivity."

Mrs. Bradshaw sighed. "Very well, miss. Let me take you to him now."

Veronica placed her hat beside Newbury's on the stand and unbuttoned her coat as they walked. Mrs. Bradshaw led Veronica up the creaking flight of stairs at the end of the hallway, past a small landing that branched off into a sizeable bathroom, and then up to the first floor, where a series of doors opened onto what Veronica assumed were the bedchambers.

Veronica hesitated. "Is he resting in bed, Mrs. Bradshaw? I'm not sure that it would be entirely appropriate for me to see him in that way."

Mrs. Bradshaw shook her head. "No, miss. He's in there." She indicated a panelled door at the end of the landing. "That's his private study. The master has been holed up inside since yesterday morning. He stepped out, and when he returned, he went directly to this room and locked himself inside. I've been unable to get a word out of him since."

Veronica looked puzzled. "Do you think he's unwell?"

Mrs. Bradshaw shrugged. "I can't say, miss. It's unusual behaviour, certainly. Not that I'm a stranger to that, these last few years." She looked circumspect. "But I worry he hasn't eaten, or taken anything to drink. I've tried knocking, but I've had no reply."

"Do you have a key?"

"No, miss. It's the one room in the house that Sir Maurice keeps to himself. He said if I were ever to go in there, I would be immediately dismissed from his service. God knows what he's got in there, but I ain't about to try and find out."

Veronica nodded. "I'm sure it's just a case of security, Mrs. Bradshaw." She put her hands on her hips. "Now, would you mind if I tried to solicit a response?"

"Please go ahead, miss. It would put my mind at rest to know the master was well."

Veronica approached the door. She put her ear to one of the panels, listening intently for any sound from within. Nothing. She pulled the red leather glove off her right hand, placing it carefully in her coat pocket, and rapped loudly on the door. "Sir Maurice? It's Veronica. Are you well?"

She paused for a moment, waiting for a response. She glanced at Mrs. Bradshaw, who offered her a noncommittal shrug. The moment stretched. She knocked again. "Sir Maurice? Are you home? I have some thoughts on the case I'd like to discuss with you today." Still nothing.

Veronica frowned, addressing her next question to Mrs. Bradshaw. "You're sure he's in here? Could he have left during the night?"

"No miss. His bed is undisturbed, and his coat and hat are still on the stand downstairs."

Veronica tried the handle. It turned, but the door wouldn't open.

"He always keeps this door locked, miss, even when he's inside. If he asks for tea, I leave it out here on the landing and he collects it at his leisure."

Veronica smiled. "Mrs. Bradshaw. All this talk of tea is making me thirsty. I don't suppose you would be so kind as to put the kettle on the stove for me?" She rubbed the back of her neck. "I'll continue to try to raise a response from Sir Maurice. I'll be sure to call if I have need of your assistance."

Mrs. Bradshaw looked uneasy. "Are you sure, miss? Somehow it doesn't seem appropriate to leave you up here alone."

"Please do not concern yourself with propriety, Mrs. Bradshaw. I am sure Sir Maurice would trust me enough not to idly wander through his private rooms. I assure you I will remain just here on the landing and attempt to find out what is preventing him from answering our calls. Once the tea is prepared, we'll take stock of the situation and agree on a course of action."

"Very well, miss. I'll be in the kitchen if you need me."

Veronica watched as Mrs. Bradshaw disappeared down the stairs, her long skirt swishing around her as she walked.

She knocked on the door again. There was still no response from within. She glanced behind her, judging the length of the landing. There was plenty of room for a run-up. She slipped her other glove from her left hand, popped it in her pocket and wriggled out of her coat, draping it over the side of the banister. She adjusted her blouse. Then she walked to the other end of the landing and, with one last glance down the stairs to make sure that Mrs. Bradshaw was completely out of sight, took a run at the door, presenting her shoulder to the wooden panels. The door creaked in its frame, but didn't give way. She tried again, this time throwing all her weight in front of her as she slammed into the door. It burst open with a loud splintering sound, banging against some unseen piece of furniture inside and kicking back at Veronica, who was struggling to maintain her balance. She caught the door as it came back at her and leaned on it heavily, her shoulder aching from the impact. She hoped that Mrs. Bradshaw hadn't heard the noise in the kitchen two floors below, that the sound of the kettle whistling on the stove had been enough to mask the racket. She'd know soon enough, if the housekeeper came running up the stairs to see what all the fuss was about.

Gasping for breath, she looked around, searching the room for Newbury.

The first thing that struck her about the study was the sheer amount of bizarre paraphernalia that lined the shelves. Aside from the vast array of books, there were all manner of esoteric objects on display. Jars containing what looked like the amputated tentacles of an unidentifiable sea creature, the skull of a chimpanzee, bottles filled with strange-coloured liquids, arcane symbols cast in precious metals, little stone idols that appeared to date from sometime in pre-history—the list was endless. The second thing that struck her was that Newbury was lying face down on the floor, in the centre of an large pentagram that had been drawn on the bare floorboards in white chalk. The carpet had been rolled back to reveal the symbol, although it wasn't immediately clear if it was freshly drawn or had been hidden under the Turkish pile for some time. Objects lay all about the prone man: an empty glass and wine bottle, a sprig of rosemary, some matches and a brown medical bottle half-full of liquid.

She rushed to Newbury's side, kneeling on the floor and rolling him over onto his back. His breath was shallow and his face was cold and glistening with perspiration. She searched for his pulse, feeling around his unshaven throat until she found it, counting out the rhythm under her breath. She loosened his shirt and placed a hand on his cheek. "Oh, Newbury, what have you been up to?"

He moaned, his eyes flickering under their lids.

Veronica heard footsteps on the stairs. Mrs. Bradshaw had obviously realised something was amiss. She called up ahead of her. "Everything alright up there, miss?"

Veronica knew immediately that she couldn't allow Mrs. Bradshaw to see Newbury in such a state, or let her see the inside of his study, either. The contents of the room were alarming enough to Veronica herself, and she already had a very good notion of Newbury's expertise in the dark arts and all the mysterious paraphernalia associated with them. The scene inside the room would probably be enough to send poor Mrs. Bradshaw running straight to the police.

Veronica propped Newbury's head on a cushion that she

grabbed from the nearby daybed and stepped out into the hallway, closing the door behind her. She stood in front of the damaged lock, ensuring that Mrs. Bradshaw couldn't see where the frame had been splintered during her assault on the door.

"Everything is fine, Mrs. Bradshaw," she said as calmly as possible. "You will be pleased to hear that I have managed to rouse Sir Maurice. He is suffering from a slight fever and has been dozing in his study. I'm attending to him now. I'm sure that he will shortly be anxious for some light food to aid him in his recovery." She smiled. "For now it would be of much benefit to him if you could fetch us another cup and saucer to go with that pot of tea."

Mrs. Bradshaw eyed her inquisitively. There was an awkward silence. Then, realising that it was probably better to go along with Veronica's instructions than defy her employer's wishes and enter the study herself, she nodded her head in assent. "Right you are, miss. I'll leave the tea on the landing for the two of you." She turned and made her way back down the stairs.

Veronica called after her. "Thank you, Mrs. Bradshaw. And if you could see yourself to fetching a flannel and a bowl of cool water, that would be most helpful, too." She slipped back into the room, not waiting for Mrs. Bradshaw's response.

Newbury hadn't tried to move. He was only semi-conscious, possibly even delirious. She bent over him, grabbing him firmly under the arms, and hauled him up onto the daybed a few feet from where he was lying. She paused for a moment, trying to catch her breath after the exertion. Making sure he was comfortable, she set about collecting the objects from the floor, placing them neatly on the coffee table by the side of the fire. She picked up the little brown bottle and inspected the label. It was peeling, but she could easily make out what it contained.

"Laudanum." She shook her head. She had no idea what Newbury had been up to with the pentagram, but it was clear to her that the laudanum was responsible for his current state of ill health. She rolled the carpet back into place, hiding the elaborate chalk symbols. She had a lot of questions for her employer, but first she had to make sure she could bring him round. She crossed the room and went to his side. Taking her handkerchief from her sleeve, she gently mopped his brow, brushing his hair back from his forehead with her other hand.

"So you do have an Achilles' heel, after all, Maurice." She dabbed tenderly at the beads of sweat running down his face.

Searching out a blanket was a relatively easy task. She laid it over him as he shivered, then set about stoking the fire, which had burned low in the grate without attention. Long ago, when her sister had first begun having seizures, the doctors had treated her with laudanum, and she knew all too well the pains of withdrawal, having spent long hours by Amelia's bedside as she came round from the large doses she'd had administered to her in an attempt to quell her visions. She watched Newbury as he lay there on the daybed, his breath still shallow as his lungs fought for air. He'd clearly taken too much of the dreadful stuff. Now it was just a waiting game as his body purged itself of the drug. Veronica, making herself comfortable in a chair by the fire, would stay by his side as it did so.

CHAPTER 13

When Newbury woke, he was appalled to find Veronica asleep in the chair by the fire. He had no idea how much time had passed. He sat up, bleary eyed, and then sank back into the warm confines of the daybed, unable to move. His head was spinning, and he felt sick to his stomach. He ran a hand through his hair, which was damp with perspiration, and then rubbed at his eyes, trying to shake the feeling of lethargy. He'd lost track of events and couldn't remember how he'd ended up where he was. The physical symptoms, however, were entirely familiar; he knew he'd overdone it on the laudanum.

He glanced around the study. Everything had been restored to order. After propping him up on the daybed, Veronica must have rolled the carpet back into place to hide the chalk pentagram that he'd drawn on the floorboards. He wondered if that had been for Mrs. Bradshaw's benefit. If so, it suggested that she'd seen it herself. He could only think how shocked and appalled she must have been to see the items that he had on display in there. That, coupled with the fact that Veronica was sitting across the room from him, meant that he'd have a lot of explaining to do. Worse still, Veronica had seen him at his lowest ebb. He wondered if he'd ever be able to earn her respect again. He cursed himself for his weakness. Still, what was done was done, and he supposed it was his own foolish actions that had landed him in this position. Now he had to face his embarrassment with humility. He sighed.

Craning his neck, he tried to work out how Veronica had entered the room. His first thought was that Mrs. Bradshaw must have kept a spare key, one that he wasn't aware of, but then he saw that the doorframe was splintered and the lock was hanging loose where the screws had been torn out of their housing. The door itself was propped closed with a large stone vase that Veronica had taken from one of his displays. Absently, he wondered if she'd realised that it was nearly two thousand years old. Not that it mattered. She'd obviously used her shoulder to barge her way in. She was a strong woman, and he was thankful to her for the consideration she had shown. He'd underestimated her resourcefulness. He wouldn't allow himself to do it again.

Newbury shifted on the daybed, watching Veronica as she slept in the chair, the rise and fall of her chest as her breath came in little flutters, her head lolled gently to one side. The firelight cast dancing shadows all about her. He wanted to stay in that moment, for time to stand still so that he could lie there, basking in the firelight and watching the pretty girl who had come to his rescue—without having to face her when she woke and explain his failings. He imagined watching the light dying in her eyes as he revealed the truth: that aside from his more salubrious pursuits he was a habitual opium-eater and a dabbler in the occult. He had drawn the pentagram on the floor in an effort to divine a solution to the case, and when it hadn't worked, frustrated that he couldn't seem to find the clarity of mind that he had been searching for, he had given himself up to the drug, intent on dreaming his way to the solution. Of course, such is the delusion of the addict, and he had found no salvation in debauchery. He was no closer now to having a solution than he was when he set out from the palace that morning. If indeed it was still the same day; he had no idea how long he'd been unconscious and whether, outside, it was even day or night. He coughed, fighting back nausea. The racking movement caused little explosions of pain in his head.

The sound of his coughing caused Veronica to stir. Her eyes flicked open. She looked dazed for a moment, before the sight of Newbury seemed to register and she realised where she was.

In a moment, she was out of the chair and had rushed to his side. "Maurice. You're awake."

He looked up at her and smiled. "Indeed. Although I fear I could hardly be further from my true self. I'm sorry you had to see me like this."

She laughed, obviously relieved. "You did give me an awful fright. But you'll be well soon enough. When you're feeling up to it, Mrs. Bradshaw will prepare some food and draw you a bath."

Newbury looked anxious. "Mrs. Bradshaw? Did she—?"

"No." Veronica shook her head, cutting him off. "You need not worry about that. Mrs. Bradshaw didn't see a thing. She thinks you have a fever."

"And you?"

"I think you have a fever of your own devising." She smiled tenderly. "Although I assure you that I'm in no position to judge. We all have our secrets and vices." She paused. "I admit I have no idea what you were up to with that pentagram, however."

Newbury coughed again, easing himself back into the cushions. His eyes were glassy and tired. "I was searching for answers." He paused, and she listened to his ragged breath for a moment whilst he made up his mind about whether to tell her any more than that. His eyes flicked over her face. "I was trying to find out who or what was behind the crash."

Veronica narrowed her eyes, suspicious. "And?"

"And the exercise proved fruitless. I'm afraid we're no closer now than we were when we last spoke." He sighed. Veronica took his hand.

"What of the laudanum?"

Newbury grimaced. "A moment of weakness, is all." He met her gaze. "I shall take the matter in hand." He looked away again. "Now, did you say something about a bath?"

"Yes, I'll call down to Mrs. Bradshaw now." She rose from her knees and brushed herself down.

As she turned towards the door, Newbury sat forward, catching her hand. "Veronica?"

"Yes?"

He smiled, his face sincere. "Thank you."

She nodded. "You're welcome."

Her fingers trailed in his as she walked away, leaving the room in search of Mrs. Bradshaw.

"Thank you, Mrs. Bradshaw."

Newbury smiled as his housekeeper presented him with a large plate piled high with a fluffy omelette and crisp bacon. On the table she placed a rack of toast, blackened to perfection. It was late to be having breakfast—almost three in the afternoon—but she was used to such irregularities and had been sure to offer Newbury her sympathies upon discovering he'd been unwell. Happy that she had discharged her duty, she slipped away from the dining room, casting a final glance at Veronica as she pulled the door shut behind her. It was clear that she didn't understand what Veronica's role in this whole matter had been, and that she had mixed feelings about the scenario. On the one hand, Veronica had proved indispensable in helping her to look after Newbury, and had been the one to finally rouse him from his study. On the other, it seemed somehow inappropriate for her employer to so freely allow his female assistant the run of his household, and for her to allow herself to be so familiar with the gentleman, particularly in company. Nevertheless, she had a great deal of respect for Newbury and had been in his employ for many years, so she had decided to trust his sense of propriety and say nothing that may cause offence. She took the stairs two at a time, eager to get back to her chores, and to some semblance of normality, before the day was out.

Veronica sipped at her tea, watching Newbury from across the table as he attacked his meal with vigour. He had spent the last hour taking a bath, shaving and then dressing in his private rooms. He looked almost restored to his former self, save for the dark rings that still sat heavily beneath his eyes. Veronica was sure that a hearty meal would be good for his constitution and aid in his recovery from the effects of the laudanum. She had passed the time whilst he washed and dressed by perusing the spines of the rare books in his study. It was a wide and varied collection, containing many books she had never heard of and was sure could not be found in the annals of the British Library. Whilst she had been aware of Newbury's speciality in dealing with the occult and paranormal, she hadn't been aware of the sheer *intensity* of his fascination. If finding him semi-conscious inside an enormous chalk pentagram hadn't been evidence enough, the esoteric volumes in his private library had proved beyond a shadow of a doubt that he was one of the foremost experts in the field throughout the whole of the Empire.

She placed her empty cup on the saucer. Newbury looked up.

"So, tell me, what came of your visit to the palace yesterday?"

Newbury finished chewing his food. "Very little, I'm afraid, although I did manage to tease out of Her Majesty the reason for her unusual interest in the case." He reached for his coffee, taking a long draw. Veronica leaned forward, waiting for him to continue. "Apparently the body of a Dutch Royal was found aboard the wreckage. A cousin of the Queen, in fact." He paused, waiting for her reaction.

Veronica frowned. "But wasn't *The Lady Armitage* a passenger-class vessel? Why would a member of the Royal Family take a second-class transport to Dublin?"

Newbury smiled. "Precisely. But it's not much of a lead. We can't even begin to consider interviewing the family, and besides, they have even less of an idea about the whole thing than we do. The man had been missing in London for days before it happened. Her Majesty has promised the boy's mother an explanation, and it's up to us to find one, as soon as possible." He didn't look particularly confident. Taking his cutlery, he continued to tackle his breakfast. Veronica poured herself another cup of Earl Grey. They sat in silence for a few minutes, each of them racking their brains for ideas.

Veronica was startled by a knock on the door. Newbury looked up, but didn't speak. A moment later, Mrs. Bradshaw entered, bearing a silver tray that was covered in letters—the post Veronica had seen on the hall table when she'd first arrived. It seemed like days had passed since her arrival that morning.

"Your post, sir. I thought you may like to open it whilst you finished your breakfast?"

"Very thoughtful, Mrs. Bradshaw. Thank you." He watched her leave and then turned his attention to the tray she had placed on the table beside him, studying the contents intently. Five or six letters lay scattered upon it. He placed his cutlery on the side of his plate and poked at the envelopes, stopping when he saw one that bore a hand he didn't recognise.

He glanced up at Veronica. "Excuse me for a moment, my dear, whilst I take a look at this rather interesting missive." He used his finger to tear the envelope open and withdrew the letter he found inside. It was dated the previous day, and written in a perfect copperplate, with big artistic flourishes, on plain white paper. Newbury scanned the short paragraph that composed the body of the letter, then folded it in half and passed it to Veronica.

Veronica unfolded it and spread it out on the table before her.

Sir Maurice,
I request your presence at the Orleans Club, 29 King St, S.W., tomorrow at four. I find myself in possession of in-formation that may pertain to your current investigation, regarding the crash of the passenger airship, The Lady Armitage. I'd appreciate the opportunity to aid you in bringing the perpetrators in this matter to justice.

Yours,
Mr. Christopher Morgan

She looked up. "Do you know this man?"

"Indeed not. Although . . ." He thought for a moment. "I believe I know him by name and reputation." He took another sip of his coffee. "A speculator and a dilettante, if I'm not mistaken. I believe he owns an art gallery across town." He smiled, dabbing his mouth with his napkin. "Nevertheless, Miss Hobbes, we have our lead, and no time to spare. If we're to make it to the Orleans Club by four, we should be on our way directly. Are you fit?"

Veronica smiled back, delighted to see Newbury so engaged and full of energy once again. She nodded. "Are you?"

Newbury laughed, shrugging his shoulders. "Fortified by eggs and bacon. Let us not procrastinate any longer." He stood, pushing the remnants of his meal to one side. "Come on, let's fetch our coats."

Veronica watched Newbury's back as he left the room, calling for Mrs. Bradshaw. She hoped he was up to another sojourn, and whilst she admitted to herself it was wonderful to have the old Newbury back, she felt drained by the whirlwind that surrounded him. She'd rather, for his health, that they put the meeting off until the following day, but with no return address on the letter, it would be difficult to get word to Morgan in time—and in truth, it was too good an opportunity to miss. It was the only lead they had, and if they chose to enjoy the confines of Newbury's home for much longer, the trail would almost certainly grow cold again. Reluctantly, she climbed to her feet and followed after him, anxious to keep a watchful eye on proceedings, and on Newbury himself.

CHAPTER 14

In their haste to get across town, Veronica had allowed herself to be subjected to the noise and bluster of one of the steam-powered carriages that Newbury appeared so heartily to enjoy. It had proved as uncomfortable as ever, and now, on the doorstep of the Orleans Club, she found herself rearranging her dress and trying to put herself hastily back in order. It was cold, and fog was beginning to settle over the streets in wispy tendrils, slowly encroaching upon the city like ivy creeping across an old brick wall.

The Orleans Club, Newbury had informed her on the way over, was the offshoot of a gentlemen's club based in Twickenham, the town dwelling for members of the latter who, it seemed, were welcome to invite guests to the establishment so long as they were of the male variety. Any women were referred directly to the ladies' room and kept well out of earshot of the banter that took place in the main lounge. Veronica found the whole idea ridiculous, but she also knew that she wasn't about to overturn hundreds of years of tradition simply by complaining about it. She was aware that Newbury attended a club, and that he found it a worthwhile pursuit, in terms of both business and pleasure. Not only that, but it was important that they got to speak with Morgan, one way or another. She supposed she'd just have to live with it, for now.

The building itself was typical of this type of establishment; a Georgian town house that sat mid-terrace between what appeared to be private dwellings on either side. Sash windows revealed little about the activities inside, covered by heavy drapes, and there were no signs or indicators that they had even come to the correct address, other than the number *27* on the door, as suggested in Morgan's letter. Clearly the members of the Orleans Club liked to carry out their business behind closed doors.

Newbury stepped up to the blue-panelled door and rapped loudly with the knocker. Almost immediately, it creaked open and a butler appeared in the opening. Light spilled out onto the steps around their feet. Newbury presented his letter and informed the man that they had come for a private conference with one of the club's members, Mr. Christopher Morgan.

The man studied Newbury and Veronica with what seemed to be a measure of disdain. "I'm afraid we have yet to enjoy the pleasure of Mr. Morgan's company today, sir."

Newbury pulled his watch from his pocket, popping open the engraved case and glancing at the ivory face inside. "I see we're a little early. Perhaps Mr. Morgan intends to meet us here at four, as his letter suggests, or perhaps he is running a little late. Either way, I do believe that we'd like to wait."

The butler nodded, opening the door a fraction wider to allow them to pass. "Sir can wait in the lounge, and I'll be sure to inform Mr. Morgan of your presence when he arrives. I'm afraid your companion will have to wait in the ladies' room."

Newbury put his hand on Veronica's arm. "As I suspected, my dear. I'll try not to be too long about it. Why don't you ask around in there and see if you can get a measure of this fellow from the other ladies? It may be that you can find out something useful while you're waiting."

Veronica nodded. "Of course." She allowed the butler to escort her to the door of the ladies' room, whilst Newbury disappeared down the hallway in the direction of the main lounge. The butler held the door open for her, and she stepped through.

The ladies' room was clearly an underused commodity. The room itself was small, and whilst lavishly furnished, it bore the musty odour of emptiness; Veronica had the sense that the place was more of a showroom than a location where ladies actually went to pass the time, at least by choice. She suspected that the room was provided as a service to those unlucky men who didn't seem able to go about their business without their wives following on behind them, limpetlike. That or it was listed as a benefit in the members' book, and as such had to be upheld for those rare occasions when a lady actually found herself in the unenviable position of needing somewhere to wait for her companion whilst he went about his business inside. Whatever the case, there were only two other ladies present in the room when Veronica entered, and both looked up, startled, to see a newcomer whom they might endeavour to coerce into a discussion of some sort. They both stood, placing the books they had been reading on the chairs where they had been sitting. Veronica smiled warmly. "Good afternoon, ladies."

The two women looked at each other, and then turned back to Veronica. The one on the left, who was wearing a long dress cut in pale yellow silk, returned Veronica's smile. "Likewise, I'm sure." She indicated the chair beside her. "Please, won't you join us for tea?"

"I'd be delighted." Veronica walked over to the table and the two ladies returned to their seats.

The woman in the yellow dress poured Veronica a cup of tea from the silver pot on the stand beside her chair. "My name is Mrs. John Marriott, although you may call me Isabella."–

she glanced up—"This is Miss Evelyn Blackwood."

Veronica took the proffered cup and saucer. "Thank you. My name is Miss Veronica Hobbes. It's a pleasure to meet you."

Evelyn Blackwood, a young dark-haired woman in a red jacket and matching skirt, looked Veronica up and down. "Is this your first time at the Orleans Club, Miss Hobbes? I haven't seen you here before."

Veronica nodded. "Yes, indeed. My associate is here to meet one of the members. I thought it wise to wait for him in here."

Isabella Marriott gave her a conspiratorial wink. "So, dear, who exactly is this mysterious 'associate'? You can be sure that your secret is safe with us."

Veronica almost laughed out loud. She had no reason to hide her association with Newbury, and it was clear that the two ladies, so starved for company, were fishing for gossip and intrigue to keep themselves amused. It would do no harm to let them think what they would. In fact, it may help to draw them out on their thoughts about Morgan. "I'm here with Sir Maurice Newbury, the academic and anthropologist."

Isabella and Evelyn exchanged glances. "A sir? Well, didn't you do well for yourself, Miss Hobbes?" Both of them began to giggle like schoolchildren. Veronica was finding the whole experience incredibly trying. "So tell, us, Miss Hobbes. Is he devilishly handsome?"

Veronica took a sip of her tea, wishing for a moment that it was something stronger. "Well, I suppose he is, rather." She tried to look coy, playing along with the conversation.

Evelyn clapped her hands together. "How exciting! A new romance in the Orleans Club. Just wait until we tell Juliana!"

"Now, now, Evelyn, don't get carried away." Isabella placed a hand on her friend's knee. "Miss Hobbes is only just getting started." She looked at Veronica expectantly.

Veronica saw her chance to turn the conversation in a

different direction. "Well, Sir Maurice is here for an important meeting with Mr. Christopher Morgan. I've heard a lot about the man, but I've never had occasion to meet him. Is he a fine fellow?"

Isabella looked impressed. "Oh, Miss Hobbes, one of the finest. Mr. Morgan is a pillar of our community, both here and in Twickenham. He owns an art gallery in town, and all the ladies who've been lucky enough to visit the place say it's full of the most wonderful paintings. Mr. Morgan, is a true gentleman. I'm sure that if your Sir Maurice is having any dealings with Mr. Morgan it is a good reflection on them both."

Veronica smiled. "I'm delighted to hear it, Miss Marriott. I appreciate your candour."

Evelyn leaned forward, clutching her empty teacup to her knee. "Do you think Sir Maurice might decide to become a member of the Orleans Club? I'm sure the other gentlemen would make him most welcome, and I'd love to introduce you to Juliana."

Isabella cut in before Veronica had chance to answer. "Juliana is Evelyn's elder sister. She recently married an industrialist named Greene. She has pretensions of becoming a novelist."

"Really?"

Evelyn nodded enthusiastically. "Actually, I believe she's really rather good. She gives Margaret Oliphant a run for her money, anyway." She patted the book beside her on the chair and smiled.

Veronica tried to look engaged by the idea. "I'm sure that she's very talented indeed, Miss Blackwood." She placed her cup and saucer on the table. There was a rap at the door. The three women looked up to see Newbury framed in the doorway.

"Miss Hobbes. I'm sorry to disturb your conversation, but I believe our business here is done."

Veronica tried to hide the relief on her face. As she stood,

Isabella leaned in and whispered surreptitiously, "You're right, dear—he's terribly dashing."

Veronica smiled knowingly and turned to face both of the ladies. "Good afternoon, ladies. It's been a pleasure."

Evelyn glanced from Newbury to Veronica. "You must come and see us again, Miss Hobbes. Sir Maurice, do say you'll bring her again."

Newbury coughed to cover his laughter. "All in good time, I'm sure."

Evelyn smiled triumphantly. "That's settled then. Next time Juliana may be here. I am sure she'd be delighted to tell you about her writing."

"I'll look forward to it." Veronica turned on her heel and joined Newbury in the hallway, before the two of them took their leave of the Orleans Club and headed out into the cold afternoon.

"So, how did you find Morgan?"

They were waiting for a cab by the side of the road. The fog had settled even lower during the time they had passed inside the Orleans Club, and the street seemed deserted, wreathed in a thick smog. Veronica was standing close to Newbury, partly in an effort to fight off the penetrating chill, but partly for the comfort of having him nearby. The fog made her uncomfortable these days, what with all the talk of revenants and glowing policemen. She had resolved to spend as little time out in it as possible, for the time being, at least.

"I'm afraid I didn't find Morgan at all. He didn't keep our appointment. Either he was detained elsewhere, or simply decided that his information wasn't so inflammatory after all."

Veronica frowned. "That sounds unlikely, especially after hearing about him from the ladies inside the club."

Newbury chuckled. "Yes, you did seem to ingratiate yourself with them rather."

Veronica sighed. "I admit that I find that sort of woman most difficult to engage. I think it was their sheer desperation at seeing another female face that led them to embrace me so quickly."

Newbury shrugged. "Did they reveal anything useful, other than recommendations for the latest romance novel or the usual society gossip?"

"Not as such. Although they did go on at length about Morgan, assuring me he was an excellent fellow, a perfect gentleman and a 'pillar of their community.' Doesn't sound to me like the sort of chap not to keep his appointments."

"Indeed." Newbury paused at the sound of horse's hooves. He stepped into the road for a moment, catching the attention of a cab driver. He came back to stand beside Veronica as the cab drew up before them, coming to rest beside the curb. "Well, it's been a difficult day for us both, Miss Hobbes, and I suspect, with the dark drawing in, that it's a little too late to go searching for Morgan now. What do you say that I drop you at home and we set out again first thing tomorrow morning for Morgan's gallery? We shouldn't allow the trail to go cold, no matter how tenuous it actually is."

Veronica nodded her assent. After the day she'd had, she'd be glad for a hot bath and an early night. "Will you be alright, Sir Maurice?"

He caught the meaning behind her words as he opened the door of the cab for her. "I'll be fine, Miss Hobbes. Absolutely fine."

"In that case, I think it is an excellent plan. I'm sure we could both do with the rest."

They mounted the cab and gave the driver directions. Then, falling into a casual silence, each of them watching the fog roll by the windows of the cab, they set out for Kensington, and home.

CHAPTER 15

Good God, Newbury. You look done for!" Bainbridge had never been a man to keep his thoughts to himself.

"A rough night, Charles, followed by a long day. Think nothing of it." Newbury stood to greet his guest. "How the devil are you?"

"Troubled, if truth be told. Can't seem to shake this damn Whitechapel case. I'm starting to think you may have been on to something, you know, with all that 'glowing policeman' business." He dropped himself into a chair in Newbury's lounge, sighing, and Newbury took a seat opposite him. He knew Mrs. Bradshaw would already be organising drinks. He hadn't been expecting Bainbridge to call, but he wasn't disappointed by the development. His old friend offered good company, and he was in need of a distraction to prevent him from pondering too long on the other events of the day.

"Well, I have no doubt Mrs. Bradshaw will be preparing a brandy. We can discuss it at our leisure before a warm fire. I only wish I could do more, but I'm up to my neck in this other affair."

"You're a good man, Newbury. But tell me, I've heard nothing further on the airship disaster. What news?"

"Little, I'm afraid to report. Her Majesty is eager for a

quick resolution, but the leads are few and far between. She's adamant there's foul play involved, but I admit I'm still unsure. I take it Foulkes hasn't turned up anything useful?"

Bainbridge shook his head. "Indeed not. He's a good man. Thorough. If there was anything to be found, he'd have turned it out by now. I'm afraid it's in your hands, Newbury. Ah, look . . ."

They turned to see Mrs. Bradshaw enter the room bearing two large glasses of brandy. Bainbridge took one from her, smiling, his bushy moustache quivering as he did so. "An asset to you, Newbury." He raised the glass to Mrs. Bradshaw. "I'm in dire need of a housekeeper like you, Mrs. Bradshaw. Many thanks." He took a long draw of the brandy, blinking as the alcohol assaulted his palate. Newbury sniffed at his glass and then placed it on the low table between them. He wasn't sure his damaged constitution was ready for it just yet. Mrs. Bradshaw quickly made herself scarce.

Newbury leaned back in his chair, making himself comfortable. The room was small and cosy, with three chairs, a roaring fire, a small bureau and a portrait on the wall showing his grandfather in his military attire. The man had fought in Afghanistan during the expansion of the Empire, and was in many ways responsible, if indirectly, for Newbury's fascination with the occult. John Newbury had died in action, and his small chest of belongings had been returned to the family back in London aboard an old steamer. Still only a boy, Newbury had wondered at the secret contents of the chest, which his father had kept locked and hidden under his bed. One day, when his father was away on business and his mother was receiving visitors in the rooms below, Newbury had taken the key from the drawer in the nightstand and crawled underneath his parents' bed, searching out the chest and unlocking the ornate clasp. The contents were to change his life forever.

Aside from the more typical paraphernalia of war–a pistol, a dagger, a medal–the chest contained three books of a kind young Newbury had never encountered before. The knowledge within them would send him spiralling into a world full of mystery, full of magic and creatures of the night, rituals and charms. They contained a secret history of the world, a catalogue of the occult and a guide to all the bizarre, arcane practices that demonstrated the thin line between life and death. For weeks, Newbury would return to the chest underneath his parents' bed, digging out his grandfather's books and reading by candlelight, filling his head with wonders. He still had the books, now, safe in his study, reclaimed from his father's belongings after both his parents had died. The chest had remained in place for another thirty years, undisturbed, and the day he had finally laid his mother to rest he had returned to the family home to collect it. By this time, of course, Newbury had assembled a vast library dedicated to the arcane, but these particular volumes he had never found again, and they now held pride of place in his collection. He wondered if they were the only three copies of the books that still existed, anywhere in the Empire.

Snapping out of his reverie, Newbury glanced at Bainbridge, who had downed the rest of his brandy and was watching him inquisitively. "Lost you for a moment, Newbury. Everything alright?"

"Yes. Yes, indeed. I was lost in thought. Apologies, old man." He clapped his hands together, demonstrating that Bainbridge had his full attention. "So tell me, what's troubling you about the Whitechapel case?"

Bainbridge stared at the empty glass in his fingers, turning it over so that it caught the light. "We're just getting nowhere, Newbury. More and more bodies are turning up, dumped all over the place, and we don't even have a suspect. The witnesses, such as they are, all report seeing a ghostly blue figure emerge from the fog, and then they damn well run for their lives. Who can blame them? Some report hearing the screams of the victims as they run, but that's about all we've got to go on. It's the same every time—the victim is strangled, apparently without motive, and none of their belongings are taken or disturbed. There is never any trace of the killer left on the scene, and we haven't been able to find anything that links the victims to one another either. I admit to being completely confounded by it all." He looked exasperated, and Newbury, taking pity on his old friend, got out of his chair and searched out a bottle of brandy from a small cabinet on the other side of the room. He placed it on the table in front of a thankful Bainbridge before dropping back into his seat.

"Well, I can see why you're grasping at straws." He smiled. "Miss Hobbes had an interesting notion a few days ago that the killer may not be the original 'glowing policeman' at all, but a new one, an example of the same phenomenon at work, involving different people entirely. Have there been any constables killed in recent months?"

Bainbridge looked thoughtful. "Not that I'm aware of. Although it's certainly worth double-checking. I'll have a man look into it tomorrow."

"Excellent. Other than that, have there been any changes at all in the pattern of the murders? Any minor detail that you haven't mentioned to me as yet?"

Bainbridge poured himself another drink. "Not as such, although the most recent body was different from the rest."

Newbury leaned forward, his interest piqued. "How so?"

"It was a gentleman. All of the victims so far have been paupers, down-and-outs. This chap was a member of a private club with connections to a number of well-respected families. He had no real business being in Whitechapel in the early hours of the morning. We're wondering if he was actually killed elsewhere and then moved across town to give the impression that he was just like all the other victims."

"What was his name?"

"Christopher Morgan. Owned an art gallery not far from here, I'm given to understand."

Newbury practically leapt out of his chair. "Charles! Morgan asked me to meet him this very afternoon! Now I know why he didn't keep his appointment. There has to be a connection. Look here—"

He sprang out of his seat and rushed to the pile of papers he'd left on the bureau. He rifled through them, discarding most of them on the floor in his haste. After a moment, he put his hand on the envelope he'd received that afternoon, containing the letter from Morgan. He handed it to Bainbridge, who eyed it curiously.

"Go on. Open it, Charles!"

Bainbridge slipped the letter out of the envelope and cast his eye over it warily. He seemed to take a moment to let it sink in, then folded it neatly, put it back inside the envelope and placed it on the table beside his drink. "So Morgan had a secret about the airship disaster, and then he turned up dead at the hands of the glowing policeman on the same day he was supposed to meet with you to reveal it."

"Or at the hands of someone wanting us to *believe* it's the glowing policeman. He may well have been killed elsewhere and deposited at Whitechapel, just as you suggested."

"It can't be a coincidence."

"Only further investigation can help us to establish that, my dear man." Newbury was animated now, and he reached for his brandy, hoping it would help to steady his jangling nerves. "Charles, I need to see the body."

"Impossible."

"How so?"

"Because it's already been delivered to the morgue for a

post-mortem examination. They'll be cutting him open at first light."

Newbury shook his head. "Then we go now. It's imperative that I get to examine the corpse. It could shed light on both of our cases."

Bainbridge nodded, although he was obviously reluctant to venture out again at this hour. He glanced at his fob-watch. It was approaching seven o'clock. "What about dinner? Could we stop somewhere on the way?"

"Afterwards, Charles! This could be the breakthrough we've been waiting for. Let's not waste another second!"

Bainbridge downed the last of his brandy and stood to join Newbury at the door. "My private coach is downstairs. We'll take that directly to the morgue. They won't be happy to see us at this hour, but I'm sure we'll be able to talk them around. Shall I send for Miss Hobbes?"

Newbury thought for a moment. "Let's not. We'd only disturb her unduly. I can fill her in when we meet tomorrow morning."

Bainbridge nodded, and together they set out in search of clues.

The morgue was a cold and dreary place, in keeping, Newbury supposed, with its function as a repository of the dead. This was the place where murder victims or other suspicious deaths would be sent by Scotland Yard for closer examination, before the cadavers were forwarded to a funeral parlour and prepared for burial. Paupers, of course, tended to go directly from the table to a wooden box, and then into the ground, without the dignity of an elaborate service. The state did what it could, but as the politicians insisted on reminding everybody, it was not a charity.

Newbury looked the place up and down as Bainbridge spoke with the mortuary attendant, showing his credentials in an effort to solicit the man's help. The room had a clinical feel, with white-tiled walls and floor, steel instruments set out carefully on wooden trolleys and a pair of marble slabs, empty and awaiting the freshly dead. Newbury shivered despite himself. The room reminded him of a bizarre underground station, with a curved roof and tiled archways leading to other rooms. The entire building seemed to echo with their footsteps, silent save for the voices of the other two men as they agreed, finally, that Newbury could examine the corpse of Christopher Morgan.

The mortuary attendant—a tall, lean man, freshly shaved, with his blond hair swept back in a widow's peak and a pale complexion that suggested he spent the majority of his time indoors—led them through one of the open archways and into an adjoining chamber, where one of the slabs was covered by a white sheet. With a serious look in his eye, the attendant drew back the cover and allowed them to gaze upon the cadaver that had once been Christopher Morgan.

"Is this the man you're looking for?" His voice was nasal and thin.

Bainbridge was starting to get impatient with the man. "We'll have to take your word for it. We have no record of his likeness. Neither of us was in attendance at the crime scene."

The attendant nodded. "Then please feel free to inspect the body for as long as you deem necessary. I shall return to my post and await news that you have finished." He stopped, glancing sharply at Newbury. "I hope you find what you are looking for.'

Newbury met the man's gaze. "Thank you." He turned to regard the body, waiting for the attendant's footsteps to disappear into the next room before looking up at Bainbridge, who was opening and closing his fist with impatience. He drove his cane down hard on the tiled floor. "Despicable fellow. Even after I established my position, he continued to question me regarding our visit. I have it in mind to speak with his superiors about his conduct."

Newbury put a hand on his friend's arm. "It's late, Charles, and our visit is very irregular. Let us concentrate on the task at hand."

Bainbridge nodded, clearly not placated. "On with it, then. Let's get this done with so we can get to dinner. This place always gives me the chills."

Newbury reached over and rolled the white sheet down to the dead man's knees. It was evident almost immediately that Morgan had been a man of fortune: his black suit was perfectly tailored, probably Saville Row, and his hands were perfectly manicured and impeccably clean. His hair had clearly been worn short in a side parting, but now it had been disturbed, either in the struggle that preceded his death, or during the transportation of the body to the morgue. The man still wore a fine gold ring on his right hand and an expensive chain looped from his fob-watch to his waistcoat pocket. Newbury glanced at Bainbridge. "So it wasn't a robbery, then."

"No. Just like the others. The only difference here is that Morgan had more on him worth stealing."

Newbury felt around in the man's pockets. They were practically empty. One held a handful of loose change whilst another held his wallet. To Newbury's dismay, there was nothing inside that suggested Morgan's reasons for wanting to speak with him at the Orleans Club earlier that day: just a couple of business cards, some banker's notes and a grainy sepia photograph of a woman sitting on a wicker chair, smiling at the camera. He stuffed the wallet back into the pocket where he had found it.

"Well, nothing so far to shed light on the airship disaster. Let's see if the manner of his death brings us any closer to an answer in the other matter, shall we?" Newbury inched around the table, examining the corpse in minute detail as he did so. He stopped beside the head, taking the chin between his thumb and forefinger and moving the head from side to side, as if he were trying to make Morgan shake his head. "The neck's not broken, but there's some pretty serious bruising around the throat. I'd wager it's a crushed windpipe. The assailant appears to have caught him with both hands and throttled the life out of him. Poor chap. It doesn't even look like he got a chance to fight back." He leaned closer, examining the bruised flesh around the throat. The skin was starting to take on a waxy pallor as rigor mortis set in. His brows furrowed in concentration.

"What is it? Have you seen something?"

Newbury stepped back from the mortuary table. "Take a look at the bruised areas around the throat."

Bainbridge handed Newbury his cane and leaned heavily on the marble slab, lowering his face to examine the corpse more closely. "What am I looking for, man? I can see plenty of bruises. Looks to me like the chap was strangled, just as you said."

"Indeed, but if you look a little closer, you'll see what I'm interested in. There are flecks of blue powder spotted about his throat. It shimmers if you shift slightly in the light."

"My God, Newbury. I think you're on to something."

Newbury smiled. "It's not much, but it certainly suggests our killer may have a more corporeal explanation than we'd previously imagined."

Bainbridge stepped away from the corpse. "So what's to be done?"

Newbury circled the table again, finding the white sheet and folding it neatly back over the corpse. "Miss Hobbes and I will pay a visit to Morgan's gallery tomorrow and interview the staff. I need to establish what it was he was so keen to talk to me about. It may have been what got him killed, and if so, there's a definite link between the glowing policeman and the wreck of *The Lady Armitage*." Bainbridge nodded, listening intently. "I'd suggest that you have your men test this blue powder at first light. Let's see if they can't establish a manufacturer. That way we can run through their customer records and begin to narrow down the list of potential candidates for our killer."

Bainbridge grinned. "Marvellous. Newbury, I knew you'd be of service to me when I knocked on your door this evening. Now–" He took the other man by the shoulders and led him away from the mortuary slab, his cane clicking on the tiled floor as they walked. "–what about that dinner you promised me? How about that little place you like by Kingsway?"

CHAPTER 16

It was mid-morning before Newbury rose, pulled on his dressing gown and sauntered to the bathroom to begin his daily ablutions with his razor and flannel. The previous day had been a drain on him, both physically and mentally, and today he had chosen to lounge for a while in bed, reading a book. He was, of course, eager to press on with the case, but by the same token was sure that Morgan's gallery could wait for a few hours whilst he ensured that he was fully recovered from the excesses of the laudanum. He had finally emerged around ten o'clock, enjoyed a leisurely feast of porridge, fruit and toast and then, after opening his post, had taken a short constitutional stroll before hailing a cab to Kensington to call for Veronica. His mind felt sharp and alert, his body taut and wiry. His trip to the morgue with Bainbridge had proved enlightening, and he was sure they were getting closer to the heart of the mystery surrounding the wreck of *The Lady Armitage,* and also the Whitechapel strangulations and the glowing policeman. It was clear that the two investigations were linked, somehow, and he hoped that a visit to Morgan's gallery would help him to establish the nature of that link. It would take a day or two for the police to analyse the blue powder he'd found on Morgan's corpse, but in the meantime, he'd agreed with Bainbridge that he'd press on at the gallery, and that they would keep each other informed of their progress. The discovery of the powder had been playing on his mind since the previous evening, and he couldn't help wondering if he'd somehow missed the evidence on the first few bodies that he had inspected. Were there specks of the stuff on the collars or clothes of those other victims? He certainly didn't recall seeing anything around their throats, save for bruising and the obvious signs of a fight, although he knew by now that it was too late to check. The bodies would have been interred in the local cemetery, and he was loath to start digging up graves on the off chance that he'd still be able to find evidence of a fine blue power on their clothes. In fact, in all likelihood, their clothes would have been burnt and their corpses dressed in their best suits before burial. He clacked his tongue. He supposed it may be that the killer was getting careless or arrogant, confident that no matter what trace he left of himself at the scene, the police would be unable to catch him. He may have taken care to remove all the evidence at the scenes of the first few murders, but after weeks of continued activity with no sign that the police were on to him, he may have grown lazy. Newbury had seen that before: the mad gleam in the eye of the killer, the notion that he was somehow invincible and above the law. It wouldn't surprise him if the killer turned out to be totally insane.

On the other hand, of course, he'd inspected the other bodies *in situ* at the various murder scenes, in the dark and the fog, and it could be that he'd simply missed the evidence without the aid of the lamps and the clinical gleam of the morgue. So be it. He knew it was a waiting game now: waiting for the police laboratory to identify the powder, or else waiting for the killer to make his next move. He closed his eyes as the cab rumbled on towards Kensington, wondering which it would be.

Veronica's apartment was on the ground floor of a large terraced house, built during the Georgian period, with tall sash windows and the brickwork rendered in smooth white plaster. The fumes of the passing ground trains and steam-powered carriages had begun to stain the white walls up above, turning them a dirty grey, and Newbury knew that Veronica would disapprove most heartily of this development. He found a delicious irony in that. Veronica was such a forward-thinking woman, and put such great stock in the liberation of the fairer sex, but in other ways she had yet to accept the tide of progress that was currently washing through the Empire. Industry and technology were revolutionising the world, an unstoppable force as certain as life and death, and in Newbury's view, the only options were to embrace it wholeheartedly or else be left behind. He wasn't old enough yet to get stuck in his ways.

When Newbury did finally rap on Veronica's door, it was clear almost immediately that she had spent most of the morning awaiting his arrival. Moments after her housekeeper had come to the door, Veronica appeared in the hallway, dressed in a short grey jacket, white blouse and long grey skirt.

Newbury smiled at her from the door. "Good morning, Miss Hobbes. I'll wait for you outside."

He held the cab whilst she collected her belongings and put on a long woollen coat to protect her from the winter chill. The wind was bracing, and Newbury took the opportunity to seek shelter in her doorway whilst he waited. She joined him a moment later, smiled, and then climbed up into the cab without saying a word. Newbury, grinning, gave the driver instructions and clambered in behind her.

Settling into his seat, he turned towards her, only to find her watching him intently from across the cab. He removed his hat and placed it neatly on the seat beside him.

"You look well today, Sir Maurice. I'm delighted to see it." She was wearing a kindly expression.

"Thank you, Miss Hobbes. I do believe that I am fully recovered. Please, let us speak no more of the incident"—he looked somewhat sheepishly at the floor—"if you can bear to forgive me my foolishness."

Veronica blinked, looking from his face to the window and back again. "I see no reason to dwell on it, Sir Maurice." She smiled, altering her tone. "What plans do you have for the day ahead?"

"Ah, well, yesterday evening brought with it developments of a sinister kind."

Veronica leaned in, intrigued. "Go on."

"After parting company with you here in Kensington, I returned directly to my lodgings, with plans to settle in for the evening, only to find Sir Charles calling on me half an hour later for dinner. It was an entirely unexpected visit, but certainly not an unwelcome one, and I invited him in to join me. During the course of our conversation, he inadvertently revealed the reason for Christopher Morgan's non-appearance at the Orleans Club yesterday afternoon."

"Which was?"

"The simple fact that he was dead." Newbury allowed that to sink in for a moment. Veronica searched his face expectantly, waiting for him to continue. "Killed, apparently, by the glowing policeman."

Veronica gasped. "Where? What happened?"

"We're not sure. His body was discovered in Whitechapel like each of the others, but it seems doubtful that he would have been there of his own volition, especially in the early hours of the morning. I suspect he was murdered because of the secrets he held, and his body was moved to Whitechapel in an effort to disguise that fact."

Veronica shook her head. "So are you suggesting the two investigations may be linked?"

Newbury shrugged. "Perhaps. I admit I have my

reservations. Morgan's death is not a perfect fit with the pattern of the other murders. For a start, he was a gentleman, where the other victims were all paupers. I have no doubt that his death is in some way related to our investigation of *The Lady Armitage* disaster; it seems far too much of a coincidence that Morgan would write to me claiming to have evidence regarding the matter just a day before he died. I think the question is whether or not his death is truly related to the glowing policeman murders, or whether the circumstances of his death are just an elaborate cover adopted by someone trying to throw us off the scent." He scratched his chin. "I wish I'd had chance to talk with the man. Still, he may have left us a clue all the same."

Veronica raised her eyebrows.

"I visited the morgue with Bainbridge last night to examine the body. We found specks of a strange blue powder around the throat and collar of the corpse."

"Meaning? . . ."

"Meaning nothing, as yet. But it could be the method by which the killer is disguising himself as the glowing policeman, covering his face and hands in this iridescent powder. It would certainly fit the descriptions we've had from the various witness reports. Scotland Yard are running some tests in an attempt to identify the manufacturer of the powder."

"So you're convinced now that the glowing policeman is not of supernatural origin?"

Newbury shook his head. "I'm convinced *Morgan's* killer is not of supernatural origin. We've seen no evidence of this powder on the other bodies from Whitechapel, so I'm reluctant to make any assumptions about whether or not they were killed by the same hand. We can't rule out the idea, but neither can we jump to conclusions. Still, the powder gives us a lead, of sorts. Whether it aids us in simply resolving the mystery surrounding the airship crash, or whether it also leads us to the Whitechapel strangler, time will tell." He smiled. "Whatever the case, I'm hoping we'll find some further answers at Morgan's art gallery today, or at least some more clues to point us in the right direction."

"One thing is certain. There doesn't appear to be a simple solution to any of this." Veronica shrugged, folding her hands on her lap.

Newbury smiled. "There rarely is, my dear Miss Hobbes. There rarely is."

Newbury looked up, startled as the cab came to a sudden juddering halt. He peered out of the window. The cab had come to rest before a large red brick building. It was a single storey structure, no bigger than a public bath-house, with a sloping roof of grey slate tiles and an elaborate entrance porch in the classical style, with four large Corinthian columns and a series of low steps up to the door. Ivy formed a web-work across the fascia of the building, trimmed to accommodate the entranceway itself, and a small pleasant garden gave the impression that both the gallery and grounds were kept in impeccable order. A sober-looking sign by the front gate read THE CHRISTOPHER MORGAN GALLERY OF FINE ART.

"Miss Hobbes. I do believe we've arrived."

Veronica looked round. "Do you think there'll be anyone here? Given the circumstances, I mean?"

"I have no idea. We shan't let it stop us, though. Come on."

Newbury paid the fare and, having dismounted the cab, moved to stand beside the wrought-iron gate, surveying the scene before him. The cab driver steered the horses around a large turning circle at the end of the driveway and guided them off towards the city once again, their hooves clacking on the cobbled road.

Newbury took a moment to enjoy the view of the building

and its grounds. He noted that the flower-beds were still bursting with colour, even at this late point in November. Overhead, pigeons cooed noisily as they wheeled in the sky, high above the bustle of the city. Veronica crossed the path to stand beside him. After a moment, he held out his arm for her, and she took it appreciatively, locking her arm in his, and together they set off towards the gallery, their feet crunching on the loose gravel of the path as they walked.

Moments later, to their surprise, they found themselves joined in the courtyard by a burly-looking policeman who had apparently seen them coming and stepped out from the shadow of the doorway, where he must have been standing for some time. He nodded politely and cleared his throat. "The gallery is closed today, sir. I'm afraid you've had a wasted journey."

Newbury smiled. "On the contrary, my good man. We're here on business." He withdrew his arm from Veronica's and fished around in his jacket pocket before producing a black leather wallet filled with crisp yellow documents. "Here, allow me to show you my papers."

The policeman stepped forwards and took the proffered papers from Newbury. He glanced over them briefly, his eyes widening at the sight of Her Majesty's seal and signature, before handing them back to the other man. There was a minor alteration in his posture. "Please forgive me, sir. How can I be of assistance?"

Newbury folded the wallet away into his pocket once again. "Thank you. We're fully appraised of the situation regarding Mr. Morgan's death. You need not divert your attentions away from your duties on our behalf, Constable. Nevertheless, can you tell us if there have been any further developments since yesterday evening? Did any of your officers find anything of interest inside?" He nodded at the building, as if clarifying his question.

The policeman shook his head. "No, sir. Inspector Lewis spent much of yesterday interviewing the staff and searching the gallery for evidence, but there appears to be nothing out of order. It doesn't seem likely that the victim was killed on the premises, and we've been unable to establish a motive for any other suspects, either. Much the same as the rest of those Whitechapel killings, if you ask me." He glanced over his shoulder at the gallery. "We're keeping an eye on the place all the same, mind you."

Newbury frowned. "Would you mind if we took a look around? We won't disturb anything, but I think it would aid our own investigation."

The policeman stepped to one side to let them pass. "Be my guest. The staff all turned up for work today, too, so you'll find most of them inside. Not sure what's to become of them, really."

"Yes, a sorry state of affairs." Newbury led the way towards the gallery entrance, mounting the steps. "Thank you, Constable." He pushed on the door and stepped inside, Veronica following close behind him.

The foyer was a spacious room, with a large reception desk and two doors leading off to either side of the building. Newbury guessed these led to the two exhibition galleries he'd seen advertised in the papers, one featuring the work of a Frenchman, Gustave Loiseau, the other a British artist named Paul Maitland. The reception desk was unmanned, and the place was quiet. It was as if the building itself were in mourning for the loss of its patron.

Newbury crossed the room, his heels clicking loudly on the marble floor. He stopped before the door on the right, turning towards Veronica. "Shall we take a wing each, Miss Hobbes? I've never been enamoured of the Impressionist school, but I'm interested to see why this Frenchman has been causing such a stir throughout London." He grinned. "If you happen across Morgan's office, don't touch anything. I think it's best we tackle that together."

He didn't wait for Veronica to respond before disappearing through the open door, the sound of his footsteps ringing out into the cavernous space of the foyer.

Veronica waited until the sound of Newbury's footfalls had diminished, and then she turned in the other direction, heading towards the left wing of the gallery.

Passing through the doorway, she realised that the gallery itself comprised a series of interconnected rooms, each one featuring an array of paintings hung neatly on white walls. Many of the paintings were landscapes, and she recognised a number of them as views of the English countryside. The palette was subdued, but even so, against the stark white of the walls the colours leapt out at her like vibrant splashes of light. She supposed that was the point.

She toured the room, paying no real attention to the details in the paintings. She found the mood of the place serious and maudlin. There was nothing of Christopher Morgan in here; only the artist and the works he had chosen to display.

An archway led through to another room, longer this time, although the paintings continued in the same vein: trees and landscapes, the occasional building. There was no doubt in Veronica's mind that the artist had great ability, but personally the pieces left her cold. She moved on, hoping to find evidence of people in the next room.

She was not disappointed. The exhibition appeared to terminate in this third and final chamber, and she could hear voices coming from behind a tall panelled door that was marked with the word PRIVATE on a small brass plate. She approached the door and knocked loudly with the back of her hand. The chattering ceased.

After a moment, she heard footsteps approaching the door from the other side, and then it creaked open, its hinges protesting loudly, and a boyish face with ginger hair and startling blue eyes appeared at the opening. "Yes?"

Veronica was a little taken aback by the man's directness. "Oh. Good morning. I'm here with the Crown investigation, looking into the matter of Mr. Morgan's unfortunate death. I'd appreciate it if I could come in and ask you a few questions?"

The man's face fell. "More questions?" He opened the door to its full extent and stepped aside to allow Veronica through. "We spent a good deal of yesterday talking to the police. Do we really need to go over it all again?"

Veronica glanced around the room. This was obviously the staff and office area behind the scenes of the main gallery. Three other people were seated at a large table, two men and a woman, all watching her with interest as she took in her surroundings. There were two other doors exiting the room, both marked with brass plaques similar to the one on the door she had just come through. One read STOREROOM, whilst the other read MR. C. MORGAN, ESQ., PROPRIETOR.

She turned towards the man with red hair. "I'm afraid so, although we'll do our best to keep it to a minimum." She glanced at the other expectant faces around the table. "My name is Miss Veronica Hobbes. May I take a seat for a few moments whilst we wait for my companion?"

There was a brief pause, and then the woman stood. "Please do, Miss Hobbes. We know you're here to help." She frowned at the redheaded man before indicating a chair. Veronica accepted it gratefully. The woman returned to her seat, as did the redheaded man, who plopped himself down opposite Veronica, scowling. The woman continued. "I'm Cynthia. This is Jake." She pointed to the man on her left, a slight rakish-looking chap in a grey suit, who nodded in acknowledgement. "This is Stephen," she said next, this time indicating the man on her right, who gave the impression of being a labourer of some sort, dressed in a waistcoat and shirt and with a swarthy look about him. "And this," she said, shaking her head and pointing at the redheaded man, "this is Adam."

Veronica tried her best to give a sympathetic smile. "I suspect things are a little up in the air for you all at the moment." She directed her question at the woman. "Did you all know Mr. Morgan very well?"

Cynthia nodded. "As well as anyone knows their employer. He was a good man, Miss Hobbes, and he didn't deserve what happened to him." She glanced at Jake, who picked up the conversation.

"We'd all heard stories about this glowing policeman, read the reports in the newspapers about the killings in Whitechapel, but none of us can understand how Mr. Morgan got involved in all that business. He never mentioned it to any of us. It's just senseless."

"And now no one seems to know what will happen to the gallery. Mr. Morgan's son is in Africa, and his wife died last year of pneumonia. We're waiting for the solicitor to tell us whether we're out on the street or not." Adam shook his head.

"Tell me, had Mr. Morgan exhibited any unusual behaviour in the last few weeks? Have there been any strange occurrences at the gallery?"

They heard a noise and looked around as one to see Newbury standing in the doorway. He'd obviously been listening to the conversation for a few moments.

Veronica turned back to the others. "This is Sir Maurice. He is responsible for our investigation."

Cynthia shrugged, looking from Veronica to Newbury. "No. Nothing out of the ordinary."

"Unless you count that automaton device that Mr. Morgan brought back to the gallery a few weeks ago?" The man called Stephen spoke in a quiet, unassuming voice that seemed somewhat at odds with his swarthy, manly appearance.

Newbury paced into the room, resting his hands on the back of an empty chair. "Go on."

The man looked at the table-top as he talked, clearly nervous. "Well, Mr. Morgan bought one of those new automaton men a few weeks ago, and brought it back to the gallery to serve drinks during the private viewings. He wanted it to be a talking point amongst the guests."

Veronica leaned closer to hear. "And what happened?"

Stephen glanced at her. "After a few days, it started to behave erratically. It failed to carry out Mr. Morgan's instructions and began shambling around the place like it had lost its balance. It started to emit strange sounds, high-pitched whistles and suchlike." He toyed with his fingers. "Then, on the following day, it attacked Mansfield, the desk clerk, when he came in to look at the books. Mr. Morgan and I had to prise it off of him and lock it in the storeroom until the manufacturers could come and collect it. It made a hell of a racket in there."

"Was anybody hurt?"

"Just cuts and bruises. But Mr. Morgan was hopping mad. He sent a telegram to the company he'd bought it from. He refused to have a replacement. Said the things were dangerous and should be banned."

Newbury stood back from the table. "Do you know the name of this manufacturer?"

Stephen met his gaze. "I do, sir. Chapman and Villiers. I remember it clear as day."

Newbury walked over to the door marked STOREROOM. "Is this where you imprisoned it?"

"Yes."

He opened the door and glanced inside. Veronica craned her neck to see. The contents of the cupboard were exactly as one would expect: a mop and pail, a broom, a shelf full of cleaning products. The inside of the door, however, was marked with a series of long gouges, scratches where the automaton had clearly tried to break out of the cupboard, raking its brass fingers across the wood. Newbury caught Veronica's eye. He closed the door.

"Is any of this actually relevant?" Adam sat back in his chair, clearly put out by the conversation. "What difference does it make now? Mr. Morgan was murdered by the glowing policeman, and no talk of automatons and clerks is going to bring him back."

Cynthia leaned across the table and took his hand. "Adam, everything is going to be alright." The young man pushed his chair back petulantly and got to his feet, strolling pointedly from the room. Cynthia sighed, waiting for the sound of his footsteps to fade before speaking. "He's young, and he's taken it hard. He was fond of Mr. Morgan, and he's worried about losing his earnings." She shrugged once more. "We all are."

Veronica stood. "I can assure you that we'll do everything we can to find the culprit. You've been very helpful. Now, if we can just take a quick look inside Mr. Morgan's office, we'll leave you to your mourning."

Jake nodded. "The door's open. Go ahead. I'm not sure you'll find anything of use in there, mind you. The police have been through it once already."

Veronica navigated her way around the table, and together, she and Newbury left the three remaining employees to their thoughts.

Jake's words had proved more or less correct, and the two investigators had found nothing of real use in Morgan's sparsely furnished office. The desk had been piled high with correspondence, but much of it had already been rifled through by the police, and it consisted mostly of bills, receipts and speculative letters from artists, soliciting Morgan to exhibit their work. Veronica had managed to locate the receipt, and consequent refund slip, from Chapman and Villiers, and was appalled by the expense Morgan had gone to in acquiring the unit. It was no wonder he had complained bitterly when the thing began to malfunction: the device had cost him more than Veronica was paid in a year. She had passed the documents to Newbury, who had folded them carefully and slipped them into his pocket for later use.

As they strolled along the private driveway outside the gallery, Newbury's disposition seemed to brighten. "Well, Miss Hobbes. Another interesting development, wouldn't you say?"

Veronica smiled. "Absolutely. I believe I could now hazard a guess as to what it was that Morgan wished to talk to you about yesterday."

"Indeed?"

"Well, it sounds to me as if Morgan had cast-iron proof that the automaton units are not, as Monsieur Villiers had us believe, impervious to malfunction."

"Precisely my thoughts, Miss Hobbes. It seems as though our friends from Battersea were a little economical with the truth."

"To my mind, that puts Chapman and Villiers themselves very much in the frame for Morgan's murder. They certainly had a motive. It also suggests that the pilot of *The Lady Armitage* may indeed have been subject to a malfunction. Shall we pay them another visit this afternoon?"

Newbury shook his head. "No, my dear Miss Hobbes. It's too soon for all that. We need more evidence before we can build a case against them. Motive on its own is not enough. Certainly, they had a lot to gain from Morgan's death, but we still don't know what the link to the Whitechapel case may be, if any. I don't want to compromise either investigation by charging ahead prematurely. No, I suggest we part company for a short while."

Veronica looked concerned.

Newbury laughed. "Don't worry, I'm not about to go charging off without you. I'm overdue a stop at the office, and I'm anxious to see if there is news from Miss Coulthard. Are you free this evening?"

"Yes, of course."

"Then how would you like to accompany me to a soiree? The Hanbury-Whites are hosting a party at their house in St. John's Wood and I was planning to attend."

Veronica looked a little taken aback. "Thank you, Sir Maurice. I would be delighted to accompany you." She smiled, fiddling with the buttons on her coat.

"Excellent. I will call for you in a cab around seven."

"Just be sure that it's one of the horse-drawn variety, and not one of those terrible modern contraptions. I can't bear the noise and the smell."

Newbury chuckled. "I most certainly will."

They turned from the driveway onto the street, which was bustling with mid-afternoon traffic. Newbury hesitated. "Can I drop you now?"

Veronica shook her head. "No. I'm intent on a stroll. You go ahead."

"Are you sure? It's quite a walk back to Kensington."

"Positive. I could do with the exercise."

Newbury nodded, and Veronica watched as he hailed a cab, and, with a brief wave, disappeared inside. Then, wrapping her coat around her shoulders, she set off into the blustery afternoon, a wide grin on her face.

CHAPTER 17

The party was in full swing when, later that evening, Newbury and Veronica arrived in St. John's Wood, climbing out of their cab to stand in the shadow of the extravagant family home of the Hanbury-Whites. The moon was a bright disk in the sky, wreathed in wintry mist, and Veronica's breath plumed in the frosty air. She turned on the spot, taking in the view.

Carriages and hansom cabs were arriving and departing in a constant stream, depositing guests on the gravelled driveway at the foot of a large flight of stone steps. Visitors dressed in their best finery flowed up these steps, disappearing into the grand entranceway as if it were the maw of some ancient famished beast. Inside, silhouettes chattered to one another behind brightly lit windows, and the hubbub of voices was spilling out into the night, an undulating cacophony of pleasantries, compliments, vitriolic sleights and whispered asides. Butlers stood in the open doorway, greeting the guests and taking their coats as they drifted through to the party inside.

The house was magnificent. Built about a hundred years before, it had all the wonderful proportions of Georgian architecture that she had come to adore, the same that had inspired her to take the lodgings she now kept in Kensington: tall sash windows, a glorious front porch, a squat rectangular shape. It lacked the ostentation of the more recent buildings that had been springing up all over London, and she approved wholeheartedly. She couldn't wait to see inside. Years ago, her parents had introduced her to London society, and she had visited a great many of the grand houses in the city, but with the news of Amelia's illness, they had spent the last year in solitude, retreating from the social scene, and the effect had been to leave Veronica without a means to engage with it herself. She was grateful to Newbury for the opportunity to join him this evening, and for giving her the chance to wear something other than the functional attire she often found herself donning for the office. Worse, her recent activities in the field—climbing through the wreckage of burnt-out airships or visiting manufactories on the other side of the river—had left her feeling less than ladylike. Tonight, she'd decided, as she looked herself over in the cheval glass at her apartment, she would redress that balance. She turned to Newbury, who was standing alongside her. "Thank you for bringing me here."

He smiled warmly. "You're welcome, my dear." He was wearing a smart, black evening suit; formal, but with a forgiving cut. Around his throat he wore a perfectly knotted bow tie, and a top hat balanced precariously on one side of his head. He looked the perfect picture of a gentleman. He turned to look Veronica up and down, now that he had an opportunity to admire her properly in the light of the street-lamps. She was dressed in an immaculate flowing gown of yellow silk. It had a low neckline, exposing the soft pink flesh of her throat and chest. The bodice was fitted, with skirts that flowed all the way to the floor and skimmed the ground as she walked. The ensemble was finished with a single string of opalescent pearls and a pair of matching earrings. Her hair was tied up in an elaborate coiffure.

"Miss Hobbes, I must add that you look wonderful this evening." Newbury, attempting to hide his embarrassment, offered his arm, and together they climbed the steps towards the bustle of the house.

Inside, it was immediately clear to Veronica that the party was very much the zenith of London society that evening. Everywhere she looked, she saw faces she recognised, as well as ten others she did not. The place was bustling with ambassadors, politicians and gentlemen, not to mention their multitudes of wives and daughters. She stood for a moment on the threshold of a large room, arm in arm with Newbury, and together they surveyed the scene. Brass automata wove through the press of people, elegantly side-stepping the little conversational clusters that had formed, bearing trays full of drinks and food. Veronica watched as one made a lap of the room, its glassy, spinning eyes shimmering in the reflected light of the gas-lamps, the porthole in its chest revealing the crackling blue of the electrical charge generated by its winding mechanism. For all the stories she'd heard that day about the unit that had malfunctioned at Morgan's art gallery, she was still impressed by the machines and the smooth manner in which they seemed to integrate with the party and its revellers. She watched people snatching drinks from the trays as the automata brushed past them, hardly pausing in their conversations to consider the miraculous nature of the devices that were wandering amongst them, pandering to their every need. There were at least ten of the devices waiting on the guests, and Veronica couldn't help wondering at the expense the Hanbury-Whites must have gone to in having them there. She had seen the price of an individual unit that morning and could only suppose that the automata were there on loan, and did not actually belong to the household itself—that would surely be too much.

She leaned in towards Newbury, keeping her voice low. His hair smelled faintly of lavender. "I admit to feeling a little nervous in the presence of so many automata. After hearing the stories this morning at the gallery, I mean."

Newbury nodded, acknowledging her concern, but it was clear he was feeling playful. "My dear Miss Hobbes, it's not the automata you should be worried about. They may be dressed in their best finery, but I assure you, half the men in this room are more dangerous than those devices could ever be." He smiled. "Come on, keep your wits about you and we'll do a lap."

He led her in a circuit of the room, nodding politely at the other guests as they passed each one in turn. Newbury was clearly an established figure amongst the society crowd, and was greeted innumerable times by men whom Veronica did not recognise: men wearing ancient wispy beards, men dressed in immaculate military attire, men who gave the impression of being nothing but ridiculous fops. In turn, Newbury was polite, but he did not allow himself to be drawn into conversation, having just the right air about him of a man who needed to be somewhere else and could not stop to pass time in idle chit-chat.

After making a circuit of about half the large room, they paused momentarily by the fireplace and were approached by one of the automata. Newbury claimed two flutes of champagne from the proffered tray, passing one to Veronica. The automaton paused, cocking its head to regard them. For a moment, it remained there, eerily still. The moment stretched. Veronica thought she could hear the sound of its mechanisms whirring away inside, but then it turned away and moved on, drifting towards another small gathering of guests who looked as if they were in need of more refreshment. Veronica shivered, and took a long draw from her glass.

After passing a few words with a man named Dr. Russ, who had seemed rather engaging and had complimented Veronica enthusiastically on her dress, patting Newbury on the shoulder like an old friend, the two of them exited the room through a second door, winding their way farther into the large house. They walked along a short hallway filled with the billowing smoke of cigarettes, dodging the crowd that had spilled out from the other rooms, and coming to a set of double doors, behind which more chattering voices could be heard.

"I believe this should be worth seeing, Miss Hobbes." Newbury, grinning, pushed on the doors and they swung open, revealing a large chamber filled with row upon row of wooden chairs, arranged to accommodate a large piano and two stools in the corner of the room. Music stands had been set up, and sheets of notation had already been placed *in situ.* Many of the seats in the room had already been taken, but there were a few empty rows near the very front of the chamber. The guests were mostly engaged in talking amongst themselves, but a number of them looked up as the newcomers entered the room.

Newbury cleared his throat. "Come on, let's find somewhere to sit. I'm told the performance will be a real eye-opener."

Smiling, Veronica allowed herself to be led.

Newbury, nodding and greeting the other members of the assembled audience as they shuffled along the central aisle, located two chairs in the very front row and indicated that Veronica should take a seat. She lowered herself carefully into the chair, ensuring that her skirt did not crumple too severely beneath her. Newbury took his place beside her, first taking a printed order of play from the pile on a nearby table. He flicked through it quickly, and then placed it on his lap, folding his hands over it. He turned to Veronica, his voice lowered. "Looks like they're starting with Elgar. Could be worse." He grinned.

Veronica shook her head. It was clear Newbury was enjoying himself, but not, as far as she could tell, for the same reasons as the other guests. He did not seem to want to engage with the society crowd, at least any more than he deemed necessary. Instead, Veronica got the distinct impression that he was toying with them, laughing at their self-congratulatory attitudes, and whilst she did not believe he actually thought himself above his peers, it seemed as if he were remaining purposefully aloof from them. It was an interesting side to his character, and one that she had not expected to see.

Veronica heard the doors swing open behind her and a hush descend on the room. She glanced over her shoulder, almost gasping out loud at the sight she saw. A man in his fifties, with greying hair and a slight limp in his left leg, was leading two automata into the room. They walked with the typical mechanical gait of the others of their kind, but were each dressed in a neat black suit and tie, and one was clutching a violin and bow firmly between its padded brass fingers. She tracked them as they strode down the central aisle between the rows of chairs, taking up their positions in the corner. The automaton holding the violin took a seat on a stool before the music stand and readied itself, tucking the instrument neatly underneath its chin. The other lowered itself into place before the piano, its brass feet clicking as it found the pedals, its fingers resting silently on the ivory keys. The man who had entered the room with them took his place beside the piano, paused, and seemed to steady himself with a deep lungful of air. He looked around the room, ensuring that the audience was prepared, and then turned back to the two automata. With a sharp flick of his wrist, he cued them to begin their performance.

Newbury glanced at Veronica, a smile on his face.

The violin stirred. Veronica settled back into her seat, watching intently. The automaton drew the bow back and forth across the strings with an expert touch, and she found she was holding her breath, not wanting to exhale, lest she somehow shatter the magic of the moment. She closed her eyes, allowing the music to wash over her. It was deeply affecting, and delivered with incredible precision. The piano joined in then, the other automaton timing its performance so that it seamlessly segued along with its companion at the violin. The music soared, both arresting and beautiful, and Veronica could barely believe that it was being delivered so perfectly by two inhuman devices, designed, so she had thought, for simple labour and not for complex tasks such as this. Waiting on guests was one thing–even maintaining an airship in flight–but delivering a piece of music with such skill and power made her think twice about the nature of these brass machines. She'd assumed the automata lacked any real sense or emotion, lacked the sentience of living things, being simply machines that could be programmed with punch cards to *imitate* human behaviour, rather than having any awareness of self, or of how their behaviour would impact others. Judging by the skill with which they handled their instruments, however, she began to doubt that assumption. She'd always maintained that music was more than just the sum of its parts; not so much a technical skill in isolation, but an emotional one, too, an art form that blended passion with ability. She was astounded by the quality of the automata's performance, and moved by it as well.

She glanced around the room, trying to get a measure of the audience's response. Like her, many others in the room were entirely engaged with the performance. Newbury had closed his eyes and seemed lulled by the melody. She twisted in her seat, looking back towards the double doors by which they had entered the chamber. To her surprise, Joseph Chapman was standing there, his hands clasped behind his back, looking ill at ease in his formal attire. He seemed to be staring directly at her. Veronica blinked, and then looked away. She tried to focus on the performance, but had the bizarre sense that Chapman's eyes were burning holes in the back of her head. Her face flushed. She glanced back. Chapman was still staring over at her, his face blank, showing no sign of emotion. Feeling uncomfortable, she looked away, nudging Newbury with her elbow. Surprised, he turned to face her, his eyes questioning.

She whispered, and pointed over her shoulder with her thumb. "Chapman."

Newbury strained in his seat, searching the back of the room for the man. After a moment, with no success, he glanced back at Veronica, shaking his head. Unnerved, she leaned on the back of her chair, trying to see what had become of the industrialist. The woman in the chair behind her made a *tut*ting sound and shifted obviously in her seat, making her displeasure with the fidgeting Veronica clearly evident. Veronica sank back into her chair, frustrated. Newbury placed his hand on hers in a placating gesture. A few moments later, the automata finished their first piece, and both Newbury and Veronica joined in with the enthusiastic applause. Then, when the moment seemed appropriate, Newbury stood, held his hand out for Veronica, and lifted her out of her chair. As politely as possible, the two of them slipped away from the scene, leaving the room to silent glares from the other members of the audience. Veronica heard the music starting up again as the door fell shut behind them.

The hallway was still bustling with guests. Newbury leaned in closer and spoke into her ear. "Are you alright?"

Veronica shrugged. "Yes. Just a little unnerved. It wasn't a friendly look he gave me. He seemed somehow . . . sinister. It was as if he were trying to threaten me in some way."

Newbury frowned. "Are you sure it was Chapman that you saw?"

Veronica nodded. "Certain."

Newbury straightened his back. "Well, in that case, let's see if we can't find out where he's hiding now." He took Veronica by the arm and led her back towards the main thrust of the party, passing a gaggle of squawking women in the hallway as they did so. Newbury cringed as the ladies seemed to grow momentarily silent, whispering to one another conspiratorially as they brushed by. Veronica wondered what inane secrets they were sharing at Newbury and Veronica's expense. The giggling resumed again almost as soon as Newbury and Veronica had reached the other end of the hall.

The party had swelled in the few minutes they'd been away from the main reception room, with more and more guests arriving and others yet to drift away from the main hubbub and farther into the bowels of the great house. The room was hot and bustling with people. The automata waited patiently in the wings, surveying the crowd, ready to step forward at any time to offer the guests more refreshment. Newbury strained to see over the heads of the nearby dignitaries. After a moment, he stopped craning his neck and leaned in to whisper to Veronica. "No sign of Chapman in here. At least that I can see from the doorway. Shall we do another lap and try to get a better look?"

Veronica nodded. "I'd feel better about it if we did. At least that way I'd know I'm not imagining things."

Newbury gave her a reassuring look. "I'm sure that's not the case. We don't have to confront him about it, but we can certainly try to keep an eye on him, if indeed he's here. Come on."

They edged into the room, taking two further flutes of champagne from the tray proffered by the automaton near the door, and began the process of slowly weaving their way through the crowd, working clockwise around the edges of the room. Veronica held on tightly to Newbury's arm as they manoeuvred through the press of guests, keeping their eyes peeled for any sign of the industrialist. It wasn't long before they'd circled back as far as the main entrance. Finding a little more breathing space there, they decided to take a moment to pause. Guests were still arriving as they stood with their backs to the door, surveying the room. Newbury sipped at his drink, regarding the little huddles of people nearby. "Perhaps he left?"

"Or perhaps he's watching us from elsewhere in the room?" Veronica shivered at the thought.

Newbury frowned. He looked as if he were just about to reply when he stopped suddenly and turned away at the sound of shouting from the other side of the room. A hush descended on the party like a thick blanket, smothering the chatter. It was difficult to make out what was being said, but a man was clearly engaged in directing a torrent of abuse at another man whom he felt had somehow done him a disservice.

"–and another thing, sir! Your company's literature clearly states that in circumstances such as this, full recompense is assured. Yet I continue to find no such recompense is forthcoming! A damnable business, and you, sir, are a damnable man!"

Newbury raised his eyebrow at Veronica. Neither of them could see anything through the gathered throng. There was a wave of gasping sounds, and then the crowd suddenly parted as two automata, their trays now abandoned, moved forward, their brass feet clicking on the marble floor, a middle-aged gentleman in a black suit between them. The automata each held one of the man's shoulders as they forcibly marched him towards the exit. The man was squirming, clearly in discomfort, and the spinning eyes of the automata glinted in the low light, their features frozen, unmoveable. Behind them, Joseph Chapman stood with his hands on his hips, a wry smile on his face. He glanced at Newbury and then nodded politely, his eyes flicking away to watch as his two brass guardians escorted the other man from the building. Then, as the guests all looked upon the scene with a kind of horrified fascination, he set off after his clockwork devices, exiting the party through the main entrance. Outside, the sound of the man's protests trailed away down the street. The party took only a moment to recover, and then the hubbub began in earnest once again, the society gossips quickly moving to engage one another with talk of the scandal.

Newbury looked at Veronica, bemused. "Well, my dear Miss Hobbes, you were certainly right about Chapman being in attendance here tonight, but it seems as if the problem has miraculously solved itself."

Veronica smiled. "Yes, you could say that, I suppose. But what do you make of it all? It strikes me that the unfortunate captive of those automata may be a likely witness in our developing case."

Newbury nodded. "Yes, it certainly seems that way, doesn't it? I get the distinct impression that the poor gentleman may have had a similar experience to Mr. Morgan."

Veronica looked thoughtful. "Indeed. Do you think he's in danger of suffering the same fate? Should we go after them?"

Newbury shook his head. "No, I'll wager the man is in no danger, this evening at least." He took a long draw from his flute of champagne. "Even if Chapman is somehow connected to Morgan's death, this outcry was a little too public for anything to come of it now. The connection would be obvious to everyone. The automata will take the man around the corner and he'll flee to his abode, angry and embarrassed. No doubt Chapman will take the opportunity to gloat to anyone who'll listen."

Veronica placed her empty glass on a sideboard behind her. One of the automata immediately made a beeline over to reclaim it. "It is interesting, though, isn't it? I mean, after finding us in the other room watching the performance. It's almost like Chapman arranged for us to see this little charade. Did you notice how he made a point of catching your eye?"

"I did. I wonder what it is he's up to." Newbury was

watching the crowd again as he talked. "Let's see if we can discover the identity of Chapman's protagonist before the night is out. That way, we can pay him a visit in the morning."

"And now?"

"And now we have a party to attend." He smiled, holding out his arm. "I believe we were in the middle of doing a turn around the room. And you, my dear Miss Hobbes, look as though you could use another drink."

Arm in arm, they rejoined the gathered crowd and searched out another glass of champagne, keeping a wary eye on the automata as they tried to enjoy the rest of the party.

CHAPTER 18

Newbury woke with a thick head and a dry mouth. He rolled over, burying his face in his pillow. Then, as if surfacing from a glassy pool of water, he suddenly became aware of the world outside of his own head. Someone was rapping insistently on the door to his bedchamber. He rolled onto his back, peeling back his eyelids. It was still dark; there was no light streaming in through the window, and he hadn't yet had sleep enough to banish the residue of the alcohol he had consumed the night before. Early morning, then. He sat up, running a hand through his hair.

"Sir Maurice? Are you there?" The rapping continued.

Newbury frowned. "Yes, Mrs. Bradshaw. I'm awake."

There was an audible sigh of relief from the other side of the door. "Very well, sir. Sir Charles is here to see you. I've asked him to wait in the living-room. Shall I assure him that you will attend to him shortly? I understand that it is a matter of some importance."

Newbury pinched the bridge of his nose between his thumb and forefinger. He groped around in the semi-darkness for his pocket-watch, finding it on the bedside table. He peered at it intently, trying to see the hands. It was just after five. It must be important, for Charles to be calling at this hour. "Please do, Mrs. Bradshaw. I'll be with him momentarily."

Mrs. Bradshaw's footsteps fell away from the door, and Newbury slumped back into his pillows, rubbing his eyes. Then, sighing, he slipped from underneath the warm woollen blankets of his bed and stood beside his dresser, shivering in the chill. He blinked a few times until his eyes had adjusted properly to the dim light, and then searched out his dressing gown, flung it around his shoulders and shoved his feet into the slippers he kept underneath his bed. A moment later, he was following behind Mrs. Bradshaw, squinting in the bright light of the gas-lamps as he stumbled down the stairs to meet his friend.

Bainbridge was pacing anxiously before the fireplace, which was dull and cold and full of nothing but ash at this early hour in the morning. He held a brandy in his hand, but appeared not to have taken a swig of it, as yet. He looked up when Newbury came into the room, his moustache bristling at the sight of his old friend, still dressed in his bedclothes and suffering from a mild hangover.

Newbury looked the other man up and down. "There's been another murder in Whitechapel."

Bainbridge looked astounded by this rather minor piece of deduction. "How did you–?"

Newbury sighed. "Why else would you be here at this hour, Charles?" He shrugged. "Your boots are still clean, and you look like you've dressed hastily: your tie is askew and you've notched your belt on the wrong hole." Bainbridge looked down at his belt, and then shook his head in exasperation. "I take it you've only recently been made aware of the situation and have come to pick me up on your way over to the scene?"

Bainbridge nodded. "Indeed. As you say. So jolly well go and fetch up some clothes and make yourself presentable, man. I've already sent a cab for Miss Hobbes." He took a swig of his brandy and leaned heavily on the mantelpiece.

Newbury nodded, smiling, and then disappeared once again from the room.

A few minutes later, the two men took their leave of Newbury's Chelsea home and mounted the cab that Bainbridge had left waiting for them on the road outside. Its steam engine spluttered noisily as the driver gunned the controls and sent the vehicle careening into the cold, dark morning. Newbury, his head still groggy from the alcohol and lack of sleep, fell back into the seat inside. He had dressed hastily and still wore the shadow of a beard around his face and throat, but had more or less managed to make himself presentable. He looked up when Bainbridge tapped on the window with the end of his cane. "Not sure how much longer I can put up with this abominable weather, Newbury." He glanced out at the smoky, fog-filled streets as they rushed by. "This damnable fog makes our police work doubly hard. Gives these criminal types the cover they need for sneaking around the city at all hours." He sounded weary.

Newbury nodded, but didn't speak. He watched the shapes of building flit past, hidden by the gossamer mist that seemed to soften the edges of everything, making the real world outside the cab seem insubstantial, otherworldly.

"Are you well, Maurice? You seem unusually quiet."

"Quite well, Charles. I attended the soiree at the Hanbury-Whites' last night. I fear I may have led Miss Hobbes rather astray; we indulged in one too many glasses of champagne amidst the merriment."

Bainbridge laughed heartily. "Then I shall conserve my sympathy for more worthy subjects! I take it there was much merriment to be had, in that case?"

Newbury grimaced. "A little. Most interesting, however, was the scene between a certain Mr. Musgrave of Islington and

Joseph Chapman, of Chapman and Villiers Air Transportation Services."

"How so?"

"It appears Chapman sold Musgrave one of those automaton devices. It later malfunctioned and killed his best hound. The word from the society gossips is that Musgrave had been trying to claim compensation from the company and, having received no satisfactory response, took the opportunity to set upon Chapman in front of everyone at the party."

Bainbridge sat forward, resting on his cane. "So what happened?"

"Not a great deal, if truth be told. Chapman had Musgrave escorted from the party by two of his automata and then made his own exit from the proceedings. We didn't see him again all night."

"How peculiar. Do you think it's relevant to your case?"

Newbury nodded. "*Our* case, Charles. You're forgetting Christopher Morgan. It transpires that the same situation is true of Morgan, although in his case, it ended in a rather more grisly fashion. He'd also had an automaton malfunction at his gallery and had successfully negotiated a refund from Chapman. However, when he heard about *The Lady Armitage*, he wrote to me asking to meet, intending to divulge his miserable experience with the device, and the rest you are already aware of. He ended up dead and dumped in Whitechapel."

Bainbridge clenched and unclenched his fist. "So it seems as if Chapman is involved in Morgan's death, and that he may be behind the airship disaster, too. What of Musgrave? Do you think he's in danger?"

"That's just it. I can't see how he could be, not after the performance made by Chapman at the party last night. If he turned up dead now, it would give us cause to pull Chapman in immediately. If he is guilty of Morgan's murder, I can't believe he'd be so insouciant about it."

Bainbridge took a moment to let that sink in. "But what about the other murders? They don't follow the same pattern as Morgan's. Do you still think Morgan's killer tried to use the existing spate of murders as a cover for his own crime?"

"That's what I'm trying to work out. We've got very little we can actually pin on Chapman yet, and if we move too soon, we'll simply cause him to clam up. We need to build a solid case against him, if indeed he is responsible for Morgan's death. Whilst we've certainly established that the automaton device that was piloting *The Lady Armitage* could have caused the crash through malfunction, in truth, we've got no real way of linking Chapman to Morgan's murder, as yet. It's a matter of time and patience." He shuffled in his seat, adjusting his collar. "As to whether the other murders are connected, too, I still have my doubts. Perhaps we'll find out more at the scene we're about to attend. Did your men find out anything useful about the blue powder we found on Morgan's corpse, by the way?"

Bainbridge shook his head. "Not as yet. So far, they haven't even been able to identify the powder itself, let alone the manufacturer, but they're aware of the importance of the matter. Some of them think it may have come over from China."

"Good. Make sure you tell me the minute you hear anything."

The men fell silent, both gazing out of the window at the sleepy city, both wishing they were still at home in their beds instead of rushing through the morning fog towards Whitechapel and another unhappy death.

After a few moments, Bainbridge looked up, catching Newbury's eye. "Oh, I received another invitation from Miss Felicity Johnson in yesterday's post, for a small gathering she's having on Tuesday evening. Did you find yourself invited to the same?"

Newbury tried to keep a serious face as he met the other man's eye. "I did not."

The two men faced each other across the cab. Bainbridge was first to give in, looking away in an attempt to stop himself from sniggering. By the time they reached the outskirts of Whitechapel, the two men were roaring with laughter in the back of the cab, both of them finding the hilarity a welcome distraction from the more serious elements of their lives, and the knowledge that they were once again headed towards a scene of terror and death in one of the poorer parts of the city.

With a grinding of gears and a spluttering of the engine, the cab rocked to a halt on the cobbled road alongside another, waiting vehicle. Bainbridge was first to jump out into the foggy morning, crossing the cobbles to the door of the other carriage. He rapped loudly before swinging the door open and stepping up into the cab. A moment later, as Newbury was arranging his hat by the curb side, he watched as Veronica emerged from the other vehicle, closely followed by the Chief Inspector.

Veronica crossed the street to stand beside him. "Good morning, sir. How are you?"

Newbury arched one eyebrow. "Capital. And you, my dear Miss Hobbes?"

"Perfectly well, thank you, Sir Maurice." Veronica smiled brightly. Newbury grinned. She gave no impression that her alcohol consumption the previous evening had affected her in any way.

Bainbridge approached them, bearing three small oil lanterns, his cane tucked neatly underneath his left arm. He handed one of the lanterns to each of them and then fiddled with the shutters on his own until the light was emanating in a warm halo all around it. It reflected back in the fog, giving it a strange, fuzzy glow, as if he were clutching a ball of light itself and not a lantern at all. He turned to the others. "Right. Turn these up like mine so we can keep an eye on each other as we walk. This blasted fog is so thick this morning that we run the risk of losing each other if we don't stick together." He looked from Veronica to Newbury and back again. "It wouldn't do to be losing either of you in the fog out here. We don't know what else might be lurking around the corner." His face was steely, determined. "I've told one of the cabs to get on its way, whilst the other waits for us here. We'll head to the scene of the murder, take a look to see if there's anything new to be deduced, and then be on our way, as quickly as we can. No use hanging around out here when there's a couple of men already in attendance by the body." He took his cane from under his arm. "Come on. One of them is waiting to show us the way." He set off, hugging the edge of the curb as he walked, in an effort to stay on track in the blinding fog. He was joined a moment later by a uniformed bobby who had been waiting around the other side of the cab. Newbury and Veronica followed behind them, their lanterns held up in the gloaming.

It was only a matter of minutes before Bainbridge's lantern came to a halt and Newbury and Veronica sidled up beside him. A scene resolved out of the fog. The confluence of three buildings and the cover of an arched alleyway had created a barrier of sorts against the thick smog. It still lay heavy in yellow wispy strands, but with the light of the three lanterns, plus the one held by the other uniformed constable already in attendance, Newbury was able to ascertain the key elements of the scene.

A body lay on the cobbles a few feet away from where he was standing. Moisture from the fog had caused the skin to take on a damp sheen, and the waxy complexion suggested that the corpse had been *in situ* for some time before being discovered. That was only to be expected, Newbury supposed, given the visibility out there that morning. The neck of the corpse had been violently twisted and was lying at odds to the rest of the body. Clearly the neck had been snapped before the body was dropped to the ground. The man himself was undeniably a pauper, aged around thirty years old and wearing a scruffy beard and long straggly hair.

Bainbridge moved off to talk with the other policeman, who was standing with his back to the wall a few feet away from the corpse, looking nervous and cold. Newbury caught snippets of the conversation as they talked: Bainbridge questioned him in detail about the circumstances of the death, how the alarm was raised, who found the body, which of the men was first on the scene. It was a thorough interview and, whilst it didn't appear to yield any further clues, it ensured they weren't making any assumptions before examining the corpse. The two constables did not mention the glowing policeman to Bainbridge, and it seemed as if there were no reliable witnesses to call on. Newbury waited for Bainbridge to return, his cane clicking on the cobbles.

"I'll take a look at the corpse, if you've no objection, Charles?"

"Of course not. That's why you're here, isn't it?" Newbury could tell that the other man was feeling the pressure.

Veronica stepped forward. "What can I do to help, Sir Maurice?"

"If you can stomach it, can you go through his pockets whilst I examine the wounds?"

"Of course." She circled around the body and dropped to one knee, setting about the task of emptying the dead man's pockets and searching out his wallet beneath the layers of dirty wool.

Newbury leaned in towards the body. He loosened the man's collar and examined the soft flesh around the throat.

It was badly bruised and broken. He took the man's head by the chin and moved it from side to side. Then, mumbling something to himself, he took up the man's left hand and examined the fingernails. The hands were filthy, but it was clear he'd been in a fight. The knuckles were bloodied, and there was some sort of residue under the fingernails where he had scratched his attacker during the fight.

By this time Veronica had located the man's wallet and had moved to one side to examine the contents. Newbury looked up at Bainbridge, who was leaning over him impatiently, his lantern dangling over Newbury's head. "Found anything?"

"Indeed. Just give me a moment to confirm my suspicions." Newbury rested the man's lifeless hand upon his chest, and searched around in his own pockets for his penknife. "Here, hold that light steady for me, Charles." He beckoned the other man closer. Taking up the dead man's hand again, Newbury unclipped the blade of his penknife and ran the point of it underneath the fingernail. He then returned the hand to its place beside the victim and lifted the blade to the light, examining the residue he had scraped free. "Ah. Just as I thought."

"What is it, man?" Bainbridge was frowning, unclear what it was exactly that Newbury had found.

Newbury rose to his feet. "Here, give me the light and take a look at the man's throat. I think you'll see something of great interest around the larynx."

Bainbridge placed his cane on the ground beside the corpse and leaned in. "The what?"

"The Adam's apple."

Bainbridge took a moment to look over the body. Then, without saying another word, he pushed himself up to stand beside Newbury. "Blue powder."

"Precisely. Dusted around the collar and worked into the broken skin, where the assailant's hands had clutched him around the throat." He held out his penknife, handing Bainbridge his lantern back. "And here, too, under the fingernails. He scratched at the killer's hands as he struggled to get free. That's probably why the killer had to break his neck in the end, because he was fighting back too hard."

"Well, I suppose it means our 'incorporeal' killer has struck again."

Newbury nodded. "Indeed. But this time the profile is exactly the same. This man was clearly a pauper, judging by his clothes and the state of his hands. Veronica, did you find anything?"

Veronica came to join them, clutching the dead man's wallet. "Only a few coins. Nothing of note. He certainly wasn't robbed, though."

Bainbridge shook his head. "So here's the link to Morgan, then, and Chapman through that. The blue powder is a dead giveaway, regardless of what it actually is."

Newbury looked thoughtful. He turned back to look at the corpse. "Perhaps. We certainly may have missed the blue powder on the earlier victims. But there is a distinct problem with your theory about Chapman, I'm afraid. This man has been dead for at least eight hours, judging by the rigor mortis and the pallor of his skin. Chapman couldn't possibly have done it."

"Why not?"

Veronica put her hands on her hips. "Because he was with us at the party." She paused for a moment, shaking her head. "Very clever."

Newbury gave an impressed sigh. "Indeed. Very clever. We wondered why Chapman was making a point of being seen. Now, I think, we have our answer. He's toying with us, inviting us to call him out. He knows he has a watertight alibi, for this and, no doubt, for Morgan's death, too. And whilst we have good reason to believe the airship crash could be the result of an automaton malfunction, all we have is reasonable doubt. Without the evidence from the wreckage, we have no way of proving our argument." He ran a hand over his stubble, adjusting his collar. Veronica shivered in the cold.

"So, what, we lay a trap?" Bainbridge said, frowning and frustrated.

"I'm not sure it's that easy." Newbury blinked, and noticed that Veronica's lantern was beginning to gutter in the damp. "Come on, we can talk further on the way back. Let's get out of this damp fog and somewhere warm for breakfast."

Bainbridge concurred, and went to have a brief word with the two constables before rejoining Newbury and Veronica and starting out for the cab once again. The fog was still thick and cloying, and away from the shelter of the mouth of the alleyway, they were soon smothered by it once again. Nevertheless, following the line of the curb led them easily back to the waiting cab, their lanterns bobbing in the quiet darkness. The cab driver was huddled on his dickey box against the cold, the engine running noisily, steam spouting into the cold air through tin funnels on the top of the contraption. He looked up when he heard them coming, grateful for the opportunity, no doubt, to be on his way.

Newbury was first to the coach door, and held it open for Bainbridge and Veronica. They both extinguished their lanterns before mounting the step, and Newbury held his aloft to ensure they could see. Then, just as he was about to follow suit, Bainbridge slapped his knee in frustration. "Damn it! I must have left my cane beside the body back there. Watch out, Newbury, I'll just run back and fetch it."

Newbury held his hand up to steady the older man. "No fear, Charles. You stay where you are, and I'll dash back and collect it for you. It'll only take me a moment." He turned and held the lantern aloft before moving to retrace their steps along the curb. He heard the coach door click shut behind him.

After a moment, Newbury had been almost completely

swallowed by the dank fog. The sounds of the steam engine had faded to a dull thudding as the pistons fired relentlessly, turning over the large mechanical machine. He crept along, hoping to avoid surprising the two uniformed constables at the scene. A moment later, he emerged from the fog into the mouth of the alleyway. What he saw was one of the most horrifying scenes he had ever witnessed in his life.

Three monsters—it was the only way he could think to describe them—were in the process of gutting the two constables, whose corpses had been dashed to the ground, blood spattered across their torn faces, spilled out over the cobbles all around them. Steam rose from the warm innards as the revenants pulled loops of intestine free from large rents in their bellies, feasting on it all indiscriminately, stuffing it into their mouths with abandon. The creatures looked as if they may once have been human, but all sense of their humanity had now been lost. Their flesh was peeling in long ribbons, their hair falling out around their shoulders, their clothes hanging filthy and torn from their abused bodies. The virus had done its work well, and these monsters were now no more than dead carriers of the plague, capable of nothing but killing and feeding on their victims. They had the stink about them of half-rotted corpses, and this foul smell, mingled with the stench of blood and faeces, caused Newbury to gag violently. He fought back the urge to vomit, not wanting to draw attention to himself. The three creatures were intent on their feeding frenzy, and he didn't want to give them cause to make him their third victim of the day. Tentatively, he glanced from side to side. The area was entirely surrounded by the thick fog, and he had no sense of whether there were more of the creatures lurking in it. He was only a few feet away from the corpse of the murder victim, and he could see Bainbridge's cane on the cobbles beside it. He assumed the revenants were ignoring the body because it was hours old, and with two fresh victims, there was no need for them to feed on the bloated flesh of the dead.

Gingerly, Newbury inched forward, trying not to make a sound. He was intent on getting out of there as quickly as possible, and whilst he wasn't really concerned with retrieving Bainbridge's cane, he knew it would make a handy bludgeoning weapon if he found himself cornered with nowhere to run. The sound of the creatures feeding on the ruined corpses of the two policemen filled his ears. He repressed the fear that was creeping up his spine. He needed to keep a clear head.

He reached out slowly and, keeping his eyes on the backs of the three revenants, felt for the cane with his fingertips. At first he found nothing but cold, slick cobbles, but he patted the ground for a moment longer and eventually his fingers closed on the hard wood of the cane. He rose slowly to his feet, bringing the cane along with him. Trying not to let the adrenaline make him run, he tightened his grip on the lantern and turned slowly away from the nightmare scene, directly into the path of another revenant.

Newbury stumbled backwards but it was too late, and the creature, its foul breath sour in his face, leapt forward and clamped its jaws onto his left shoulder. He cried out in agony as the monster's teeth bit down through his clothes and into his flesh, drawing blood. Its hands quested for a grip on his torso, its talons raking into his flesh, tearing his overcoat as if it were paper. Newbury kicked out with all his might, getting a measure of leverage on the creature and forcing it back with his booted foot. The monster allowed itself to be pushed back momentarily, releasing Newbury's shoulder from its vicelike jaws, before coming at him again, its teeth bared in an ominous black snarl.

His shoulder aching with the vicious bite wound, Newbury reacted as quickly as he could, swinging the cane down across the creature's temple, striking it hard with the round brass handle. It staggered to one side with the force of the blow, the bones around the eye socket shattering where the brass knob had impacted. Newbury tried to glance over his shoulder to make sure the other three creatures were still busy with their existing meal and were not closing in on him from behind. They were not, but the one in front of him ranged up again in no time at all, and he found himself dodging out of the way of its flailing talons. His shoulder throbbed, and he could feel the warmth of his blood seeping down the inside of his shirtsleeve.

He struck the revenant again with the cane, this time breaking loose a few teeth, which rattled to the stones below, but it seemed to have no real effect on the creature. Its bloodshot eyes glared at him as they circled each other, Newbury trying hard not to stumble over the corpse that lay behind him on the ground. The creature lunged once again, aiming its jaws towards his throat, hoping to incapacitate him by tearing his windpipe and jugular out with its teeth. Not knowing what else to do, Newbury dropped the lantern and threw himself backwards, using the corpse of the dead pauper to cushion his fall. He then rolled quickly to one side, scrabbling back up to his feet as quickly as possible, brandishing Bainbridge's cane before him. He could see out of the corner of his eye that the other three creatures were still busy with the remnants of the policemen. He knew it wouldn't be long before they turned their attention to this new quarry, however. He had to despatch the one in front of him soon, or he risked ending up like the bobbies.

He circled, fixing his attention on the revenant before him. It was waiting, hulking over the body of the dead man, looking for another opportunity to pounce. Blood was running down the side of its face where he'd caved in the orbit of its eye, and he noticed for the first time that it had a letter opener half-buried in its neck. Clearly this was not the first time it had cornered someone unexpectedly.

Newbury readied himself, planting his feet firmly on the cobbles. He'd managed to snatch up the oil lantern again after his brief tumble, and realising that he was no match in strength or endurance with the creature, he'd decided to try something else.

The revenant pounced, uncoiling in mid-air like a half-human panther, baring its teeth and flexing its claws. Newbury swung wildly with the lamp, connecting with the monster's shoulder and spattering its hair and face with hot oil. There was a sudden *whoosh*ing sound, and all at once the creature was on fire, its rotten skin and lank hair spreading the angry flames that seemed to spill out from the lamp like a wave of liquid light. Within seconds, the creature's entire head and shoulders were in flames, and it staggered about, unable to see as its eyes boiled away in the heat. Newbury took the opportunity to run, darting past the burning monster and staggering away into the fog. His shoulder burned where the creature had bitten him, and his right side was agony where its talons had gouged a tear in his flesh. Drawing a huge breath and fighting against the spinning darkness that threatened to drag him into unconsciousness, Newbury started back in the direction of the cab.

CHAPTER 19

🔔

Without the aid of the lantern, Newbury found it difficult to get his bearings in the thick fog. He stumbled along the road, doing his best to anchor himself to the curb in an effort to stay on track. He was bleeding profusely from the wounds in his shoulder and side, and he leaned heavily on Bainbridge's cane, attempting to propel himself along in an effort to get away from the terrible scene behind him as quickly as possible.

The fog wreathed everything in its clinging oppressive blanket, and Newbury found it almost impossible to see. This in itself wouldn't have troubled him, but now, in the midst of escaping the clutches of the revenants, he had no idea whether he was being followed or not. The creatures could have been shambling along behind him these last few minutes, drawn to the scent of his spilt blood.

He glanced behind him. There was nothing but a sea of white. He tried not to think of the nightmares that were hulking within it. If he got lost in the fog now, the likelihood would be that he'd never be able to find his way out of it again. He tried to focus on getting back to the cab: to Bainbridge, Veronica and safety.

Presently, after what seemed like an age, he became aware of the choking sound of the cab's engine, and breathed an audible sigh of relief. The sound would be enough to guide him through the remaining fog and darkness to his friends. Clutching at his shoulder, he marched on, confident that Veronica would be able to help him stem the flow of his blood when they managed to get him up into the cab. He almost laughed. The whole episode seemed so bizarre, now, dislocated from reality, left behind in the fog. He squeezed his shoulder a little tighter, feeling woozy from the loss of blood.

A moment later, he was snatched rudely back to the present by the sound of a shrill, piercing scream from somewhere up ahead. It cut through his dizziness like a knife. Newbury felt his hackles rising. One thought crossed his mind: *Veronica*.

Shaking off his pain and lethargy, Newbury forged on, forcing himself to run towards the sound, blindly throwing himself through the hazy curtain of fog. He skidded to a halt when the cab came into view.

Two revenants were menacing his friends, clutching at the cab door and shaking the vehicle back and forth like children with a toy-box, trying to get inside. The driver had clambered hurriedly onto the roof of the cab in an effort to put himself out of the creature's reach, but now found himself clinging on for dear life as the vehicle rocked from side to side. His fingers grasped the brass rails, and his shouts for help were growing more and more desperate as he slid across the flat roof, doing his best to stop his feet from dangling too far below. The thick shroud of fog prevented Newbury from seeing into the cab itself, but the shouting emanating from inside it made it clear to him that both Bainbridge and Veronica were trapped in the carriage, doing their best to keep the monsters from getting in.

With no other options available to him, Newbury rushed forwards, bringing Bainbridge's cane to bear and driving it with all his might into the lower back of one of the monsters. It penetrated the beast's rotten flesh, forcing a gob of putrescent fluid out of the exit wound on the other side, but seemed to cause the creature no visible sign of pain or distraction. Newbury pulled the cane free with an almighty heave and instead drove his boot into the back of the monster's knee, causing it to buckle to one side.

The creature freed its hold on the carriage, finally turning to see what had caused it to stumble. It bared its teeth in a grim caricature of a smile. Newbury was appalled to see that, once, the monster had been a woman. It wore the tattered remnants of a blue gown, ripped open to expose its distended belly. Its feet were bare and rotten, black and peeling, with toes missing where rats had evidently chewed on the foul flesh.

Newbury paced back a few steps, trying to draw it away from the cab. It stumbled towards him, snatching out with its talon-fingered hand in an effort to grab hold of him.

Newbury shook his head. "You'll have to be quicker than that." He whipped the cane around again, connecting loudly with the monster's wrist and snapping the brittle bones there with a sickening *crunch*. The hand fell limp, and the creature withdrew momentarily, as if bemused by this new development. By this time, however, the other revenant had become aware of what was happening and had moved away from the carriage to join its fellow, evidently deciding that an unprotected quarry represented easier pickings than a sealed cab. They closed on Newbury together, working like pack animals to come at him from both directions at once.

Panicking, Newbury was unsure how to fend them off. He held Bainbridge's cane out before him, the brass knob swinging to and fro like a club, but he knew this wouldn't hold them off for long. He had no lantern this time to use as a weapon, and the two creatures were between him and the cab. He'd just have to make it up as he went along. He feinted to one side, causing the revenant on his right to swipe for him, and then pushed forward, slamming the cane into the back of the creature's head. The momentum of its attack, coupled with the force of Newbury's blow, carried it forward, and it sprawled out on the cobbles, smashing its face hard on the ground.

Newbury wheeled on the other one, just in time to see the back of its hand slam forcefully into his face. The impact sent him careening across the road. He landed heavily, jarring his left elbow on the stones and fighting to keep his breath. He snatched up Bainbridge's cane from where he'd dropped it in the gutter, and rolled to the right, just before the creature was on him again, slashing at his already-bloody shoulder. His clothes fell away in shreds, and his arm bloomed with pain as the monster's talons tore away chunks of flesh. Knowing that the impact of the cane itself would have little effect, Newbury instead hooked it behind the revenant's ankle and rolled forward onto his knees, pulling on the shaft of the cane with all his might. It seemed to have the desired effect, toppling the shambling monster heavily onto its side. Newbury, gasping for breath, tried to stagger away, but the first creature didn't stay down for long, and the other was already back on its feet and heading in his direction. He backed up, desperate for an idea. He knew he was going to lose if the fight came down to brute force and endurance.

Behind him, he heard the pistons on the cab firing noisily as the driver readied their escape. Beneath this, just out of earshot, he could hear Veronica and Bainbridge clamouring for attention. He didn't have time to try to make out what they were saying before one of the revenants dived at him, landing bodily on top of him and sending them both sprawling back towards the ground. Newbury managed to get a hold on the monster's throat and it gnashed its teeth dangerously, its putrid breath almost enough to send him spiralling into unconsciousness. He'd lost the cane somewhere in the fall, but with his other hand free he had no option but to try to lever the creature off of him. He punched out, hard, his fist crumpling through slick, rotten flesh and burying itself deep inside the creature's belly.

It thrashed around on top of him as, grimacing, Newbury forced his hand deeper inside of it, questing for its spine. Seconds later, he found purchase on the brittle bony structure and, pushing his fingers deeper into the rotten fibrous tissue that surrounded it, managed to grasp hold of it with his fist. He pulled as hard as he could, pushing against the creature's throat with his other hand for leverage. There was a dry cracking sound, as if old timber were being snapped underfoot, and the spine splintered in his hand.

The creature's legs stopped thrashing, twitched a couple of times, and lay still. Its arms continued to claw away at him, however, its teeth ominously close to his face. Newbury, gasping for breath against the weight of the creature on top of him, withdrew his hand from the rotten belly, trying not to think about where it had been. His damaged shoulder was perilously close to giving in. He put his right hand on the ground and pushed himself over, rolling with the creature until their roles were reversed and he found himself on top of the foul thing, his left hand still tight around its throat.

Glancing up to get a measure of what had happened to the other one, he jumped back off the beast and fumbled around, looking for Bainbridge's cane. It was nearby on the cobbles, close to where he had fallen. He retrieved it quickly, then backed up, waiting for the other revenant to loom out of the fog.

The creature he had been struggling with—the one that had formerly been a woman—was still trying to right itself, pulling itself up on its arms and finding that its legs would no longer support it. Relentless, it started to shuffle towards him, using its arms to pull it along the ground. It was an obscene gesture, and Newbury was unable to watch. He turned to look behind him, trying to work out where the cab was in the fog. He leaned on the cane for a moment, catching his breath. Perhaps the other creature had slipped away, driven by the desire to find its own prey, when it looked as though its fellow had Newbury pinned to the ground? But that seemed unlikely.

He heard Veronica calling his name, somewhere behind him in the cloudy soup. He set off, staggering towards her voice, but stopped when he became aware of the shape of the other revenant, about ten feet away from him, silhouetted in the fog. It had its back to him. He edged around it, following the sound of the churning pistons nearby. Gingerly, he placed one foot after the other, doing his utmost to remain silent as he circled the monster. Then, stumbling on a loose stone, his foot scuffed on the cobbles. The creature twitched at the sound and spun around to face him. Newbury, exhausted, waved the cane from side to side, trying to hold it at bay. He didn't think he had the strength to take another one down.

He heard Bainbridge calling to him from the carriage. "Newbury! Newbury! Use the cane."

He couldn't help but laugh at this most inappropriate advice. "I'm using the bloody cane, man!" He stepped back, trying to keep his distance from the creature. He knew it was likely to pounce at any moment.

Bainbridge's disembodied voice came back to him. "No! Twist the knob on the end of the cane. Quickly!"

Newbury peered along the shaft of the cane. The bulbous brass knob didn't look extraordinary in any way. Nevertheless, desperate to find a way out of his current nightmare, he swung it back towards him, clutched hold of the cold metal knob and twisted it sharply to the right.

There was a clicking sound from within the shaft itself. Clasping the knob, Newbury pointed the end of the cane at the revenant, unsure what he expected to happen next. The shaft twisted and then began to spin, sections of the wood unpacking along its length and folding out to create a kind of chambered structure along the middle of the cane. Brass filaments ran along the inside of this structure. The spinning reached a crescendo and, with an electrical hum, an arc of blue light spat from one end of the chamber to the other, fizzing along the length of the shaft and crackling at the terminus of the device, the small pointed section at the very end of the cane.

Smiling, Newbury raised the weapon towards the revenant just as the creature decided to give up waiting for an opportunity to catch Newbury off guard and threw itself towards him, claws outstretched. The point of the shaft impaled the monster through the chest, and there was a loud *bang* as the electrical current flowed into the rotting carcass of the creature and fried what was left of its nervous system. The creature lost its momentum and dropped to the ground, dead for the second time. Blue light arced in its open mouth, and the blackened, dirty hole in its chest was smouldering, dark smoke rising into the air to mingle with the thick fog. Newbury's lungs filled with the scent of charred meat. He looked down at the body. The electrical current had set the creature's hair on fire, and little flames were licking at the edges of its tattered clothes. It wouldn't be long before the flames took and the creature's papery, rotten flesh became nothing but dry kindle.

He stood over the body and pulled the lightning cane free. Then, confident that the monster was finished, he staggered over to where the other one was still struggling to pull itself along the ground and drove the cane into its back, just below the base of the neck. Blue light sparked dramatically. The creature thrashed around for a moment before the twitching subsided and Newbury knew he had put it out of its misery. He stood for a moment, gathering his strength.

Then, not even bothering to deactivate the weapon, Newbury

staggered towards the sound of his friend's voices, hopeful that, this time, he'd be able to make it back to them unmolested.

Bainbridge and Veronica were waiting by the cab when Newbury staggered out of the fog. He was faint and bleeding from multiple injuries, the blue electrical light dancing and fizzing in the darkness along the length of Bainbridge's cane. They both rushed towards him, their eyes flitting nervously from side to side, worried that more revenants may come hulking out of the fog at any moment. Bainbridge swept the weapon out of Newbury's hand and twisted the brass knob, compacting the device so that it folded away neatly, dissipating the electrical charge and ensuring none of them would accidentally bear the brunt of its force. Within a matter of seconds, the peculiar device was nothing more than a cane once again.

Newbury, his vision swimming, practically collapsed into Veronica's arms, and together with Bainbridge she lifted him up into the cab. They laid him carefully across one of the seats, and Bainbridge used the top of his cane to rap on the ceiling of the carriage, letting the driver know they were all safely back on board. A moment later the engines gave a wheezing gasp, and the vehicle trundled away into the rising dawn.

Veronica was on her knees beside Newbury, tearing strips off his shirt to use as makeshift bandages on his wounds. He looked a mess: his torso was covered in scrapes and bruises and he was pale from the loss of blood, which pooled on the floor after soaking through his torn clothes and running free. Veronica tried to stem the flow with her hands, applying as much pressure as she could to the tear in his shoulder.

"Oh, Maurice." She seemed at a loss for words.

Newbury turned his face towards her. "I'll be alright. Everything will be alright." His voice was nothing but a croak. He cast his eyes at Bainbridge, who was sitting in the seat opposite them, leaning heavily on his cane. "Quite a contraption, Charles. Wish I'd known about it earlier." His face cracked into a weary smile. "Where did you acquire it?"

Bainbridge shook his head, smiling in amazement that Newbury had even the strength to hold a conversation. "Dr. Fabian. Never had much chance to put it to the test, but the old girl seemed to do alright by you out there, didn't she?"

Newbury nodded, wincing as Veronica tied a strip of fabric tight across the wound in his shoulder. "She certainly did."

Veronica glanced at Bainbridge, concern etched on her face. "That's the best I can do, here. We need to get him to a hospital."

Bainbridge scoffed. "Might as well take him to a butcher's shop. No, we need to get him to the Fixer."

"The what?"

"The Fixer." Newbury turned his head to look her in the eye. "One of the Queen's surgeons . . ." He coughed, shifting on the seat in an attempt to alleviate the pain. "Tell her, Charles."

Bainbridge picked up the explanation. "The Fixer is one of the Queen's personal surgeons, on hand to help Her Majesty's agents in times such as this. He works for Dr. Fabian. He's the best medical man I've ever had the misfortune to meet, and he's got a place out in Bloomsbury, not far from the museum."

"Does the driver know where to go?"

Bainbridge nodded. "Barnes? Yes, he's one of ours. Why do you think he didn't bolt when he had the chance earlier, when Newbury had those damnable revenants after him?" He paused, glancing over at Newbury, his brows furrowed. "I take it the two uniformed chaps weren't so lucky?"

Newbury shook his head, but didn't speak. Bainbridge knew this meant the worst. "Damn!" He rammed his cane against the floor. "Poor bastards." He glanced at Veronica. "I do apologise, Miss Hobbes." She waved her hand dismissively.

Newbury had closed his eyes. Veronica brushed his hair

back from his face. She met Bainbridge's stare. Her voice was only just above a whisper, as if she didn't really want to know the answer to the question she was asking. "What about the plague? Doesn't it spread when the revenants bite someone? Will he be infected?"

Newbury eyes flicked open again. He tried to prop himself up on one arm, but cringed when the pain in his side became too much. He returned to his previous position, supine on his back. He searched Veronica's face with his eyes. "Don't worry. I'm immune to the plague. I won't be infected."

Bainbridge leaned closer. "Immune? How so?"

Newbury swallowed, then reached up and pulled at his ragged shirt, exposing a large expanse of his chest. It was streaked and matted with blood, but it was easy to see the sickle-shaped scar of white tissue just above his left nipple, even in the dim light. "I was bitten before." Veronica's eyes were wide with shock. "Years ago, in India. My family had purchased some land out there, just about the same time that I'd found myself enamoured with stories of the occult. When the opportunity arose to pay a visit, I jumped at the chance. I spent two years in Delhi, exploring the Indian myths, searching for truth in the ancient stories of their culture." He sucked in his breath as the cab rolled over the uneven cobbles, jostling him in his seat. "At around the same time a plague was spreading through the slums, a virus that turned people into shambling cannibals, forcing their skin to stop regenerating and blowing the blood vessels in their eyes." He coughed, raising a hand to his mouth.

"The revenants." Veronica mopped his brow.

Newbury nodded. "The revenants. I was out visiting a temple in the hills when I was set upon by one of the detestable creatures. It bit me here on the chest, but I was young and quick-witted enough to be able to get away. I managed to find my way back to my family's rooms in Delhi, whereupon they immediately called for the doctor. The Indian physician told us that his research had shown that the virus incubated in the brain for eight days before massively altering the physiology of the victim."

"What happened?"

"They threw me in a cell and gave me nothing but bread and water to survive. For eight days, I ran the most appalling fever, and then, on the eighth day, the fever broke and I began to recover. Soon after, the doctor sent me home. He told me I was one of only a handful of people he knew who had survived the plague." He glanced from Veronica to Bainbridge. "I'm convinced that this is the same virus, spread here from India, and that, provided my wounds don't kill me first, I'll live to fight another day." He flexed his fingers, frowning at the pain in his shoulder.

Bainbridge nodded. "Of course you will, my man." He looked serious. "Of course you will." He patted Veronica on the shoulder reassuringly and then looked up, smiling. "We all know that the Fixer can perform miracles, don't we."

Newbury sighed. The cab trundled on towards Bloomsbury, and towards the mysterious surgeon who, Bainbridge assured them, would be able to make things right once more.

CHAPTER 20

The sun had risen by the time the cab pulled up outside the Bloomsbury home of the Fixer, reducing the fog to wispy trails of vapour that seemed to linger in the air like white tendrils. Newbury had passed out a short while after they had set out from Whitechapel, and Veronica had continued to tend to him, staunching his wounds and trying to limit his blood loss by continuing to use strips of his shirt as makeshift bandages. She was covered in blood herself, now, her skirt, blouse and hands sticky with the gritty residue. Bainbridge thought it was a credit to her that she seemed entirely unfazed by this development.

Newbury's breath was shallow, his skin had lost its colour and his eyes had sunk back in their sockets. Black bruises had emerged all over his exposed body where he had taken a severe battering from the revenants. Bainbridge hoped the Fixer really was able to work miracles. Newbury would need one if he were going to live.

Taking his cane, Bainbridge stood and swung the carriage door open, glancing from side to side to see if anyone was watching. There were a few early risers going about their business, but the street was mostly deserted. He turned back to Veronica. "Stay here. I'll go and make arrangements." She nodded silently and he ducked out of the cab, nodding at the driver as he mounted the step down to the road and made for the entrance of the large house. The building was tall, with three storeys above ground and a basement below, which Bainbridge knew would be their destination today. The house stood at the end of a long terrace, and as Bainbridge mounted the steps up to the front door, he heard the engine of the cab chugging behind him and watched as the driver reversed the cab around the corner, parking it near the iron staircase that led down to the basement level.

He rapped loudly on the door with the end of his cane. There was a momentary pause, and then the door clicked open and a middle-aged man in a black suit appeared in the opening. "Ah, good morning, Sir Charles. Won't you come in?"

Bainbridge stepped over the threshold and into the opulent foyer of the house. It was a grand building, worthy of royalty itself. The floor had been laid in a shimmering white marble, and a huge staircase swept away towards the upper levels of the house. Panelled doors led off into other, private rooms. A chandelier hung from a perfect ceiling rosette, and a small table had everything arranged just so. The entire place smelled of freshly cut flowers. The presentation was immaculate.

Bainbridge caught sight of himself in the large mirror hanging on the opposite wall, and shuddered. He looked terrible. Once he'd deposited Newbury with the Fixer, he'd see Miss Hobbes back to her lodgings and head home himself for a sleep and a long soak in the bath.

The manservant who had admitted him to the house—a stout man of around fifty, with a receding head of grey hair—looked Bainbridge up and down, as if trying to ascertain the reason for his visit. "Are you well, Sir Charles? . . ."

"Yes, yes, no time for all that, Rothford. I've got Sir Maurice Newbury in the cab back there, practically torn to pieces. He's in urgent need of the Fixer."

Rothford snapped to attention. "Quite right, sir. Better

bring him around the side entrance, quick-sharp. I'll notify the master immediately. I believe you know the way?"

"I do."

"Then go, sir, and I'll make the necessary arrangements."

Bainbridge nodded. "Thank you, Rothford."

"I'll hear no word of it, sir." He clicked the door open again and ushered Bainbridge out.

Bainbridge hurried down the steps and round the corner to where the cab was still waiting, its engine burring noisily. Overhead, an airship swept low over the city, whipping his hair back from his face. He was glad he'd left his hat in the carriage earlier. He hopped up onto the step and spoke to the driver. "Keep an eye out, Barnes. Wouldn't do to have anyone see what we're up to."

The driver nodded. "Aye, sir. I'll give you the word when you're clear to make a move."

"Good man." He ducked into the carriage. Newbury was still unconscious. Bainbridge put a hand on Veronica's shoulder. "All will be well, Miss Hobbes. We've brought him to the right place. The Fixer will do his work, and Sir Maurice will be back on his feet in no time at all." He glanced down at the supine man. "Here, can you help me with his head whilst I lift him down?"

"Of course." Veronica moved to cradle Newbury's head as Bainbridge placed his cane on the opposite seat and moved to scoop his unconscious friend up into his arms.

He staggered under the weight, trying to get his footing, and then was able to rest Newbury's head in the crook of his arm as he moved towards the open door. Gasping a little for breath, unused to the exertion, he called out to the driver. "Barnes? Are we set?"

"Aye, sir. All clear."

Bainbridge stepped cautiously down onto the step beneath the carriage door, and then onto the street below. Without looking back, he approached the side of the house, mounting the first rung on an iron staircase that descended from street level down to the basement of the large house. His feet clanged loudly on the steps as he struggled to manoeuvre Newbury down the tight enclosure. Then, reaching the bottom of the flight of stairs, he used the edge of his boot to bang on the wooden door that awaited him there. A fraction of a second later, the door swung open, revealing a dark space beyond, and Bainbridge, shifting so as not to strike Newbury's head against the doorframe, slipped quietly inside.

A few minutes later, Bainbridge emerged from the same doorway, having deposited Newbury with Rothford to await the ministrations of the Fixer. He crested the top of the iron staircase, dusted himself down, and, red-faced from the exertion, hopped back into the cab with a nod to the driver. The engine spluttered to life as Bainbridge took a seat, careful to avoid the spilled blood that was congealing on the floor. Barnes would have his work cut out for him, cleaning that lot up.

Veronica was sitting with her hands folded in her lap. She looked nearly as white as Newbury had, shocked to the core and uncertain about Newbury's condition.

Bainbridge attempted to offer her his warmest smile. "My dear Miss Hobbes. I should think Sir Maurice will owe you a large debt of gratitude when he eventually comes round from all this. Your efforts in stemming his wounds are surely what kept him alive during the course of the journey over here. Now, the Fixer can do his work and make him whole again."

Veronica pursed her lips. "Sir Charles, I think it is we who shall owe Sir Maurice a debt of gratitude. His actions at the murder scene are what saved us all from disaster. He willingly put himself in the way of those monsters to save us from harm. Saving his life in turn was the very least we could do, if indeed we have managed it." She looked away, still dignified, even whilst caked in the dried blood of her employer. "I hope this 'Fixer' is everything you've made him out to be."

Bainbridge nodded, carefully weighing her words. "You're quite right, of course, Miss Hobbes. Forgive my insolence. I did not mean to demean the actions of our brave friend, only to embolden you with talk of your own. I was aiming to give reassurance, where perhaps none was needed. I'm afraid I've forgotten how to talk to ladies, ever since my wife died. I now spend all my time in the company of other men."

Veronica returned his gaze. Her demeanour softened. "Sir Charles, I fear it's not a case of knowing how to talk to a lady. I'm simply concerned for the well-being of Sir Maurice." She tried, ineffectually, to brush some of the dried blood from her clothes. "So tell me, what does this Fixer do?"

Bainbridge smiled. "He fixes things."

Newbury woke with a start.

He sucked at the air.

His head was throbbing, although he felt as if he'd somehow been infused with a warm, liquid glow; warmth that started in his belly and seemed to seep upwards towards his head, gloriously taking the edge off his pain and leaving his mind to wander in a drowsy state of semi-consciousness. He knew the sensation of old.

Opium.

Newbury peeled open his eyes, and then immediately shut them again. The light in the room was blinding, clinically sharp, and it seared the back of his retinas like a hot knife. He drew a ragged breath, pulling the air down into his lungs. His chest felt like it was on fire. Cautiously, he tried to open his eyes again, reaching up to shelter them from the glare with cupped hands. Stinging tears ran down his cheeks. He blinked them away. Finally, an image resolved.

He was lying on his back on a hard metal table. A face was looming over him. He tried to sit up.

"No, Sir Maurice. Try to lie still. Everything is going to be alright."

Newbury felt a hand on his chest, holding him still on the table. He blinked up at the strange face that was hovering over him. The man was in his late forties, balding, with a neatly trimmed black beard. A bizarre mechanical contraption sat on his head, like a wire frame that encompassed his temples and forehead, with various accouterments and glass lenses attached to it on folding levers and arms. The man reached up and flipped one of these lenses down over one eye.

"Who are you? Where am I?" Newbury had a panicked edge to his voice.

"I'm the Fixer, and you're in my workshop, underneath my home. You have nothing to worry about."

Newbury breathed a sigh of relief, allowing himself to relax. He'd never had occasion to visit the Fixer before, but he was well aware that the man existed: a personal surgeon of Her Majesty's who made himself available to her agents in times of dire need. He remembered Bainbridge speaking about him in the carriage, just after the attack. What was not good was the fact that, if he was here, his situation was potentially very grave indeed.

Newbury quickly discovered that his abdomen and shoulder lanced with pain every time he made even the slightest motion with his body. He tried to lie still, giving himself over to the warmth of the opium, but the Fixer had been wise and had dosed him with only enough to take the edge off the pain, and not enough to render him unconscious again. He felt gloved hands tearing at his clothes and the faint stirring of a breeze on his exposed flesh. Nevertheless, the room itself was warm, and listening to the sounds around him, he had the sense of a workshop full of bizarre mechanical devices. There was a faint electrical hum, accompanied by the occasional sound of a belching valve as it issued forth a cloud of hot steam, as well as the constant *tick-tock* of numerous clockwork engines powering objects that he could not see from his limited vantage point on the table. Newbury tried not to imagine what the man was about to do to him with the strange machines that were making such sounds.

The Fixer appeared in his field of vision once again, wavering slightly under the influence of the opium, and then disappeared. Newbury could hear him shuffling around the other side of the table. The Fixer cleared his throat, and then began to speak, offering a running commentary as he examined Newbury's wounds. His voice, Newbury noticed, was gruff and gravelly, the voice of a man who'd smoked too much heavy shag in his time. "Hmmm. A vicious bite in the left clavicular area, there. Serious tears to the flesh and muscular tissue. Excessive blood loss." He paused for a moment, poking sharply at the wounds on Newbury's chest. "Deep gouges in the chest. Numerous flesh wounds. A severe laceration in the left side of the chest and abdomen. My, my. You have been busy."

Newbury stirred uncomfortably. He waited until he heard the other man move away from the table, his footsteps ringing on the tiled floor, and then, with a significant effort, managed to prop himself up on one elbow.

The Fixer stood at the foot of the table, fiddling with an array of surgical tools, which pinged noisily on a steel tray. Beside him on a wooden trolley was a rack of steel hypodermic syringes, which contained a range of strange, multi-coloured fluids. Newbury took the opportunity to take a better look at the man who called himself the Fixer.

Aside from the contraption on his head, the man was wearing a tarnished leather smock and matching leather gloves. Newbury couldn't help thinking that he had more of the appearance of a butcher about him than of a physician. He had a ruddy complexion and the manner of a public schoolboy. Newbury suspected he spent a great deal of time in his workshop, and very little time engaging with the world.

Unsure what was likely to happen next, and unwilling to ask, Newbury cast his eyes around the room, trying to get a measure of his surroundings.

The basement was lit by a series of long, unusual gas-lamps that arced across the ceiling from one wall to the other, curved glass tubes that terminated with gas valves where they met the walls at each end. An array of strange machines and surgical tables filled the space in between. One of these—a large brass contraption about the size of a small table, with two glass vats full of bubbling fluid atop it—had long coils of tubing that snaked out from the belly of the machine and away into the dark corners of the room. Another, smaller contraption was fitted with wheezing bellows of the sort Newbury had seen attached to Queen Victoria's life-preserving engine. It even rose and fell with the same constant rhythm of Her Majesty's breathing machine, although in this instance, it appeared that the bellows were helping to power an unusual electrical device, the lights on it flickering from orange to blue as the exposed filaments danced with the current.

The alarming contraption above Newbury's own table was connected to an extensive brass framework, a kind of large gun on a moveable rail, with fat tubing trailing from the back of it and disappearing into a nearby hatch in the floor. The device had a trigger fitted to the undercarriage and the end of it terminated in a spread of fine needles, bunched together to form a neat point. Newbury shivered.

The Fixer turned to notice him looking. "Impressive, isn't it?" He turned to encapsulate the room with a gesture of his arms, indicating the various machines. "This is what Dr. Fabian gets up to when he isn't busy attending to Her Majesty or running errands for the likes of you and Sir Charles. Works of genius, every one of them."

Groggily, Newbury met his gaze, and felt immediately disorientated by the sight of the man's strange eyewear, which magnified the appearance of his right eye so that it seemed at least three times the size of his left. "So, what's next? Surgery?"

The Fixer smiled. "Of a sort. I'm going to knit your shoulder and chest back together with my stitching machine." He indicated the gunlike device on the rail overhead. "Then I can give you a blood transfusion and a dose of one of Dr. Fabian's excellent compounds."

Newbury narrowed his eyes. "What will it do?"

"Fix you, of course." The man beamed. Newbury held his gaze, a serious expression on his face. Sighing, the Fixer continued. "It's derived from a rare flower that Fabian discovered out in the Congo last year. When the powder is dissolved in saline and transfused into the human body, it boosts the existing immune system, helping the blood cells to clot and bind, so that muscles and bones can reconnect very swiftly indeed. I wish we'd know about it before—could have saved a lot of trouble with Ashford all those years ago." He paused, tapping his foot on the tiles as if planning his next move. "Come on. Let's get you under the knife. You'll know the effects of the treatment soon enough, anyway."

Cautiously, Newbury laid his head back against the hard surface of the table. The Fixer moved round to stand beside him, reaching over to wash his shoulder wound with a wet cloth. The antiseptic fluid burned angrily where it came into contact with the damaged, puckered flesh. Newbury winced and clenched his jaw, grinding his teeth as the other man reached up and took hold of the stitching machine. Newbury closed his eyes. He heard the device firing up, the *rat-a-tat-tat* of the needles scraping back and forth as the Fixer applied pressure to the trigger, testing the pneumatic power.

He brought the gun closer to Newbury's shoulder, and then, without any further warning, he jabbed the device into the soft tissue underneath the skin of Newbury's left arm. The needles began to puncture the lacerated flesh in a torrent of relentless pinpricks.

Newbury screamed out in agony as the device stitched a series of fine filaments deep into his clavicular muscles; slowly, deliberately, knitting his shoulder back together. The Fixer began to move the device along the extent of the wound, closing the flesh where the revenant's mouth had torn it open. Blackness swam around the edges of Newbury's vision.

He swooned, and everything went dark.

When Newbury came round again, he was lying on a bed, his head resting on the soft, downy pillows, a thick woollen blanket pulled up over his waist. Thin rubber tubes jutted rudely from incisions made in each of his wrists, trailing off toward large machines on either side of him, one of which was giving off a deep mechanical rumble and a gentle gasp of warm air. He tried to sit up, but felt his shoulder pulling tightly where the Fixer and his stitching machine had done their work. He flexed his fingers and tentatively moved his arm, feeling that he'd regained a lot of strength in the limb. The pain in his shoulder and abdomen had mostly subsided to a dull ache. He lifted the corner of the blanket warily and looked down at the line of puckered flesh where the machine had sewn him back together again. It was bruised and purple, and had an ungainly web-work of black stitches weaving across it, but it was far better than an open wound, and in truth, he felt almost normal again.

"Marvellous, isn't it?" Newbury looked up, noting for the first time that the Fixer was sitting in a chair by the side of the bed, watching him intently as he explored his handiwork. His strange headpiece was on the table beside him. He looked considerably more normal without his leather smock and gloves. "It won't leave much of a scar there, either, what with the watertight stitches and the transfusion of Dr. Fabian's healing compound that you're receiving." The Fixer smiled. "It'll be sore for a few weeks, though."

Newbury folded the blanket back over his lap. "How long before I'm up and about?"

"A couple of hours. There's no reason to keep you here, once the transfusions are complete and we've found you some suitable clothes. You should go home and rest, let the compound do its work." He waved at Newbury's abdomen underneath the fawn-coloured blanket. "It should hold up, even if you do find yourself in another scrape. Those stitches aren't designed to give out on you. You'll need to come back in a couple of weeks to have them out again, whatever the case."

Newbury grimaced at the thought of it. He lifted his arms, presenting his wrists to the other man. "Which one's which?"

"The machine on your left is giving you blood. The one on your right is giving you the saline solution."

Newbury glanced at the machine to the left of him. It seemed to be vibrating gently, humming as it pumped the fluid along the coiling black tube and up into his arm.

A panel near the Fixer's chair was decorated with a series of dials, all of which had been turned to various positions that made no sense to Newbury, at least from where he was sitting.

He met the other man's eye, indicating the transfusion machine "Why is it so noisy?"

"Ah. That's the refrigeration unit. I use that to keep the blood from congealing. It doesn't last long out of the body. Luckily for you, Rothford is a willing donor, and his blood type is compatible with most people's."

"Rothford?"

"My manservant."

Newbury nodded.

"You'll meet him shortly. Now, though, you need to lie back and rest. I'll come and disconnect you shortly, once we're both convinced that you're ready to take a walk." The Fixer stood at the foot of the bed, smiling, and then disappeared into the gloom.

Newbury allowed his head to fall back onto the pillow. The effects of the opium had worn off, and his skin crawled with craving. He longed for the warm glow of the drug. He thought of the small bottle of laudanum on the shelf in his study, thought momentarily of what he might do when he got home . . . and then thought of Veronica, and the manner in which she had found him just a couple of days ago. It wouldn't do to descend into that madness again. Sighing, he closed his eyes and willed himself to sleep, listening to the sounds of the gurgling fluid that was currently seeping into his bloodstream.

A couple of hours later, dressed only in a plain white robe, and with thick yellow poultices applied to his wounds, Newbury followed the Fixer up a small internal staircase and into a waiting area that was set out like a gentleman's reception room. Rothford, the Fixer's manservant, was waiting for them there, his hands folded neatly behind his back. He stood when the two gentlemen came into the room.

The Fixer spoke first. "Rothford, this is Sir Maurice Newbury. He'll be needing your attention, as well as some assistance finding suitable attire. Please treat him as a guest in this house."

Rothford gave a single nod of the head, and then glanced at Newbury, a twinkle in his eye. "Very good, sir."

The Fixer clapped a hand on Newbury's arm, carefully avoiding the wound on his shoulder. "I'll leave you in Rothford's capable hands. Be sure to take some time to rest."

He turned to leave, and Newbury reached out to stop him. He offered the Fixer a sincere smile. "Thank you, I–"

The other man shook his head. "Don't thank me. Simply try to make sure that you don't need my attentions again in the near future, especially before you're back to have those stitches out."

Newbury laughed, causing his chest to burn with pain. "I'm not planning on it, I'll give you that much."

The Fixer smiled. "For men in our profession, Sir Maurice, that has to be enough. Good day to you."

"Likewise." Newbury watched as the man disappeared from the room, descending the stairs towards his workshop once again.

Rothford approached from the other side of the room. "If you'd like to come with me, Sir Maurice, I'll show you to our dressing room."

Newbury nodded and followed behind Rothford as he led him through a door, along a short passageway and through another door into a small room on the left. It was furnished with a wardrobe, cheval glass mirror and dressing table. Rothford crossed to the wardrobe and opened the doors with a flourish. Inside, Newbury could see that it was filled with all manner of formal suits and dresses, white shirts and underclothes. He wondered how many "visitors" the Fixer regularly received.

Rothford searched through the rack of clothes for a moment, before withdrawing a black suit on a hanger and holding it up beside Newbury. "There. I should imagine this will do. I'll lay it on the chair over here." He draped it over the back of the tall chair by the dressing table. "Please feel free to help yourself to a shirt and underclothes. When you're decent, you'll find me in the reception room at the other end of this short hallway. I'll organise some breakfast. Bacon and eggs?"

"Thank you." Newbury nodded, unsure what else to say.

He watched as Rothford exited the room, clicking the door shut behind him.

Then, gingerly, he disrobed, eyeing his wounds in the cheval glass. The line of bruised, puckered flesh that ran down the left side of him looked angry and sore. Yet, strangely, he felt decidedly more alert than he had in days. He supposed that had a lot to do with Dr. Fabian's miraculous healing compound. He made a mental note to attempt to find out the name of the flower it was derived from. It would make an interesting study, and he could do worse than to have a small amount of the compound available to him at his Chelsea lodgings.

Taking care to dress slowly so as to avoid pulling on his stitching, Newbury was soon feeling more like his usual self, and with the promise of eggs and bacon just along the hall, he realised he was absolutely famished. Finding a pile of his personal belongings arranged on the dressing table, he slipped these into the pockets of the borrowed suit and set off in search of Rothford, Earl Grey and food.

CHAPTER 21

Veronica sat beside Amelia on a wooden bench on the grounds of the asylum, wrapped up against the chill. They were watching the other inmates as they circled the airing court like a flock of birds, each following the others as they walked, their feet crunching noisily on the gravel. Nurses kept a watchful eye from one end of the courtyard, gossiping amongst themselves and dressed in thick winter coats. Their breath plumed in the frosty air.

Veronica glanced at Amelia, who—even dressed in a heavy coat and shawl—was shivering with the cold. She put her arm around her sister, hugging her closer for warmth. Veronica knew that she shouldn't have come. She could think of a hundred reasons why she shouldn't be there that day, why she'd have been far better off staying away, yet none of them seemed quite so important as the reason she had finally given in and made the journey across town. Now, here, she could barely face her sister, who had been delighted by the unexpected visit and had clutched her brightly, kissing her fondly on the cheek. Tired and emotional after a difficult morning, Veronica had chosen to walk with Amelia in the gardens before broaching the true reason for her visit.

After Sir Charles had deposited her at her Kensington

lodgings, Veronica had found herself alone in her apartment, her housekeeper out running errands around town. She had stripped out of her filthy clothes, poured herself a scalding hot bath, and sat weeping on the bathroom floor, her knees drawn up to her chin, tears streaking down her blood-caked cheeks.

She sat like this for at least an hour, cycling through the full gamut of emotions, from relief to anxiety and then back again. She had been so terrified by those detestable creatures as they attacked the cab, trying to peel the door away to get at her and Bainbridge inside, that she had done little to aid in the battle. She cursed herself for being so weak. She was a strong woman, a fighter, but she had seen no way out of that dreadful scenario, and had almost given herself over to her fast-approaching fate, when Sir Maurice had appeared out of the fog and taken on the two monsters single-handedly, drawing them away from the cab.

She felt ashamed that her first thought had been to flee, to get away from there as quickly as possible whilst she had the chance, to abandon Newbury to the monsters in an effort to save herself from harm. Reason had reasserted itself, however, and she had remained in the carriage, knowing that there was little she could do to help him as he fought the creatures in the fog-enshrouded street. She had come close to rushing out there to aid him when she heard him crying out in pain, but she knew that she would only have served as a distraction and that, had she taken on one of the creatures herself, she would have surely lost out to its brutish strength and animalistic will.

The worst horror, however, had been seeing Newbury in such a desperate condition after he'd managed to make it back to the cab. Even now she feared for his life, feared what this Fixer character may do to him, and worse, feared that his words of reassurance regarding the revenant plague were simply that—words—and that before long he would succumb to the terrible blight and, regardless of how tightly she had tied his bandages and how well she had staunched the flow of his lifeblood, she would lose him anyway.

She couldn't bear the thought that Newbury might transform into one of those horrifying creatures, and she knew that he, too, would rather die than let that happen. So she had resolved to visit Amelia at the asylum, to take advantage of her sister with a long list of difficult questions, and to try to ascertain what the future held.

Amelia was watching the other inmates as they went about their laborious routine. "Tell me I'm not reduced to that, Veronica. I feel like a little bit more of my life is sapped away from me each and every day I spend in this terrible place."

Veronica hugged her sister closer. "You're not, Amelia. You're not like that at all."

"Then why do I have to live like this? What have I done wrong to deserve to be locked up in here? It's basically a prison cell."

Veronica didn't know what else to say. "I'll get you out, Amelia. I promise. I'll find a way to get you out."

Amelia shifted slightly in her arms and smiled. "I know you will, Veronica. I know it's just a matter of time."

Veronica looked at her sister quizzically. "Do you know something? Have you seen something in one of your visions?"

Amelia shook her head. "You know it doesn't work like that, Veronica. I only remember snatches of what I see, dreamlike sequences and unconnected images. In one of them, I see you and me, walking down the street together, away from this place."

"Can I ask you something? Something I promised I'd never ask you?"

Amelia slipped out of Veronica's embrace, stiffening slightly on the bench. "What is it?"

"Have you seen what becomes of Sir Maurice? In the future, I mean." Veronica couldn't meet her eye.

"No. Nothing." Amelia shrugged. "Well, that is to say that I do not recall seeing anything. Why, what happened?"

Veronica was exasperated. She balled her hands into tight fists. "Try for me, Amelia. This is very important. Try to remember if you've seen him during a recent episode. Anything at all. Even just a glimpse."

Amelia looked pained. "Veronica, I've never even met the man. This is not something I know how to control. It happens, and then it is as if the episode somehow leaves a residue in my mind, fleeting images I can sometimes remember. It's not as if I can recall the entire episode at will."

Veronica tried to fight back the tears. "I know, Amelia, I know. I'm so sorry." She turned away, breathing deeply to steady herself.

Amelia put her hand on Veronica's arm. "Don't be. Clearly something terrible has happened, and I want to do everything I can to help."

"You already have. I suppose now it's just a matter of time."

"What happened? Tell me."

"Sir Maurice was attacked by three revenants this morning. They practically tore him apart, but he managed to get away. He was fighting for his life, bleeding all over the carriage—all over me—but we managed to get him to the surgeon."

Amelia put a hand to her mouth. "Will he make it through?"

Veronica was solemn. "I don't know. Worse than that, though, is the threat of plague. I have every fear that he might have been infected."

"Oh, God."

"That's why I came to you, Amelia. I had to know if you'd seen him in one of your visions, had to know if he was going to be alright. I should never have come. It was unfair of me."

"Sister, you've done so much for me. Is it not fair that I at least attempt to repay that love and loyalty from time to time?"

"It doesn't work like that, Amelia. You don't owe me anything."

"I know *exactly* how it works, Veronica. That's why I love you so."

Too late, Veronica noticed that Amelia was starting to take short, shallow gasps at the air, beginning the process of inducing an episode. She clutched her by the shoulders. "No! Stop it, Amelia! Stop it now!"

Amelia shook her head, gasping for breath.

Veronica held her tight. "I'm sorry, sister."

"...I...know..." Amelia began to shake, her body shuddering as her muscles went into spasm. Her eyes rolled back in their sockets, showing the milky-white underside of her eyeballs. She rocked back, saliva running from the corner of her mouth.

Veronica glanced around to see if any of the nurses had noticed. They were still engaged in conversation by the main asylum doors. She clutched Amelia close, trying to keep her safe.

Amelia began to babble. At first it seemed incoherent, a long chain of moaning sounds and half-formed words, but then Veronica began to make sense of what she was saying.

"...from the sky...like a child's balloon, tumbling...tumbling towards the ground...water...shouting...confusion."

Veronica shook her head, trying to get through to her sister. "No Amelia, that's already happened. The airship has already crashed!"

"...water...dripping water...a clockwork man." She gasped, gulping air down into her lungs, her entire body shaking as the fit took complete control of her body. "...a dark place...a woman's voice...Veronica!" The shuddering stopped. Amelia turned towards her sister, her unseeing eyes fixed on Veronica's face. It was the most eerie thing Veronica had ever seen. She let go of Amelia, reflexively forcing herself backwards on the wooden bench. She heard footsteps on the gravel behind her.

"It's all in their heads, Veronica. Tell him. You must tell him. It's all in their heads." Amelia collapsed back into spasms once again, and Veronica, shaking, looked round to see two of the nurses rushing to Amelia's aid.

They gathered her up as quickly as they could and laid her out on the lawn beside the wooden bench, holding her down as she continued to spasm.

Veronica leaned over them, desperate to see if Amelia had anything more to say, unprepared for her sister to go through all this agony on her behalf without even finding an answer. But it was not to be. Amelia's episode began to subside and the twitching of her body slowed. She didn't utter another word. Veronica slumped back onto the wooden bench, thankful, at least, that her sister seemed to be unscathed.

Amelia's breath was shallow and she looked dazed, unsure where she was or how she may have got there. She looked up at Veronica, the nurses still pinning her arms to the ground.

"Veronica?"

"Yes, I'm here, Amelia. Are you okay?"

Amelia blinked, looking at the faces of the two nurses who were holding her down on the cold grass, awaiting the arrival of the doctor. "I'll be alright." She met Veronica's gaze. "Did you find what you were looking for?" Her eyes were questing, searching for approval from her older sister.

Veronica looked away. "I'm not sure, Amelia. I don't know what it all meant."

Dr. Mason came running towards them, then, his face flushed. He scowled when he saw Veronica sitting on the bench in the middle of the scene. "Hello, Amelia. I think it's time we got you inside." He turned to Veronica. "Your sister will be taking her leave of us now."

Veronica gave one decisive nod. She stood as the nurses

helped Amelia to her feet. "I love you, sister." She stepped forward and kissed Amelia on the cheek. "Be well."

"I'll try."

Veronica turned and walked away from the scene, her hand on her head to keep her hat from fluttering away in the breeze.

CHAPTER 22

The next morning, Newbury rose early, still tender from the ministrations of the Fixer the previous day. He went directly to the bathroom and washed his wounds, and then applied a thick layer of the yellow poultice to each of them in turn. The substance smelled faintly of beeswax, although he could only guess at what else it comprised. He felt vibrant and nervous with energy, partially the result of too much rest, and partially, he imagined, the continued effect of Dr. Fabian's compound. His wounds had begun to heal already, too, although there was still a long way to go before he'd be back to anything like his normal physical form.

Newbury had spent the remainder of the previous day holed up in his study, pacing the room, smoking his pipe and doing his utmost to stop himself giving in to his cravings for the laudanum, which sat in its little brown bottle on the shelf across the room, teasing him with promises of warmth, forgetfulness and solitude. He had sorted through a number of papers from his years in India, searching out references to the revenant plague and attempting to lose himself in reminiscences of the period. Mrs. Bradshaw had prepared him a lavish roast beef dinner, and he had taken it in the dining room, the first time for months that he had made a point of sitting down to eat a proper meal in his own house.

By morning, however, he felt he could carry on like this no longer. He was concerned that boredom would indeed drive him to the dreaded opiate that he was attempting so pointedly to resist. Instead, he had resolved to head to the office, to deal with any outstanding correspondence, ensure that Miss Coulthard was bearing up, and otherwise busy himself with work on his now-overdue academic paper.

He secretly hoped that, in doing so, he would happen upon Miss Hobbes with news of the case, and together they could spend the day mulling over the developments so far, gathering their thoughts whilst his constitution was restored and agreeing on a course of action for the following day. If nothing else, he knew Her Majesty would not look too kindly on him wasting another day in lackadaisical pursuits when he had a case to solve, injured or not.

It was still too early in the day to expect Mrs. Bradshaw to have risen to make breakfast, so instead Newbury settled for organising himself a pot of Earl Grey and rummaging up a few slices of toast, which he ate with a smear of marmalade whilst reading the morning papers. Then, confident that he was well enough for a brief stroll, he fetched his coat and hat and set out, drawing in the fresh morning air and celebrating the fact that he was still alive. The previous day's events seemed like a lifetime ago, a dark and distant memory, and if it were not for the occasional twinge in his upper torso as he walked, he could almost have believed that it had been nothing but a fantasy.

Presently, tiring from his walk, Newbury hailed a cab to take him the rest of the way to the museum. The streets were still quiet, but the sun had risen and the fog was already lifting. He bounced along in the back of the cab, wincing every time the horses ran over an uneven patch of cobbled road and the wheels juddered, jolting his injured body painfully.

The museum grounds were still deserted when the cab

pulled up outside the main gates. Newbury stepped down and paid the driver, who doffed his cap and set the horses trotting off towards Charing Cross Road, their hooves clattering loudly in the otherwise empty street. Newbury crossed the courtyard and mounted the steps up to the main entrance, smiling warmly at Watkins, who was on hand even at this hour to welcome early arrivals. Pulling his gloves off and loosening his scarf, Newbury made his way down to the basement floor and along the short corridor to his office. Taking his key from inside of his jacket pocket, he turned it easily in the lock, pushed the door open and stepped inside.

It was clear Miss Coulthard had visited the office in the last couple of days. The correspondence had been neatly stacked in the appropriate trays, the cups and saucers had been tidied away and there was a note on her desk, in her handwriting, addressed to him. He picked it up, unfolded the card and scanned the neat copperplate briefly, before dropping it into the wastepaper-basket beside the door. No word on her brother Jack, it seemed.

Newbury clicked the door shut and draped his coat and hat on the stand. He crossed to his private office, noting that there was a pile of papers for him to sign, obviously left there by Miss Coulthard, and growing in size every day he was away from the office.

He disliked the menial administrative duties of his position at the museum, but in other ways it held his interest when he wasn't on a case, allowed him to come and go as freely as he liked and gave him access to many files and artefacts he would otherwise find it very difficult to obtain. Not only that, but it served as a perfect cover for his position with the Crown, meaning that, rather than having to hide himself away from society as many of the other agents did, he could instead continue to ingratiate himself with the nobility of London, all of which, he felt, provided him with a greater opportunity to do his duty for Her Majesty and the Empire. Connections, in London, were everything, and he found they opened doors where others would find them locked.

Flexing his damaged shoulder muscle to stop it from stiffening up, he lowered himself heavily into his chair. He flicked through the pile of papers on his desk, sighing in dismay. There wasn't even enough there to keep him engaged for an hour, and whilst his paper on the druidic tribes of Bronze Age Europe was in dire need of further work, he still hoped to find an opportunity to get back on the case before the morning was out. He drummed his fingers on the desk. He needed to talk to Musgrave.

Newbury looked up at the sound of the main door clicking open. He glanced at the grandfather clock through the open door of his office. It was still too early for it to be Miss Hobbes. Perhaps, in an effort to distract herself from the difficult situation at home, Miss Coulthard had decided to come to the office early that morning?

He stood, moving round from behind his desk to greet the new arrival. He stopped short when he heard a familiar clacking sound, like brass feet clanging against the porcelain titles of the floor.

Automaton.

He backed up, wondering how one of the clockwork men had managed to get into the museum, let alone track down his office on the basement floor. The feet continued to clatter on the tiles, slowly, deliberately, and Newbury realised that, judging from the sounds of their shuffling movements, there must be more than one of the devices.

A moment later, one of the units appeared around the corner behind the coat stand. Newbury stiffened. It seemed to survey the office, its spinning eyes flicking from one corner of the room to the other. When it caught sight of Newbury, it began to move again, turning around slowly and approaching him, its arms hanging limp by its side. Another one shuffled into the room behind it.

Newbury braced himself. "What are you doing here? What do you want?"

The automaton cocked its head slightly, as if trying to compute his words. Then, stopping about six feet away from him, it raised its right hand before its face. There was a soft, almost pneumatic *snick*ing sound as thin, knifelike blades slipped out from the ends of its fingers, turning its hand into a vicious razor-sharp claw. Newbury crept backwards until his legs encountered the edge of his desk. The automaton resumed its slow, relentless march towards him. Behind it, the other unit moved farther into the room, blades clicking out of the ends of its fingertips to form an identical gruesome-looking weapon. He noted with dismay that the right hand of that second unit was already smeared in blood. He supposed that answered his question about how the devices had found their way into the museum.

Knowing that he was already seriously injured and therefore unlikely to be able to hold the automata off for long, Newbury decided to go on the offensive. He waited a moment until the nearest unit was only a matter of feet away from him and then charged it, trying to use his speed and body weight to his advantage.

The automaton saw him coming, however, and twisted out of the way, contorting itself in a manner a human being would find impossible to emulate. Newbury, unable to stop his momentum, slammed into the side of Miss Coulthard's desk, jarring his injured shoulder and spinning awkwardly to the ground. The desk overturned, sending sheaves of paper blooming into the air.

Just in time, Newbury realised he'd landed at the feet of the second automaton, and he rolled to the left, narrowly avoiding its falling hand, which chopped down against the tiles with terrifying force, splintering the porcelain in a cloud of dust. Newbury, still on the floor, grabbed out for the automaton's leg, yanking it forward and unbalancing the device, sending it smashing down to the hard floor beside him. It immediately began to climb to its feet, twisting its shoulder joints to give it better leverage. Newbury climbed to one knee and thrashed out, bringing the coat stand crashing down in front of him just in time to block the path of the other automaton, which was charging him from across the room. He had to think fast.

Leaping to his feet, he cast around for a weapon. His abdomen and chest were on fire as his movements pulled on the stitches, tearing at his damaged flesh. The automata, scrambling over the coat stand, had been reduced to tireless killing machines, stripped of their harmless guise as servants. Their gears churned as they both came at him again, swinging their bladed hands towards him, one of them only a matter of inches from his face.

He fell back, banging his head awkwardly against the wall. Trying to ignore the burst of sharp pain that flared at the back of his skull, he dived to the left, sending the kitchen equipment skittering across the tiles as he tried to take cover behind the small gas stove, forcing himself over the top of it and onto the floor on the other side. Between the stove and Miss Coulthard's overturned desk, he found himself trapped in the corner of the room, with nowhere else to turn. The one thing in his favour was the fact that the automata seemed unable to work out how to climb over the furniture, instead choosing to reach over and slash at him with their razor-sharp finger blades. He tried to stay out of their reach.

Newbury glanced around in desperation, still looking for something he could use to defend himself. Above him on the wall was a mediaeval axe with a long wooden shaft. He grabbed for it, hastily pulling it free of its mount and showering himself with a spray of plaster. Balancing it in both hands, he swung the unfamiliar weapon in a wide arc, using it to parry the outstretched hands of the mechanical men. It was weighty, and it strained his already exhausted body to lift it properly. Nevertheless, at present, it was all he had to keep the automata at bay.

He hefted the weapon as high as he could and brought it down heavily upon the chest of the automaton on his left. There was an almighty crash. The wooden handle of the ancient weapon splintered in his hands with the impact, sending the iron head banging loudly to the floor. The automaton staggered backwards for a moment, a large dent in its brass casing, but then, just as quickly, was able to reassert itself and come at him again over the top of the stove. This time, catching him on the backswing, the automaton's hand struck him hard in the arm, and he cried out as the blades sliced his flesh, drawing blood. He snatched his arm back instinctively and managed to scramble out of the reach of the machine.

He could hardly believe the resilience of the device: the blow from the axe had practically collapsed its chest, even cracking the glass porthole that contained the electrical light that powered its clockwork mind, but the unit seemed unconcerned and continued to mount its attack. Newbury threw the broken shaft of the axe at the other automaton, which knocked it aside to no effect. He knew it was only a matter of time before the machines worked out how to shift Miss Coulthard's desk out of the way to get to him.

Newbury searched the walls for more weapons, thankful now that he had been able to coerce the museum's curator into allowing him to have a small display of anthropological items in his office. A few feet away, over Miss Coulthard's desk and on the wall above the fireplace, was a flail. The weapon was a few hundred years old, but Newbury knew from examining it in the past that the shaft was still firm. He hoped the star-shaped iron ball on the end of the chain would make an effective weapon against the automata, puncturing the relatively soft brass of their skulls and damaging the delicate cogwork in their mechanical brains. It was a blunt tool for a blunt job. He just had to work out how to get to it.

He measured the distance with his eyes. If he leapt up onto the overturned desk he could be at the weapon in two strides, but equally, he ran the risk of one of the automata catching hold of his leg as he tried to rush by, pulling him to the ground whilst he was unbalanced and sticking him with its vicious claws. He looked over at them. The two machines continued to try to swipe at him from behind the stove. The situation wasn't about to improve, unless he made a decisive move. He had to risk it. There were no other weapons anywhere in reach, makeshift or not, and if he waited any longer the automata would, by sheer relentlessness, find a way to reach him. Jumping up onto the desk didn't seem like a good option, however, especially in his present condition, so instead he decided to see if he could reach the weapon by other means.

Standing, his back to the wall in an effort to stay out of the reach of the questing brass fingers, Newbury edged over towards the chimney breast. Keeping himself as flat as possible, he reached an arm around and used his fingertips to feel for the flail. If he stretched onto his tiptoes, he could just about touch it, but he needed to get past the desk to be able to get a proper grip on the thing. He stared into the impassionate faces of the brass machines, watching their mirrored eyes spinning as they clutched for him, their minds programmed only to kill. If he got out of this alive, Chapman and Villiers were going to have a great deal to answer to.

Newbury surged forward, feeling the blades of both automata impaling the flesh and muscles of his upper arms. Pain blossomed, causing everything to go momentarily white, but he forced himself through it, knowing that this would be his only chance at survival. He hoped Dr. Fabian's compound would continue to work its miraculous healing powers on these fresh wounds.

Reaching down, using his momentum to drive himself forwards, he grasped hold of the underside of the desk and flipped it up towards the two machines, connecting with them both at waist height and sending them sprawling to the ground. Not waiting to see how quickly they would be able to get up, Newbury jumped up and grabbed hold of the flail, pulling it down from the display hooks on the wall. He gave it an experimental swing in his right hand, and then, charging forwards towards one of the mechanical men, he arced the ball and chain above his head, slamming it across the side of its skull with as much power as he could muster as it struggled to get up from underneath the desk. The skull split with a dull thud, cracking along the seam between the access plate and the rest of the brass head. Newbury gave a triumphant gasp, trying to free the spiked ball from where it had embedded itself in the inner workings of the machine's head. The damaged automaton kicked spasmodically a few times, its feet clacking on the tiles, and then it was still.

Newbury didn't have time to celebrate. He looked over his shoulder to see the other automaton pulling free of the desk and climbing easily to its feet. He noted it was the unit that he had struck earlier with the axe, and decided to aim his weapon at the glass plate in its chest, tackling an existing weak point in the hope of disabling it faster. He had no idea whether this would have the desired effect, but it had to be worth a try. His arms ached where the gashes in his flesh were weeping blood down his sleeves. He knew he couldn't go on much longer.

Newbury yanked the flail free of the fallen machine, noticing that in doing so, he had exposed something fleshy and wet inside. He didn't have time to look, however, as the other automaton was coming up on him fast. He swung the flail in a wide arc around his head, feeling his shoulder scream in protest as he slammed the weapon against the automaton's chest, shattering the glass plate and causing electricity to arc out into the room in a spectacular display of shimmering blue light. The machine stumbled from side to side for a moment, tottering on its feet, before collapsing to the floor, its brass skeleton still fizzing and crackling with raw electricity.

Newbury dropped the flail and sank to his knees, exhausted. He remained there for a few moments, straining to catch his breath. The electrical current continued to crackle over the destroyed skeleton of the second automaton.

He looked around the ruination of his office. Miss Coulthard was not going to be happy. He flexed his shoulders, cringing with the pain, and held his arms up before him, cautiously exploring the knife wounds through the fabric of his shirt. They didn't seem so severe as he'd imagined, although the pain was excruciating. He tried to push it to the back of his mind. He looked over at the spilled workings of the machine whose skull he had destroyed. There was definitely something wet and organic seeping out from underneath the brass fittings.

Cautiously, Newbury used the edge of the overturned desk to pull himself upright, and tentatively approached the brass skeleton. He prodded it with his foot, making sure that there was no spark of life left inside of it. It flopped lifelessly onto its back. Deciding it was probably safe, he leaned closer, using his fingers to pry the skull open a little farther so he could see inside. He turned the head towards the light. Then, appalled, he dropped the skull to the floor with a loud clatter and stepped away from the gruesome sight, putting his sleeve to his mouth in disgust. His fingers dripped with sticky fluid.

Instead of the clockwork mechanisms that he had been expecting to find inside of the automaton's skull, there was a pinkish-grey, fleshy human brain. Newbury fought back the rising bile in his throat. Then, needing to confirm his suspicion, he retrieved the flail from where he'd discarded it on the floor it a few feet away, and set about splitting open the head of the other unit. A couple of sharp blows later and the skull had given way, revealing the same disturbing sight as the first time: the spattered grey matter of a human organ. He leaned one arm against the wall, trying to process the information. Human organs inside of clockwork men. An airship crash. A series of brutal strangulations in the slums.

Suddenly, a thought began to resolve itself in his mind, the stirrings of a theory taking shape. Wasting no further time, he snatched up his coat from the floor and ran from the office, taking the stairs two at a time, grimacing as his wounds throbbed painfully. He crossed the huge foyer of the museum, hurtled through the main entrance and burst out onto the street, startling a flock of pigeons that had settled in the courtyard. Without pausing, he ran directly to the nearest cab and leapt on board, flinging himself into the seat. The driver leaned down and glanced in through the window.

"Where to?"

"Scotland Yard, as quickly as you can stir those horses into action!"

CHAPTER 23

Charles!"

Newbury burst into the office of the Chief Inspector and stumbled over to his desk, still dripping blood from the fresh wounds in his upper arms.

Bainbridge looked him up and down with an expression of dismay on his face. "Good God, man. Shouldn't you be resting? Look at the state of you. You're bleeding all over the place. Didn't the Fixer do his work?" Bainbridge stood, as if he were about to move to Newbury's aid.

Newbury, gasping for breath, staggered across the room and slumped into a Chesterfield beside the fire. "I'm fine, Charles." He wheezed, red-faced from running. "But I think I have the solution."

"What?" Bainbridge came round from behind his desk, pushing his spectacles further up his nose. "Look here, before you start any of that, what's going on with all this blood? Are you hurt?"

Newbury emitted a gasping laugh. "A little. I've just fought off two of those automaton devices in my office."

Bainbridge looked flustered. He repeated himself. "What?"

"It seems we're getting a little too close to the truth. Someone sent two automata to my office in an attempt to assassinate me. They weren't your typical automata, either; they had hidden blades in their fingers, and worse, human brains in their brass skulls."

Bainbridge shook his head, lowering himself into the other chair by the fire. He reached over to a small table in the corner and took a decanter and two glasses, pouring them both a large brandy. "I think, Newbury, that you'd better start at the beginning."

Newbury accepted the drink gratefully and took a long draw from the glass. He rested his head against the back of the chair. "What do you know about Pierre Villiers?"

"Only what you've told me. That he's a genius. That he was exiled from his own country for experimenting on waifs and strays. That he created the automata for Chapman to market. Nothing more than that."

Newbury nodded. "It's that bit about experimenting on waifs and strays that is interesting me at the moment. What *exactly* was he doing? What was so bad that his own countrymen had him banished from Paris, renowned the world over as a place of free-thinking and bohemian eccentricity?"

"You've lost me." Bainbridge raised his eyebrows, shaking his head.

"No, Charles. I think this has a bearing on our case. Villiers has a fascination with the inner workings of the mind. He told me he's always wanted to build the perfect automaton. What if the device he showed me in his workshop wasn't it? What if it couldn't do everything he wanted it to? Perhaps it was that drive for perfection, and his experiments on those wastrels back in Paris, which provided him with the necessary knowledge to successfully transplant a human brain into a clockwork housing. Perhaps *that* is his idea of the perfect automaton device?"

Bainbridge looked appalled.

"I saw it with my own eyes, Charles. I cracked open their

brass skulls on my office floor and saw the human organs inside. I think that's why we didn't find the pilot in the wreckage of *The Lady Armitage*. Chapman probably had his man Stokes remove it before anyone else got to the scene. If we'd found it there, we would have taken it away for investigation, and would likely have discovered what they were up to."

Bainbridge took a swig of his drink, grimacing at the thought. "But where are they getting the organs from?"

"I can't be certain, but I suspect that's where the link to the glowing policeman murders comes in. It all makes a horrible kind of sense. They employ someone to murder paupers in the Whitechapel slums, using strangulation as the method of despatch so as not to damage the brains. Then they make an arrangement with the mortuary attendant to harvest the brains of the victims as they come through the morgue. It's a neat arrangement, however despicable it may be."

Bainbridge went red in the face. "I knew that damn mortuary assistant was up to no good!" He glared at Newbury, obviously incensed. "So you think the reason for the airship crash is a malfunction in the bridge between the human brain and the automaton frame? Did the pilot simply lose control?"

Newbury shook his head. "I can't answer that with any certainty, although I suspect Villiers is far too clever for that to be the case. I don't think it was the interface that went wrong. I think it was the brain."

"You mean they had trouble keeping the brain alive outside of the body?"

"Not at all. Think about it, Charles. There's a plague burning through the Whitechapel slums. Remember what I told you about the Indian doctor? The revenant virus incubates for up to eight days in the human brain. God knows how many of those harvested organs were already infected when they were wired up to the automata." He paused. "Judging by the manner in which Christopher Morgan's device went awry, I'd say we are dealing with something far more alarming than a simple malfunction. I think a number of those automata are carrying the revenant plague."

"My God, they're like ticking bombs." Bainbridge shook his head. "But Newbury, they're all over the city."

"I know, Charles. I know. We'll need to enlist the entire Metropolitan police force to aid us in decommissioning the whole lot. But first we've got to tackle Chapman and Villiers. I say we get over there this morning and try to catch them on the hop. They won't yet be aware that their assassination attempt this morning was a failure."

Bainbridge nodded. "Very well." He eyed Newbury warily. "Are you sure you're fit?"

Newbury smiled. "I'm far from fit. But I'll live."

Bainbridge downed the last of his brandy. "What does Miss Hobbes make of all this?"

Newbury nearly spat his drink across the room. "Oh, God, Charles. I hadn't even considered. What if they sent the automata after her, too?" He jumped to his feet. "We need to get over there now, as fast as we can."

"Right you are." Bainbridge placed his empty glass on the table and made straight for his cane. He grabbed his coat from the stand, not even bothering to put it on as he charged out the door. "Come on. I'll get us a police carriage. We'll be there in no time."

"I pray that's time enough." The two men hurried from the room.

CHAPTER 24

Kensington High Street was bustling with people by the time the police carriage came hurtling through the traffic, rocking furiously from side to side as its wheels bounced on the uneven cobbles, causing Newbury and Bainbridge to shift uncomfortably in their seats. They had barely spoken a word between them during the short journey from Scotland Yard, each of them choosing to mull over the situation in silence. Newbury, on his part, did not wish to give voice to his obvious concern for Veronica. It was as if talking about the possibility of her being under threat would somehow make the situation more tangible, more likely to become a reality. Instead, he sat clenching and unclenching his fists in nervous anticipation, hoping desperately that his lack of consideration would not result in her coming to any harm. He knew he would not be able to live with himself if it came to that. He cursed himself for being so caught up in his own concerns about the case.

A few moments later, the carriage shuddered and came to a stop. The horses stamped their feet impatiently as the driver tugged on their reins, trying to hold them still. In the back, Newbury climbed to his feet. He was the first through the door, helping Bainbridge down to the street beside him. He glanced at the door to Veronica's apartment, just a matter of feet away. "You'd better make sure you have that miraculous cane handy, Charles. If Miss Hobbes is in trouble, we may find ourselves in need of it."

Bainbridge nodded, and then turned to the driver. "Wait here."

The driver doffed his cap in acknowledgement.

Together, Newbury and Bainbridge approached the house. Newbury had taken only a few steps towards the door when he stopped suddenly and waved at Bainbridge to remain still. "Shhh. Can you hear that?"

Bainbridge listened intently.

Coming from the other side of the door was the faint sound of a woman shouting. The words themselves were indiscernible against the background noise of the busy road, but it was enough to send both men into a course of immediate action.

Newbury wasted no time. He charged at the door, using his good shoulder to slam against the wooden panels. The door flexed resolutely in its frame, but didn't give. He tried again, and then, on the third attempt, the lock gave in and the door bounced open, revealing the scene inside.

Veronica was standing in the hallway, her feet planted firmly apart, pointing a glowing poker at the throat of a man in a policeman's uniform. The man, who was tall and well-built, had backed up against the wall, trying to keep the angry woman at bay. It was immediately obvious that he was no real police constable, and what was more, he had painted his face and hands with an iridescent blue powder that shimmered as it caught the light.

Newbury gasped. *The glowing policeman.* The man's uniform was scorched across the front where he had already taken a blow from Veronica's hot poker. They'd clearly been engaged in the struggle for some time, and it seemed that, presently, Veronica had the upper hand.

Unsure what to do, Newbury called to Veronica and rushed

forward to help try to pin the glowing policeman. "Veronica! Be careful!"

Surprised, Veronica turned to see Newbury charging towards her. The man in the policeman's uniform saw this distraction as a chance to get away and took it without hesitation. He seized Veronica's wrist and twisted it sharply, causing her to cry out and drop the weapon on the floor. Then, giving her a harsh shove that sent her sprawling to the ground, he turned and bolted, flinging himself along the hallway towards the kitchen and the back door.

"You oafs! I had him pinned!" Veronica shouted as she picked herself up, frustrated, rubbing at her sore wrist. Newbury, leaving Bainbridge to attend to the lady, took flight after the escaping murderer, barging past Veronica and careening down the hallway in quick pursuit, banging his injured shoulder painfully off the wall as he ran.

"Oh no you don't!" He heard Veronica call after him, followed by the sound of her footsteps as she charged after him.

Newbury skidded into the kitchen, throwing his arm out to catch hold of the doorframe and slow himself down momentarily. The back door had been flung open, and the man was scrambling over a wall. Newbury followed suit, darting out into the backyard and leaping up to grab hold of the brickwork. He hauled himself bodily over the wall and dropped into the alleyway behind the house, catching sight of the man doubling back on himself and heading off in the direction of Kensington High Street. Puffing, Newbury picked up his pace, pushing himself to run after the fleeing criminal as fast as his tired, injured body would propel him along. He wasn't about to let his physical condition prevent him from resolving this case, and the glowing policeman was a fundamental part of the puzzle. The man's testimony would be crucial in helping to bring the main players to justice, before he swung from the gallows himself for his crimes.

Newbury, not waiting to see if Veronica had made it over the wall, skidded around the corner into a side street, just managing to keep the uniformed man in view. He charged on, narrowly avoiding a pile of wooden crates that someone had abandoned in the middle of the road and nearly losing his footing on the slick cobbles in the process.

The other man disappeared between two buildings up ahead. Newbury raced after him, his chest and abdomen screaming in pain. He could feel some of his stitches pulling free as he pushed his body beyond the limit of its endurance. He could hardly believe that only yesterday he had been laid out, dying in the Fixer's workshop, and today he was running through the streets of Kensington in pursuit of a multiple murderer. It was a testament to either the Fixer's miraculous abilities or Newbury's own stupidity. He tried his best to bury the pain as his feet pounded the ground, his entire body shaking with the thudding of his shoes against the hard road.

Newbury burst out onto the busy thoroughfare, glancing in both directions to try to ascertain which way the other man had run. Almost too late, he caught sight of him leaping up onto a passing ground train, snatching hold of the side railing attached to one of the carriages and pulling himself up onto the roof. The long train of interconnected carriages snaked along behind him as it trundled noisily down the road.

Not stopping to consider the risk, Newbury ran after it, launching himself from the pavement and just managing to catch hold of the iron railing that ran around the rear end of the vehicle. He tried to haul himself up, his feet trailing in the road as the vehicle steamed ahead, the driver unaware of his newest passengers. He heard Veronica shouting something from behind him, but he was already out of earshot as the train rumbled on along the road.

Gasping, Newbury hoisted himself higher, wedging his foot on the buffer and pulling himself into a standing position, balancing tentatively on the railing. He heard banging and shouting, and looked round to see the people inside the carriage had opened their side window and were leaning out, jeering at him to let go. There was a similar commotion coming from farther up the train, and Newbury reasoned that the passengers had seen the strange blue-skinned policeman leap up onto the roof and were now calling for the driver to stop the vehicle.

Being careful not to lose his hold, Newbury used one hand to explore the roof of the carriage. It seemed firm, and had a thin lip running around the edge of it that he could use as a handhold to pull himself up. It was the only way he was going to be able to catch up with the man he was chasing, and he didn't want to risk losing him if the devious blighter decided to jump off the train farther up the road to make good on his escape.

Newbury swung his other arm up, finding his grip on the roof of the carriage. He manoeuvred his feet until he could gain some purchase on the railing and then began to pull himself up and over, using his leg muscles as much as possible to avoid pulling on his weak shoulder. After a minute or two, he managed to swing first his chest and then his legs up onto the roof of the carriage. He lay still for a moment, catching his breath and casting around for a sight of his quarry. The roof was mostly flat, with a slight camber to each side to allow rainwater to run off into the street below. Newbury looked over the side. The cobbles rushed by at speed. It wouldn't do to fall.

The glowing policeman was clinging to another roof, about three carriages farther up the train. He was on his knees and had his back to Newbury, clutching the lip that ran around the edge of the carriage roof. He shifted from side to side with the movement of the train.

Newbury knew that it would be difficult to get closer to

the man without attracting his attention, but he also knew that moving quickly would provide him with his best shot at success. If he could get near enough to knock the policeman over the head—he had lost his helmet somewhere during the run—he could potentially disable the man before he even realised that Newbury was there.

Tentatively, he pushed himself up onto his knees, trying to work out whether it would be safe enough for him to walk along the roof of the carriage without falling. The train was still trundling along at a reasonable speed, but the road was straight, and as long as they didn't bounce over any potholes, it was worth the risk. Not that he had any other options in mind.

Slowly, he got to his feet, keeping his eyes on the man up ahead. He took a quick step forward, almost stumbled, but managed to keep his balance by waving his arms out beside him. He crept towards the rim of the carriage, looking down at the gap between the roof he was standing on and the next one along in the train. It was at least four or five feet. The ground swept past below. He was going to need a running jump to clear it. If he missed he'd end up caught amongst the hard buffers or tumbling to one side and cracking his head on the cobbled road, or worse, dashed beneath the train's wheels. None of them seemed like a good way to go.

Sighing, he edged away from the gap, taking a few steps backwards. He looked around to establish that there were no trailing wires that could inadvertently snare him as he made his dash, and then, with a deep breath, he careened forward and leapt into the air, throwing himself as far as he could towards the next roof in the long line of carriages. He came down with a loud *smack,* landing on his right side and skittering across the bitumen-covered roof, sliding towards the edge of the carriage.

Thrashing around, he managed to get a grip on the lip of the roof, planting his feet as best he could to gain leverage.

The landing had knocked the air out of his lungs, so he sucked fruitlessly at the sky, lying on his back, trying desperately to pull himself round. He could hear shouting from the passengers beneath him, panicked by the sudden bang on the roof of their carriage. He wondered how long it would take the driver to start weaving from side to side again, or else bring the vehicle to a halt.

Newbury rolled up into a sitting position. He realised immediately that his attempts at subtlety had been wasted; the noise he'd made leaping across the gap had been enough to startle the man in the policeman's uniform a few carriages ahead. He had not, however, made any move to try to flee, as Newbury had anticipated he might; instead, he had turned to face the Crown investigator, a look of grim resignation in his eyes, as if ready to take him on if Newbury decided to come any closer. As far as Newbury saw it, however, he had no choice but to continue. He wasn't about to be intimidated, and whilst he'd had his absolute fill of combat during the course of the last couple of days, he would do what was necessary to bring the man to justice.

Newbury found his footing and this time didn't stop to ponder the jump. He ran at the end of the carriage, diving over the gap and throwing himself, spread-eagled, onto the roof of the next one in the long train. This time he was prepared for the impact and recovered much faster from the landing, although he felt the wounds in his arms open up again as he grasped for a handhold, warm blood weeping down the length of his forearms. They burned angrily, and Newbury felt like he'd forgotten what it was like to live without pain.

He looked up, making sure that the glowing policeman hadn't jumped across from the next carriage to meet him. Thankfully, the man had chosen to wait it out on the other roof. He was hovering near the lip of the carriage, his fists ready, his stance set firm. He looked like a prize-fighter, silhouetted against the morning sun. There was no way Newbury would be able to make the jump across to tackle him. If he flung himself over as he had with the other carriages, he'd run the risk of colliding with the man, knocking them both to the ground and their deaths. It was simply too treacherous, and he needed to come up with an alternative course of action as quickly as he could. He moved over to the end of his carriage to stand opposite the counterfeit policeman, swaying slightly with the movement of the train. The gap between them opened and closed as the train bounced over the cobbles, bringing them dangerously close together and then pulling them apart again with every bump and twist of the road.

Their eyes met. The man scowled angrily, his expression filled with fury and ire. It was clear to Newbury that he was the sort of man who made his living from violence: his face was a patchwork of scars and old wounds, and his nose had been broken on numerous occasions. He was unshaven, and underneath the shimmering blue powder he had painted over his exposed skin, his neck was covered in a string of dark illegible tattoos.

Newbury shouted to him over the noise of the churning engine. "Look here. There's no way we're both getting down from here alive, unless we choose to do it together. I can help. They'll go easy on you if you cooperate."

The other man grunted. "You mean they'll give me a shorter rope to dangle from?" He shook his head. "Not me. I ain't going willingly to no noose." His accent was clipped with the sounds of the East End, his voice a gruff bark.

Newbury nodded. "So be it." He glanced from side to side, looking for anything he could use as a weapon. There was nothing obvious to hand. He shifted slightly as the train rocked forward. The movement brought the two carriages momentarily closer together, and the man took the opportunity to swing out, catching Newbury off guard with a hard fist in his gut. Newbury toppled backwards, clutching at his waist. He used his feet to shuffle back from the edge whilst he regained his composure, keeping his eye on his adversary. The glowing policeman eyed him with a sarcastic smile. Newbury clambered to his feet. He edged closer to the gap once again, his arms drawn up in front of him in readiness. He wasn't sure how much power he'd be able to muster in his damaged shoulder, but he flexed his neck muscles in anticipation and, when the opportunity arose, dashed forward and took a swing at the other man.

At that moment, however, the carriage veered suddenly to the right, and the gap between the two men widened dramatically as the engine turned a corner up ahead and sent the train of carriages careening out in a wide arc behind it. Too late to stop his momentum, Newbury toppled into the gap, falling between the two carriages. He lashed out, scrabbling desperately to find purchase on anything that would prevent him from falling to the ground. In his panic, he managed to grab the ledge that ran around the roof of the other carriage, his body slamming hard into the rear end of the carriage itself. He held on tentatively by his fingertips, thrashing his feet around beneath him as he tried to find something firm that could take his weight.

The face of the glowing policeman appeared over the lip of the carriage roof, leering down at him. The man was laughing at his apparent stroke of good fortune. It was almost a comical sight, this human face shining blue in the early morning sunshine. If Newbury hadn't been hanging precariously by his fingertips, he would have laughed out loud.

The policeman approached the edge of the roof and stamped his boot down hard on Newbury's left hand, crushing his fingertips painfully against the metal rim. He ground his foot, trying to force Newbury to let go. Newbury could feel the skin shredding from his knuckles underneath the man's roughly shod boot. He cried out in agony, barely managing to keep a hold on the roof. His eyes filled with involuntary tears of pain. The man lifted his foot away for a second, giving the slightest of reprieves, but then smashed it down again heavily, using his heel to force Newbury's fingers away from the edge.

Newbury, blinded by panic, swung out from the end of the carriage, clutching the roof with only one hand. Below, the road was a blur of dark stones that sped past as the train gathered speed and momentum. If he fell, his life was forfeit. Determined to hang on for all he was worth, Newbury tried again to swing his legs onto some footing. This time he connected with the iron buffers and managed to get his feet up onto one of them, sighing with relief as he secured himself against the end of the carriage. He was far from safe, but neither was he about to tumble to a miserable death.

The other man, not seeing that Newbury had managed to get himself into a position with more leverage, prepared to stomp down on Newbury's other hand. Newbury waited until the man lifted his foot and then swept out with his free hand, grasping him by his ankle and pulling sharply forwards, toppling the man onto his back so that he splayed out on the carriage roof with a considerable *bang*. Newbury used the opportunity to pull himself up to safety as the glowing policeman, dazed from the fall, rolled to one side and scrambled to the other end of the roof in an effort to buy himself time to recover. A moment later, he climbed back to his feet, shaking his head.

Warily, the two men faced each other. The glowing policeman was clearly the bigger of the two, his strength probably far exceeding the academic's, but Newbury didn't have time to ponder the odds. He charged forward, catching the other man off guard and driving his fist up and under his chin. It connected with a *crack,* and the man staggered back, disorientated. Newbury continued his assault, punching the criminal as hard as he could in the kidneys, trying to bring him to his knees. Unfortunately, the second of these blows had quite the opposite effect than was intended.

Losing his footing, the glowing policeman skidded backwards on the bitumen roof, his feet giving way beneath him as he misjudged the camber and overbalanced. Wheeling his arms like a flapping bird, he fell over the side of the carriage, hurtling towards the cobbles below. Newbury dashed forward, reaching out to try to catch hold of the falling man, but his fingers managed only to graze the collar of the stolen police uniform before the man was gone. There was a sickening crunch as he hit the ground below.

Newbury sucked in his breath and leaned over the side of the train as they hurtled away, straining to see what had become of the glowing policeman. He had to avert his eyes from the scene almost immediately. The man had landed awkwardly on the back of his head, splitting it open on the cobbles like a cracked egg. His body was a twisted pile of torso and limbs, the neck obviously broken, and oily blood seeped from the head wound to stain the stones underneath.

Collapsing back onto the roof, Newbury cursed himself yet again for letting a vital clue slip out of his reach. He felt no remorse for the death of the man who had posed as the glowing policeman; as far as Newbury was concerned, the villain deserved everything he got. Nevertheless, lying there bleeding and shivering on the top of a speeding train, Newbury couldn't help but feel frustration that the whole affair had resulted in nothing, except perhaps the death of a killer who could otherwise have provided evidence against Chapman and Villiers before he went to the gallows. He had to hope that the evidence he had already collected would be enough to condemn the two industrialists in court.

Mustering what remained of his strength, Newbury crawled to the far edge of the carriage and shouted down to the driver and guard, both of whom sat in a small cabin atop the main housing of the engine itself.

"Driver! Time you stopped this bloody train to let me down, isn't it?"

The man looked up at the battered and bruised face of Newbury, leaning down over the top of the carriage. He stuttered, unsure how to respond. The guard reached for his truncheon.

Newbury sighed. "Let me down and I'll show you my papers, man! I'm working on behalf of the Crown."

This was clearly enough for the driver, who applied the brakes and slowly brought the train to a stop, to much shouting and consternation from the passengers. Newbury lowered himself carefully over the edge of the carriage roof, clambering down onto the engine casing and using the fireman's steps to lower himself to the street below. The driver looked him up and down, mystified that a man claiming to work for the Crown should be found in such a diabolical state, crawling around on top of the 9:20 to Marylebone.

The guard climbed down from the cab and walked around the front of the train, his truncheon in hand. He came to stand before Newbury. "Papers, you say?"

Newbury fished his papers out from his inside jacket pocket and waved them at the portly fellow, whose eyes widened at the sight of the Royal Seal. He glanced up at the driver, nodding slowly.

Newbury outlined the situation. "Now, look here. I have to get back to my associates. You need to alert the police as quickly as you can. There's a dead man in the street back there, dressed as a police constable. His face is painted up to look blue. Tell the bobbies that Sir Charles Bainbridge of Scotland Yard wants the body taken to the morgue immediately. Can you do that?"

The man nodded, clearly unsure how to react.

Newbury, shaking his head, had little choice but to rely on

the man. "This is a matter of state importance. Now, go to it!"

The guard glanced back at the driver, and then at the carriages full of passengers. He shrugged. Then he ran off in the direction of the dead man. The driver cranked a lever on the front of the engine, allowing steam to hiss noisily from a vent in the roof, and then the train rumbled slowly away, gathering speed and momentum as it did.

Newbury took one last look at the passengers, many of whom were leaning out of their windows heckling him as the train pulled away. Then turned and searched out a passing cab, leaping aboard and directing the driver to make haste in the direction of Veronica's apartment, where he hoped to find both Bainbridge and Veronica herself awaiting him.

CHAPTER 25

The door was still hanging loose on its hinges when Newbury ducked into Veronica's apartment a short while later. He winced as he walked along the hallway, heading towards the sound of voices that were coming from one of the reception rooms at the back of the house.

He could hear Bainbridge fussing over Veronica from within. "Really, Miss Hobbes. I do suggest we call a doctor."

Veronica's response was terse. "Sir Charles, I will not be fussed over unnecessarily. I assure you I am quite well."

Bainbridge sighed extravagantly. "Very well. As you wish." Newbury could imagine him rolling his eyes in consternation. The conversation lapsed into silence.

Newbury approached the door to the lounge and knocked loudly before entering. Veronica jumped to her feet. "Sir Maurice! Oh . . ." Her mouth fell open in slack-jawed amazement when she laid eyes on his bedraggled appearance. She crossed the room, took him by the arm and led him slowly to a nearby chair. Her face was a picture of concern.

Newbury smiled. "Do I really look that bad?"

Veronica looked away, refusing to be drawn on the question, but Bainbridge was more to the point. "You look like you've gone ten rounds with an Indian tiger. Are you badly hurt?"

Newbury couldn't help but laugh. "That's the second time you've asked me that today, Charles, and the answer remains decidedly the same: no more than can be expected." He shifted in his seat where the leather upholstery was pressing painfully against his wounds. "I think we'll get today's excitement out of the way, and then I'll be paying another visit to the Fixer, to see if he can't dose me up with some more of that miraculous compound of his. I took a bit of a beating out there today." He fell silent, watching the fire gutter in the grate as the others waited for him to go on.

Bainbridge pulled at the edges of his moustache impatiently. "Are you going to elaborate, then? Did you lose him somewhere?"

Newbury watched Veronica as she made her way back to her seat. He shook his head. "No. He's very much dead."

Bainbridge nodded, his face unreadable. Veronica looked aghast. "What happened? I lost you on the High Street when you jumped aboard the train. I couldn't keep up in this damnable dress." She looked down at her torn, dirty skirt with disdain.

"He scrambled onto the roof of the train. I followed suit, we scuffled and he fell to his death. It's a damn shame. It would have been far more useful if I'd managed to restrain him instead. I would have liked the opportunity to question him about the case." He glanced at Bainbridge. "I left instructions for the body to be taken to the morgue." Bainbridge nodded his approval.

"You fought him on the top of a moving ground train?" Veronica's voice was strained.

Newbury nodded. "Indeed."

"What were you thinking of! You could easily have gone over the side with him!"

Bainbridge raised an eyebrow at this outburst from Veronica. "Miss Hobbes, it is clear to me that you are still suffering from a certain degree of shock, which is only to be expected following the nature of this morning's attack. Perhaps you need some time alone to recover?"

Newbury smirked as Veronica bit back on her retort. She glanced over at him, her eyes flashing. "My apologies, Sir Maurice. I did not mean to question your judgement."

Newbury gave a half-hearted laugh. "Oh, but you are quite correct in this matter, my dear Miss Hobbes. It was a rather foolhardy exercise, and one I shall be in no hurry to repeat, I assure you. I've had quite my fill of hand-to-hand combat for the time being. What galls me terribly is the fact that I did not even manage to apprehend the villain for my troubles."

Bainbridge spluttered. "On the contrary, old boy! Your actions have resulted in the removal of a major criminal element from the streets of London. You are to be congratulated. A job well done!"

Newbury shrugged noncommittally. He turned towards Veronica. "And Miss Hobbes, I assume you are quite well? Were you hurt in your struggle with the man?"

Veronica shook her head. "No, I'm well enough, thank you. A little shaken, perhaps. I'm pleased to report that you and Sir Charles arrived before the situation degenerated into actual violence. I should have hated it if I'd found cause to actually use that hot poker on the man." She shot a sardonic glance at Bainbridge, who seemed impervious to the witticism, or else was simply choosing to ignore it.

Newbury smiled. "You certainly seemed to have everything under control when we arrived, Miss Hobbes. I'm only sorry that I had to involve you in this terrible business. If I'd imagined at the outset of this investigation that it would in any way put you in danger, I would, of course, have refrained from including you in proceedings."

Veronica sat forward in her seat, clasping her hands together in front of her. She looked anxious. "Not at all, Sir

Maurice. I wouldn't have it any other way. I couldn't bear to be excluded now."

Newbury nodded slowly. "Very well, then." His lips curled, as if satisfied that he had done his duty in giving Veronica the opportunity to back out. "Let us order the events in our minds. Miss Hobbes, can you tell us exactly what happened here? Before I chased the villain from the scene, I mean. It could be pertinent to the case."

Veronica sighed. "I'm not entirely sure, I'm afraid." She glanced from Newbury to Bainbridge. "I was in this room, taking a cup of tea before the fire, when I heard a sound from the hallway. I turned to look just as the man you saw, dressed as the blue policeman, barged in and came at me with his fists. I grabbed the poker from the fire and used it to drive him back into the hallway. That was when the two of you arrived. He must have found his way in through the back somehow."

"What about your housekeeper?"

"Mrs. Grant has only just arrived for the day. She's in the kitchen at the moment, searching out a temporary prop for the door. She doesn't begin her duties until half past nine on a Thursday."

Newbury sank back into the clutches of his chair. He glanced at the clock on the mantelpiece. "Do you think Mrs. Grant could find it in her heart to prepare a pot of Earl Grey for two gentlemen in urgent need?" He glanced over at Bainbridge. "Charles and I have a great deal to talk to you about."

Veronica frowned. "I am sure Mrs. Grant will be only too happy to accommodate you. But what is it that you need to discuss?"

Newbury ran a hand over his face, sitting forward in his chair. "I think we'd better start at the beginning."

Newbury recounted his theory to Veronica over a pot of tea, in much the same way as he had explained it to Bainbridge earlier that morning in the offices at Scotland Yard. Veronica nodded solemnly as she took it all in, and Newbury could see by the look on her face that she thought it made a terrible kind of sense, when all the facts were considered alongside each other.

"So you're essentially saying that Chapman and Villiers organised the glowing policeman murders as a means of obtaining human brains for use in their automaton devices?"

Newbury nodded.

"And that you believe the reason that some of the automata have been malfunctioning–thus causing the airship crash, amongst other things–is because a number of those organs were carrying the revenant plague?"

"That's about the size of it, my dear. Of course, questioning the man who was posing as the glowing policeman would have helped to establish the link with more certainty, but the clues are all there: the human organs in the automata that attacked me; the blue powder around the throat and collar of the murdered Christopher Morgan, who had previously threatened to expose Chapman and Villiers, the glowing policeman coming after you this very morning. It all fits together perfectly. I suspect if we were able to disinter the bodies of the glowing policeman's earlier victims, we would very quickly be able to establish that the brains had been removed from the bodies. The fact that those organs have all been sourced from the Whitechapel slums, where the revenant plague is rife, coupled with the fact that we know the virus has an eight-day incubation period, suggests that the revenant symptoms might not present until days after the automaton units were sold to their clients." Newbury sat back, crossing his legs and taking another mouthful of Earl Grey.

Veronica shook her head. "It's all in their heads! Ha! I should have realised earlier." She sighed. "It's all in the heads of the automata."

Newbury frowned. "What was that, Miss Hobbes?"

Veronica met Newbury's gaze. "Oh, nothing. Something for later, perhaps. It has no bearing on the case." She clapped her hands together. "So, what is our next move?" She glanced at Bainbridge.

"Chapman and Villiers. It has to be. As Newbury has already pointed out, the moment they get wind of the fact that their assassination attempts this morning have failed, they'll have to make a run for it. We need to get to them first, if we're not already too late."

Newbury shook his head. "No, they're both as arrogant as each other. Chapman probably thinks he can take us on at our own game, and Villiers, I suspect, doesn't care one way or another. I doubt they'll run. In fact, if we're lucky, they'll play right into our hands."

"And directly into a noose, too, if I have any say in the matter." Bainbridge tapped his foot on the carpet, coughing loudly. "Shall we make haste?"

Veronica stood. Newbury did the same. "If I may make use of your bathroom facilities before we leave, Miss Hobbes? I would very much like to wash away some of this blood and grime before making the journey across town."

Veronica smiled. "Of course. Let me show you where to go." She led him from the room, showing him along the hall to the small bathroom.

Newbury hesitated before the door. He turned to regard her. "Thank you, Miss Hobbes. I won't keep you for long." He held her gaze for a few seconds, noticing for the first time the pretty smattering of freckles across the bridge of her nose. "I'm very glad you survived this morning unscathed."

Veronica laughed softly. "And I'm very glad that you survived at all." Her voice was barely a whisper, as if she didn't want Bainbridge to overhear their conversation. She put her hand on his arm. "When we left you with the Fixer,

I . . . I thought I might not see you again."

"I know." He looked pained. "I'm sorry I put you through all of that. I'll be well enough with a little time."

Veronica shook her head. "You have nothing to be sorry for, Sir Maurice! It is I who should be thanking you. Your efforts against the revenant creatures were enough to save all of our lives." She leaned over and kissed him gently on the cheek, her lips leaving a cool, damp impression on his skin.

Newbury cleared his throat, embarrassed. "In that case, Miss Hobbes, after the manner in which you found me in my study the other morning, I do believe we're about equal." He offered her a wide grin. "Now, if you'll forgive me, I really must attend to my wounds. I fear this suit is already beyond saving, but I'd like to give it my best shot all the same."

Veronica laughed, this time not bothering to hide her amusement. "You'll find some fresh bandages in the cabinet beneath the sink."

Newbury stepped into the bathroom and clicked the door shut behind him. He listened to the sound of Veronica's footsteps disappearing along the hallway before undressing in front of the mirror, setting the tap running and tending to his raw and bloody wounds. It was only just after ten o'clock in the morning, and already it was proving to be a long, painful day.

CHAPTER 26

The sun was a watery, baleful eye that glared down at the Thames through a bruised eyelid of rain clouds as Newbury, Veronica and Bainbridge rolled over the Chelsea Bridge in the back of the police carriage, on their way to Battersea and the Chapman and Villiers manufactory.

Newbury watched Bainbridge leaning out of the carriage window, straining to take in the sight of the embankment as it came into view. He followed the other man's gaze. The scene across the river was murky, the mist and rain forming a thick veil across the landscape. The rain had begun to fall not long after they had set out from Veronica's apartment, and the three of them had quickly decided to huddle together in the waiting vehicle. Bainbridge had stopped only to send word to Scotland Yard, requesting uniformed assistance, but they all knew it would be some time before the Yard were able to muster their men. In the meantime, Newbury had been eager to press on, to head directly to Battersea and confront Chapman and Villiers before the two of them realised the police were finally on to them.

Newbury looked up at the dark clouds that were scudding across the sky, brooding with intent. The rain would continue well into the afternoon, if he was any judge of the weather.

Across the river, the warehouses of Chapman and Villiers were squat mounds of red brick, imposing even amidst the industrial buildings that sat to either side of them. A number of airships were still tethered to the roofs, tousled by driving wind and precipitation. They bobbed fluidly but remained fixed in place by long coils of rope.

"Impressive, isn't it, Charles?"

Bainbridge turned to look at him, his expression fixed. He nodded. "Bigger than I had imagined."

"Indeed. Wait until you see inside. The manner in which they construct the new dirigibles is magnificent." He allowed his eyes to wander to the floor, biting back his enthusiasm. "If only they'd contented themselves with that, eh, rather than trying to revolutionise the world with their clockwork men?" He shook his head.

"Newbury, people like that will never be content with their lot. Whatever they say, it's not about changing the world. It's about wielding power. They may call themselves philanthropists, but in truth they're just as greedy as the rest of us, just as hungry for money and validation. In this case, probably more so."

Newbury met his friend's eyes. "You're right, of course. About Chapman, at least. But I think Villiers is a different matter entirely. I don't see that he's at all interested in money or validation. I think he sees his work as a personal challenge. He has no grand schemes to change the world; he wants only to be left alone to his amoral experiments, as terrible as they are."

Bainbridge sighed. "That may be so, but it doesn't alter the fact that together they've committed the most heinous of crimes. There's no redemption to be had here. They're both for the noose."

Newbury nodded and leaned back in his seat. He glanced at Veronica, who had been listening to the conversation from her place beside him. She didn't seem to have anything she wanted to add to the discussion and instead turned away, pretending to distract herself with the view out of the window. He wondered for a moment about what she was thinking.

Newbury closed his eyes, lulled by the motion of the carriage. His wounds ached desperately. He hoped that the affair would be over soon so that he could spend a few days holed up in his lodgings, convalescing in his study. For now, though, he had work to do, and he knew that whatever evidence the three of them had at their disposal, Joseph Chapman was not going to willingly accept his fate.

The cab rolled on, its wheels clicking loudly on the cobbled road as they neared their destination.

The reception area of Chapman and Villiers Air Transportation Services was devoid of activity when Newbury burst in followed by both Bainbridge and Veronica. Chapman's clerk, Soames, sat in his usual position behind the mahogany desk, his hands forming a thin steeple on the desk before him. He glanced up nonchalantly as the door clicked shut behind the visitors.

"Ah, good day to you, Sir Maurice." The man's eyes flicked over the faces of three newcomers, like a lizard assessing its prey. "I am afraid that you will find Mr. Chapman is unavailable today. I hope you have not had a wasted journey." He offered Newbury a sickly smile.

Newbury turned to Veronica, inclining his head in the direction of the stairs. She grasped his meaning immediately and crossed the room in a few quick strides, mounting the bottom step and starting up in the direction of Chapman's office.

"Really, Sir Maurice!" Soames stood, placing his hands on the desk before him. "I assure you that Mr. Chapman is not here. There is no need to contest my word on the matter."

Newbury glared at him but said nothing.

A moment later, Veronica appeared at the top of the staircase and gave a curt shake of her head. Chapman obviously wasn't in his office. Still, Newbury couldn't find it in himself to trust the clerk.

"Where is he?"

Soames looked exasperated. "I honestly can't say. He arrived this morning as usual, took his tea in his office and then went about his business. I haven't seen him for at least two or three hours. He told me to keep his diary free for today."

Newbury clenched his fists, exasperated.

Bainbridge put his hand on Newbury's shoulder. "What now?"

Newbury shrugged. "Villiers, I suppose."

Soames sighed dramatically. "Gentlemen, without an appointment, I really must insist–" He stopped short when Bainbridge raised his cane, leaned over the desk and placed the tip of it against the man's chest, tapping it gently as if weighing how much force he would need to shatter the clerk's breastbone.

"Look here. If you have any sense about you at all, you will stop with your insipid drivel and make haste away from this place before you find yourself implicated in affairs you'd rather stay out of!"

The clerk looked appalled, then stepped back from the tip of the other man's cane, his legs bumping into his chair behind the desk. He opened and closed his mouth as if unsure how to respond to the threat. "I . . . oh . . ."

"Shut up, man! My name is Sir Charles Bainbridge, and I am a Chief Inspector with Scotland Yard. My colleagues and I intend to locate Mr. Villiers for an interview. You can either assist us by pointing us in the right direction, or you can choose to create a situation for yourself. I fear the latter option will not work out for the best."

Soames shrivelled away from the Chief Inspector, clearly terrified by the man. "I believe you'll find him in his workshop on the other side of the manufactory site, sir."

Bainbridge nodded and withdrew his cane. The other man sighed visibly with relief. "Good man. Now, heed my advice and take your leave. I assure you that you do not wish to be associated with this business any more than you already are. As it is we'll need to have you in for questioning." He turned to Veronica, who was crossing the room to join them once again. "Are we set?"

Veronica nodded.

"Then come on, Newbury. Lead the way."

Newbury shook his head in disbelief. "You never fail to impress me, Charles." He held his arm out for Veronica, fearing that, without her aid, his injuries may soon overcome him. She took it, and together they set off in the direction of the manufactory proper, following the route they had taken during their previous visit, when Chapman himself had been serving as their guide.

The hangar was suffused with the same biting chill as the city outside of the walls, but at least, Newbury considered, it was sheltered from the wind and the rain. He pulled his overcoat tighter around his shoulders and watched as the others did the same. Below, on the hangar floor, a new gondola was under construction, and the scene was nearly identical to the one Newbury and Veronica had witnessed a handful of days before, although the workmen in this instance were still assembling the basic shell rather than fitting the interior. Newbury leaned over the rail, searching the floor for signs of Chapman. He was nowhere to be seen.

Bainbridge approached the edge of the metal walkway, clasping the rail with his left hand. He surveyed the industrious scene below. "You're right, Newbury, it's a very impressive operation, indeed."

Newbury nodded, fighting back a shiver. He knew he'd lost a lot of blood, and consequently he was feeling the cold somewhat more than usual. The bandages and salves he had applied at Veronica's apartment had helped to stem the tide, however, and he was convinced that the worst of it was over. "Yes, this is where they assemble the passenger gondolas. The next hall is where they build the frames for the main body of the vessel." He waved his hand. "Come on. We have to pass that way to get to Villiers's workshop, anyway."

They made their way along the metal walkway and down onto the main floor of the hangar, where the workmen seemed to ignore their presence entirely, preferring to continue with the task of constructing the gondola. The place was filled with the loud din of industry, and Newbury wrinkled his nose at the smells of oil and scorched wood.

The next hangar was equally busy, with the skeleton of a vessel being hoisted into place by the pneumatic cranes that ran around the edges of the large room. Bainbridge looked up, clearly impressed, as Newbury led him past the foreman, who was bellowing instructions to the men working the cranes, trying to make himself heard over the noise. Sparks dripped from welding arcs high above them. They edged around the machinery and exited the main airship works, passing along the short corridor that led them out into the smaller room that housed the automaton production line.

The room was crowded and hot, the steam-driven presses firing noisily as they worked at incredible speeds, pistons pumping furiously as they pushed out the brass components that would be used in the assembly of the clockwork men. A swarthy-looking man in a pair of grey overalls looked up when they entered the room, downed his tools and passed the chest plate of the automaton unit he was working on to another, smaller man who had been assisting him.

He approached the group of three interlopers, wiping the

grime and oil from his face with the back of his sleeve. "Can I help you?"

Newbury stepped forward. "Yes. We have an appointment with Monsieur Villiers. The clerk on the desk in reception sent us through."

The man eyed them warily. "An appointment, you say? Can I see some identification?"

Bainbridge bustled forward impatiently. He pulled a leather wallet from his pocket and flicked it open, presenting it to the man. Inside was an official badge and papers from Scotland Yard, bearing the crest of Her Majesty. The man looked perplexed, as if he were unsure whether he should let the Chief Inspector and his companions through to see his employer, or why they should even be interested in speaking to the reclusive scientist. Eventually, though, he seemed to come to a decision. He stood aside and waved them at the door to Villiers's workshop with a shrug. "He's in there."

"Thank you." Newbury inclined his head in gratitude and approached the door to the workshop. He didn't bother to knock, instead reaching out for the handle and giving the door a gentle shove. It swung into the room to reveal the same cluttered workbench they had seen before, buried beneath a vast array of components, but no sign of the man they were looking for. Newbury ushered the others through, then closed the door behind him.

Bainbridge was frowning. "Where the devil are those damnable fellows hiding?" He cast around, trying to make sense of the cluttered workshop. He looked flustered, as if he thought that the two men had somehow managed to get away.

Newbury was just about to respond, when Veronica tugged on his arm. "Look!"

He followed her gaze to where she was pointing. The automaton in the corner—the demonstration model they had seen during their previous visit—was rising out of its chair and moving towards them, its left arm outstretched, its fingers opening and closing like the shining brass pincers of a crab. Its feet clacked on the tiled floor as it walked. Bainbridge, seeing the sinister-looking device making a beeline for him, grabbed his cane with both hands and gave the brass knob a sharp twist to the right. "Oh no, you don't!"

The shaft of the cane began immediately to unpack itself, and now that he had a better opportunity to observe the mechanism, Newbury was even more impressed. Small hinges unfurled at the top of the cane, causing thin brass rods to uncouple from the main shaft of the weapon so that they formed a kind of metal cage around the device. The central column began to spin rapidly, generating sparks of light within the cage itself. There was a sudden flicker, and then blue light arced along the length of the weapon, running back and forth along the conductor rod with a sharp electrical hum, from the handle all the way down to the tip of the shaft.

Bainbridge, raising the weapon before him like a rapier, wasted no time. He jabbed the point of the cane towards the chest of the shambling automaton, the sharp tip actually managing to pierce the brass plate and bury itself deep in the heart of the clockwork device. Pulsing electrical energy leapt from the cane into the delicate internal mechanisms of the automaton, which either overloaded the device or caused its delicate clockwork brain to seize. There was a grinding sound from deep within the machine, the stink of burning oil, and then the device gave a spasm and dropped to the floor, rendered useless by Bainbridge's attack.

Newbury stepped forward and leaned over the unit. The blue light that had flickered beneath the porthole in its chest had gone out, and its eyes had ceased spinning.

He looked up at Bainbridge, who was busy repacking his cane. "Good show, Charles!"

Bainbridge smiled. "Now you see why I always endeavour

to have the device by my side. One never knows when it may come in handy."

Veronica sidled up beside them. "When you two gentlemen are finished congratulating one another, I have something interesting to show you." She stepped away again, crossing the room to where the automaton had been sitting when they first entered.

Newbury couldn't help but emit a short chuckle when he saw the scowl on Bainbridge's face. He joined Veronica by the automaton's chair. "What is it?"

"Here." She ran her hands over the wall, demonstrating the thin outline of a door, hidden in the wall behind the automaton's chair. "I wonder if this is where we'll find our quarry."

Newbury put a hand on her shoulder. "You're to be congratulated, Miss Hobbes. I'll wager this is *exactly* where our quarry will be hiding. Stand back, won't you?" He waved the others back from the wall to give himself room to manoeuvre the chair out of the way. Then, returning to the wall, he ran his fingers around the edges of the door.

Bizarrely, it appeared to have been cut directly out of the wall, as if someone had simply chopped a section of the wall away and then reattached it on a pair of well-placed hinges. It was decorated in the same dark wood panelling as the rest of the room. Newbury admired the handiwork; it was an exceptional piece of engineering, and if Veronica had not noticed the thin outline of the door, it was likely they would have abandoned their search of the workshop and moved on.

He ran his hands over it again. There were no obvious switches, handles or triggers in the vicinity. Not knowing what else to do, Newbury gave the door a push and felt it give a little. He pressed more firmly, until there was a clicking sound, and then stood back as the door swung free towards him. He caught hold of it in his left hand as it came towards him, peering cautiously into the brightly lit chamber revealed on the other side.

Pierre Villiers stood beside a low mortuary slab in a room that had been fitted out like a hospital surgery. White tiles covered the floor, walls and ceiling, and bright gas-lamps burned with intensity in fixtures situated along each of the walls. A trestle table had been set up beside the slab, holding an array of tools, knives, lenses and other items of surgical equipment, and Villiers himself was stooped over the empty skull of an automaton, preparing to transfer a human brain into the cavity. The organ itself rested beside him on the slab, suspended in a large glass demijohn filled with a yellowish fluid that bubbled effervescently, as if it were connected to an air supply of some sort. The entire set-up reminded Newbury disconcertingly of the morgue: cold, clinical and filled with the overwhelming stench of death.

Villiers did not look up as Newbury, Bainbridge and Veronica filed into the room, their shoes clicking on the porcelain tiles. He was alone, with no sign of Chapman to be found. Newbury cleared his throat. After a moment, Villiers looked up with the briefest of glances, before turning away and continuing with his work. He talked as his fingers danced around inside the automaton's brass skull. "Sir Maurice. I did not expect to be seeing you again so soon."

Newbury laughed. "I think, Monsieur Villiers, that you did not expect to be seeing me again at all."

The Frenchman shrugged. "As you say."

"They're not quite so infallible as one has been led to believe, are they, these automata you've created?"

Villiers reached for one of the tools on the trestle table beside him and began cranking something noisily within the brass head. "No. But they are beautiful, though, are they not? A wonder of modern science? Do not tell me that you are not intrigued, Sir Maurice, that you are not at least a little bit interested in how I managed to make them work." He glanced up, looking at Newbury, although his eyes seemed to be focused on something else that the others could not see. He cleared his throat. "Here, let me show you what I am doing."

Bainbridge started forward, brandishing his cane, but Newbury put an arm out to stop him. "Just a few moments, Charles. It pays to know what we're dealing with."

Villiers laughed heartily. "I knew it!" He moved around the mortuary table, turning the automaton's head towards Newbury, so that the Crown investigator could see clearly inside the empty skull. There was a short brass spike at the base of the cavity, with four exceptionally fine filaments trailing out from a separate point just below the tip of the spike itself. Villiers put his hand inside the cavity. When he spoke, his voice was full of arrogance and pomp. "The human organ is placed in this cavity, here, lowered gently onto the brass spike to hold it firmly in place. The wires are then threaded precisely through the cortex until they engage with the sensitive response centres in the left and right hemi-spheres of the brain. Electrical stimuli, generated by the movement of the automaton device itself, are then fed back and forth along these wires to create a simple neural interface that enables the organ to receive input from the world outside of the machine's casing." He clacked his tongue against his teeth. "I call this my 'affinity bridge,' the device by which my creations may learn to interact with the external world." He grinned, as if satisfied that his audience was giving him his due attention. "Once it is working we pack the rest of the cavity with a preserving jelly to ensure the organ does not degenerate or become damaged if the device is required to make any sharp movements." He paused, drumming his hand on the table before reaching for the large glass jar that held the harvested brain. He slid it across the table-top so they could see. Newbury heard Veronica swallow.

"But what about the original personality, the person whose brain you have stolen? Doesn't that present itself once the organ is connected to this 'affinity bridge'?"

Villiers practically scoffed. "We bypass the original personality, of course! Consciousness is simply a by-product of the human organism. It is not necessary for life to be self-aware. It is certainly not necessary for an automaton to be self-aware. In truth, in attaching a human brain to the affinity bridge, I am simply engaging the neural structure of the organ, making use of the existing nervous system and the brain's inherent processing functions. It is a much cheaper and less time-consuming option than building a new component to do the same job, although, as you've seen, the latter is indeed possible." He smiled. "At its most basic level, Sir Maurice, the human being is essentially a machine."

Newbury nodded, appalled by Villiers's arrogance and yet somehow still intrigued enough to want understand the elaborate details of the process the man had developed: the melding of man and machine. "So what went wrong?"

Villiers glowered at him. "Nothing! My device functions perfectly."

Bainbridge, impatient and keen to draw the conversation to a close, decided to speak up at that point. "Poppycock! What about the airship crash, and all these reports we've had of your machines going haywire?"

"The human organs!" Villiers sounded enraged. "Joseph brought me faulty organs." He banged his fist on the mortuary slab. "In the early days, I had no mind to enquire where Joseph was obtaining the human brains that I needed for my work. Frankly, I had no reason to care. At least not until some toffee-nosed art dealer began claiming his machine had been exhibiting dangerous and unruly behaviour. I had the machine brought here for testing, and when I opened up the skull cavity, I found the organ riddled with signs of the revenant plague. I asked Joseph where he'd laid his hands on the organs, and that's when he told me he'd engaged a third party to retrieve them from the Whitechapel slums. Of course, by that time, the plague had already begun to spread far and wide, and we had no way of telling which of the devices might already have been affected. We had no choice but to continue."

Veronica spoke softly. Her voice sounded remarkably calm. "So that's why *The Lady Armitage* went down?"

Villiers nodded. "Yes. Joseph had the pilot unit removed from the wreckage before the police arrived. The device was returned to my workshop. The casing was badly damaged by the flames, but there was no mistaking the signs. The brain had practically been reduced to a sponge inside of the brass skull, all malformed and rotten with plague."

Newbury glanced at Bainbridge before stepping forward towards Villiers. "If the technology had developed in different circumstances, without the need to resort to murder, you would be heralded as a genius, Monsieur Villiers. I'm ashamed to say that the path you have taken in this instance, however, has reduced you to nothing but a common criminal." Newbury put his hand on the automaton's head to hold it still. "You do understand that you're going to have to come with us?"

Villiers nodded slowly. "May I just—?"

There was a terrifying *bang*.

The sound seemed to reverberate around the entire room. Villiers slumped to the floor, blood streaming from a bullet hole in his forehead, just above his right eye. The white tiles on the wall behind him were spattered with a bright spray of blood and brain matter. Veronica screamed. Newbury spun around on his heel to see Chapman framed in the doorway, clutching a revolver that he turned to point directly at Newbury's face. Smoke curled in lazy curlicues from the end of the discharged barrel.

"Never could keep his mouth shut, the arrogant bastard." Chapman flicked his hair away from his face, eyeing the three of them carefully. Veronica shifted slightly, and Chapman waved the gun at her. "Not a single move, Miss Hobbes, or your beloved Newbury gets a bullet in the head, just like poor old Pierre." These last few words were delivered with a nasal sneer. He took them all in with a sweep of the barrel. "Now we're going to do things my way." He indicated with his head. "Newbury. Over there, with the girl."

Newbury eased himself around to stand beside Veronica. "Whatever happens today, Chapman, this is going to follow you. You can't keep running forever."

Chapman shook his head. "Oh, please. Don't patronise me, Newbury. You really should know better than that." He turned to Bainbridge. "You. Old man. Your turn next. Get over there and join them in the corner." Bainbridge turned slowly towards the industrialist. He made a cautious step towards Veronica and Newbury, then altered his momentum at the last moment, whipping up and out with his cane and connecting hard with Chapman's outstretched wrist.

There followed a brief moment of chaos when, for Newbury, the world seemed to suddenly stop. It was as if the whole scene had been cast into silence. The revolver went off, sending a bullet ricocheting off the tiled walls and causing Newbury and Veronica to duck involuntarily to avoid being hit. Chapman let out a howl of pain and clutched at his wrist, letting the revolver fall to the floor so that it skittered across the tiles towards Villiers's corpse. Bainbridge readied himself to strike another blow.

Then reality came crashing back in, and Chapman, reacting faster than the others, turned and ducked out of the doorway, leaping over the skeletal frame of the ruined automaton and fleeing the workshop as quickly as his legs would carry him. Bainbridge stooped to retrieve his revolver.

Newbury and Veronica looked at one another, and then, making up their minds at exactly the same moment, they gave chase, each of them sprinting out of the door in pursuit of the fleeing criminal. Bainbridge was quick to follow, hefting the gun in his right hand.

Behind them, the corpse of Pierre Villiers stared unseeing through the open door, his jaw slack with death, blood pooling around the exit wound at the back of his splintered skull.

CHAPTER 27

Newbury was the first out of the door. He charged after Chapman, throwing himself around the edge of Villiers's workbench and out into the main automaton production facility. The presses were pounding noisily, pistons firing in quick succession and clouds of steam hissing into the air, obscuring large swaths of the factory floor from view. It was obvious the men working the machines had not heard the gunshot over the racket of the production line, and none of them showed any signs of having noticed Chapman racing through the facility, either. If Newbury didn't find him quickly, the industrialist would be able to lose himself in the factory with ease.

Glancing frantically from side to side, Newbury finally caught sight of the man darting out through a side door in the far wall, which led to the river outside. He followed swiftly behind Chapman, his entire body protesting at the strain as he dodged around the machines, nearly slamming into a man who was lifting a partially assembled automaton frame from a conveyor belt. The worker cried out as he ducked out of the way, sending an array of components clattering to the floor. Newbury kept chasing Chapman towards the exit on the other side of the factory floor.

The door was still swinging to and fro as Newbury burst through, skidding to a halt on the other side just in time to prevent himself from careening forward into the river. He planted his feet in the muddy bank. The water churned furiously a few feet from where he had come to a stop. Outlet pipes jutted rudely from the factory wall, spewing brown sludge into the river.

The weather had deteriorated even further since their arrival at the manufactory, and rain lashed at Newbury's face in the driving wind. He cupped his hand to his eyes, trying to work out what had happened to Chapman. Surely he couldn't have thrown himself into the river? There was no sign of the man in the water, or of any boat that he may have kept berthed here for such an occasion. Of course, if Chapman *had* gone in, he might already have drowned, given the fierce weather.

There was a scuffing sound from behind him. Newbury felt his hackles rising. He spun around to see Veronica coming out of the factory through the door he had just used himself. He offered her a slight shrug, but the gesture was lost as he hunched against the wind and the rain. He glanced along the length of the building, trying to work out where the other man had managed to flee. It was then that he noticed a cast-iron ladder had been bolted to the wall, just to the left of the exit, beside one of the main outlet pipes. He looked up, turning his face towards the grey sky as he tried to make out where it led. The ladder ran all the way up to the top of the building, disappearing from view where it curved over the lip of the factory roof.

Joseph Chapman was edging his way up the wet rungs, pulling himself up the metal frame towards the roof, where, Newbury realised, an array of newly built airships awaited him. Clearly that was how Chapman intended to effect his escape. He was already about halfway towards his salvation. The wind was blowing him awkwardly from side to side as he climbed, his hands slipping on the slick rungs, but despite the obvious danger Newbury knew that he couldn't risk letting the man get away. If he made it to one of the airships, he could be halfway to the Continent within a couple of hours. It wouldn't take much for him to lose himself from there, disappearing into one of the darker corners of the Empire or, worse, to Asia and beyond.

Newbury turned to Veronica, trying to make himself heard over the rattling wind. "Get back inside. Wait for me in there." He pointed towards the door, where Bainbridge was standing, framed like a silhouette in the doorway. Then, without waiting to hear or acknowledge her response, he leapt up onto the bottom rung of the ladder and began to climb.

The going was treacherous. The wind dragged at him as if it were trying its very best to prise him free of the ladder. The rain had caused the metal rungs to become wet and slick, and the downpour continued to needle at his face, stinging his eyes and making it difficult to see. Within minutes, his clothes had soaked through, and he shivered as he hauled himself upwards, clattering after Chapman on the ladder as fast as his damaged, aching body would carry him. The side of the factory was terribly exposed, and Newbury tried not to think what would become of him if the wind did manage to throw him from the ladder. In all likelihood, he would be dashed on the ground below, or else blown out into the river and a watery grave.

It was clear from the way in which Chapman had slowed that he was tiring as he approached the top of the building. Trying to ignore the burning pain in both shoulders, Newbury pressed on. He was closing on the other man, slowly but surely. He knew he couldn't allow his ailing body to slow him now.

He watched through squinting eyes as the industrialist reached the lip of the roof and threw himself bodily over the top of the ladder, disappearing temporarily from view. A moment later Newbury did the same, hauling himself over the top of the ladder, swinging his legs around underneath him and landing heavily on his rear atop the tiled roof of the factory. He gasped for breath. The wind was howling amongst the chimney stacks, and a confusing web of ropes strained against the pull of the bobbing airships, which filled the sky overhead like a blanket of glittering clouds. He searched the rooftop for a sign of Chapman. About thirty feet away, the industrialist, soaked to the bone, his long hair now lank and slicked to his face, had just finished loosening the tether on one of the airships, and was busy climbing aboard. Newbury watched him mount the short flight of wooden steps beside the iron berthing ring and step across to the gondola, watching his footing as the airship listed dangerously from side to side in the wind.

Newbury was unsure whether Chapman had even realised that he had been followed this far; he appeared to have an almost casual, nonchalant air about him. Newbury hoped that it would be this that would prove to be his undoing, allowing the Crown investigator to gain the element of surprise.

Newbury got to his feet and charged after the other man. He scrambled up the wooden steps and flung himself towards the open door of the gondola, just as the vessel banked awkwardly to the left, buffeted by a wild gust of wind. He slammed into the side of the vessel, his hands questing frantically for purchase, one of them catching hold of the threshold at the base of the door, the other slipping dangerously free of the wet doorframe. The airship began to drift away from its berth, pitching and groaning as it rocked back and forth in the harsh wind.

Newbury dangled from the doorframe, buffeted by the wind as he tried desperately not to fall. He thought he heard the sounds of someone shouting from below, but the driving rain and his precarious position meant he had no time to pay heed to whatever was going on down there on the rooftop.

With a huge effort he swung out against the harsh wind, the fingers of his free hand catching hold of the doorframe. He clawed to find a more substantial grip. His fingers caught on something firm and loose; the wooden rung of a rope ladder. He tugged on it, gasping in relief as it came free from its housing just inside the door. He pulled it near, allowing the ladder to unfurl, flapping away beneath him as the airship drifted across the rooftop, narrowly missing another large vessel that was berthed beside it. He fought to get his feet on one of the rungs. Rain thrashed over his back and he cried out as more of the stitches in his abdomen tore free with the strain. His shoulder burned.

Fighting against the pain and fearing he might blow free at any moment, Newbury jammed his feet into the rope ladder and hauled himself up, rolling into the open door and collapsing onto his back, just as the vessel banked again. He was soaked to the skin, his clothes wet through, and blood was running freely from any number of wounds that had torn open during the climb.

The door was still open behind him, the rope ladder dangling free over the rooftop. Rain blew in on every gust, spattering the inside of the foyer with water. Chapman was nowhere to be seen.

Panting for breath and grimacing with the strain, Newbury climbed to his feet, catching hold of a sideboard that had been anchored to the deck just inside the foyer of the vessel. He found his footing as the airship righted itself once again. He brushed water away from his eyes. The rain drummed noisily against the wooden panels of the gondola.

Suddenly, the airship bucked wildly as the engines kicked in with a high-pitched whine. Newbury grasped hold of the sideboard to stop himself from falling, drawing ragged breaths as he held himself steady. The vessel powered out over the river, away from the manufactory.

Tired, hurt and unsure whether he had enough energy left in him for the fight, Newbury turned and set off down the passageway, towards the cockpit, Chapman and–he hoped–the end of the affair.

CHAPTER 28

The door to the cockpit was shut when Newbury finally made his way along the passageway to confront Chapman. The engines hummed noisily and the vessel had righted itself, even though it still shuddered disconcertingly with the to-and-fro of the wind. Now it was climbing in altitude, rising high above the factory and the city below.

Newbury was near exhaustion and anxious to get Chapman into custody. He knew the man had lost his firearm back at the factory, and suspected that he would not have hidden a replacement aboard a brand new airship, a vessel that could have only been completed by his factory a handful of days before this, its maiden voyage. Nevertheless, it was a gamble. Newbury knew that he was far from his physical peak, and whilst Chapman was a dilettante and a fop, he was also unscrupulous and cunning. Newbury only hoped that he still had surprise on his side. Readying himself, he reached out, took the door handle, and gave it a sharp twist. He stepped back and allowed the door to swing open towards him. It clattered against the wall of the passage.

Chapman sat at the controls inside the small cockpit, his hands dancing over the vast array of levers, buttons and cranks that adorned the panels before him. Above, dials were set into a polished wooden dashboard, showing altitude, speed and fuel levels. Beyond that was the viewing port: a series of large reinforced glass windows that offered a vast panoramic view of the city below, a kind of surreal bird's-eye perspective of the landscape that Newbury had never been granted before. The Thames wound away into the distance, whilst nearby the factories and industrial buildings of Battersea pumped ribbons of steam into the air. Farther afield, the City of Westminster was like a jewel amongst the rows of closely built houses: proud buildings and public parks, museums and parliament. The city glittered in all its majesty, whilst all the while, the storm clouds formed a dark, brooding vault across the sky.

"Pretty, isn't it, Sir Maurice?" Chapman laughed gently underneath his breath as he spoke. "I often like to come up here—when the weather is better, admittedly—to take in the view of the city. London really is an amazing place to call home. The hub of the modern world. I shall be sorry to have to leave."

Newbury stood in the doorway. "Why don't you take the ship down, Chapman? There's nowhere left to flee. If you come quietly now, we can make it easier on you."

Chapman laughed, louder this time, and shook his head. He turned in his seat to eye Newbury. "You know it never works like that, Newbury. Villiers was a fool, for all his genius. He would have walked willingly to the noose. Not me."

Newbury clenched his fist by his side, knowing well what was likely to come next. "Then I'm afraid we find ourselves at an impasse." He crept forward, ready to make a move.

Chapman got to his feet, careful to keep his pilot's chair safely between the two of them. He smiled slyly. "Indeed we do." He lashed out as he spoke, sending his fist flying towards Newbury's face. Newbury ducked quickly out of the way, feeling the fist brush his cheek, ever-so-narrowly missing its target. He thrashed back at the other man, connecting hard with his sternum and causing him to stagger backwards, banging against the control panel. It wasn't a graceful move, but it was certainly functional.

Chapman shook his head, disorientated, and then quickly regained his composure. He straightened himself and stepped away from the controls. The airship juddered, and both men realised at the same time that Chapman's fall had in some way knocked the controls out of line. Chapman glanced at the panel, and Newbury took the opportunity to pounce, coming at him hard, his fist slamming brutally into Chapman's abdomen. Chapman buckled, gasping, but sent a blow of his own into Newbury's gut as he doubled over.

Newbury fell back against the doorframe, jarring his shoulder painfully. He wrenched himself about to face Chapman, and the sharp movement finally proved too much for the Fixer's handiwork. He felt his stitches giving out and blood began to gush from the long wound in his side. His vision swam, and the world was momentarily limned in blackness. He sank to the floor, clutching his abdomen in agony.

It took Chapman only a moment to realise what had happened, and he swept in on Newbury, taking full advantage of the other man's wretched condition. He struck the Crown investigator with a brutal backhand across the face, sending him sprawling to the floor, his cheek smarting from the impact. Newbury coughed blood onto the floorboards in a sickly stream. Chapman laughed. He drove a booted foot hard into Newbury's stomach, taking the wind out of him and leaving him gasping in pain and shock. Newbury tried to roll away, to find a means to get himself upright again, but the passageway was too tight, and his body protested. He simply couldn't muster the energy to move, no matter how much his mind screamed at his legs and arms to react. He was trapped in the narrow passage, with nowhere left to escape the other man's assault.

Chapman circled him, taking the opportunity to gloat. He stepped over Newbury's prone form, turning him over with his boot like some common animal found dead by the roadside. He spat at Newbury, and then set about pummelling him with a series of vicious kicks, punctuating his words with powerful outbursts of violence. "What you don't seem to understand, Newbury, is that the sort of people who would benefit from the work Villiers and I were doing couldn't give a hoot about the loss of a few peasant lives, especially if it ends up making their own lives more comfortable. There'll be no public outcry. There'll be no noose. Her Majesty herself will probably give me a medal for my services to the Empire!"

Newbury groaned, but couldn't find enough of a pause in the beating to emit a response. He brought his knees up to his chest in an effort to protect himself from the constant rain of blows. His side felt warm with spilling blood.

"I suppose I'd better throw you—"

There was a dull, wet thud, and then the kicking ceased. Newbury peeled open his eyes to see Chapman collapse to the floor. The industrialist banged his head against the wall as he fell, crumpling to a pile beside Newbury on the floorboards. Newbury looked up through one bruised eyelid.

Veronica stood in the passageway, a large copper fire extinguisher clutched in her hands. She must have made it onto the rope ladder before the airship drifted out over the river. She looked bedraggled, her dress torn and wet, her hair flung back messily over one shoulder. To Newbury, however, she looked like a vision of Heaven itself.

"Thank you." His voice was a wet, warbling croak. He coughed and vomited more blood onto the floor beside him.

"Don't thank me, Maurice. Just get up and help me fly this thing. If you hadn't realised, we're tumbling out of the sky like a dead weight. If we can't find a way to land the ship, all of this will have been in vain anyway." She dropped the fire extinguisher noisily to the floor. Newbury groaned and put his hand against the wall in an effort to raise himself up. His hand slipped, leaving a dark smear of blood across its pristine white surface.

"I'm going to need a little help getting up."

Veronica looked pained, but her resolve was steely. She bent low over Chapman's unconscious body and grasped hold of Newbury's hands. Placing her feet against the far wall, she heaved him up into a sitting position. From there he was able to use the doorframe as leverage to pull himself upright. He staggered to the controls, unsteady on his feet.

Veronica followed behind him. "Where do we start?"

"I have no idea." He slumped into the chair and grabbed hold of two levers that he hoped controlled the steering paddles on the underside of the vessel. He looked out through the viewing port. His vision swam. The city was coming up fast to meet them. They were set into a dangerous spiral, blown from side to side by the sharp winds, and he wondered if he was already too late to make a difference. The best option he could see at this stage was to try to steer the vessel towards the dark smear of the Thames. At least that way they'd be able to ditch it in the water without turning the whole ship into a blazing inferno. At least he hoped that would be the case. He'd never even *been* on an airship before, let alone tried to land one in a river.

Driven on by the image of the burnt cadavers he had seen in the wreck of *The Lady Armitage,* Newbury tugged hard on the levers, throwing his weight behind them as he attempted to right the vessel from its dangerous collision course. The engines coughed with the strain and the dials on the dashboard were all flickering in the red. If the engines were to get too hot, they would run the risk of explosion, which in turn would ignite the balloon of hydrogen above them. He glanced out of the viewing port to see the city screaming towards them.

He knew the engines would be no good to them now anyway. He reached over and flicked the switch on his right, cutting the power. Immediately, the whine from below them ceased.

Veronica rushed forward. "What are you doing?"

"Trust me." He stood, leaning as hard as he could on the steering levers. Through the viewing port he could see the nose of the vessel edging up against the harsh wind, but his ministrations were having little effect on the terrifying rate of their descent. He hoped beyond hope that the water would help to cushion the blow.

The airship dived into the Thames, spinning onto its side as it came down, first glancing off the surface like a skipping stone and then dipping down into the water, sending a vast wave ahead of itself as it slowed to a halt. The balloon bobbed on the surface of the river, whilst the gondola, not designed with any buoyancy in mind, quickly began to take on water, pulling slowly towards the bottom of the river.

Newbury, powering on through adrenaline alone, scrambled up from the controls, frantically searching to ensure Veronica was unhurt. He found her draped over the back of the pilot's chair, where she'd braced herself during the landing. He put a hand to her cheek, tenderly. "Come on. I hope you can swim?"

She nodded. "Help me with Chapman."

Newbury looked down at the industrialist, who was still unconscious, even with the stirrings of river water beginning to lap at his upturned face. He nodded. "If we must."

Groaning, he reached down and hooked an arm under Chapman's shoulder. Veronica did the same, and together they hauled him towards the exit. The passageway was taking on water more quickly than either of them could have imagined, and by the time they reached the gondola's main exit they found it was easier to swim, dragging Chapman along behind them. Thankfully, the door had buckled and sprung open during the landing, so it was a simple matter to navigate out of it one at a time, passing Chapman through between them. The river water was ice cold, and with the loss of blood, Newbury was beginning to feel faint, his muscles starting to seize up. He kicked furiously, resolved that he wasn't going to fail Veronica now, not when they were so close to safety.

The wind and rain were still pounding when he eventually got free of the airship. Linking arms with Veronica to form a platform for Chapman, they made for the riverbank as quickly as they could. It was only a matter of minutes before Veronica was able to haul Chapman out onto the slick mud of the bank. Newbury, barely conscious, bobbed for a moment in the ice cold water, his body finally giving up on him. He felt the blackness closing in. His head sank beneath the surface. The cold seemed to penetrate him to the core.

Then, suddenly, he was on his back, and Veronica was leaning over him, checking he was still breathing. She dragged him further up the bank, towards safety. The rain still pounded his face, the mud wet and clinging beneath his head. Stars were dancing before his eyes, and in the distance, out in the river, he could see the outline of the airship, drifting with the current and blown about by the wind. He heard the sound of hurried footsteps behind him. He didn't bother to look round.

"We made it. We made it Maurice!" She put her hand on his chest and collapsed next to him on the riverbank. Her breath was shallow. "Stay with me now. The police are on their way."

Everything went black.

CHAPTER 29

Veronica's feet crunched on the gravel as she strolled slowly up the path towards the asylum. The inclement weather had finally broken during the night, the wind and rain receding to leave behind a cold, dry morning that, Veronica considered, was far more typical of the season than the storm weather of the previous two days. She breathed in the fresh air, filling her lungs. It was crisp and filled with the promise of winter. Unconsciously, as if affected by the thought of the changing seasons, she pulled the collar of her thick overcoat up around her throat to stave off the chill. Her cheeks felt pinched with the cold.

Up ahead, Veronica could see that many of the asylum's patients were out taking their exercise on the airing courts, small groups of them clustered around the grounds, sheltering beneath the spindly autumnal trees or else strolling round in concentric circles like caged animals searching for a means of escape. The nurses watched with beady eyes and tired expressions from their usual perch beneath the sheltered stone archway.

Veronica searched the scene as she walked, looking for signs of Amelia. Her sister was nowhere to be seen. She jammed her hands into her coat pockets and approached the main building. As she brushed past the two nurses on guard duty, Veronica noticed a young man sitting on a wooden bench beside the asylum wall. He looked uncomfortable in his rough woollen clothes, and his face was ruddy with the cold. He was unshaven and unkempt–haggard, even–but for some reason he looked familiar to Veronica. She racked her brain but found she was unable to immediately place him. Perhaps it was just a case of over-familiarity; she may have seen him during a previous visit to the asylum and the sight of him had lodged itself somewhere in the back of her mind.

The man turned to look at her as she strolled past the end of his bench, and despite herself Veronica felt struck by the haunted look in his eyes. He smiled unconvincingly when he saw her looking, and then turned away, contemplating the gravel path as if it held all the secrets of the universe. Feeling a slight sense of unease, Veronica continued on her way, stopping once to glance over her shoulder at the young man. She had the vague sense that, somehow, there was more to him than immediately met the eye. Unsure what else to do, she tried to shake off the notion. She made her way under the archway, through the small courtyard on the other side, and entered the asylum through the main door, which the nurse on the door unbolted for her with a wary glance.

Once inside, she approached the reception desk a few feet to one side of the entrance. The nurse behind the desk looked cold in her thin uniform, and she shivered noticeably when Veronica came through the door, bringing with her a cold draft. Veronica cleared her throat. "I'm here to see my sister, Amelia Hobbes."

The nurse smiled. "I'm afraid visiting hours have finished for the day. You may have noticed that the patients are currently engaged in their daily round of exercise outside."

Veronica nodded. "Indeed. Although I fear my sister was not to be found in the grounds. I wonder–" She paused, trying on her best conspiratorial expression. "–could you bend the rules just a little? I'm very anxious to ensure my sister is in good health."

The nurse was about to answer when Veronica heard footsteps behind her, and looked round to see Dr. Mason approaching along the hallway.

He smiled warmly as he drew up beside Veronica. "It's alright, Nurse Willis, I think on this occasion we can make an exception." He indicated for Veronica to walk with him, and they set off together along the corridor, their heels clicking loudly on the hard, white tiles.

"Thank you, Dr. Mason. It's just that it's been a few days since my last visit, and I'm anxious to ensure my sister is well."

The doctor offered Veronica a grave look. "I'm afraid you'll find your sister in ill health, Miss Hobbes. The frequency of her episodes has increased markedly over the course of the last few days, with the most recent occurring just over an hour ago. Try not to show your concern when you see her. She's looking very gaunt and tired." They marched along the corridor for a moment, passing a number of empty wards and rooms on either side.

Veronica nodded. "Very well. I appreciate you taking the time to talk with me, Dr. Mason."

The doctor smiled. "I want only what is best for your sister, Miss Hobbes, contrary to what you may have believed about my methods in the past." He came to a halt before a door, which led off into a side room. It was painted a drab grey and had a small window set into it at about head height.

Veronica peered inside. Amelia was sitting in a wheelchair in the small room, sunlight streaming in through the window. Beside her, a nurse sat in a folding chair, reading a book. Amelia's face was turned away from the door, but Veronica could see immediately that her skin was a deathly white.

Dr. Mason pushed the door open and ushered Veronica

through. Amelia looked up to see who had entered and the nurse trailed off her reading, smiling at the sight of the visitors. Amelia's face lit up when she saw Veronica.

"Veronica! How lovely." She looked up at Dr. Mason. Veronica tried to hide her dismay at the sight of her sister. "May we sit and talk, Dr. Mason?"

The doctor nodded. "Indeed. I believe some time with your sister will do you well, Amelia." He beckoned to the nurse. "I shall return in a little while, and then it will be time for your rest." He glanced at Veronica, and then turned away, holding the door open for the nurse to leave before him. The door swung shut behind them.

Veronica glanced around the room. The furnishings were sparse, but not unpleasant. It was obviously some sort of day-room, a place for patients to come when they weren't well enough to join the others on the airing courts outside. The very fact that Amelia was here, instead of enjoying the fresh air, did not bode well for her overall health. Veronica looked at the spine of the book that the nurse had placed on the coffee table. "Jane Austen, eh? I'd have thought the library here would be full of far more turgid fare than that!"

Amelia smiled. "Oh come here and give me a hug, sister! It's so good to see you."

Veronica did as she was bade, taking her sister gently in her arms and kissing her lightly on the cheek. She cupped Amelia's face in her palms for a moment, looking her up and down, and then set about rearranging the blanket on her knees.

Amelia slapped her away. "I'm not an invalid, Veronica!" She smiled. "At least, not yet."

Veronica lowered herself into the chair beside her sister. "Oh, Amelia, what am I to do with you?"

Amelia shrugged. "I had thought I might be getting out of this dreadful place, but now I'm not so sure. The episodes have been getting more and more frequent, and Dr. Mason is clearly concerned for my health." She laughed. "But then I suppose he's told you all of that already, hasn't he?"

Veronica nodded. She didn't know what else to say. She searched Amelia's face for a moment. "You were right, you know."

"What about?"

"About everything." Veronica sighed. "Everything you saw in your visions. It all came to pass. The airship crash. The automata. 'It's all in their heads,' you said to me, over and over again. 'It's all in their heads.'" She shrugged. "It was, too."

Amelia looked puzzled. "What *are* you going on about?"

"Your visions, of course. Don't you remember?"

Amelia shook her head. She gazed at the floor. "We've talked about this before. I don't remember most of what I see during my seizures." She folded her hands on her knees, fidgeting awkwardly with her fingers. "I'm sorry."

Veronica shook her head. "Don't be." She paused, her brow furrowed. "I've got to help you somehow, Amelia. I'm going to talk to Sir Maurice, see if we can't find a better way to keep you well. There must be something we can do."

Amelia looked up. "How is Sir Maurice? After your last visit I was concerned. . . ."

Veronica smiled. "He's fine. Well—he's recovering. He had quite an ordeal, if truth be told. We all did." Unconsciously Veronica turned her arm over on her lap and rubbed at her sore wrist. Amelia looked appalled.

"Veronica! Look at those bruises. Are you quite well? What the devil have you been up to?"

Veronica quickly covered her arm in the folds of her dress. "It's nothing. I'm well enough, thanks to Sir Maurice, anyway. He saved my life."

Amelia grinned. "Quite the hero, isn't he? Do tell."

Veronica blushed. "That's enough of that. Now, tell me, are you getting enough to eat? You're still so painfully thin."

"Stop avoiding the subject, you terrible sister! You can't

tease me like this! You know it's bad for my constitution."
Amelia beamed.

"Then what will I have to tell you about on my next visit? At least this way, I can offer you something to look forward to."

Amelia laughed. "I suppose that's true, at least." She put her hand on Veronica's arm. "You must reassure me that you're looking after yourself out there, though. It wouldn't do for our parents to end up with *two* sick daughters, now would it?"

Veronica sighed. "All is well, Amelia. If you must know, I've had rather a thrilling adventure. And yes, you're right. Sir Maurice *is* rather a hero, after all." She laughed and looked out of the window, watching the trees blowing back and forth languorously in the breeze. "I'm not sure yet how I'll be able to go back to my desk at the museum after the excitement of the last few days. It all feels a little mundane at the moment."

Amelia smiled knowingly. "Oh, I suspect there's more adventure to come, Veronica. You always were the headstrong one. I can't imagine you'll be behind that desk for long."

Veronica sighed. The moment stretched into silence. She was just about to speak again when there was a gentle rap at the door, and both of them looked up to see Dr. Mason appear in the opening. "Ladies, I'm afraid it's time Amelia took a rest. It pains me to hurry you, but I think it best we get her settled before the other patients return from their exercise."

Veronica smiled at Amelia sadly and then leaned over and kissed her tenderly on the cheek. She rose to her feet. "Take care, sister. I'll return in a few days to see how you're getting along."

Amelia nodded. "Until then."

Dr. Mason held the door open for Veronica as she left the day-room without looking back, the stirrings of tears in the corners of her eyes.

* * *

The young man was still lounging idly on the wooden bench when Veronica stepped out of the asylum. She tried again to place him, but somehow his identity eluded her. She was convinced that she'd seen him before, in a different context. She took a few steps along the gravel path, and then, deciding that she'd be unable to let it rest, she turned back and accosted one of the nurses, who seemed both bemused by Veronica's sudden appearance and annoyed at having her train of thought interrupted whilst gossiping with one of her colleagues.

"Excuse me, nurse. Can you tell me: Who is that man?" She spoke in hushed tones so as not to let him overhear her words, indicating him with a wave of her hand.

The nurse looked over her shoulder and shrugged. "I have no idea, ma'am. None of us do. He was brought in last night after lights-out, and the night nurse was told to find him temporary accommodation. He was in a terrible state. His clothes were covered in blood and the wounds on his arms were severe. He looked like he'd been savaged by an animal. Not for the first time, either, judging by the scars we found when we washed him down." She shrugged. "We cleaned him up and gave him a bed for the night, is all. It was one of the locals who found him, shivering in the gutter by the side of the road. They brought him in last night, figuring he wasn't a drunk and may have been a patient who had somehow found his way out of the asylum. Seems he can't remember his name or any of his family connections. Poor sod. He'll be collected and taken to the public sanatorium later this afternoon." She searched Veronica's face for an answer. "Why do you ask?"

Veronica frowned. "For some reason he just looks . . . Oh God!" She stared at the man over the nurse's shoulder, watching him as he gazed up at the sky, lost in a world of his own devising. Suddenly something seemed to click in her head. "Oh God! Jack! Jack Coulthard!" She ran towards him, realisation dawning behind her eyes. "You're Jack Coulthard!"

The man turned to look at her, his eyes searching; confused and unsure how to take this outburst from a strange woman he had no idea whether he should know. "I am?"

"I believe so, yes." She grinned, almost disbelieving the coincidence. "Your sister showed me your photograph. She's waiting for you to come home."

The nurse rushed over to Veronica. "You're saying that you know this man?"

"I know his sister, yes. She's been searching for him for a week. She's beside herself with concern." Veronica turned to face the nurse, who was looking as bemused as the patient. "Quickly, call for a cab immediately. We have to send for her now."

The nurse nodded and disappeared under the archway to fetch assistance, her feet crunching noisily on the loose stones.

Veronica took a seat beside the young man on the bench, almost bursting with excitement. "Oh, Jack, your sister is going to be so delighted to discover you're alive."

The man returned her gaze, a bright smile lighting up his face. He looked lost, but hopeful.

Nearby, the other patients continued to circle the airing courts, indifferent to the fact that their newest arrival would, in just a matter of hours, finally be reunited with his loved ones.

CHAPTER 30

Newbury leaned heavily on the mantelpiece and took a long draw on his pipe, watching the smoke curl in lazy circles in the still air of his Chelsea living-room. He was wearing a long blue dressing gown and slippers, and was warming himself by the raging fire that Mrs. Bradshaw had built up for him earlier that evening. Across the room, Bainbridge sat easily in one of the Chesterfields, his cane propped by the door, a brandy clutched firmly in one hand, a cigar in the other. He observed Newbury through a pungent wreath of smoke.

Newbury was tapping his foot impatiently, unable to allow himself to relax. He clearly wasn't taking well to his period of convalescence.

Bainbridge sucked on the end of his cigar. "So, truthfully, how are you man? You seem irritable."

Newbury laughed. "No, not irritable, Charles. Just anxious to get out of these rooms! I feel like I've been trapped in here for weeks, pacing backwards and forwards, waiting for something new to come along that I can sink my teeth into. My wounds are healing in a satisfactory fashion, and with any luck, I'll be fighting fit again in no time. I need something new to engage my mind. I fear I'll be climbing the walls before long if something doesn't come along soon."

Bainbridge shook his head. "Newbury, you astound me! I'd have thought after your experiences this last week you'd be eager to get some rest. I know I am!"

Newbury chuckled. "You know me, Charles. I never have been able to stand still for long." He glanced at the end of his pipe, a frustrated look on his face, and then tapped out the spent tobacco on the mantelpiece, banging the vessel repeatedly against the palm of his left hand. He moved stiffly across the room, still wincing with the movement, and lowered himself into the armchair opposite Bainbridge. He searched out his leather tobacco pouch from amongst the debris on the coffee table, and began the process of refilling his bowl. "So tell me, Charles, what of Joseph Chapman?"

Bainbridge took a swig of his brandy, shuddering as the alcohol sent tickling fingers of warmth into his belly. He looked grave. "Chapman's for the noose, and he knows it. His crimes were some of the most severe and inhumane I've yet encountered in my career, and in this city, that's certainly saying something. What galls me, though, is the man's consistently pompous attitude. He sits there during his interviews gloating about his crimes, about how clever he was to outwit us for so long. The man is a monster."

Newbury struck a match, lit the bowl of his pipe and tossed the dead match into the fire with a brief glance over his shoulder. He puffed to kindle the flames before replying. "They often are, Charles. They often are. Shame about Villiers, though. He was an entirely singular man."

Bainbridge pulled a face. "For the life of me, Newbury, I cannot understand where you developed such profound respect for the man."

Newbury closed his eyes. When he opened them again, he was studying the floor. "It's complicated, Charles. Villiers was an evil man, but he was also incredibly accomplished. In fact, I'd go as far as saying he was a genius, in his own way. And with genius comes a certain amorality that is sometimes difficult to judge. Genius is, in many ways, akin to madness. Both states of mind demand a disconnection from reality, from the real, physical world, an ability to lose oneself in thought." He shrugged. "There is no contesting the fact that Villiers's crimes were of the most appalling variety, but I only wonder what may have come of it if his genius could have been harnessed for the good of the Empire, instead of being misapplied in such a terrible way. . . ." He trailed off, lost in thought.

Bainbridge chewed on the end of his cigar. "Good riddance to him, is what I say. Chapman did us a favour when he removed the man from proceedings, and that's all I have to say on the subject." He paused. "Still, it's good to see another case through to its resolution, isn't it?"

"Hmmm?" Newbury returned from his reverie, his eyes darting to meet Bainbridge's expectant face. "Oh, yes indeed. Although I hasten to add that there *is* still one small part of the mystery that perplexes me. I've yet to discover the reason why a Dutch nobleman was to be found on board the wreckage of a passenger-class airship bound for Dublin."

Bainbridge placed his glass on the table and leaned forward. "I may have something to help you with that, old man. The one good thing about Chapman's boastful tirade is that we've been able to glean a few facts from his testimony. He claims *The Lady Armitage* had been engaged by a coterie of local noblemen, men who were keen to see as many revenants removed from the streets as possible, for use as a plague ship. Chapman had been using the automata to round up the revenants like animals, forcing them onto the airships and shipping them off to Ireland, where his men were setting them loose in the countryside—if they didn't dump them at sea during the course of the voyage. Not sure that explains how your Dutchman found himself involved in the matter, but it may help you get to the bottom of the mystery, eh?"

Newbury looked animated. "Indeed it does, Charles. Indeed it does!" He sprang out of his chair, clamped his pipe between his teeth and began pacing back and forth before the fire, all sense of his stiffness gone. The silence stretched. After a moment, he turned to Bainbridge, gesturing frantically with his hands. "Charles, allow me to ask you a question. Why should a visiting nobleman take to the streets of Whitechapel by evening, choosing to travel alone, without the protection of a Royal escort?"

Bainbridge frowned. "No reason at all, unless he had a taste for the wicked side of life, if you catch my meaning." He coughed into his hand, embarrassed at the implication.

"Precisely! If the man had harboured a longing for visiting cheap whores whilst staying in the city, he would surely have slipped out of his lodgings unaccompanied, in an effort to keep his inappropriate activities under wraps. If the newspapers were to discover his secret, it would cause the palace a terrific scandal, and if any unscrupulous aides were made aware of it, they might have chosen to use the information against him at some point."

"Blackmail, you mean."

Newbury nodded. "Indeed. So we've established that if the man *did* engage in such carnal pursuits, he would be sure to hide the fact from his aides, stepping out alone only at the most opportune moments, such as late in the evening after his men had retired." He smiled to himself, pleased with his deduction. "Could it be, then, that the man inadvertently contracted the revenant plague during one of these nightly sojourns to the slums, so that when the automata came to round up the miserable fellows a week or so later, he was wandering the streets, transformed into one of the detestable creatures?"

"You could be right, Newbury! Certainly no one would recognise the man in that state."

"Until, that is, they removed his charred corpse from the

wreckage, which would show no signs of the viral infection that had thus far been ravaging his body. An identifying item of jewellery would be all that it would take for the coroner to proclaim that Her Majesty's missing cousin had been found."

Bainbridge retrieved his brandy from the table. "My God, Newbury. I think you're on to something. But how the devil do you prove the man had such inappropriate desires in the first place? That's quite an accusation to level at a member of the Royal Family without any real shred of evidence. I can't imagine Her Majesty will accept your story on supposition alone."

Newbury chuckled. "That's just it, Charles. I believe I have all the evidence I need. I've spent the last couple of days scouring my records for background on the Dutch royal family, identifying potential victims. Her Majesty had been less than forthcoming about which particular cousin had been involved in the incident, but her words provided me with a number of important clues. I knew we were dealing with a young man, a minor royal, but someone who would be sent to London on diplomatic duties all the same, probably due to the importance of their mother. After taking all of that into consideration there was only one likely candidate, a man whose name—I'm sure you will forgive me—I will refrain from repeating here." Newbury paused for breath, although it was clear he was anxious to proceed with his tale. "But during the course of my reading, I turned out a number of newspaper reports regarding a 'misunderstanding' between one of the Queen's cousins and a mysterious 'lady,' who claimed to be the bearer of an illegitimate child. The newspapers had reported the story as a minor item, alluding to the fact that the woman was a prostitute and had probably invented the entire story as a means of extorting money from the unfortunate young man. However, in light of current events, I'll wager there's truth behind the tale. And what's more, I imagine it was this very same man whose corpse was extracted from the crash site of *The Lady Armitage* just a few days ago in Finsbury Park."

Bainbridge nodded, a smile curling his lips. "I should say that will do the job."

"Indeed." Newbury returned to his seat with a satisfied sigh. He raised an empty glass. "Well, that's the end of it then." He sucked on his pipe, resting his head against the tall back of the Chesterfield.

Bainbridge shuffled awkwardly in his seat. "There is just one other thing I should mention, if you're not too opposed to hearing me out on something rather peculiar?"

Newbury peeled open his eyes, his interest piqued. "Go on."

"I'm sure you recall our conversations from a few days ago, regarding the potential origins of the glowing policeman?"

"Of course."

"At the time, before Morgan's death and the realisation that we were on the trail of a purely corporeal killer, you mentioned Miss Hobbes's supposition that the perpetrator could in fact have been a phantom killer akin to the one reported all those years ago. Another example of the same phenomena, you said, involving entirely different people."

Newbury sat forward in his chair and poured himself a brandy, listening intently to Bainbridge's account. "Quite so." He considered his friend, concern evident in his eyes. "What's troubling you, Charles?"

Bainbridge shook his head. "It's all rather embarrassing, really. I mean, I don't know what to think. You know I'm not a superstitious man."

"For Heaven's sake, Charles. Get to the point."

"You asked me if there had been any recent murders of police constables in the Whitechapel area, and at the time I couldn't say for certain. But I had the clerks check the records and it turns out there was a man, a Mr. John Harris, who was done in with his own truncheon by a gang of youths, after he happened upon the miscreants roughing up a girl in an alleyway earlier that night. They got away with it, too, since a local shopkeeper provided an alibi. The word amongst the rest of the men was that the gang had applied a liberal amount of pressure to the shopkeeper and, fearing for the safety of his wife and daughter, he had willingly perjured himself to protect them."

Newbury took a swig of his brandy. "Let me guess. It turns out a number of these youths were amongst the victims of the glowing policeman, found strangled in the Whitechapel area, their personal effects still *in situ* on the bodies?"

Bainbridge smiled. "Close, Newbury. *All* of the youths were amongst the reported victims of the glowing policeman. I don't know what to make of it. It seems like too much of a coincidence to ignore."

Newbury laughed. "Ha! I'll wager coincidence has nothing to do with it!" He sank back in his chair. "Of course, there's no way of telling, now. It *could* have been coincidence, or it could have been the murdered man's colleagues taking the opportunity to seek revenge. But it would certainly explain why we didn't identify the residue of the blue powder on all of the victims. Revenge can drive people to do terrible things, Charles, terrible things indeed. Even, perhaps, to rise from the grave itself. Did I ever tell you of the Hambleton affair?"

"I don't believe so, no."

"Ah, well. I suspect that's a story for another occasion. Nevertheless, it serves to prove the point. There are things in this world—and beyond—for which the combined efforts of science and religion have yet to divine a suitable explanation. I have no doubt that, given time, they will." He heaved himself out of his chair, stretching his sore muscles. "But now, my friend, I must prevail upon you to forgive me. I feel the need to retire for the evening, to rest these damnable wounds in an effort to hasten my recovery and put an end to my captive misery." He sniffed. "The guest room is yours if you want it."

Bainbridge rose to his feet and clasped a hand on his friend's shoulder. "No, I'll take my leave, dear boy." He smiled warmly. "Look after yourself, and keep an eye on that wayward assistant of yours. She'll be causing a scandal or two of her own if she doesn't check herself from time to time."

Newbury laughed heartily. "Indeed. She might at that."

Bainbridge downed the remainder of his brandy and crossed the room, collecting his coat and cane. "Well, Newbury. Until next time."

"Good-bye, Charles."

The Chief Inspector took his leave. Newbury waited until the sound of his footsteps had receded down the street. He banked the fire, making sure the embers were burning low, and turned out his pipe in the grate. Then, leaving the living-room behind him, he climbed the stairs and passed along the hallway towards his bedchamber. He stopped outside the room and placed his hand on the doorknob. A little farther along the landing, the door to his study was propped shut, still loose on its hinges following Veronica's dramatic entry a day or two earlier. He'd have to have it fixed in the next couple of days, once he'd regained the rest of his health.

Hesitantly, he withdrew his hand from the handle of his bedroom door and crossed the landing, his wounds itching where scabs had formed over the open cuts. He pushed his way through the unwieldy study door and propped it shut again behind him. He turned up the gas jet on the wall, causing a dim radial glow to light the room. The room was just as he'd left it.

He crossed to the daybed and took a seat, eyeing the little brown bottle on the table in the corner. In the dim light, he could just see the peeling label, the familiar liquid inside. There was also a half-drunk bottle of red wine on the table beside it, stoppered with a used cork. It had probably spoiled during the intervening days. He rubbed a hand over his face and glanced at the door sheepishly, knowing he should head for his bedchamber, and stood, pacing towards the landing. His stomach twisted in knots. He drew a deep breath, trying to fight off his cravings, playing out the consequences in his mind. He'd promised Veronica. . . .

He glanced back at the bottle in the half-light. It sung to him of cosy oblivion and warmth. It was like the call of a siren; unrelenting, full of terrible beauty. The need burned within him, made every inch of his skin crawl.

He stood on the threshold of the room for a few moments, tortured and confused by his own desires. Then, finally, he crossed the room, collected the two bottles, and settled himself on the daybed, aware that, for a short time at least, he could banish the guilt that gnawed at him from within. The laudanum would bring stillness. The laudanum would remove all sense of fear, all sense of doubt. The laudanum would excise the pain, and tomorrow, he told himself as he carefully poured a measure from the dull, inconspicuous bottle, was another day entirely. Tomorrow he could start again.

CHAPTER 31

Veronica glared at the pile of unsorted papers on her desk and sighed. The office was deathly quiet, lacking the banter she had become accustomed to, with only the constant tick-tock of the grandfather clock and the occasional sound of Miss Coulthard shuffling papers in the adjoining room punctuating the monotony.

She leaned back in her chair and glanced over at Newbury's empty desk, which had lain undisturbed since they were last in the office together the previous week. Correspondence had temporarily been forwarded to his Chelsea home whilst he spent time convalescing away from the museum, and the lack of his usual cheer lent the place a mournful air, as if it were missing something fundamental, the heart of it temporarily removed. The office itself had been restored to something approximating order, following Miss Coulthard's return to work and the removal of the automaton remains by Scotland Yard, who were keen to gather evidence for the case against Chapman. Not that they needed to worry, Veronica considered; she was certain that they would be able to uncover enough at the manufactory to send him to the gallows ten times over, especially when one took into consideration the testimonies of Sir Maurice and Sir Charles, both respected members of society and gentlemen to boot.

Veronica leaned back in her chair, drumming her fingers idly on the desk. The days following her visit to the asylum had passed in a sedentary fashion, and whilst she had enjoyed hearing tales from an effervescent Miss Coulthard about the return of her brother Jack, in truth, she was finding it difficult to give her administrative tasks their due attention. It had only been a handful of days since the apprehension of Joseph Chapman and the resolution of the case of *The Lady Armitage,* and she already found herself speculating on what the future may hold. She longed to see Newbury again, to lose herself in another mystery. She knew it was idle speculation, but it helped fuel her motivation for the laborious research work she was obliged to carry out whilst she waited for Newbury himself to return to work.

Deciding that she shouldn't put it off any longer, she set to work, taking a stack of manuscript pages from the top of the nearest pile and leafing through the content in an effort to identify any references that Newbury might find useful in the writing of his most recent essay, regarding the ritualistic practices of the druidic tribes of Bronze Age Europe.

There was a polite rap on the inner door. Veronica looked up to see Miss Coulthard hovering in the doorway, a large sheaf of papers clutched tightly in her arms.

"Miss Hobbes, I'm just running these along to the museum archive. I'll be back shortly if you find you have need of me."

Veronica smiled. "Of course. Thank you, Miss Coulthard." She indicated the large stack of papers on her desk. "I won't be going anywhere for a while."

Miss Coulthard gave her a knowing sigh and then left, her heels clicking loudly on the tiled floor. Veronica returned distractedly to her reading.

A few minutes later, she heard the door open and shut in the adjoining room, followed by the sound of footsteps on the threshold of the office. She continued reading, her eyes flicking over the carefully crafted copperplate on the page before her. "You were far quicker than I'd imagined, Miss Coulthard. Now, if you could find it in your heart to put the kettle on the stove...." She looked up at the sound of a man clearing his throat, her voice trailing off. "Sir Maurice! I—we weren't expecting you back so soon!"

Newbury smiled. "My dear Miss Hobbes. There is only so long a gentleman can sit in his rooms, staring at the walls, before the experience becomes entirely unbearable." He removed his hat and indicated his desk with a wave of his hand. "Besides, that essay isn't going to write itself." He beamed at her, his eyes twinkling.

Veronica grinned. "Tell me. How are you feeling? Are you recovered?"

"A little stiff. My wounds are healing well enough, although it's a damnable irritation. Still, I imagine I'll be back to my usual self before long. Provided, that is, that I don't find myself scrabbling around on the top of any moving ground trains in the near future."

Veronica laughed. "Well, sit yourself down, and I'll prepare a nice cup of Earl Grey. Miss Coulthard should be back soon. She's just popped along to the archive to file some papers." She climbed to her feet, stretching her back after spending too long sitting hunched over her desk.

"Indeed. I ran into her in the passageway. It's most excellent news about the safe return of her brother. I understand that you were instrumental in seeing him home?"

Veronica came out from behind her desk. She shrugged. "Yes, I suppose you could put it that way. I happened upon him in the most unlikely of spots, and having seen one of Miss Coulthard's photographs, I was able to place him. His memory has yet to return in full, but I'm told he's otherwise in good health. It transpires that Miss Coulthard was correct all along, that he was indeed savaged by a revenant in Brixton, but somehow managed to get away. It seems the two of you have a good deal in common, too: aside from spending time in India, you've both encountered revenants on more than one occasion and lived to tell the tale. Jack is also immune to the plague. Miss Coulthard says that the doctors are talking about fashioning a vaccination from his blood."

Newbury nodded, smiling. "Remarkable. I'm most delighted for Miss Coulthard." He paused, running a hand over his face. "So, tell me, how did you find Amelia? Is she bearing up?"

Veronica tried to maintain her smile, but her face faltered. "Not well, I'm afraid. She grows weaker with every visit I make. I don't know what else I can do for her. I think just being in that place is enough to suck the life out of her."

Newbury stepped closer and tenderly placed his hand on her arm. "We must see what we can do to help. I'll give the matter some attention directly."

Veronica's breath became shallow. She edged nearer to Newbury, her heart hammering in her chest. Her lips were dry. "It's good to have you back, Sir Maurice."

"I–"

Then the door swung open and Miss Coulthard bustled noisily into the office. Veronica hurriedly stepped back from Newbury, smoothing her dress. Her face flushed.

Miss Coulthard seemed not to notice anything untoward. She smiled. "Good to have you back, Sir Maurice." She glanced at them both in turn, and then shuffled over to the stove. "Tea, anyone?"

Newbury laughed. "Yes, please, Miss Coulthard. That would be perfect." He crossed into the other room and dropped his hat on the stand, shrugged out of his coat, and then, moving carefully so as not to put stress on his wounds, he wandered back through to his desk and lowered himself into his chair.

Veronica returned to her seat. They eyed each other across the office, neither of them knowing what to say. Miss Coulthard whistled tunefully in the other room as she set the kettle on the stove and searched around in the cupboard for some cups and saucers.

Newbury was first to break the silence. "Did Bainbridge stop by to inform you of my theory about the Dutch Royal cousin and *The Lady Armitage*?"

Veronica nodded. "Indeed he did. He was rather less than forthcoming when it came to detailing the activities the man had been pursuing in the Whitechapel district, but I was able to tease out enough information from his inferences to work out what he was trying to say."

Newbury laughed. "That certainly sounds like Charles. He never could talk to a lady."

Veronica looked suddenly serious. "I suppose that explains why all of the passengers had been tied to their seats on the airship. The fact that they were plague victims, I mean."

"Yes, I suppose it does."

Veronica toyed with the corner of one of the manuscript pages on her desk. "So how did Her Majesty take the news? It's rather a scandalous affair for the family, isn't it?"

Newbury shrugged. "I visited the palace yesterday. Her Majesty seemed to take the news impartially. She was rather too busy admonishing me for the state of my health, if truth be told." He chuckled. "I doubt there'll be any word of it in the press. Whether the facts are deemed appropriate for the boy's mother, we'll have to leave for others to decide."

Veronica nodded. "So, what's next?"

Newbury laughed again. "Druids. The Bronze Age. Pages and pages of arduous notes." He leaned back in his chair. "After that, who knows? I'm sure that something will turn up." He shifted to see Miss Coulthard entering the office, bearing two cups of Earl Grey on a wooden tray.

Veronica smiled, reaching for another sheaf of papers on her desk. She shuffled them into a neat pile before her. Looking up, she met Newbury's eye from across the room. "I do believe it will, Sir Maurice. I do believe it will."

EPILOGUE

The life-preserving machine laboured in the semi-darkness, hissing and wheezing as the bellows rose and fell in time with the toilsome breathing of its occupant. Her Majesty Queen Victoria eased herself forward, wheeling her chair closer to the figure that was standing in the shadows on the other side of the audience chamber. Her face resolved in the gloom. She was wearing a stern expression. "We are most satisfied with the resolution of this investigation"—her voice was shrill and echoed around the empty room—"yet we remain concerned for the well-being of our agent. Tell me, Miss Hobbes, do you believe that Sir Maurice acquitted himself in a manner becoming a representative of the Crown?"

Veronica swallowed and stepped forward into the wavering light of the gas-lamps. "I do, Your Majesty. Sir Maurice is a credit to his nation."

The monarch nodded. "Very good. That is most reassuring." She put her hand to her mouth and gave a wet, spluttering cough. The machine wheezed as it tried to compensate for the brief fit. Her chest heaved, her lungs filling with oxygen. She continued, catching her breath. "Even so, Miss Hobbes, we encourage you to remember your duty. We must ensure that Newbury remains steadfast in his beliefs. We fear that the dark arts have a terrible allure, and, lest you forget, your primary role in this assignment is to protect Newbury from falling for such devious charms. One would hate to imagine that we were allowing another dissenter to propagate in our midst."

Veronica frowned. "What word is there of Dr. Knox?"

The Queen shook her head. "No word. He is lost to us. We have dozens of agents searching for him, all across the Empire, but he proves as elusive as he ever was. He has managed not to show his hand for over a year now. One wonders what he is plotting in the darkness."

Veronica shrugged. "Perhaps he is already dead."

"No." The Queen was firm. "He is a wily devil, and he has darker forces at his disposal. We have no doubt that he is alive, somewhere out there, hiding in the quiet places, unseen to our agents." She straightened herself in her wheelchair. "What is clear to us is that Newbury must be steered in a wholly different direction. He cannot be allowed to succumb."

"Yes, Your Majesty. I can assure you that this matter remains my sole concern. I will ensure that Sir Maurice does not fall prey to that particular trap."

Victoria raised an eyebrow. "You seem overly confident in your own abilities, Miss Hobbes. Perhaps you already have the man wrapped around your little finger." She laughed, and the sound was like boots crunching on gravel.

Veronica looked away, a pained expression on her face. "Perhaps. Yet I think his heart is true. He will not be swayed by petty obsessions or a vain desire for power. He is not Aubrey Knox. He serves you well, Your Majesty."

Victoria nodded. "Then you may go, Miss Hobbes, and be about your business." She wheeled back a few feet, indicating that it was time for Veronica to leave. Veronica crossed the room. Victoria waited until she was nearing the door. "Oh, and Miss Hobbes? One other thing before you take your leave."

Veronica turned back to regard her, finding it difficult to place her in the dim light. "Yes, Your Majesty?"

"This 'affinity bridge' that Newbury spoke of. The device that facilitates the interaction between the human brain and an artificial body. Have they all been destroyed?"

"No, Your Majesty. The Chapman and Villiers automata are currently being decommissioned, but it is proving to be a lengthy process. It will be some months before they are all accounted for."

The Queen offered her a weary smile. "Good. Please ensure that you keep at least a handful of them in working order. One never knows when the technology may prove useful."

"Indeed, Your Majesty. I will endeavour to do so." She glanced at the door. "Will there be anything else?"

"No. That is all. Thank you, Miss Hobbes."

"Good day, Your Majesty."

Veronica pulled open the door and hurried along the passageway, keen to get away from the palace and back to the museum, to Newbury and to her newfound life of adventure.

Newbury and Hobbes will return in
The Osiris Ritual

ACKNOWLEDGEMENTS

No book is written in isolation, and I owe thanks to a great many people, not least to the miraculous Emma Barnes for all her support (how do you fit it all in?), Michael Rowley for being a true friend, Mark Newton for being a fantastic sounding board, Lou Anders for continuing encouragement, Chris Roberson and Allison Baker for their shared love of British TV (amongst many other virtues), Nathan Long for his judicious pencil, my family for their ongoing support, and Fiona, my wife, for taking me seriously when I needed it most, and for not taking me seriously the rest of the time.

ABOUT THE AUTHOR

George Mann was born in Darlington and has written numerous books, short stories, novellas and original audio scripts. *The Affinity Bridge*, the first novel in his Newbury and Hobbes Victorian fantasy series, was published in 2008. Other titles in the series include *The Osiris Ritual*, *The Immorality Engine*, *The Executioner's Heart*, *The Casebook of Newbury & Hobbes* and the forthcoming *The Revenant Express*.

His other novels include *Ghosts of Manhattan* and the forthcoming *Gods of Karnak* and *Ghosts of Empire*, mystery novels about a vigilante set against the backdrop of a post-steampunk 1920s New York, as well as the original Doctor Who novels, *Paradox Lost* and *Engines of War*, the latter featuring the War Doctor alongside his companion, Cinder.

He has edited a number of anthologies, including *Encounters of Sherlock Holmes*, *Further Encounters of Sherlock Holmes*, The *Solaris Book of New Science Fiction* and *The Solaris Book of New Fantasy*, and has written two Sherlock Holmes titles for Titan Books, *Sherlock Holmes: The Will of the Dead* and *Sherlock Holmes: The Spirit Box*.

Occasionally he finds time to breathe.

GEORGE MANN
THE OSIRIS RITUAL
A NEWBURY & HOBBES INVESTIGATION

Death stalks London and the newspapers proclaim that a mummy's curse has been unleashed. Sir Maurice Newbury, gentleman investigator for the crown, is drawn into a web of occult intrigue as he attempts to solve the murders. And he soon finds himself on the trail of a rogue agent – a man who died to be reborn as a living weapon.

Meanwhile, Newbury's able assistant, Miss Veronica Hobbes, has her own mystery to unravel. Young women are going missing from a magician's theatre show. But what appears to be a straightforward investigation puts Miss Hobbes in mortal danger. Can Newbury save his assistant, solve the riddle of the mummy's curse, capture the deadly man-machine and stop the terrifying Osiris Ritual from reaching its infernal culmination?

Available November 2015

GEORGE MANN
THE IMMORALITY ENGINE
A NEWBURY & HOBBES INVESTIGATION

On the surface, life is going well for Victorian special agent
Sir Maurice Newbury, who has brilliantly solved several nigh-
impossible cases for Queen Victoria with his indomitable
assistant, Miss Veronica Hobbes, by his side. But these facts
haven't stopped Newbury from succumbing increasingly
frequently to his dire flirtation with the lure of opium. Veronica,
consumed by worry and care for her prophetic but physically
fragile sister, Amelia, has no idea that she is a catalyst for
Newbury's steadily worsening condition.
Veronica and Newbury's dear friend Bainbridge, tries to cover
for him but when the body of a well-known criminal turns up,
Bainbridge and Veronica track Newbury down in an opium den
and drag him out to help them with the case. The body clearly,
irrefutably, belongs to the man in question, but shortly after
his body is brought to the morgue, a crime is discovered that
bears all the dead man's hallmarks. Bainbridge and Veronica
fear someone is committing copycat crimes, but Newbury is not
sure. Somehow, the details are too perfect for it to be the work
of a copycat. But how can a dead man commit a crime?

GEORGE MANN
THE EXECUTIONER'S HEART
A NEWBURY & HOBBES INVESTIGATION

When Charles Bainbridge, Chief Inspector of Scotland Yard, is called to the scene of the third murder in quick succession where the victim's chest has been cracked open and their heart torn out, he sends for supernatural specialist Sir Maurice Newbury and his determined assistant, Miss Veronica Hobbes.

The two detectives discover that the killings may be the work of a mercenary known as the Executioner. French, uncannily beautiful, her flesh covered in tattoos and inlaid with precious metals, the Executioner is famed throughout Europe. But her heart is damaged, leaving her an emotionless shell, inexplicably driven to collect her victims' hearts as trophies.

Newbury and Hobbes confront many strange and pressing mysteries on the way to unearthing the secret of the Executioner's Heart.

Available Now

GEORGE MANN
THE REVENANT EXPRESS
A NEWBURY & HOBBES INVESTIGATION

Following their bloody encounter with the beautiful but deadly Executioner, Sir Maurice Newbury's assistant Veronica Hobbes is close to death, her heart removed and replaced with an unstable mechanism. Desperate to save her life, Newbury and Veronica's sister Amelia board the immense L'Esprit du Paris, a sleeper train bound for St. Petersburg, in the hope that the illustrious Gustav Faberge might have the answer.

But Newbury's enemies are also on board. As they steam across Europe, Newbury and Amelia must do battle with an outbreak of vicious revenants, a cultist who is determined to reclaim a stolen item, and a figure from Veronica's past, a woman hell-bent on revenge… With time running out for Veronica, Newbury and Amelia will need all their strength and cunning in order to survive the Revenant Express.

Available 2016

GEORGE MANN
THE CASEBOOK OF NEWBURY & HOBBES
VOLUME I

A collection of short stories detailing the supernatural
steampunk adventures of detective duo, Sir Maurice
Newbury and Miss Veronica Hobbes in dark and
dangerous Victorian London. Along with Chief Inspector
Bainbridge, Newbury and Hobbes will face plague
revenants, murderous peers, mechanical beasts, tentacled
leviathans, reanimated pygmies, and an encounter with
one Sherlock Holmes.